VENGEANCE IS HERS

ROBERT CHAZZ CHUTE

NOTIFICATION

COMMENDATION

Chute gives us a story worthy of Stephen King. A read both thoughtful and fun. ~ Linda Beer Johnson, Amazon reviewer

Robert Chazz Chute has an innate ability to produce realistic and diverse characters. I always enjoy reading his novels. ~ Steve G, Amazon reviewer

Robert Chazz Chute is such a skilled spinner of tales that the reader is more than willing to suspend any possible disbelief to go along for the ride. ~ David Pandolfe, author of *Jump When Ready*

It's not very often one finds a writer with such a dark side that has such a great sense of humor. ~ Glenn Roberts, Amazon reviewer

He makes the stuff that is obviously fiction, believable. ~ W. Nickels, Amazon reviewer

The author has a definite talent with words and ideas. ~ Love to Read!, Amazon reviewer

His words lift and dance off the page, bringing the story to life. ~ Kindle Customer, Amazon reviewer

The world-building is horrifically well done with twists and turns and deceit around every corner. ~ Wanda, Amazon reviewer

RCC blends characters' beliefs & worries concerning society's failures, plus vivid action scenes skillfully. ~ RMerkl, Amazon Reviewer

Nothing but sheer exhaustion could tear my eyes from the captivating dance of words choreographed by Robert Chazz Chute. ~ Halph Staph, Amazon reviewer

Wonderful action constantly holds your interest. ~ Sharon Finn, Amazon reviewer

The complexity and attention to detail throughout absolutely blow me away. ~ Kindle customer, Amazon Reviewer

Very few authors impress me with their actual writing style, it's usually always about the story. But this author paints such beautiful vivid pictures with words that I found myself not only enjoying the story but enjoying the way the words created images in my mind. I know that sounds corny, but it is true. ~ B.H., Amazon reviewer

The author does an excellent job building the characters and getting you invested and involved. ~ Michele L. Hebert, Amazon reviewer

I just can't say in words what a powerful author this is! ~ Delinda L. Calkins, Amazon reviewer

For Earl and Roy, my two fathers, both off to solve the greatest mystery.

DISSOCIATION

This is not an instruction manual.

All acts of vengeance detailed herein were performed by fictional
trained sociopaths.
Do not attempt.

POPULATION

Molly Edwina Jergins
Our poetic protagonist on a journey of revenge and discovery.

Keith Faun
Hockey goon, narcissist,
Molly's nemesis.

Barry Graves
Keith's first victim and the fulcrum, forced to flee.

Lloyd Gregory Faun
Keith's abusive alcoholic father, toxic enabler, and Molly's chief
target.

Marjorie Farrah Faun
Small-town socialite, Keith's mother, Lloyd's wife, in that order.

Charles (Chuck) Lyman Jergins
Molly's father, a wounded veteran, an injured carpenter, keeper of
some secrets.

Kayla (Kay) Eliza Jergins
Molly's ailing mother, keeper of many secrets.

Gordon Beaufort Hobbs
Sheriff for Poeticule County, lazy, useless, and the worst of the town
gossips.

Dylan Caffrey
Once, another of Keith's victims. Someday, one of Molly's allies.

Rosemary (Rose) Rainier
Poeticule Bay Consolidated's school librarian, a protector on a slow
train bound for tragedy.

Sarah Emily Rainier
Rose's daughter, taken in by Keith's deception.
Abused wife in need of escape.

Anthony (Ant) Rainier
Rose's son, a chatty, jealous coward who needs Molly's help.

Vincent Arthur Jergins
Chuck's brother, Kay's caregiver, kind crank, and kind of a crank.

Dr. Richard Whelan
Dean of Greenbriar College, petty bureaucrat, misogynist, and racist
AKA the Mad King.

You
Reader, observer, soon to consider whether to forgive your many,
many enemies or use the strategies that lie ahead for nefarious
purposes.

WATER

With mean enemies made and fine friends lost,
we teeter at the edge of the end.
Naming our sorrows and counting the cost,
we are broken because we would not bend.

1

SEDUCTION

On her ninth birthday, Molly Jergins was almost eaten by a shark twelve feet from shore in St. Petersburg, Florida. It was a best-of-times, worst-of-times situation.

Shark attacks are incredibly rare, but when they occur, most happen in shallow water. At the time the large triangular fin appeared behind her, Molly was up to her chin. She tipped her head back so the little waves would not spill salt water up her nose and down her throat.

After stopping in St. Petersburg to visit one of her father's Army buddies, Molly had been promised a couple of days at Walt Disney World. Until the shark appeared, this was possibly the happiest day of her young life.

Her father had borrowed his brother's Airstream trailer for the summer. Her mother complained it smelled of mildew, but to Molly the big, polished aluminum trailer looked like a spaceship.

Her parents, Chuck and Kay, took turns at the wheel of their pickup. Both were nervous about hauling the big trailer down U.S. Route 1 from Maine. Her mother's knuckles were especially tight on the steering wheel of their pickup truck.

Molly had heard her mother swear occasionally, but from the

driver's seat of their Ford, Kay lambasted other drivers profanely and profusely. Listening to her mother curse someone who had cut her off was a delight. By acknowledging the world's dangers in her presence, her parents made Molly feel more like an adult.

They'd parked the Ford and the Airstream in her father's friend's driveway. Her mother complained of the heat and was eager to leave St. Petersburg for Wekiwa Springs State Park. However, Chuck insisted they give Molly a break at the beach.

We focus on big choices. Where to live, whom to marry, when to divorce, how to die. But seemingly small decisions can have a big impact, too.

"When they're flyin' around in formation," he said, "the pelicans look like pterodactyls. The kid will love it."

"The beach here isn't like back home," Kay told Molly. "It's all tattoos and the smell of coconut sunscreen oil. Don't be long."

As she waded into the warm waters of the Gulf of Mexico, Molly thought her father was right. Watching the pelicans on the hunt, skimming the water, it was easy to imagine the dinosaurs from which they'd descended. When Molly said so, Chuck nodded and added cheerily, "History is full of horrors."

The little girl looked up at her father, her face a question mark.

He shrugged and patted her shoulder. "You get older, you'll understand how messed up things are."

She scanned the pristine sand. Far out, two catamarans were racing, knifing through the light waves. Sunlight played on the water's surface under a warm breeze. "Looks nice to me."

"I mean things are messed up compared to what they could be. I was raised believing in the *Star Trek* future. Instead, we got people talkin' about rocketing to Mars. Mars is just the worst parts of Utah, but with no oxygen," he said sourly.

"Anything else, Mr. Sunshine?

"Sure! You buy life insurance, but it's really death insurance. People go to what they call a teaching hospital. The patients would friggin' freak if they called it a learning hospital. Doctors make mistakes and not everyone in authority has your best interests at heart."

"Dad!"

"Relax. You're nine now and growing up too fast! I'll lose you to the world soon, but stay my little girl a little longer, please. I got no spare kids lyin' around, so you're it and it's all on you! You'll be embarrassed to be seen with me in public — "

"Already am!" she teased.

But she wasn't as precocious as her father gave her credit for. At nine, Molly Jergins still thought bad things were confined to the past. She had yet to seriously consider that the future, too, held horrors.

Drawn by her splashing, a curious shark was swimming up behind her at that moment.

Molly was long and lanky for her age. She felt like a ballerina on tiptoes in the shifting, sloping sand. Another minute and she would have been treading water.

Chuck had bent his knees to go up to his neck, just six feet from shore. When he spotted the triangular fin break the surface behind his daughter, he stood. He didn't wait to analyze the danger. Hands outstretched and coming toward her as fast as he could, he shouted, "Molly! Come here!"

But she didn't move toward him. Startled, she turned to follow his wild-eyed gaze. She saw the fin. It wasn't far from her, and it was approaching.

Molly wasn't sure which was faster, to try to run back to shore or swim. There was no time for a conscious choice. She tried running to shore. Between losing traction in the loose sand and the wall of water holding her back, every movement felt too slow.

The seas conceal millions of secrets. Beasts lurk in the dark. The drowned disappear into watery graves. Dead people and broken ships find their final resting place on ocean beds. On her ninth birthday, little Molly learned that sometimes monsters made of teeth come for the innocent.

Both father and daughter wanted to deny that reality. It couldn't be a shark, could it? A porpoise or a dolphin, maybe? No, the fin was too sharp, too distinctive. They'd seen plenty of depictions of sharks in movies. Watched from the safety of a living room couch, the sight was interesting. In real life? A fish up from the depths hunting for meat?

Molly peed a little. Butt and jaw clenched, she discovered that she could walk underwater with her feet fairly far in front of her. Not far enough, of course, but to the girl, it felt like she was tilted back at an extreme angle.

By the look on her father's face, she could tell the fish was coming closer. She could picture the shark going for her legs, chomping down, crushing her bones. Driven wild by her blood, it would shake its head, working at what tender connections bind the flesh until her legs no longer belonged to her.

Chuck reached for his daughter's hand, and in one mighty heave, pulled her up out of the water. He tossed her behind him as hard as he could manage. Molly splashed down in water up to her waist.

The only sound in the world was her father's voice, "Get to shore! Get to shore!"

She did. So did he.

When Chuck and Molly turned to look back, the shark had disappeared. The ocean was once again a shifting blue mirror under bright sunlight.

Shaking, Molly whispered, "A monster made of teeth."

Chuck turned to her, his eyes still like pie plates. His first words were, "Don't tell Mom!"

It was as if they'd knocked over the snake plant in the living room, and some soil had spilled on the rug. As if they were both children, afraid of getting in trouble.

And then something wonderful happened. They flopped down in the warm, sugary sand and laughed and laughed and laughed.

"She'd never let me go to the beach again, would she?" Molly giggled.

"Dunno. She might kill me for insisting on takin' her little girl down here. On the other hand, I wouldn't put it past your mom to get her shotgun from the trailer. I can see her lookin' to shoot a fish!"

"Where is it?" Molly asked.

"What?"

"The shotgun. I could do it."

Chuck chuckled and waved her away. Then he quoted *Jaws*, a movie she had never seen. In a gravelly voice, he mimicked, "Lifeless eyes, black eyes, like a doll's eyes."

That set them off again. They laughed until their relief washed away all the sudden adrenaline that comes with facing cruel mortality.

For some reason neither could quite articulate, they kept their shark encounter a secret from Molly's mother for the rest of their lives. They told a lifeguard about it down the beach, but Kay never knew. Precious and private, it was a memory and a moment for father and daughter alone.

Years later, after a mean night by a colder sea, Molly would keep another secret from Kay Jergins. Stumbling into their kitchen at dawn, Molly was too afraid to admit the murderous truth. Had she been honest, she would have marched upstairs, woken her mother, and confessed. Molly failed to meet that moment. She told herself she was sparing Kay from the worst day of her life.

"I met two monsters made of teeth on the Drifting Cliffs. I killed somebody — actually, a couple of somebodies."

Molly did not say that.

Neither did she admit that she let another monster get away.

2

INSTIGATION

The average person lives 27,375 days and few are memorable. The worst day of Barry Graves' life — the day he could never forget — was rooted in evil. Evil, but nothing supernatural. Choices were made, and mean actions taken. All too human, in fact.

News of the crime spread, but law enforcement wasn't interested in pursuing a conviction. The town sheriff commented that the boy was "roughed up." A better person would have called it assault. To Barry, it sure felt like attempted murder with a cruel dollop of humiliation.

People say, "It can't happen here." But bad things happen everywhere, even in forgotten nooks of the world like Poeticule Bay, Maine.

The town clung to the edge of the Atlantic along a six-mile half-moon crescent of rocky coastline. A miniature lighthouse — a replica of the town's actual lighthouse — decorated the town's Welcome To and Come Again signs. Stiff ocean winds spun the seagull whirligigs that decorated many a front yard.

At first glance, the town — a village, really — seemed a tiny retreat from the many dramas of the new century. Nestled at the foot of Poet's Mountain, it certainly looked safe enough. A lot of places used to be like that. For instance, many didn't know about the upward trend of suicides among Poeticule County's young and elderly.

Honesty about some local nobody taking his or her life could kill. One suicide could spur two more. Information could act like a virus among the vulnerable. Secondary suicides used to be called copycats. Now the phenomenon was called social contagion. However, the media still reported far away celebrity suicides. For some reason, that was okay.

Suicides were secrets, so no one but the Graves family doctor knew Barry had considered finishing the job Keith Faun had started. Alone and isolated, the boy came close to taking his life. Three things stopped the boy from taking his own life: He had no gun, there weren't enough dangerous pills in the house, and his parents' love. If they hadn't elected to run away from Poeticule Bay, the kid surely would have found a way.

In those gloomy days and cold nights, it seemed like the sky was always gray over an empty gunmetal ocean. Some locals, mourning a bygone era with rose-colored glasses, speculated there was something wicked in the air. As if choices were curses wafting up from the ocean depths, appearing with the foul smells of red and brown tides.

Besides the dying fishery, the area's cottage industry was cottages. People came from three states away to their summer retreats. In summers gone by, Poeticule County's population would quadruple. At one time, the little town supported two taxis. Harsh winters nearly emptied the town and the surrounding countryside, but vacationers returned with the warm weather.

But nothing is forever. Most young people moved away as soon as they could, searching for work, for love, for anything and everything small towns can't offer.

Some said it was simply the fish die-off that killed the town. Toxic runoff from creekside farms had turned the water hypoxic. Once a busy port for a thriving fishery, algae blooms killed aquatic life and turned the bay into a dead zone.

Some elders felt the town's downward spiral on a spiritual level, with 9/11 as its turning point. "The whole country's going to hell," they'd say.

Several towns nestled up and down the coast and along the crooked roads of rural Maine offered more charm. As the fish stock depleted, Poeticule Bay became more often a waypoint than a destination.

To glimpse the infamous dead zone, a few curious travelers still took the coastal route instead of the much faster interstate highway. The roiling black the Atlantic pulled their gaze. Most thought there was nothing more to the town than what they could see of weathered buildings and fading paint from the twists of Shore Road at forty miles an hour.

Some motorists stopped for gas or to stretch their legs on their way up the coast to Bridge Falls or Legger's Notch. A few took pictures of themselves at the foot of the white tower of the lighthouse.

Once a manned station, the lighthouse had become automated in 1995. The base of the lighthouse had been repurposed as a tourist information office from May to September. Janice Bull, a retired teacher and a descendant of the last lighthouse keeper, manned the information desk. When asked how brisk business was, she always answered the same, "Quiet. Too quiet."

Some summer people kept returning, though. It was impolite to ask for details, but those returnees were probably too stubborn, too poor, or too tired to look elsewhere for a better family retreat. Circumstance, desperation, and tradition contains an inertia that keeps good things past their best-before date.

In retrospect, it's clear that most of Poeticule Bay's residents — both summer and year-round — held to one key lie. They told themselves they were safe. They talked as if what Keith Faun did to the skinny fifteen-year-old was a unique aberration and not a sign of psychopathy.

The lies we tell ourselves are the most dangerous deceits. The come-from-aways didn't hear much about the assault on Barry

Graves at first. That sort of news was for the locals to whisper among themselves.

However, some infections cannot be contained. From warm breath to cold wind, the town gossips broadcast the bad word as if their highest aspiration was to become living radios.

They relayed the details of the attack as they shook their heads in disgust. Some of that outrage was performative. Others, weak fools who imagined themselves hard men and no-nonsense women, spoke of Keith Faun's crime with glee. With few exceptions, most townsfolk didn't really care much about what Keith did to the Graves boy. It hadn't happened to them, and no one relished the prospect of drawing Keith's father's ire.

It is one of the curses of small towns that prominent families skate on the fantasy of "coming from a good home." Though no one claimed to love the Faun family, they were an institution. They'd been in the Bay for generations, and for some unknown reason, that sort of legacy carries weight with idiots.

Lloyd Faun's father, Jim — ruthless and lucky to boot — had grown rich from the lumber business after pioneering sawdust logs for fire starters in wood stoves.

Big Jim Faun had served as mayor for three decades before his death. He was a brawny, loud man. Jim prospered as better and more polite men stepped aside to make way.

When Big Jim passed away, his son Lloyd became head of the Welcome Wagon Committee and president of the Poeticule Business Guild. His handshakes were painful exercises in domination. As the town shrank, the Faun family's power and influence grew.

Though the town seemed destined for ruin, Lloyd was determined to either turn Time's tide or preside at Poeticule Bay's wake.

After receiving a massive inheritance from his father, Lloyd had branched out, selling franchises of his laundromat and dry cleaning business across New England. With the wealth that Big Jim had built, Lloyd could have lived anywhere, but Poeticule Bay was his kingdom, and Keith Faun a prince.

Earl MacAdam, AKA Old Earl because he was the town's most

elderly resident, once said, "Folks around here claim Lloyd's ornery, but I was born in Scotland, so I just call him an asshole." (MacAdam and his family emigrated to Maine when he was nine months old, but he proudly claimed to be "Scotch" all his life.)

Every king has a queen. Lloyd's wife Marjorie was a fading beauty with a laugh that could pierce eardrums. The balancing yin to Lloyd's angry yang, she played the part of town socialite. Her circles bridged the worlds of the locals (cliquish, caustic, and judgmental) and the summer people from New York (wealthy, entitled, and oblivious).

"Marjorie's a character, that one," MacAdam observed. "She buys her friends by the drink. Whether she's playing badminton, tennis, or pickle ball, she always seems to have a racquet in one hand and booze in the other."

Aided by precocious puberty, Lloyd and Marjorie's son Keith had inherited the athletic and towering Faun family frame. It seemed he'd skipped from boy to man having never slowed down to be a tween. When Keith entered a room, people thought, *There's a big'un*. The young Faun did not walk school hallways. He lumbered.

As a muscled brute, Keith was the high school hockey star. No one doubted the handsome boy was bound for great things. NHL scouts had already traveled to Bangor to watch him in the playoffs. The consensus was that he wasn't the best skater or scorer, but as a goon, he was unmatched.

Keith could deal out savage beatings. Much later, locked in a small room with his hands bound behind his back, Keith would reflect on his life. He would briefly consider that if he'd kept his fighting to hockey rinks, fewer people would have died, and he indeed would have been a star.

The Fauns may never have done anyone much good, but locals said the Faun family had "done well." They had the nicest house in town so, as often happens, money was mistaken for merit and worth was mistaken for value.

The Graves were poor, so they received no benefit of the doubt. When news spread of Keith's assault, too frequently, the first question asked was, "What did that little Graves kid do to deserve all that?"

Victims are often blamed for their misfortunes, as if their wounds and bruises sprang from a moral failing. Everyone heard of Keith's sins on the wind, but too many turned their backs to the nasty gale. "Nothing we can do about it. That's the way it goes sometimes."

Lloyd and Marjorie protected their son instead of allowing Keith to be punished. Lloyd even threatened to sue the Graves for defamation and false accusations.

"I got a Bangor lawyer on speed dial for all my troubles," Lloyd bragged, "and deep pockets to keep my enemies in court until they die, maybe even then some."

Frightened for Barry's safety, the Graves family left town one night without a word of farewell to anyone. Smug and thinking themselves untouchable, the Fauns assumed silence equaled total acquiescence.

Ordinary people have few choices. They can mind their own business and hope others will stop injustice. They can hide or bend over and take it. Those options keep them in their dull prisons, but in matters of injustice, nothing is what ordinary people ordinarily do. For folks who measure each day's weight, worth, and waste, this is very sad news, indeed.

However, one extraordinary person lived in Poeticule Bay. She would later go by many aliases, but when she was innocent, her name was Molly Edwina Jergins. Fueled by righteous outrage at Keith's crime, Molly was damned, mad, and damned mad.

3

REVELATION

Barry Graves was almost three years younger than his attacker, four inches shorter, and forty pounds lighter. At Keith Faun's hands, Barry suffered a broken nose and cracked cheekbone, two black eyes, a twisted ankle, and bruises that turned him black and blue.

As with any assault, the damage that can't be seen lasts longest. The pain of humiliation never really goes away.

Keith's parents tried to play it off as a boys-will-be-boys spat. When that didn't fly with Barry's parents, Lloyd accused Barry of flirting with their son, propositioning him. As if that would be enough to justify such violence. Apparently, Keith had learned his homophobia and cruelty at home.

High school girls got unwanted attention all the time. Girls got hit on and even groped at school frequently. That didn't give them license to leave their pursuers gasping in the dirt, crying, bloody, and unable to stand.

The school didn't consider the assault a matter for the police. Instead, Principal Kieran Costa suspended Keith for three days. The hockey coach also pulled him from a couple of games. For his vicious assault, Keith received a vacation from the classes he hated. When he returned to the ice, his buddies celebrated him as a hero.

Barry's parents complained, of course. To try to bring a quick end to the matter, Principal Costa threatened Keith with expulsion if he didn't apologize to Barry. Keith complied and said he was sorry. However, his telling smirk sucked any power a mere apology might convey.

Too easily placated, the principal then tried to shame Barry into shaking his bully's hand. To the kid's credit, Barry steadfastly refused. Curling a busted lip, he looked Costa in the eye and said, "There's nothing more satisfying than a disingenuous apology."

Next, Costa called a school assembly to make a galactically stupid pronouncement. "I don't want violence in my school." He spoke as if they were all guilty, which made Molly furious.

"I want an end to fighting," Costa continued, "so don't fight. It's the *second* punch that starts the fight."

The feet of Barry's chair scraped against the top of the basketball key as he got to his feet. He still had to favor one leg, but he stood as tall as he could. He tried to hold back his tears, but he was not successful. "*What?* It's the *second* punch starts the fight? Really? I didn't fight. I got beat up!"

The hockey team sat together at the back of the gym. As Molly listened to them snicker, a new energy, dark and swirling, surged through her. She wanted to torment every one of them, but she sat silent, balling her hands into tight fists as she fought the urge to hurl curses at them.

Barry's moment was not over. "Was I supposed to take a beating? In your world, are there victims? *I'm right here!*" He pointed to his broken nose. "Can you see me, Mr. Costa? Do I exist? Is that the problem?"

At that, every guy on the hockey team laughed and jeered. The whole auditorium buzzed with excited whispers. Much of the laughter was of the nervous variety. Too much of it was gleeful.

Molly admired Barry for standing up to the principal. He couldn't defend himself against Keith, but his words were strong. She clapped for the kid. However, she started too late, and the assembly's applause was scattered and weak. To her great regret, seeing she was among too few allies, Molly stopped clapping too soon.

Her cheeks burned with embarrassment. She knew she should have stood with Barry. She should have added her voice to his protest. Instead, Molly remained silent.

A teacher shushed them, but the boys on the hockey team continued to whisper and sneer. Mr. Costa tried to appear conciliatory. "Barry, we'll talk about this later, in private."

"We *have* talked," Barry replied angrily. "But what are you going to *do*?"

"Sit down, Barry."

The principal's plan for peace was silly. He was basically telling the bullies that they could pick on weaker children. He may as well have said, "Take your beating and stop whining. We'll give your attackers a slap on the wrist. This is the way of the world."

Molly couldn't sleep that night. She tossed and turned and fantasized about all the unlikely scenarios that she could visit upon Keith Faun. She imagined sneaking over to the Faun house and super gluing all the doors to his house shut. What if she were to break a pane of glass and run their garden hose through it to flood their basement? She pictured the look on Keith's face if she took out his knee with a lead pipe just before a championship game.

But it was too early in her education to graduate to violence. Instead, Molly responded the only way she knew at the time. The next Saturday morning, she went to the school early and slapped two rainbow signs of her own making on Keith Faun's locker.

The first read:

I'M A SMALL TOAD WHO BEATS PEOPLE UP TO FEEL BIG AND MANLY.

The second read:

HOMOPHOBIA IS WEAKNESS!

Covered in layers of transparent industrial tape, the signs could not be ripped down easily. Slipping out of the school, Molly was satisfied she'd done something useful.

That early effort backfired. Monday morning, Keith flew into a blind rage and went after his favorite victim again. He found Barry in the school library. Certain of the culprit, Keith charged at him. The kid slipped beneath the table where he'd been reading. The bully missed grabbing him by inches.

If Keith had waited and gone after him off school grounds, Barry might have been killed or crippled. That would have been Molly's fault, but she got lucky.

Trembling with fear, Barry popped up on the other side of the table. Keith gave chase, but Barry kept the big table between them. When Keith launched himself over the table, Barry wisely retreated behind another reading table. If the bully's intentions hadn't been so murderous, it might have seemed funny, like a flailing fight in a sitcom.

Rosemary Rainier, the school librarian, saved Keith from becoming a murderer that day. With the air of someone much larger than her small frame, she put herself between the assailant and the assailed. Keith sputtered curses. Instead of giving him a moment to explain himself, Mrs. Rainier took Keith by surprise. She hauled him out of her domain by the hair.

Believing Barry had pasted the signs to his locker, the goon vowed bloody revenge. To give him time to cool off, Keith received another suspension. That was the extent of his punishment.

Barry denied having anything to do with the vandalism to Keith's locker. Costa didn't believe Barry and gave him a stern talking-to before sending the boy back to class.

The Graves family's troubles went on and on. Barry lived in fear that the whole hockey team would come after him. Lloyd and

Marjorie Faun claimed that Keith was the real victim. They proclaimed far and wide that a lawsuit would soon materialize and seek damages for slander and defamation. Silly or not, dealing with the Faun's claims was a financial burden Barry's family couldn't afford.

Lloyd Faun made rumblings with his buddies at Poeticule Bay's business association. John and Marie Graves, Barry's parents, were new to the area and trying to make a go of it in the real estate business. Lloyd made it known they should be unwelcome. Not willing to get in the middle of a spat, Lloyd's sycophants complied.

The Graves family would find no justice in town. By the time Keith returned to Poeticule Bay Consolidated High School, Barry had begun attending a school in Bangor.

Molly's failure literally made her sick. She could barely eat for days after she learned Barry and his family had been chased out of town. She didn't understand the forces that allowed the school principal and the police to look the other way.

Economics and convenience fueled the authorities' apathy. Lloyd sponsored the elementary school's baseball team and had headed the campaign to fix the community pool. He was also chairman of the town's rink committee. He bought the Zamboni himself and raised money for ice time each winter. Hockey was big in the Bay, and Keith was the team's star.

The school administration did not guarantee Barry's safety because he wasn't as valuable to the system. The town valued the Fauns. They didn't even know the Graves family.

Molly didn't know Barry, either. A grade above Barry and one grade below Keith, she only passed them in the halls. As small as the school was, she really only knew the names of her immediate classmates.

Almost everyone dressed alike, and few dared to show off any individuality except for Barry. Nothing outrageous, just maybe a little feminine and fussy. He didn't swear, wasn't interested in sports, and was a little chubby. That was enough for the bigots.

Maybe it wasn't any of that so much as that he was an easy target. Barry was small for his age. The older boys snickered derisively when they talked about the kid, laughing at his pain. "He cried like a baby!" someone said.

And with his injuries, who wouldn't? But it's that easy, Molly thought. *One day you're minding your own business and the next you're traumatized.*

Shaken by how uncaring those in charge had been, Molly was thankful to remain invisible. But a seed had been planted: What if the notorious Faun family were targets for a change? They were unfamiliar with the sensation of being victims. Molly decided she could fix that, so she began plotting. The bullies would finally know wrath.

She lost sleep mulling the problem. *Turnabout is fair play,* she thought, *and revenge is the best success.*

4

EVALUATION

Molly's revenge fantasies were complex. In her imagination, she always won, and her targets saw the error of their ways. They moaned for absolution, repented, and made restitution. Was it sadism? Not if her cause was just.

Those constant reveries built up pressure, as if she were a balloon about to pop. The urges were undeniable, almost sexual. She had to find an outlet, or she thought she might burst.

Reading a book of science fiction one day in the school library, Molly came across a passage that spoke to her. In the story, some authority figure told a young girl, "Life's not fair." The fictional heroine replied, "But we are supposed to try to make it that way."

It wasn't just the Fauns that were the problem. She decided to start small with Keith Faun's puck buddies. Her only rule was that her targets had to be deserving.

She also had to be cautious and anonymous. As her mother, Kay, would say, "Stay true to the eleventh commandment. Don't get caught."

Molly began by slipping anonymous notes into the jocks' desks. After school, it was easy to leave notes in their homeroom.

At first, she warned the bad actors to stay away from Keith Faun and be better or she would report them to the principal. That didn't work. Those first attempts were as weak and toothless as her school's anti-bullying policies.

Molly took stronger measures. Her anonymous messages to her targets became more vague. She left the puckheads a number of vague threats that took darker turns:

People are watching you and don't like what you're doing. We know where you sleep.

We know where you were last weekend. I watched you through my rifle scope. Be kind and polite, and we will move on to more deserving targets.

Even your parents don't like you. Your mom complains to my mom about you all the time. Try being kinder, and maybe you won't get kicked out. They're talking about sending you away to military school.

I saw what you did. Do you want everyone to know? Keep acting like an asshole and see what happens.

Do you think your parents know? They could find out easily. Do you think they'd kick you out or just pull you off the team and ground you until graduation?

Does your girlfriend know about the cheating? Be nicer to people or she'll find out.

Do you think the cops know yet? You're just one

phone call away from getting in deep trouble. You won't be able to handle it. You know that, right? You think you're a tough guy, but you wouldn't do well in prison.

You didn't know you were confessing, but one of your buddies recorded you in his car. Are you sure you know who to trust?

Be kinder or drugs will be found in your locker and not by you.

I have pictures. You don't want the whole town to see the pix I have of you? Pretend you're not an asshole and act nicer.

Through that writing campaign, Molly learned that fear of consequences from an unseen enemy could be a powerful force for good. Unknown to her targets, she remained safe while they studied the faces around them and wondered who was watching. For the bullies, it must have felt like getting punched while blindfolded, never knowing from where or when the next strike might come.

Whether those deserving targets had actually done something criminal wasn't relevant to the effect she sought. It was not necessary that her targets possess a conscience. Molly suspected some of them lacked that capacity. Whether or not they *felt* guilty, their paranoia softened much of their antisocial behavior at school.

No one dared to report her notes to the principal, but she couldn't claim she succeeded in turning bad people into good ones. Molly's nasty note campaign didn't deter everyone. The human skid mark, number one on her hit list, remained Keith Faun. He had already gotten away with so much, a poison pen wasn't going to get him to stop. Besides, she was determined to make his punishment more proportional to his crime.

Molly knew she couldn't beat Keith in a fair fight, but she wasn't looking for a fair fight. Barry's family had had to flee so her aim was to banish the Fauns from Poeticule Bay, too. For their sins, the whole Faun family became Molly's target.

5

INSPIRATION

The Fauns lived in a huge house on Main Street. It was an old town lot with a big front lawn that sloped toward the street. One spring night, a couple of weeks after Barry and his family fled, Molly made that lawn her canvas. Two big bags of salt served as her paint.

She'd thought long and hard about what the message on their lawn should say. Supporting Hitler might be too over the top. She'd already tried declaring Keith weak and fearful. That tactic had back-fired miserably. Burning "Whites Only" into their lawn would be too obvious.

Molly knew of few people of color who lived in the Bay. She didn't want to risk putting innocents in the crossfire. However, ISIS was in the news, and those terrorists made Mainers itchy.

The budding avenger replayed the scenario over and over in her head. She pictured Marjorie Faun rising first, wiping sleep from her eyes, contemplating her first cup of coffee. She could almost see Marjorie in her nightgown and terry robe parting her living room curtains. The woman must have been mystified when she saw cars slowing in front of her house. Drivers gawked as their passengers pointed at the message burned into their lawn: *WE SUPPORT ISIS!*

The steep angle on the slope of the lawn made for an excellent sign to the townspeople. By sundown, everyone in Poeticule Bay and a couple of neighboring towns were jabbering about it. People being people, some actually believed the Fauns might stand behind the message.

The day after Molly painted their lawn with salt, Keith didn't come to school. His whole family spent that day digging up their front yard and yelling at passersby, angrily protesting their innocence. Funny thing about innocence: The more you proclaim it, the less convincing you sound.

The next night, Molly spiked the car tires in the Fauns' driveway. At first, she worried about trying to drive a nail into a tire and how much noise she would make. She donned her ski mask and crept out of her bedroom window armed with a hammer and a pocketful of nails.

Late at night, she set off to train, just another young runner prepping to be a high school track star. She'd scooped deck nails from her father's shed. Wary of watchful eyes, Molly paused at the end of the Fauns' driveway. All was quiet. No lights shone from the windows of nearby houses.

The Fauns' red Lexus and classic 1961 Lincoln Continental, cream with whitewall tires, sat in the driveway, as vulnerable as baby chicks. Inspiration struck. She didn't need the hammer. All she had to do was wedge nails tightly under each tire, poised to puncture as soon as the vehicle rolled back. In less than a minute, she was off running again.

On the way back from school, Molly spotted the Faun family's cars at Bruce Motors. Her campaign had escalated far beyond taping signs to a locker or leaving anonymous notes. She'd crossed a Rubicon of sorts. Ruining the Fauns' lawn and flattening eight tires had escalated her ambitions. In her eagerness to avenge Barry, she'd committed vandalism of an expensive sort.

Molly hardly slept that night, convinced she'd taken her campaign too far. She had reason to worry. The next day, the school was abuzz with the rumor that Barry had come back to town to mess with the Fauns' vehicles. She worried law enforcement would go after the boy and his family.

However, it didn't take long for that story to unravel. The Bangor police department had interviewed the Graves family and cleared them of any wrongdoing. By sheer luck, Barry had been off on a school trip to museums in New York City on the night Molly sabotaged the tires.

Molly could have stopped then. More sane and sober people would say she'd done more than enough. However, those people hadn't seen Keith's smug look the day he returned to school after his suspension.

The goon bragged to the puckheads how he'd run Barry's whole family out of town. He showed no remorse, and it wasn't just bravado. He actually thought he was the hero of the story. Worse, several of his buddies agreed. They had learned nothing, so Molly resolved that her lessons would continue, *had* to continue.

But prudence made her pull back a little. Molly's next act of vandalism was more devious than expensive. A few nights later, after she assumed the Fauns had begun to drop their guard, she targeted Lloyd Faun's pride and joy.

Eleanor's Cleaning and Gleaming was the first of his chain of laundromats with locations in Bangor, Augusta, and Kennebunkport. It was dinnertime when she ran toward the big red and white signpost outside of Eleanor's. Until his son became a murderous homophobe, the most trouble Lloyd had to deal with was his dispute with the Baptists. That story had powered the rumor mill for weeks: Lloyd versus the Baptists.

Reverend Ernest Bailey was head of the congregation at Poeticule Bay Community Worship Hour. The church stood close by Eleanor's and the pastor objected to Lloyd's sign:

DROP YOUR PANTS HERE! WE WON'T JUDGE YOUR SHORT-COMINGS!

Pastor Bailey showed up at Lloyd's door, pleading in the name of decency that he change his sign to something less salacious. Lloyd crowed about the brief confrontation for weeks. "I'm a Presbyterian,"

he declared, "and I thought *we* were humorless. I slammed my door
in Bailey's face! I opened it again and told him I didn't give a shit! I
slammed it again, laughed a lot, then opened the door again to shout
that all Baptists would burn in Hell!"

His fellow Presbyterian congregants tutted and fretted and
allowed that Lloyd shouldn't have said such a thing to the gentle
pastor. They didn't come out and declare he was wrong about the fate
of Baptists in the afterlife, just that he shouldn't have said it.

Few — not even many Baptists — were so fervent that they
agreed with Pastor Bailey's prudishness. The town was generally on
Lloyd's side in the piddling matter of censoring his sign. As a matter
of decorum, however, many agreed privately among themselves that
Lloyd didn't have to be such a cackling dick about it to the poor old
fusspot.

Reverend Steven Gunter, Lloyd's pastor, gently reminded Lloyd
about the Bible's entreaty to love thy neighbor. Lloyd announced
grandly that he would capitulate. The next Sunday, the sign read:

*10% OFF DRY-CLEANING FOR PRESBYTERIANS! BAPTISTS PAY
MORE AND BURN IN HELL!*

The townspeople sighed and said things like, "Well, that's just ole
Lloyd for ya."

Molly agreed with her father's assessment. Chuck Jergins said,
"I've known Lloyd since high school, and at least I can say he's consistent. Never knew a man so determined to be a contrary asshat. I tell
ya, that whole family are a bunch of kitten drowners."

It was still daylight as Molly jogged behind the strip mall
containing Lloyd's laundromat. Dinnertime was dead time. Whether
they were around the table or taking in the news, no one was
watching the back alley behind Eleanor's.

Lloyd's Lincoln Continental was parked at the rear door of the
business. The possibility that he could pop out at any moment was
Molly's primary concern. She dealt with the door first. She'd acquired
a tube of superglue from her father's workbench and used all that
was left of it around the lock. In the time it took her to bend to untie
and retie her shoes, the glue had set.

Confident she would not be interrupted, Molly slipped her father's smallest crowbar out of her sleeve and, after a sweaty moment, popped the hubcap off the right front wheel. After delivering the planned payload, she pounded the hubcap back in place.

Gluing the door had been wise. Lloyd must have heard the metallic pounding out back. The doorknob turned, but the door did not budge. Molly wasn't quite finished, but she kept cool and finished getting the hubcap back in place.

"What the Jesus lord-leaping Christ is going on out there?" Lloyd yelled as he pounded on the door.

Molly hadn't planned on it, but disasters provide excellent opportunities to improvise. She stepped close to the door, and in as low a register as she could muster, replied, "Your...clan...will...be...banished."

It was improvisation, but Molly had learned a lot from playing D&D with her father. That particular proclamation would later get her shot, but Molly was happy as she jogged away.

6

REALIZATION

Lloyd Faun didn't suspect anyone had sabotaged his beloved car until he began following the locksmith's truck out of the alley that night. Molly had slipped four heavy bolts and a couple of screws behind the hubcap. Those metal bits made a mighty rattle in the old Lincoln.

Most people would naturally assume it was a problem with the engine. That had been Molly's intent. However, Molly's previous acts of vandalism made Lloyd more paranoid. Upon hearing the rattle, he did not drive the two blocks over to Bruce Motors. Instead, he called the sheriff to ask how long it would take the Maine State Police to get a bomb squad to Poeticule Bay.

"Word is, Lloyd is in quite a tizzy," Molly's mother told her the next night. With a wink, Kay added, "I bet it was the Baptists."

Chuck Jergins barked out a laugh from his recliner. "Lloyd let his imagination run away with him."

Kay looked annoyed. "How'd you hear about it, anyway?"

Molly's father gave a knowing smile. "You know Gordon Hobbs is the biggest gossip in town. You wanna know what's going on about anything around these parts? Catch the sheriff in the barber's chair.

Our town cop fancies himself quite the raconteur, and I guess he's not wrong. Holds court down at Ernie's every whipstitch."

"It's just that everybody loves crime stories," Kay replied. "It's not the sheriff who's so shit hot, it's his material. Gordon cornered us at a bean supper for the fire department a couple of years ago and wouldn't shut up about all the gory details about that Atkinson case."

"Yup!" Chuck caught Molly's mystified look and filled her in. "They caught Ariella Atkinson standing over her husband with a deer rifle. She didn't care to defend herself. She didn't care about anything. I don't even know why these things go to trial. When the prosecutor asked if she was a good shot, Ariella said she could light a match with a bullet at fifty yards."

"It was a competency thing," Kay interjected. "They were trying to decide if Ariel was crazy or just mean. Poor old thing didn't go to jail. After she soiled herself and sat in her own stink in court, Judge Grimshaw couldn't wait to send her off to the Waterville loony house."

"Maybe her husband deserved it," Molly suggested.

Her hand trembling, Kay made a seesaw motion. "Well, yeah, some, there is that. Denny Atkinson was no angel, quite the devil, in fact. Blackened Ariella's eyes more than once. Those two fought like two cats in a bag."

"Denny was a lot like Lloyd," her father added. "Nobody liked him, neither. Anyway, everybody in town is having quite the laugh about Lloyd's call for the bomb squad. Better, Lloyd knows we're all having a laugh."

Kay returned to her knitting. "Shouldn't have messed with the Baptists. They talk some nice, but give 'em five minutes, and they're all about the hellfire and brimstone their own selves."

Molly's crimes had an effect on the Faun family. Marjorie refused to leave the house. Lloyd was convinced dark forces were allied against him. Keith, looking even more surly than usual, stomped around school as if under a raincloud.

The next Wednesday, in an unhinged letter to the editor in *The Poeticule County Lens*, Lloyd wrote, "In my day, we weren't all so soft.

Boys settled arguments with their fists, shook hands, and left it at that. The people trying to run my family out of town are cowards. I'm sick of sympathizers to the gay mafia!"

Lloyd made it sound like the whole town stood against him. That made Molly chuckle. She didn't have an army. She was just one lone teenager.

As a loner who preferred reading to hanging out with friends, few really knew her beyond the obvious. Molly was an honors student who excelled at track and field, a star of debate club, and tall for her age. No one asked, not even once, if she'd ever fantasized about burning down the hockey rink with every member of the high school team inside.

Lila Aaronson, the school's guidance counselor, reviewed Molly's grades. She asked if Molly had any interest in going to university. "Your grades are good, especially in math."

"I prefer English and history."

"But with these scores, you could be an engineer, for instance."

"I don't know, Mrs Aaronson. Honestly, all I really want to do is read novels, eat Chinese food, and wreak havoc."

Mrs. Aaronson stared at Molly a moment to see if she'd break into a laugh. When the girl stared back at her stonily, the guidance counselor asked if everything was okay at home.

"Just kidding!" Molly said lightly. "I'm full of light and hope. Maybe academia is my thing."

"Give some serious thought to engineering. The field needs more female energy, you know?"

"I hadn't thought of that. Thank you so much, ma'am."

As Molly left the guidance office, she was inspired, but not in a way Mrs. Aaronson would likely approve.

Molly was young and optimistic, so she thought she had a chance at changing the world. All she had to do to change behavior was to find the right pain and pressure points. Certain that dangerous times called for desperate measures, her campaign against the Fauns would continue.

The girl didn't have an army, but later, she would have a squad of like-minded people on her side. To rise to that occasion, to attain that leadership role, she would have to grow into a woman. Her trial by fire still lay ahead.

7

ORATION

Molly's enthusiasm for vengeance and the Fauns' banishment had not waned. However, with Lloyd calling in the bomb squad, she decided to give them a cooling-off period. She needed Sheriff Hobbs to stand down from high alert before deciding on her next move. While she waited, the Faun family were still spun up, punching the air, and fighting ghosts.

Lloyd, sure he was surrounded by enemies at every turn, continued to posit outlandish conspiracies about the gay mafia coming after him. Hobbs told him he thought that was more of a Hollywood thing, not a worry for sane people deep in the reaches of Maine.

Rambling about her salt-burnt lawn, Marjorie Faun showed up at the Pick-Right one day conspicuously inebriated. She cursed at a woman with a baby stroller for standing in her way. Then Marjorie threw a can of pineapple rings on the floor for reasons only known to her. She was so drunk that the grocery store's proprietor, Emery Cantly, insisted on driving her home.

Keith showed up to class looking haggard and told everyone he was tasked with guarding the laundromat after dark. "Who knows when they'll come at us next? Just because the terrorists have stopped doesn't mean they're done."

Quite right, Molly thought. She waited them out, confident they would get bored after a while without further attacks.

After a week passed, Keith looked more rested and strutted around the school's halls again. But Keith was on a campaign of his own. Still defiant and convinced of his utter innocence and victim-hood, the goon searched for enemies in every face. When he approached, people looked away and pretended to be suddenly fasci-nated with the time, their lockers, or their notebooks. To catch his eye was to invite interrogation and harassment.

Then Molly saw the results of her actions in person. A student she didn't know, so thin he appeared malnourished, looked up at the wrong time and stared Keith's way a moment too long. That was all it took. Keith caught the kid by the arm. "Do I know you, boy? Barry Graves a buddy of yours, is he?"

The school's corridors were filled with students changing classes. Everyone stopped to watch.

The boy raised his chin in defiance. "I'm Dylan Caffrey."

"I asked, you friends with Barry Graves, or what?"

"I seen him around. Didn't really know him."

Keith pushed Dylan against his open locker. "It's a one-horse town, shit-for-brains. How is it you don't know him?"

Dylan was rattled, but to his credit, the boy's voice was strong. "Don't live in town. I gotta take care of the cows. I bus home. I don't hang with townies."

"Shit kicker and shit for brains, too, huh?" Keith pushed him harder into the locker.

Molly had not spoken up for Barry, but now she had a second chance. She found her voice, "He answered you, Keith."

Keith whirled on Molly. "What are you, Jergins? His lawyer? Mind your business!"

"Funny you mention lawyers. Maybe I should be yours."

Keith's eyes narrowed. "How's that?"

She turned to the gaping crowd. She had no friends in the hallway, but when she looked from girl to girl, even among the younger kids, she sensed some solidarity against the bully. At least no one was running away, and she needed an audience to make her plan work.

"Well?" Keith's tone was low, but as threatening as the rumble of thunder from a darkening sky. She had to turn that oncoming storm before he unleashed a tempest. Keith still held the kid, Dylan's shirt balled in his tight fist.

Molly had seen too much of Keith lording his power over others to remain a bystander. Not everyone had a phone, but those who did had pulled them out. She thought she had a chance to get away with saying what she wanted if she could harness the power of witnesses. Keith had the brawn. Molly's brains would have to win the day.

Sensing her time was running out, Molly gambled with her safety. Keith didn't care about school, but he desperately cared about his reputation and playing hockey. Those were his vulnerabilities, the pain points she could press.

Her throat dry, Molly's fear rose. A quaver crept into her voice, but she managed to smile. "I'm doing you a favor, dude! You and me, let's provide evidence you *didn't* hurt anyone today. Everybody? Phones up, cameras on!"

Keith's face reddened. "What? You a narc?"

"This is for *your* sake, friend," Molly replied. "If you hurt anyone at school now, that would be your third strike, right? The principal said he wouldn't give you any more chances. You're risking expulsion. That would put you off the team. I'm curious, would you have to start your senior year all over again? Here or somewhere else? How would that work?"

The goon's jaw went slack. As his eyes darted to the watching crowd, doubt and indecision crept in. His grip on Dylan's shirt loosened a fraction. Then Keith abruptly let go and turned to focus on Molly.

Her heart pounded a rapid beat. A rising feeling of elation filled her chest. The strength of it made her think she might defy gravity, lift off, and hover above her enemy.

Molly stepped nose to nose with the goon. She could smell

onions on his breath. She forced herself to stay perfectly still. Whispering so no one else could hear, she allowed a pleading note to enter her tone. "Even your daddy won't be able to push the school board around a third time, right?"

"What are you flapping your mouth about?"

"Well, you beat up Barry Graves, and you've threatened to kill him in the library. Now you're bothering another kid. He's a lot smaller than you. I'm worried it's not a good look for you. I'm not trying to embarrass you, but why are you doing this? Does your daddy beat you? Do you need help? Do you want me to call someone for you?"

The way the bully's eyebrows shot up in surprise told Molly she'd hit the bull's eye. Keith stood staring at her — no, *through* her. For a few seconds, he may have forgotten where he was entirely.

Molly continued in the same whisper, "Does your dad worry you liked Barry? Is he worried you're *like* Barry? Would he hurt you if you thought that way?"

"You do sound like a lawyer. Nobody likes lawyers, Jergins, and I'm not on trial." His lips became a thin, white line.

"I just have to wonder why you turned out this way. Everyone is wondering why you care so much who's gay and who isn't. Why is that?"

"I have a girlfriend, you stupid bitch!"

Molly had seen him walking around school with Sarah, the librarian's daughter. Ignoring that, she persisted. "Stop and think about what you're doing, man. I'm *helping* you here."

Pushing him like this, Molly stood on a trembling tightrope. Keith might lash out at her. The mob grew restless, shuffling and buzzing.

"Someday you'll look back on all this and see how silly it all was. You don't have to be up in everybody's business. Not everyone is thinking about you. They're just worried about themselves. Leave that kid alone so you don't ruin your last year of high school. You're being scouted, right? I'm worried for you and for the team. They need you."

Keith's gaze slid to the floor.

Molly's history teacher, Mrs. Abby Simmons, pushed her way

through the crowd. "Hey! People! The bell has rung! Get to class! What's going on? I've got an empty classroom, and I get lonely talking to myself! All of you have somewhere to be!"

Molly, sporting a wide and grateful grin, turned to her. "Sure, Mrs. Simmons!"

Keith turned and walked away, and Molly called after him, "You're welcome!"

Some students snickered. Mrs. Simmons shushed them and waved them on. The crowd dispersed. A few of the juniors and sophomores touched Molly's shoulder as a silent gesture of respect as they passed. She was relieved, certain that those witnesses and their phones had saved her from getting a black eye, or worse.

"What are you up to, Molly? Did you just make a bad situation worse?" Mrs. Simmons demanded.

"Me? Nah. That guy is like an ice cream headache. He's going to get worse before he gets better. Not that anyone cares, but a lot of us don't feel safe going to this school."

By her eyes, Molly could tell the teacher didn't disagree. Mrs. Simmons didn't feel safe, either.

"You should know," Mrs. Simmons said, "when you're young and immature, you've got a lot more anger and energy. You look at the state of the world and...." She trailed off. They were alone in the corridor, but the teacher still looked around nervously to make sure no one else was within earshot.

"What is it, ma'am?" Molly prompted.

The teacher's jaw worked for a moment as she searched for the right words. Finally, Mrs. Simmons said, "I just think you should appreciate that a lot of people around here, not just students, are appalled by the incident between Keith and the Graves boy. But we're also tired and just trying to get through our days. The police and the principal were informed. The ball's in their court now. What's best is to leave it be. Not our monkeys, not our circus anymore, right?"

Molly cocked her head to one side. "You're tired?"

"Of this business? Surely and immeasurably."

"If you're tired, imagine how exhausted Barry must be. It sounds like you've given up, ma'am."

"You will, too. Everybody does. When you learn the limits of what you can do, it makes sense to set your sights lower."

"Spoken as a true educator, Mrs. Simmons! You're an inspiration!"

The teacher shot her a sour look. "Tend to your own knitting, Molly, and get your butt to class."

"I've got a free period in the library, ma'am."

"Then get to it."

She'd meant to curb Keith, not shame Mrs. Simmons. "Sorry," Molly said, "maybe you're right. I guess a lot of people do give up for whatever reason. I understand you're trying to help me."

But Molly couldn't leave it at that, could not stop herself. "As long as I'm still young and full of energy, though, I think I'll keep on being angry when it's right to be angry. Your way, powerless people stay powerless. *You* taught me that, in *your* history class."

Molly thought she had earned herself a detention, but Mrs. Simmons said nothing more, spun on her heel, and strode back to her classroom.

Whatever happens, Molly cautioned herself, *don't turn into her. Don't get so chicken of being wrong that you don't do right.*

8

CONTRIBUTION

As Molly headed toward the library for her free period, Dylan Caffrey caught up with her. "Hey! Thanks for dealing with that asshole. I thought I was dead."

"I don't think he'll bother you again, at least not at school — "

"He's big and big mad. He still could take it out on me."

"You're not wrong. Don't get caught alone in the bathroom and head straight home after school."

"I told the truth about taking the bus right after last bell. I don't hang with townies, but you're all right. Can I ask you something? You're in the debate club, right? Saw you in that assembly a while back."

"Yeah, why?"

"I was wondering how you came up with all that on the spot? It was a great speech. Stopped him so cold, like you poured *ice* over him."

"Gift of gab and a little inspiration, I guess."

"Pretty awesome."

"Thanks."

"You think he's gay? That why he did what he did to that kid?"

Molly shook my head. "No idea, dude, but I doubt it. That's kind of old. People look for reasons, but either way, it doesn't matter. You already called it. He's a colossal asshole. Keith Faun does what he wants because he thinks he's the prince of Poeticule Bay. It's not about gay or straight. I don't care about that, and I don't care what Keith Faun thinks. I doubt he thinks much at all. Whatever his dysfunction, I care what he *does*. For him, it's all about power."

Dylan sighed. "My parents say getting in fights is just part of growing up — "

"Shouldn't be."

"That's what I told them," Dylan replied. "What they don't get is everybody and anybody goes to high school. Adults don't have to deal with this shit, but we do. We have to. I shouldn't have to worry about losing my teeth just so I can come here and learn algebra I'll never use. I look at a guy like that and figure he's going to jail someday."

"Yeah or become president."

Dylan let out a braying laugh. "I don't have a bunch of older brothers to beat him up, but if I can ever do anything for you, let me know." With that, he disappeared down the hallway.

Molly ducked into the girls' bathroom and shut a stall door. Only then did the shakes hit. She was scared and giddy. Those conflicting feelings struck all at once.

She had lied to Dylan. Molly laid awake nights rehearsing variations of that little speech. She had practiced it in her head many times, sometimes even in front of the mirror.

In some fantasies, Keith was tied to a raft as frigid Atlantic water lapped over him. She smiled at the thought of standing over the bully, ready to push him out into the dead zone forever.

In other scenarios, Keith woke up naked and handcuffed to something on the gym stage. Just as the curtain rose on an assembly of the entire school, bright lights would hit his wide eyes. As he died of embarrassment, Molly would deliver a triumphant speech about the end of his tyranny at Poeticule Bay Consolidated.

Molly was disappointed she hadn't had the chance to include the part where Keith's parents would send him away to military school. In her imagination, there were more witnesses. She hadn't received the applause she'd hoped for, either. In a perfect world, the principal and the school board would publicly apologize and establish a county-wide rule of zero tolerance against school violence.

Molly glanced in the mirror as she washed her hands. *No black eye and still have all my teeth. Tiny victories*, she told herself.

For the moment, school felt safer. However, she had to keep up the pressure and turn up the heat on the Fauns. Entitled and protected by the town elders, the family's position in the community still shielded their precious hockey monster.

If there were such a title in the yearbook, Keith Faun would have been elected Most Likely to Become a School Shooter. To protect the innocent, Poeticule Bay Consolidated needed one more maniac.

I am that maniac, Molly thought.

She inspected her reflection in the bathroom mirror for a full minute. She tested a smile but didn't feel it yet. Her face was still a mask that didn't quite fit.

Did she look different? Had she always been this way? Had circumstances brought this out in her? Did anyone have this capacity? If Keith weren't a monster, would her talents have laid dormant forever?

Whatever the cause, she was proud of her acting job in the face-to-face encounter with the bully. Molly had confronted him, but she almost sounded caring and compassionate, as if she were really concerned for Keith Faun.

Addressing her reflection, Molly declared, "I'm not interested in healing wounds. I'm here to slide in the blade and twist the knife on the way out."

This time, when she smiled, there was real happiness behind it.

9

CONFRONTATION

The next day, Molly went on an after-dinner trail run through the neighborhood and in woods behind the Faun property. Scoping out their house, she spotted three new surveillance cameras. One monitored their driveway. The other two were placed at the front and back doors.

She kept running, following the trail all the way to where it met the shore. With the cool breeze in her hair, arms and legs pumping, runner's high kicked in. For a while, she felt like she could run forever, escaping to somewhere better, someplace where everyone was safe and free of worry.

Eventually tiring, she turned back. Muscle fatigue began to drain her energy, and she began to fantasize about more mundane and achievable goals, like enjoying a hot shower. As she retraced her route behind the Faun's house, Marjorie Faun stood in the middle of the trail, blocking the way.

Molly gave the woman a nod and paused, jogging in place and miming checking her pulse. The mother of the monster stalked toward her. Had she been waiting? Was this a trap? Did they know what Molly was up to?

Marjorie was one of those people who always had the harried air of someone who was late for something. Nervous energy was one thing. Keith's mother was downright jittery. Pointing accusatorially with her cigarette, she demanded, "What are you doing back here?"

"Training. What are you doing?"

Marjorie glanced at the cigarette in her hand. "The opposite of training, I guess. My husband doesn't like me smoking in the house."

Molly shrugged and bobbed her head. "Well, have a nice evening, ma'am." Before she could take three strides, the woman put up a hand to stay Molly's exit.

"Keith!" Marjorie shrieked. "*Keeeeith!* Get out here!"

It was Molly's turn to be jittery. This was only supposed to be a reconnaissance mission. She'd jogged along this path before many times and had never spotted Marjorie.

The woman screamed for her son again.

"I've got to get home," Molly said.

"Stay put. I know who you are. I saw you. Thanks to you, my son is all over social media acting the fool."

Keith appeared, jogging out from the back door barefoot, bare chested, wearing only baggy pyjama pants.

Molly had no witnesses to back her up this time, and she felt their absence. Her anxiety shot higher as the boy spotted her.

His lip curled in disgust. "Jergins? You bitch — "

"Keith!" Marjorie interrupted. "We're having a civilized discussion here."

And then he can kill me, Molly thought.

Marjorie glared. "We didn't appreciate some of your remarks at the school, young lady. The suggestion that my husband mistreated Keith was way out of line — "

"And talking like I'm gay!" Keith interjected.

"Son, please, let me handle this!" She was speaking to Keith, but her eyes never left Molly.

"You said hurtful things," Marjorie continued. "My husband is livid. He wants to sue you and your family for slander."

Molly was about to speak, but the woman held up a palm to stop her. "I talked Lloyd out of that. Getting the courts involved would only make this misunderstanding last longer and get bigger. The last thing we want is more attention to this tempest in a teapot. Besides, I know about your mother's troubles."

Troubles, Molly thought, *that was the* way *of the Bay.* Naming diseases was best left to doctors. For everyone else, uttering the technical term for a medical problem invited the same malady upon the speaker. People spoke in haunted whispers of the C-word or said someone was "poorly." On her bad days, Molly's mother stayed in bed and muttered, "The day's a-wastin', but I'm not up to nonsense."

Marjorie Faun's pitying tone was insincere, as fake as her fading blonde dye job.

"And, of course, with your father being on the dole — "

"Veteran's disability," Molly shot back. "He does what he can."

"Part-time handyman or whatever, dear. My point is, I doubt any judgment we could get against you would be worth our time. Can't squeeze pennies from the penniless."

"How kind."

"Someone is harassing us," Marjorie continued. "Ever since the Graves boy left town, I get stares from people at the grocery store. Folks I used to have game night with are suddenly unavailable for socializing. This is unacceptable. This is our *home.* We've been here for generations, and that boy's family? They're just come-from-aways. This is *our* town."

As if she owns everything, Molly thought. *As if she owns us.*

"Somebody screwed with our cars and the door to my dad's shop," Keith put in.

Molly heard her pulse pounding in her ears. *Are they on to me?*

"The whole town has a hard-on for us," Keith said. "I don't know who these guys are, but I suspect it's that — "

Marjorie held up one index finger, a warning for her son to shut up. "Careful!"

Keith went quiet, but Marjorie took up the homophobic banner for her son. "You know that pair of men who own that knickknack shop? Candles, seagull whirligigs, and touristy books? Stuff for the cottage life?"

"They're married. Definitely part of the alphabet mafia!" Keith imparted this information with the same heavy tone one might use to assert that a Russian nuclear vessel had surfaced down at the wharf.

"Those people are like us in one very important way," Marjorie said. "They stick together and so do we."

Her look and tone suggested she was trying to sound reasonable. "They might not have anything to do with the attacks on us directly. I bet they *brunch* with people who know what's really going on."

She used the word brunch as if it were something nefarious — possibly vicious — a code word only known to gay people. In other circumstances, Molly might have grinned at that.

"Whatever comes next, we're ready for them when they come for us," Marjorie concluded. "We've taken precautions. We got cameras now. No one's getting into our house without us knowing it."

"And Dad's got his shotgun ready, 'cuz that's a lot closer than the sheriff." Keith wore a murderous grin, but it faded as his mother pulled him toward Molly.

She looked in her son's eyes and nodded toward the girl. "Go ahead, what we talked about. You know what you gotta say."

Keith gritted his teeth. "I'm supposed to thank you for holding me back. You said some shitty things, and you were a real bitch about it — "

At that, his mother reached up and smacked the back of Keith's head hard. "Try again!"

Keith cleared his throat, trying to find words that approximated the gratitude his mother insisted he express. "I got a little crazy. I'm working on that. I don't like how you did it, but your little stunt probably kept me from getting kicked off the team."

"And out of school," Marjorie prompted.

He shrugged at what was obviously a low priority for him.

Barry had joked that there was nothing more satisfying than a forced apology. The same is true of empty gratitude.

Looking from mother to son, Molly wondered what they wanted from her. Agreement? Commiseration? Absolution? She felt no twinges of mercy, no regret at her petty acts of vandalism. The woman had threatened to sue her for defamation and, in the same breath, said her family was too lowly and poor to bother with.

Worse, Marjorie Faun had minimized her son's threats and violence. Barry's safety was not some sort of misunderstanding, nor was it a tempest in a teapot. The Graves family had been run out of town, but the Fauns cast themselves as victims.

Only now that they'd experienced shunning from their social circle and dealt with Molly's harassment did they want peace. And they wanted it on their terms. No real apology. No reform. No restitution.

"Well," Molly said, "I'm sure things will work out. I have to get home now. I've got a math test to study for."

"Good!" Marjorie said. "That's good. You could learn something from this one, boy!"

Keith grimaced and turned away.

Molly ran on, relieved to have escaped and more determined than ever to teach the whole family a lesson they'd never forget.

10

PREPARATION

Molly debated long and hard about returning to the Fauns' house that same night. When the police investigated, they would undoubtedly inquire if anyone had been hanging around the edges of their property.

It seemed reckless, but she had several defenses planned if the sheriff came knocking. First, her confrontation with Keith at school was an effort to *de-escalate*. Second, Molly tracked her routes, mileage, and resting and peak heart rates. She had kept a running log that went back a year. Her routes were all over town, and the trail through the woods behind the Faun house was part of a regular rotation, not an aberration. That path snaked down to the beach, so it was well-traveled by joggers, hikers, and dog walkers. In a town full of suspects, Molly would be one needle in a haystack made of needles.

Ironically, it was the Fauns themselves who would later provide the evidence that appeared to exonerate Molly. Video evidence.

The shenanigans Molly had planned was best performed in the town's deepest and darkest hours. She paced her room, full of nervous energy, waiting to make sure her parents — and the town — were asleep. She guessed this must be what it was like to stand at the door of an airplane, wondering whether to trust your parachute.

But her mother called from her bedroom, "Molly?"

Usually, her father took care of her mother in the night. However, they slept in separate bedrooms because his loud snoring disturbed Kay's sleep. Some nights, he slept so deeply he didn't hear her call. When that happened, it was up to Molly to help out.

When Molly appeared at the bedroom door, she found her mom sitting up in bed. Since the queen mattress used to be for two, her once-formidable mother looked small, almost childlike.

"Can't sleep?"

Kay shook her head. "Your father could sleep on a clothesline. Not me. And you're up? Tell me, do you feel it, too?"

"Feel what?"

Her mother gave a helpless shrug. "It's as if there's a hum in the background, I think, not quite there, but there. It's like something at the edge of your eye that you can't look at directly, can't quite catch. In olden times, I would have said it's ghosts. Lots of cause for insomnia, though."

"Did you take your sleeping pill?

Her mother waved that suggestion away. "Don't wanna use that until I really need it! I'm not alone, up to all hours. Since the water went bad, a lot of people 'round here don't sleep right. For a bunch, it's money worries. For others ... I don't know, but I think it's the bad water out there. We're all a little watery, one way or t'other."

Molly stared at her mother blankly.

"You don't feel it?" Kay gestured vaguely in the direction of the bay. "The poison? The bad energy from down deep in the dark?"

I feel the pull of the dark, yes, Molly admitted to herself. But she didn't say so.

Kay beckoned the girl closer, reaching, her arm and hand shaking. "Help me up a little, would ya?"

Molly clasped her mother's arm around the forearm, so thin, like a brittle branch. Her mother scooted her butt closer to the edge of the bed until she could grab the bedrail on the side of the mattress.

"Strayed too far into the middle of bed," she muttered. "It's nice to have the whole thing to myself most nights, but for a while there I felt like I was lost at sea!"

In high school, Kay had excelled in the heptathlon. Now, she moved slowly and carefully, as if the world might turn upside down at any moment. In a way, Molly supposed that had already happened. Betrayed by her body, Kay was trapped. At her worst, her mother complained she felt claustrophobic, as if her very skin was a garment that was far too small, too tight.

Molly wasn't sure exactly when the change in her mother's posture began. Such changes are almost invisible when you see the same person every day. Kay had definitely become more stooped. Her neck was always bent as if she'd dropped something and was searching the floor for it.

"Can I get you something, Mom?"

"I'm needful of another Katherine Hepburn treatment."

By that, Kay meant she intended to have a cold shower. Molly had looked into it at the school library. People often thought the famous actress had Parkinson's. She did not. Instead, she'd been afflicted by an essential tremor. However, Hepburn did find cold showers exhilarating and reportedly enjoyed a cold spritz more than once a day. It had nothing to do with treatment of her tremor.

Molly had explained to her mother that the frequent showers were more a beauty treatment Hepburn used to try to keep her skin looking younger. Kay was undeterred. The cold showers refreshed her.

"Would you get me a towel? One of the fancy, fluffy ones your father ordered from that store in Boston? He always forgets, but you know the ones."

Molly nipped out to the linen closet, retrieved a towel, and was back in a moment.

Once Kay was out of bed, she seemed able to walk fairly well. Sometimes her balance was off. Chuck already had a walker tucked away in the back of the shed, ready for when it was needed. Molly hated that walker. To her, it felt less like an assistive device set aside by a thoughtful husband and more like a harbinger of bad things to come.

Kay got to the door before she turned back to look Molly up and down. "You're still dressed."

Molly shrugged. "Couldn't sleep."

"PJs in the wash, or something? I feel like it's something."

"I was up studying."

Her mother studied Molly for another long moment. "What's going on with you, anywho?"

"Nothing."

"Try again."

"I don't know what you mean."

"You've never needed to study so much before."

"Algebra. I'll never use it, but somehow, it's supposed to be the most important thing in my life right now. Despite what teachers demand, can't be good at everything."

Kay waved that away. "*You* can be good at everything or anything. What's up with you? Did somebody pee in your cereal bowl?"

"I'm fine," Molly insisted.

"I ask because you have me wondering."

"I'm telling, so there's no reason to wonder."

Her mother's eyes narrowed. "The other day, I was nappin' in batches and snoozin' in snatches. You know how it goes. When night came, that evil background hum was back. I couldn't sleep a wink, so I gave up the losing proposition. Got myself up, ambulatin' and perambulatin'. Heated up the bed something awful and couldn't get cool. One curse at time, I say. That seems at least half-fair. Anyway, up and about and feeling snoopy, I peeked in your room. Your bed was dead empty and made up, not a wrinkle. What's that about? You weren't out of the house at that hour, surely? I hope not!"

"Must have been the night I fell asleep on the couch in the basement. Monster movies. Didn't want to disturb you or Dad with the TV."

"Ah, I see. And were you alone on the downstairs couch? Is there a boy somewhere hopin' to do some heavy courtin'?" Kay laughed. "That's what my father woulda called it."

Molly chuckled and replied, perhaps a little too loudly, "No, no boys!"

"I can't imagine why not. Surely there's a bunch of needy little buggers making cow eyes at you all day at school. At your age, boys mostly look good, long as you can stand the smell, of course."

Molly burst out laughing.

Her mother shushed her. "Careful! Don't wake your father. He's getting up early to work on Mrs. Iverson's fence."

Mother and daughter both paused, cocking their heads in the same manner to listen for movement in the bedroom across the hall. The slow snores remained long and steady.

Satisfied Chuck still slept, Kay grinned and continued, "Are you sure you have not, as they used to say in old romances, 'taken a lover?'"

Cringing and laughing at the same time, Molly protested in a whisper, "*Mom! No!*"

Her mother bobbed her head in approval. "And a good thing, too. At this age, boys are all hormones and no brains."

Molly could think of a few exceptions, but given her experiences with Keith and the puckheads, her mother wasn't all the way wrong.

"Do you need help getting into the shower?"

Kay scowled. "The day I need that much assistance, sedate me with all the liquor we've got in the pantry. When I can't wipe my own ass, just take me out behind the shed and shoot me."

"Don't talk like that."

"Eh, it's the depression talking. Comes and goes. Sometimes just dreaming of my next extra cheesy pizza slice is enough to make me think all this nonsense" — she gestured to her head and her body -- "is worth the toil and trouble."

"It's worth it," Molly said. "You're worth it. Dad needs you."

Her mother waved a trembling hand dismissively. "Yeah ... sure."

"Hey, are you okay, Mom? I mean, really?"

"You know I'm not into boo-hooin', but I must admit, I woke up crying one morning last week."

"What happened?"

"Nothing new, exactly, but I sure gave myself a jolt of self-pity. My last dream of the night right before I woke up at dawn. I was running through the woods toward the shore, running like a deer, running like you. It felt so real that when I came to, I wasn't even sure I was in my own bed at first. You know that feeling? I had that confusion for a few seconds. It was like I was in two places at once. Then I found myself back in my bed. I couldn't run anymore. I'll never run again."

Molly hugged her. She tried to find comforting words but came up empty, so she said nothing. At that moment, her mother felt smaller than ever.

Ebbing, Molly thought. *My mother is ebbing away like the tide pulls away into the dead zone.* Reluctant to let go, mother and daughter stayed like that for a time. It was her mother who finally broke the embrace.

Kay stared into Molly's eyes. "When you run, run for me, will you? Enjoy it. *Enjoy* it! In the day-to-day, it's gonna feel like all the clocks are broken, but that's not true. Time goes so fast. I want you to have a big life, you know? You're not just my daughter. You're my friend."

With that, Kay turned and shuffled off to the bathroom for her shower.

With a lump in her throat, Molly sat on the bed and waited in case her mother needed any more help.

It was another hour before Molly was satisfied the house was finally quiet. She crept down to the basement and dug out her father's old bulky winter coats from the back of a closet. She put on her father's old parka on top of two layers of her own coats. Then, she stopped by the shed to pick up her next weapon of choice in her mission to exile the Fauns.

Poeticule Bay's emptiness called to Molly as if the dark had the quality of osmosis. To bring about balance, the night demanded she exit the light and leave behind the safety of her home. With her mission top of mind, she slipped out the back door and into the welcoming night.

"I'm going to run," she said aloud. It was a vow to her ailing mother and to herself. She added, "I'm going to run, and I'm going to enjoy this thoroughly!"

She was dead wrong.

11

EXECUTION

The wind was up. Clouds raced across the moon. The town lay silent except for the waves crashing against the rocky shore, a sound she rarely noticed during the day. Nighttime was Molly's time.

Her father's big parka fit loosely over the layers of clothing. Underneath it all, Molly wore a Lycra jogging outfit. The parka added the most bulk. Between the winter gear, her ski mask, and Chuck's Allagash Brewing Company hat, Molly thought she could easily pass for a big fat dude, at least in the dark.

She felt awkward in her many layers and oddly comforted at first. Then, she grew hot and sweaty. The closer she got to the Faun home, the more adrenaline pumped through her blood. She felt a confusing mixture of anticipation and fear.

The anticipation leaked away as she got closer. Her stomach was all butterflies made of nerves. Molly considered turning back to give more time between her appearance on the trail and her next attack. What kept her going was Barry Graves. She loved that he'd ignored Principal Cisco's order to shake his tormentor's hand. She admired his defiance as he stood before the whole school, refusing to settle for less than he deserved.

His parents whisked Barry away for his safety, but if he knew what she was doing, Molly was sure he'd approve. She was nearly certain he'd be by her side as she stormed the castle.

But her resolve went deeper than concern for a stranger. It was spite, really. Unclear of her own motivations, Molly did not credit Marjorie's insults as her main motivator then. She'd hated how Marjorie Faun had spoken about her father as if he were some sort of freeloader. As if he didn't matter.

I have to keep the pressure up, she thought. *They have to feel what Barry and his family felt.*

She'd once heard a story about Mozart, or was it Beethoven? As a kid, he was a late sleeper. To drive her little prodigy out of bed, his mother would play only seven keys of an octave on their piano. He probably had OCD, because he was compelled by a force as irresistible as gravity to leap from his warm bed to race downstairs and complete the octave over and over.

That's what Molly's compulsion felt like, a growing, irresistible pressure. She could have restrained herself, but she felt helpless under the weight of her anger. Compulsion is not the same as conviction, but Molly had convinced herself she was doing a heroic thing, performing just actions. She didn't care where the Fauns fled, but it wasn't fair that the Graves family had to run while the monsters stayed and gloated about facing no consequences.

I'm a prodigy, too, Molly thought. *Maybe I should order business cards. All I have to do is figure out how to monetize the vengeance business.*

But her confidence did flag. Maybe she was sensing the same vague thing her mother felt, an unidentifiable wrongness.

Does Mom know something I don't?

She dismissed that notion, but her sense of danger heightened as she entered the forest trail that would lead her to her enemies. The pines and balsam firs closed ranks around her, deepening the blackness of the night. Molly kept going. Flicking on her little pen flashlight, she kept it low to the ground so she could stick to the trail and remain less visible.

The way was mostly clear, but occasionally roots crossed the path here and there, threatening to trip the unwary. A fall in all her puffy armor would pose little threat, but if she twisted an ankle, she would have to call off the mission.

Escape always had to take priority over execution. As her mother would say, "If you're going to do something dumb, be smart about it."

Soon, the backyards of houses came into view from the trail. Molly switched off the penlight and advanced slowly, cautiously. The moon slipped from behind the clouds intermittently. As the moonlight shifted, the houses transformed from dark silhouettes to pale suggestions and back in a slow, hypnotic strobe.

Molly stopped behind a tree with a clear line of sight to the Faun house. It was hard to be sure in the dark, but this might have been Marjorie's smoking tree. She knelt, watched, and waited. Too far inland, she'd left the comforting beat of the waves behind.

Marjorie's whiny voice came back to her. "*Our* town," she'd said.

"*My* town, bitch," Molly muttered.

Life's not fair, but we're supposed to try to make it that way. It was a good mantra. It strengthened her resolve.

All lights were extinguished save for the tiny red blink of a surveillance camera by the back door. It was pointed at the gate between the backyard and the top of their driveway. Molly knew she'd be stepping into its field of view but was confident in her disguise.

She pictured Lloyd, Marjorie, and Keith reviewing the recording in the morning and saying, "Who the hell was that guy?"

Satisfied she was as safe as could be, Molly pulled her can of spray paint from one of the parka's inside pockets. She was sweating but smiling, too. Now that she was in place, she was excited. It wasn't nervous energy that made perspiration suck the fabric of her T-shirt to her back. She was simply wearing too many layers.

Her only regret was that she had to shake the can to prep it. There was a little marble in there that made a racket as it mixed the paint. Molly had found the can forgotten on a bottom shelf of her father's shed. It was old but wasn't too light. Upon testing it, there seemed enough pressure to give the aerosol a good spray.

This can had been used to touch up the door to the shed to make it look more like a little barn. She was thankful her dad was a hoarder when it came to tools and the odds and ends of repair projects. It wouldn't do to buy a new can of paint on a Tuesday afternoon and use it for graffiti that night. Poeticule Bay was too small a town to be so careless.

Emerging from the tree line, Molly headed across the backyard. She adopted an exaggerated limp. She had rehearsed this scenario in her mind whilst brainstorming a list of harassment techniques. If she were captured on video, it wouldn't be enough to appear different. To complete the illusion that she was someone else entirely, it was wise to act differently, too.

Stepping from the grass onto the back patio, she arrived behind the gate. Atop the little fence, she spotted the rear of another camera that was set to monitor the driveway. After two attacks on their cars, Molly wasn't going to risk going back to that well again.

That was unfortunate. Limburger was the most pungent cheese she knew of. Stuffing it up the exhaust pipes would stink up their cars pretty well, perhaps permanently. However, her budget didn't allow for such a purchase.

Her father, always the softer touch of her parents, gave her an allowance, but what he could spare wasn't much. In past summers, Molly had picked up a few shifts at the Dairy Queen. The last job she had was working as a camp counselor and cleaner for kids at the Christian camp in Legger's Notch.

Molly considered cutting the driveway camera's cable with the jackknife she'd brought. Doing so could leave the Fauns wondering if their cars had been tampered with again. That could spark a fresh round of paranoia. However, she decided not to improvise and left that option for another night. Continual pressure better suited her ends.

The girl stepped past the black rectangle of a back window to the expanse of white wall. The only thing that interrupted her graffiti was a power meter.

The parka, combined with the other jackets, squeezed under

Molly's armpits, limiting her range of motion. Her paint job wouldn't be as big as it might have been, but no matter. Now, she just wanted to get it done.

As she got to leaving her dire message, the clouds parted. Molly was bathed in pale moonlight. The red paint looked black. The spray sounded too loud at first. The aerosol pressure weakened too quickly. Molly had to shake the can again. The little marble bouncing around in there, so loud in the quiet of the night, sounded like a primordial alarm.

The bad feeling in the pit of Molly's stomach rose to an ache. Still, she pressed on. She had come too far and now that she'd started, she was determined to finish. It wouldn't do to allow the Fauns any comfort. Incompetent harassment would not move them.

The can ran out of paint. Impatient and rash, Molly jiggled the can harder. A light popped on upstairs, but she didn't have much left to write.

She got to the middle of her last word. Almost done, she stepped into the edge of a microwave field and triggered a motion sensor. A spotlight popped on, hitting Molly in sickly yellow light.

How many seconds did she have? Awakened from a dead sleep, whoever was coming to investigate would probably pause to put on shoes or slippers. They'd look to the cameras or peer out of a window. By the time they got to the first floor, she'd surely be gone.

Molly was mistaken. The back door burst open. Lloyd Faun came up the concrete steps shouting curses. He wore nothing but boxer shorts. He carried a double-barreled shotgun.

Lloyd didn't call out, "Who goes there?" or, "The police are on their way!" He said, "Hold it right there, or I'll shoot you down where you stand."

She froze for a second as he closed the distance. If he'd kept away, he would have had her for sure. Instead, he kept on coming, one free hand outstretched, reaching for Molly's ski mask.

She didn't think about getting shot. She didn't think at all. Instead, she ducked under his outstretched arm, knocked the shotgun to one side, and sprayed what little was left of the red paint in his face.

He coughed and reeled as she took off for the woods at full speed. No time to fake a limp, her only hope was to rely on the talent to which she devoted six days of each week. Molly could run.

A dog barked somewhere nearby. Lloyd's coughing, choking, and curses followed her, but he sounded far away. She had covered three-quarters of the distance to the safety of the tree line when she heard the first shotgun blast.

Lloyd's first shot went wide. The second did not.

12

ESCALATION

At first, getting shot felt like getting hit in the back by a giant's fist. Molly stumbled forward for a few steps, recovered, and ran for the safety of the tree line.

A couple of dogs in a nearby yard barked frantically. Behind her, Lloyd Faun screamed curses. Molly ran on harder and faster than she had in any race. That was until she blundered into bushes and tree branches that slapped her face. She was forced to slow enough to find the trail in the dim light.

She realized then that she still held the empty paint can. She shoved it in an inner pocket of the parka. Panting, Molly searched frantically for her little pen light.

She imagined Keith running through the woods, catching up, tackling her, and pressing her into the ground. Head-to-head, he might have outweighed her by almost a hundred pounds. She'd be no more a threat to him than Barry Graves had been.

Molly considered leaving the trail and pushing through the forest until she reached Shoreline Road. That might give her pursuers more time to catch up. If she went to ground, how long could she hide and remain safe? The sheriff and his deputies might find her when the sun came up.

The darkness is my friend, she thought. *Darkness is my friend.*

More desperate for escape than confrontation, she remained on the trail and opted for speed over stealth. She tripped twice more before emerging on Center Street. Out of the cover of the woods, she felt exposed, almost as if she were naked.

Her breath came fast and shallowly. Her heart pounded. The layers of coats felt like a sauna. She yanked off the ski mask and drank in deep breaths of cool night air. With her burst of adrenaline wearing off, her right shoulder blade began to burn. Molly had once been stung by wasps as a child. This hurt in a similar way, only much more so.

The electric pain in her shoulder blade sang at a high buzz and stayed there. She winced and groaned but kept moving. Gulping air, weeping but stifling her cries, Molly hurried home. She clung to the edges of dark streets, ready to jump into the bushes or behind trees at the approach of any people or cars.

Not just any people! Searchers. Law enforcement.

The Fauns would surely have called the sheriff by now. Maybe an ambulance. She wondered if she had blinded or poisoned Lloyd with the paint. She felt no regret at that, only the terror of being identified and caught.

The closer she got to home, the darker her thoughts became. She might have been better off waiting with him for the police and the ambulance to arrive. She'd go to jail, but at least she would receive medical attention sooner.

Molly hurried on through side streets until she got two blocks from her back door. Then she took to weaving through backyards.

She began to slip the heavy parka down her arms but thought better of it immediately. The stinging pain reminded her again of wasp venom. She had to stifle a cry as she shrugged back into the coat.

Molly wouldn't be able to examine her wound until she got to the full-length mirror in her room. Even then, given the gunshot wound's location, she would have to borrow the hand mirror from the bathroom to assess the damage.

What am I going to do? Will I have to leave town like Barry? What will my parents say?

She sat on the back step of her house to catch her breath. If she dripped blood on the floor, she'd have to clean it up, and bending over hurt a lot. She didn't fancy working a bucket and mop.

Gingerly, she stepped into the kitchen. Looking behind her, she searched for a blood trail and found none. She breathed a sigh of relief, but she knew she was hanging on to a temporary reprieve. Molly was putting off the inevitable. She was doomed.

Maybe I'm dying, and the cops won't get to me first.

Molly took another few steps. She still didn't seem to be losing blood to the floor. She reasoned that her layers of clothes must be soaking it up.

When she turned to head upstairs, her father stood in the doorway to the kitchen in his old robe, worn and threadbare. Stock-still with a steaming mug in his hand, he commented, "You're up early."

"Early morning run."

"In my parka?"

Molly didn't speak. There was nothing she could say. Chuck gazed at his daughter steadily, reading her face. "You're in pain. Tell me."

Still, she stood frozen and mute.

"You been tormenting the Fauns, haven't you?"

Molly didn't deny it.

"Ever since that Graves boy got beat up and his family got run out of town, you've been banging around the house. You've gotten quieter but angrier. I see it."

She choked back a sob. "What Keith did and how the Fauns just got off with no consequences ... it isn't right!"

Chuck put a finger to his lips. "Mom is still sleeping."

"Sorry," Molly whispered, "but I'm not sorry about what I've done."

"I know Lloyd from way back. You'll never catch me asking you to be sorry. I went to school with him. He wasn't in my grade, but he was a terror. Elbowed me upside the head playing basketball once. He's been a legendary asshole from the time he was a pup."

"So, it's genetic," Molly said, "and now I'm dealing with his son."

Her father nodded. "All the way back to the beginning of time, Fauns have all been bad seeds, grifters, and pond scum. Never knew a good one. One way or 'nother, seems family is destiny."

Molly looked up at him sharply. She loved her father, but until that moment, she hadn't given him much credit for being interesting. Suddenly, he'd become someone she didn't know. And yet, Chuck was more like her than she ever suspected. She would soon discover he was adept in skills at which she was a novice.

Molly winced as she lowered herself into a chair at the kitchen table.

"What happened?"

She shook her head and gestured to her back. Molly expected her father to panic. Instead, Chuck stepped behind her and inspected the damage to his coat. Without a word, he gently slipped the parka from her shoulders.

She groaned. For a moment, she thought she would vomit. Molly swallowed her gorge.

"Breathe slower," he said. "When you're in pain, bracing for impact makes it worse."

Gently, he pulled off the next layer and then the third coat. Down to her T-shirt, she asked, "Is there a lot of blood?"

"Not hardly. Hold still." Chuck reached for the kitchen scissors from their place by the knife block. He cut through the polyester and cotton to expose her wound.

"How bad is it?" Molly whimpered.

"You'll live," he said. "Maybe more important to you right now, you're going to get away with whatever you did tonight."

It hurt when she took a deep breath. It hurt just as much when she let out a long sigh, but that was the sound of relief.

13

EXPLANATION

"You're gonna be a pretty shade of purple for a while, but you'll be fine."

"But Lloyd *shot* me!"

"Nah, not hardly, but in addition to the purple pain, you'll be a deep red. Red from embarrassment for getting sloppy and overeager. That and poor preparation are usually the culprit when you look to the roots of misadventures."

Molly had feared her father would freak out. Now, she was irked that he was too calm. "I did mention I was shot, right?"

"Saw lots of wounds in the Army. This is a lot less than a mortal wound. You got lucky."

"Doesn't feel like it!"

"Bad and good are both kinds of luck," he replied laconically. "Settle down, and don't catastrophize. Concentrate on the pain, and you amp it up. You'll convince yourself it's worse than it is, and that's bad for your blood pressure. High blood pressure from panic makes you bleed more."

"How am I alive, though? Or at least not crying in the back of an ambulance?"

"First off, we can't afford an ambulance, so you can forget about getting that ride. Second, you got hit with rock salt."

Chuck informed her of this in such a professorial tone that Molly began to calm down. As her mother would say, "He sounds like he knows his onions."

"You've got no pellets in you. The layers of coats did you a favor. Looks more like he got you with the end of a baseball bat. No penetration to worry about. Outside of twenty yards, it probably wouldn't have even felt like a hit from a hailstone."

Her father's demeanor flummoxed Molly. Chuck Jergins had never been one to get excited easily. He had never spanked her. She couldn't even remember him yelling in anger, not even once. Still, his calm in the middle of what she considered an emergency was eerie.

"First things first," he said. "Are the police on their way? Have we got to get your story straight?"

"I wore a mask."

"And all those coats to make you look bigger — "

"To look like a dude, yeah."

"Good. And you're sure you weren't followed?"

She shook her head.

"Say yes or no."

"No, not followed."

"So, you weren't totally stupid."

She winced as he placed a warm tea towel over her wound. "My stupidity is incomplete, yeah."

"Come Christmas, you owe me a new parka."

Relieved she wasn't going to bleed to death, she remained irritable. "How are you ... you know, how are you like this?"

"Lotta boys over a lotta Halloweens got shot in the ass by farmers with rock salt. Stealing pumpkins on a full moon virtually guaranteed it. If you mix in rice with your salt load, it's even better. The kid who gets shot with rice would run on home to sit in a bath to try to dissolve the salt and ease the pain. Then the rice would expand, and they'd really start to holler. They had lots of explaining to do while their momma pulled out the rice with tweezers. Nasty trick, but darn effective in discouraging thieves. Shoot 'em once, and they curse you out. Shoot 'em twice, and they find Jesus."

"You got shot?"

"Me? Nah!" He chuckled. "Your grandfather and I tended to be the ones doin' the shootin'. Papa's farm had some tantalizin' pumpkins."

Her father replaced the towel with another warm rag. Molly swore at the pain. Until then she had never sworn in front of her father unless she stubbed her toe very badly. With the intensity of this wound, her curses came much coarser.

Chuck got up, walked to the coffee pot, and poured her a mug. "Coffee?"

"No, thanks. I have to go to bed. I'm exhausted."

"On a school day?" He glanced at the oven clock. "Dawn's coming, and with that boo boo, you won't get any sleep. Today, of all days, not showing up to class would look suspicious. You have to be there, Molly. Pop a couple of Advil and suck it up. Now that you know you're not seriously hurt, the pain is already going away, isn't it?"

Her eyes widened in surprise. The pain had lessened somewhat.

"Imagination is a wonderful tool," Chuck said, "except when you imagine the worst for yourself."

"I don't want to go to school today. Is that my punishment?"

"Nah, that's today's lesson. Remember the eleventh commandment?"

"Don't get caught."

"Well?"

"Yeah, I get it."

"Get through the day. Then we'll talk about how to proceed."

"Proceed?"

"With your project. There are better ways. We'll figure it out. What did I just say? Imagination can be a terrible thing when you come up with the worst that can happen to you. Imagination is something else entirely when you come up with bad things to do to terrible people. I know a few things about dealing with folks like the

Fauns. I've dealt with much worse, actually. The Fauns are the kind of targets you and I can deal with together."

"What are you saying?"

"I'm jealous you started without me. Pushing back on the Fauns' bullshit? Sounds to me like Christmas morning with a new toy train under the tree."

When she was little, Molly's father had returned home from deployment with a limp. For a long time, Molly thought he had amnesia, too. When asked about his time in the military, Chuck always lied, "I forget."

Curious, Molly had persisted in questioning him until her mother pulled her aside. "When Daddy says he forgets, he means he wishes he could forget."

After his medical discharge, Chuck had picked up side gigs as a roofer. When he fell from a roof with a steep pitch, he wrenched his back in a way that never quite straightened out.

After that injury, Molly made him a new business card. It read: *No job too small, some jobs too big.*

Her father never did tell her anything about how he served his country. Later, Molly would realize that should have been a clue to the depth of his secret keeping.

14

AFFILIATION

Molly had really only known her father as a handyman. Occasionally, they'd go fishing or camping. More often, she would tag along on carpentry jobs. She would hand him tools or sweep up the curled shavings from his woodworking.

Because he was self-trained, he modestly described himself as a "half-assed carpenter." When one of his clients praised his work erecting a fence, Chuck shrugged it off. "Good enough for poor people, and rich people don't care."

The man sitting across from her now was someone new, suddenly more interesting, someone she wanted to know better. Now that she was almost grown, he had a lot to teach her.

As dawn crept over Poeticule Bay, father and daughter sat at the kitchen table. Eager to caffeinate her for the trial of getting through the day, her father served up coffee and painkillers.

"Dad?"

He grunted.

"I didn't expect you to react this way. Why ... how — ?"

"'Cuz I understand. Growing up, I hated Lloyd. Never did enough about it. Thing is, people say pretty words. Happier, nicer people cheerily order us to forgive. I never figured out how to do forgive and forget. They tell us to forget as if we're all halfwits. To me, holding a grudge means I learned the lesson the bully taught me about himself."

Molly managed a smile. "Maya Angelou says, 'When someone shows you who they are, believe them the first time.'"

"Yeah, like that," Chuck agreed. "That way, when the jerk comes back to screw you over again, you see him coming."

"And maybe do something about it?"

"Do shit unto others before they do shit unto you, yeah."

Molly's smile grew larger. "Who are you? I've never seen this side of you!"

"Good fathers aren't supposed to be so honest that they show their nasty side."

"So, you've been hiding."

He seemed to consider this a moment before giving a slow nod. "In the belly of almost every airliner you see, there is a corpse flying home one last time. Nobody talks about it, and few people know, but every plane's got at least one dead body flying home."

"Meaning?"

"Surfaces are just surfaces. Not only does nobody know what's really going on, no one even knows anyone else. No matter how close you get, you only know what somebody shows you. Unless you endure the horror of marrying a motor mouth who shares every passing thought, God bless us, you're in the dark. Mostly, living is lonely business. Don't tell your mother I said that."

"Why not?"

"Says she loves me. Claims to still believe in soulmates. Maybe she's just sayin' that so I'll take out the garbage. Me? I just think we both got lucky. You ever notice people who call each other soulmates, most of the time, happen to live within an easy drive of each other?"

He'd never been so open. "*You* need to talk more," Molly said.

"Nah, all *we* need to do is make the ride easier for each other." He tilted his head back and forth, weighing his words. "Making the ride harder for people who can't keep their hands to themselves? Well, that could be sweet consolation for the evil they do. I hate it when bad people get away with doing bad shit. Happens a lot. Seems people barely even see through the scams, crimes, and nonsense anymore."

He paused with his coffee mug halfway to his mouth. "I don't say this enough, Molly. I love you. You really are a good person. I'm proud of you for being strong enough to stand up against jackholes. I'd love to see you get away with it. Just trying to survive is tough enough. A righteous crusade shouldn't be so lonely. I'll help. You and me, Molly, together. If you try to do it on your own anymore, I'll tell Mom. You don't want that. People think she's the nice one." He smiled and winked. "They're wrong."

Chuck offered his hand. "Partners in crime?"

Molly accepted the handshake, but hoping to minimize her pain, she shook with her left hand. "But not partners in crime. We're partners in seeking justice."

He chortled. "I like the way you dress it up!"

15

EDUCATION

The following Saturday morning, Molly sat beside her father in his rusty old Ford pickup. They parked down the street from the Fauns' house, the windows steaming up. Morning dew had coated the grass, and the air was fresh. Several brown rabbits pottered around on neighborhood lawns. As the sky lightened and dawn approached, birds began to stir and sing.

Father and daughter sat in silence for a while, Chuck with his steaming travel mug of black coffee and Molly with homemade cocoa that was no longer hot.

"I'm surprised how many rabbits there are," Molly said, finally breaking the silence.

"They're crepuscular."

"I don't know what that means, but it sounds like it has something to do with veins and blood."

"People assume the bunnies are nocturnal, but crepuscular means they're most active at dusk and at dawn. When I was a boy delivering newspapers, I saw more rabbits than anyone in town. These early hours when it's quiet and no one else is around are just about the best part of the day."

A shiver ran through Molly. It wasn't the cold morning air. This was a shiver of excitement. She wasn't normally a morning person, but she anticipated that this dawn would be different.

A lot had happened in the few days since she spray-painted the back wall of the Faun's house. Word spread and the town was abuzz about her act of vandalism. The wrinkled and creaky men down at the barbershop lamented the town's soaring crime rate and how the old days were so much better.

Not everyone was sympathetic to Lloyd Faun. Some chuckled that there was no man more deserving of such aggravation. A few agreed Poeticule Bay's atmosphere and discourse would be much kinder and generally improved if the town had three fewer Fauns in it.

It made Molly smile to think she was a crime wave of one. Looking over at her father, she corrected herself. *Now we are two.*

Not everyone had heard about the spray-painting foray yet, however. *The Poeticule County Lens* only came out on Fridays bundled with the *Discount Days Supplement*, so her mission had only just appeared in the local newspaper the day before.

The fresh furor had been worth the wait. A picture of Molly's message to the Fauns appeared on the front page. Lloyd and Keith Faun appeared on either side of the spray-painted message, pointing forlornly. *Monsters hunt monsters. You will be banishe*

The top of the d on banished was merely a hint because she'd run out of time. Molly thought *banishe* made her look stupid.

"Nah, it's good for business," her father assured her. "If you can make your actions look like that of a less intelligent person, so much the better. Simply writing GET OUT would have been even better and taken less time. Anyway, rightly or wrongly, people won't tend to suspect you of a crime."

"Because I'm a girl."

"As a criminal, you would definitely fly below most people's radar. I don't have to tell you, keep it that way."

Chuck adopted the same professorial tone Molly heard from him more and more of late. Their shared disgust with the Faun family had spurred her father to open up. "I've got lots of ideas for how to deal with Lloyd, Marjorie, and their demon seed, but you've got a leg up.

Law enforcement will be looking for a boy. High jinks of this nature generally involve more testosterone."

"School shooters are almost never female," she said.

He gave her the side-eye. "You aren't contemplating shooting up the school, are you?"

She chuckled. "Give me *some* credit! I'm more clever than that."

Chuck nodded. "Then we're on the same page. Just remember the eleventh commandment."

Molly knew she'd been lucky not to have been caught so far, but her father was right. She would not crop up as a prime suspect. Girls were often harassed by boys. Kids like Barry were often bullied. Girls, women, and marginalized people were often among the most oppressed. However, it was almost always white guys on the attack — white guys imagining themselves heroes.

A moment's doubt crept in. Molly thought of herself as a hero, too. She did not share that with her father. When she tuned back in, he was pontificating on how they would avoid law enforcement.

"People who don't spell well are considered more dangerous. I don't think it's a conscious prejudice. People just feel it. Some really smart and good people are terrible spellers, but when someone can't spell or has a limited vocabulary, they probably aren't readers. It's been studied. People who read tend to have more empathy. They can put themselves in other people's shoes."

"I read plenty, but I don't have any empathy for the Fauns."

"No, but you have plenty of empathy for the kid Keith almost killed twice."

"I didn't misspell banished." Molly had already asserted this but felt compelled to repeat herself. "I was interrupted."

Chuck sighed. "You're missing the point of the lesson. People are eager to underestimate dumb people and believe the worst of them. In your case, better to appear to be too smart for any of these shenanigans. They'll never see their downfall coming if they assume you're a nerd."

"Because they think that means I'm weak, too? I hate being weak."

"Don't be weak, but never let them see how strong you can be until it's too late. Prolly best not to be seen even then."

"Always wear a mask," Molly said, "even if it's your own face and not a ski mask from Walmart. So, Master of Masks, tell me more. How do I be the spy who no one ever suspects?"

"Easy," he replied. "When shit goes down, you're just another face in the crowd, as shocked and appalled as any other innocent bystander. Before you do what you do, you have to appear polite but disinterested. Even as you extract the information you need to bring down your targets, you're just hanging out, making conversation, friendly, but not memorable. Look like you're thinking of something else more important to you."

"Nothing's more important right now than banishing the Fauns."

"Fine, just don't look like you feel that way. The police are looking for you."

"I was surprised. The sheriff hasn't even questioned me."

"Nerd cred!" Chuck said.

Molly swatted him across the shoulder. "Dad!"

Her father grinned. "I can teach you a lot, but you'll learn the most from observing your enemies. Their actions, habits, and weaknesses are there for all to see as long as they don't think anyone's looking. People give up their weaknesses all the time, especially when they're talking about their favorite subject, which is always themselves. Listen more than you talk, and you'll get everything you need on them."

Molly was disappointed that the Fauns didn't have more weaknesses to exploit. From what she'd observed, the Faun family had powerful allies. The sheriff, the town council, and the school board didn't want to make waves with Lloyd. No one seemed to mind Marjorie so much. They tended to call her a character. People cared much less for Lloyd and Keith Faun. Lloyd's tone was so argumentative that even well-meant advice sounded like an accusation. As for Keith, general opinion among the town elders was "That Faun boy don't have both oars in the water." The gossip stayed behind Keith and Lloyd's backs, though. Most Poeticule Bay residents didn't think a confrontation would be worth the hassle, or the chipped teeth.

One of those exceptions stood out, however. The article in the *Lens* had not merely reported the spray-painted assault on the Faun's home. The reporter spoke to the Fauns' neighbors, too. Mrs. Rose Rainier, the school librarian, was made of sterner stuff, and she was not pleased. She opted not to speak as an anonymous source.

Quoted in the *Lens*, Rose complained, "It was the middle of the night, and suddenly there's a racket, lots of shouting and cursing. My dogs barked up a storm. My kids woke up, too. I went to the window, and suddenly I hear a big boom. I fell to the floor wondering if me or my kids were about to get shot!"

It got better. "Firing a gun in a residential neighborhood? Over some prank easily fixed with a small can of paint? Really? Property is not more important than people. What does Mr. Faun think is going on? This is Maine, not Texas, for God's sake! I'm obviously against hooliganism in all its forms, but what I want to know is, is the sheriff going to take Mr. Faun's guns away for irresponsible use? Somebody in authority should set that man down and have a serious talk about proportionate response."

The school librarian was not the kind of person to keep the peace for its own sake, even if she did share a property line with the offender. It was a good bet Mrs. Rainier and the Fauns would not be exchanging cards come Christmas.

Rose Rainier was braver than most, but she wasn't alone in airing concerns. In the article, several nameless townspeople mentioned Keith's bullying and the Graves family's sudden departure from the Bay. A few even commented that Lloyd Faun had made many enemies over the years.

Kids at school took no little glee at the news that the school's most infamous bully had become a target. However, one anonymous source suggested the vandalism may not have targeted Keith Faun at all, but his father.

Chuck stabbed his index finger on that line in the paper. "That anonymous source was me. Lloyd's ears must be burning."

Her father had met Rory Fox on the street outside The Big Scoop. Rory was a home inspector Chuck had worked with from time to time. Rory commented, "Some punk has got Lloyd all wound up, heart beatin' like a little moth goin' at a lightbulb! Gather up all the suspects who hate ole Lloyd, and the line will reach out the door and down to the shore!"

Rory then mentioned he had just come from an interview with a reporter from the *Lens*. Chuck asked for an introduction. Under the condition of anonymity, he backed Rory's claim.

"I also told the reporter that my wife still thinks it's the Baptists who want the Fauns run out of town, but they didn't print that."

Molly was amused, but she was also running out of patience. "How much longer?"

"Justice is coming," her father replied breezily. "Given ole Lloyd's disposition, justice is going to look to him like a crazed mob."

16

SOLICITATION

Molly was antsy for what was to come, but Chuck Jergins sipped his coffee, as serene as a pond on a windless day. "Did you know that before the fish went away, half the money coming through Poeticule County was from the sale of Canadian rum? Lloyd's grandfather was the county's biggest rum runner all the way back to prohibition."

"That's how the family has so much?"

"Lloyd's father, Big Jim, made legit money from the rum-running money he got from his dad. The Fauns have always been an entrepreneurial bunch, gotta give 'em that. Nasty people, but I guess there's good money in being bastards."

"I hate them," Molly said, "but only because they're full of hate —
"

Chuck shrugged. "Besides the money, power, and real estate, hate's all they got. I imagine they'd think that's a fair trade. No bad person thinks they're bad."

He turned his head and shot Molly a big grin. "With all the Faun clan pulled over the years, it's no wonder somebody finally stood up. Overdue for a reckoning, I'd say. Lloyd's son is poisoned from the same tree, but the rotten roots go back generations.

"Big Jim Faun made trouble for my father, cheated him out of his rightful real estate down the shore."

"That when Papa moved out to the farm in the county?"

Chuck nodded. "Yeah, and as a family, we pretty much just took what Big Jim dished out. Dad could be very tough, but he knew when he was beat, and he was too smart to get pulled into a fight with a man twice his size and three times as mean. I wasn't so smart. Got into a few scrapes with Lloyd in high school."

Chuck rotated his shoulder and winced a little. Molly heard a little clunk with each circle of the joint.

"Feels and sounds like there's a couple of pennies in there that shouldn't be, huh?"

"Lloyd did that? You had a fight with Lloyd because of a feud between the families? My God! It's Shakespeare in Maine!"

Chuck shook his head. "The real estate thing wasn't really part of it for Lloyd and me."

"What other reasons did he have?"

Chuck looked away for a moment.

"Dad?"

"He figured he had his reasons."

"What reasons?"

"Nothing that justified jacking up my shoulder so bad. I was young, so I thought it healed. You get ancient like me, old sins and injuries come back to visit."

"Dad?"

"Yeah?"

"It's not too late to drive away."

"And miss the show? You gettin' nervy? This the same girl who got shot and shook it off?"

"Still aches."

"It will for a while, but you're young — "

"You said Papa was too smart to get pulled into a fight he couldn't win. Lloyd messed you up — "

"I got a few good punches in."

"My point is, am I dumb for going after Keith?"

"Yes, but you're smart enough not to get caught."

"Eleventh commandment."

"Right." Chuck turned to gaze into Molly's eyes for a moment. "It comes down to this: What do you want?"

She spoke from the heart. "The law failed Barry. The Fauns keep getting away with everything. If they get away with this, the next thing could be worse. They need to feel the heat of someone breathing down their necks. So... yeah, since the school and sheriff proved useless, it's left to somebody else!"

"You're somebody."

"Then it's up to us. Where the law fails, justice might still prevail."

"And if we don't teach 'em, how will they learn? I'm so proud of you, Molly."

She swallowed hard.

"Like an old western, running the bad guys out of town on a rail." Her father sighed. "Looks good on you. Lloyd shooting you and all, kinda wakin' me up and forcin' my hand here, huh?"

"Are *you* saying we shouldn't — "

"You're my daughter. I'll see this through with you. After this, though, you gotta promise me you'll use your book smarts and get out of this backwater. Places like Poeticule Bay are nice to visit in the summer, but living here permanent? That should be confined to retirees and the unambitious. You'll get scholarships. Take the ticket out of town when the time comes. I'm going to lose you to the world, and, truth be told, I'm in no hurry for that day. Getting you up on your feet and out there is my job, though."

Molly nodded in silent agreement.

Chuck gave her arm a squeeze. "Guess I shouldn't have been surprised at your adventures in vigilante graffiti. We got an impetuous streak in this family. Between that and the Faun family behavior?" Her father broke into a chuckle. "Your grandmother would say, 'Those Fauns do tend to inflame intemperate passions.' What that young Faun did to that boy — "

"Don't," Molly said. "I don't want to think about what Keith did to Barry Graves."

"Do think about it," Chuck insisted. "You go on a crusade, it's important to hold on to why you're on the trip. Keep a firm grip on why you're doing this."

"Why *we're* doing this."

"Right you are. *We.*"

She teared up when she thought of Barry Graves. Some kids at school said Keith "smacked the kid around." They smiled when they said it.

Adults said the younger, weaker boy was "roughed up." But it went much deeper than that. Keith wasn't satisfied with hateful slurs. Keith hadn't stopped hitting Barry even after it was clear the kid couldn't stand.

Barry was on the ground, begging to be left alone, when Keith poured a soda over him. Keith then yanked off his shoes and tossed them in a field. He tore off the beaten boy's pants.

Child, Molly corrected herself. *This was not a fight between physical equals.*

Barry was a child beaten by a thug desperate to prove himself a man. Instead, Keith revealed himself a monster.

The puckheads repeated the story with glee many times. After Keith yanked Barry's pants off, he said, "Do as I say, or your tighty-whities come off next! Then we'll all see your little thing! Now raise your chin!"

Keith and the puckheads laughed and jeered. Barry wept but did as he was told. The hockey crowd treated the assault as if it were all a big joke until Keith kicked him in the face. The toe of his boot caught the boy under the chin.

The bully's enablers went silent.

But to Keith, it was nothing, Molly thought, *as if Barry were nothing.*

The kick was so savage even the bully's sidekicks groaned in sympathy. One or two tried to pull Keith away, saying Barry had had enough.

The monster shrugged them off and pushed them away. Before he walked away, he kicked Barry in the gut once more and spit on him.

Molly gritted her teeth at the thought of Keith being let off so easily. Bruises heal. Humiliation is forever.

As if reading her thoughts, her father said, "Fussbudgets and little cluckers talking about how concerned they are is just empty vessels full of big, hollow echoes."

"Something Nana would say?"

Chuck bobbed his head. "Point is, too few people are willing to fight for the Barrys of this world."

"But some do. *We're* here."

Sitting in the early morning light, waiting for their next attack on the Fauns to unfold, Molly had never felt closer to her father. They finally understood each other.

Cars and trucks began to arrive up and down the block. Some drivers arrived alone. Quite a few arrived in pairs. Molly was surprised that, despite the early hour, three cars arrived with children packed in the back seat. People sat in their vehicles watching the Faun house. She no longer felt so conspicuous sitting in the truck with her father doing the same thing.

Her father checked his watch and yawned. "Soon."

"You sure this will work?"

"Sure? Nothing in this world is for sure. You can't even count that if you put two socks in the wash, you'll get two back. If this goes south and lands in troubled waters, I'd say to you what my father said to me: 'I loved you the best I knew how.'" He chuckled again. "Not that Sheriff Hobbs will be impressed with that sentiment."

Molly felt little comfort in that offering, but she put on a brave face. "You won't have to make that speech if we don't get caught, so —"

"Eleventh commandment," Chuck interjected.

With all his handyman work flipping houses over the years, her father had a stash of signs in his shed. One warned of staying off wet cement. Another exhorted workers to beware: HARD HAT AREA.

While it was still dark, Molly had placed a sign on the Faun's front lawn. Back to wearing many coats to disguise her true shape, her hoodie hid her face from any cameras the Fauns might have set up.

With the sun lightening the sky, stretching from pale to pastel pink, the sign was now clearly illuminated. The bold red letters announced:

HOUSE FOR SALE BY OWNER

Chuck checked his watch. It was 5:50 a.m. "Ten more minutes, then the big show begins."

17

PUBLICATION

The day after Molly found out she had never really known her father, he handed her two envelopes. Each contained cash and a letter. Neither were for Molly. They were both addressed to *The Discount Days Supplement*. The return address on the envelope was the Fauns' house.

"A little creative forgery will get you further than a kind word sometimes," Chuck said.

He had written two advertisements to appear in the Friday edition. One touted that the Faun house was for sale. The second was to declare a massive estate sale.

The advertisement's huge headline read:

BLOWOUT! BIGGEST SALE THIS YEAR! ALL ITEMS MUST GO IMMEDIATELY! NO REASONABLE OFFER REFUSED! MANY UNIQUE ITEMS TOO NUMEROUS TO LIST!

Despite that title, Chuck had included an extensive list designed to attract bargain seekers. *Guns! Civil war weaponry and uniforms! Comix!*

Classic celebrity autograph collections! Antique furniture! Weights and weight bench, barely used! Glassware, books, and appliances! Many rare items!

Molly had to smile at the subtle dig of "weights and weight bench barely used!" Lloyd had been a dedicated weightlifter since high school. He worked out like a fiend, a fact he frequently shared with anyone and everyone, no matter their interest.

With all his past injuries and the arthritis, Molly's dad wasn't so strong anymore. Perhaps that jab was a sign of her father's jealousy. She dismissed the thought and read on. A notice at the bottom of the ad was highlighted in bold:

No phone calls or early bidding will be accepted. Early birds, come get your deals at 6 a.m.! Too cold for a yard sale, so come on in!

When Molly was little, father and daughter would do a tour of the town, "garage sailing" as Chuck put it. Each spring and summer, Saturday mornings were their time to shop at yard sales and flea markets.

"The sale of secondhand stuff is the best and cheapest entertainment our town's got. Despite the cold, this one is gonna be legendary."

His coffee was cold, but Chuck finished it anyway. "The system is tried and true. People get fed up with their winter mess and get the cleaning bug. They spread their crap out on their lawn and down their driveway or open up their houses to strangers. Then the bargain seekers haggle over nickels and pay a pittance for some nonsense they gotta dust. Both parties are a little resentful about the whole process, but you make a deal. Then you take the crap home and put it up in *your* attic. Capitalism! It's what made this country great ... and then progressively shitty and shittier."

Despite their previous experience with yard sales, Molly had no idea how rabid the bargain hunter community could be. Just before six, they eyed the Faun house as they climbed out of their cars and trucks.

Chuck grinned. "See how they're side-eyeing each other? The vultures are circling, antsy to get started."

It was true. The bargain hunters sized each other up as if they were nervous runners at the starting line. "Competition is fierce, even when so little is at stake," Chuck said. "In war, fightin' tooth and nail makes sense. Here, it's about beating the other guy out of two bits over a cracked vase or an old tie pin."

No one but a visitor from New York would dare cross a land boundary until the appointed time. To break into an outright sprint would be seen as overly eager and undignified. However, at one minute to six, a couple of old-timers broke into a trot to be the first to the Fauns' front door.

With cinnamon sugar from the donuts still on his smiling lips, Chuck settled into his seat. "Lloyd's not going to care for a crowd at this early hour, especially since they're here to clear him out. We can count on ole Lloyd to overreact."

Molly nodded. "The Fauns' skill is not self-regulation."

Chuck straightened in his seat. "Self-what?"

"Self-regulation. I mean, they can't button their gob flaps."

"Ah."

It wasn't quite six, but the pressure to get deals on everything the Fauns owned had built too high. After the two old men broke ranks, the rest of the mob followed and became a swarm.

One older woman bent from the waist with great difficulty. Leaning on her cane, she began plucking the little solar-powered lights along the side of the driveway. A man slipped through the gate at the side of the house and soon emerged with a roll of garden hose in his arms.

"Everything must go," Dad said.

"As long as the Faun family goes, too, I'm good with it," Molly said.

Molly rolled down her window so they could listen to the bargain hunters ring the doorbell and knock on the door. Eventually, one bargain hunter gave into impatience and pounded on the door.

"They got up extra early for this sale. They will not be denied," Chuck observed.

From their post in the truck, Molly wondered aloud, "Do you think most people are basically good?"

"Most? I don't know about most," he said. "People can be nice, but that doesn't mean they can't also act crazy. In my experience, most aren't evil, but half are basically goofs."

18

OBSERVATION

Molly had had no idea her father was such a misanthrope. His disdain for stupidity leaked out occasionally when he read the letters to the editor in the newspaper. However, when he dealt with people in person, she'd never seen him act unkindly.

Once, when she was thirteen, she accompanied her father to collect a bill. He'd renovated a kitchen for Mrs. Jillian Rafuse. Complaining that he had taken too long to put in her new cabinets, she demanded a deep discount.

"I've been without a working kitchen for three weeks and mostly living at my sister's!" she yelled. "In what world does it take so long to rip out some old cabinets and put in the new? In what world?"

"In this one," Chuck replied in a low, calm voice.

Then he patiently explained that he'd been delayed because there was an order of operations for such projects. He couldn't put in the new counter and cabinets until her plumber had done his work. He'd offered to do that work himself, but her nephew Jimmy was an apprentice plumber.

Mrs. Rafuse had insisted on using her inexperienced relative. Jimmy first ordered the wrong tap and could only work on Sundays, off his boss's clock. Chuck didn't say so outright, but the delay was really on Mrs. Rafuse and her idiot nephew.

The debt was paid, but Mrs. Rafuse wasn't happy about it. Even as she handed him the cash, she observed that Poeticule Bay was a small town, and word got around about poor workmanship. On the way back to the car, her father muttered something about being unable to change the laws of physics, but that was all.

Molly was angry at her and worried for him. "Could Mrs. Rafuse stop you from getting other work?"

"Nah, she's fine," he said, "Once she understood how her expectations were wrong, she only dug in her heels because she was embarrassed. She'll stew a bit, maybe a long time, but she won't complain too much. Someone else might tell her she's in the wrong. Good people hate being in the wrong. Jillian Rafuse isn't a bad person. She was just mistaken. Everybody makes mistakes."

"But she was wrong and took it out on you!"

"You see any blood on me? I don't think she drew any blood. I'm okay."

"Sure, but if she's so good, why wouldn't she admit she was wrong and apologize?"

"Oh, sweet thing, that's a rare breed! That's only something truly great people do. Your expectations are too high. Are you embarrassed? Are you going to apologize?"

She said nothing. He chuckled. "When I brought up her nephew's half-assed ways, I could see it in her eyes. Mrs. Rafuse knew she was being unreasonable."

"You saw it in her eyes?"

"It wasn't just that. Did you notice how hot she came at me out of the gate? Yelling and carrying on and banging the door on her new cabinet under the sink? Then she got quieter, brought her tone way down. When she got really quiet, I answered her softly. She eased off until she was matching my energy. Before I even took the cash from her hand, we understood each other. She was being silly."

"You've got a lot more patience than me," Molly said.

"Reserve your fury for the deserving," Chuck had advised. "Ignorant isn't the problem. That's easily cured by information. It's the people who don't see they're being mean who worry me. That's another kettle of fish — mean fish."

"What?"

"Mean fish. They don't eat to feed themselves. They rip and tear for fun. They go out of their way to bother people just minding their business. Were I you, I'd worry myself more about them."

Now, as Lloyd and Keith Faun erupted out of their front door, Molly saw them for what they were. They were two mean fish, the ugliest kind that lived in the dark at the bottom of the ocean.

But these fish carried shotguns. Father and son yelled in unison, "Get back! Get back!"

Bleary with sleep and confusion, blinded by their growing paranoia, Lloyd and Keith were in a rage. They had somehow convinced themselves that their tormentors had returned to the scene of the crime.

Lloyd stood at the top of the stoop, spit flying from his lips. "One of you is watchin' and just waitin' and slobberin', hopin' we'll crack! Let me see your hands! I'm bettin' one of you has red paint on your hands!"

Those at the front of the eager crowd drew back in stunned surprise. One teenager would have tumbled backward off the bottom step had a middle-aged couple not caught him mid-fall.

Someone on the front walk implored, "Easy! Easy! We're just here for your stuff is all, Lloyd. Calm the flyin' Christ down!"

"Oh, yeah," Chuck told Molly, "In case you were wondering, you really gotten under their skin."

As the chaotic scene unfolded, several of the bargain hunters yelled for Lloyd and Keith to put their guns away. Most of the crowd sprinted for their cars.

Molly told her father to start the truck. Leaving then, they would be invisible amongst the exodus.

Chuck shook his head. "Wait for it."

Among those who remained, an argument had broken out. An old man, the boldest of the mob, refused to leave. He pulled a newspaper from his coveralls and tapped the ad in *The Discount Days Supplement* angrily.

Red-faced, Lloyd handed his shotgun to his son. As soon as his father's weapon was in Keith's hand, the front door burst open again. Marjorie Faun appeared, her hair disheveled and her robe barely closed by a loose knot of belt. She tried to yank Keith back into the house. He shrugged her off, swore, and pushed her away.

Marjorie came at her son with more fury the second time. First, she kicked Keith in the buttocks. Unsteady, her slipper came off as she fell against the porch railing. Scanning what remained of the crowd, Keith ignored his mother.

Marjorie picked up the fallen slipper and used it to smack him in the ear repeatedly with as much force as she could muster. As he whirled on her, Marjorie yanked him back through the open door. Her screamed curses cut off as she slammed the door shut.

Lloyd was marooned on the front step to face the horrified crowd alone. He looked from the paper in his trembling hand to the for sale sign on his front lawn.

There is probably a Latin medical term for what happened to Lloyd in that moment. Her father's description was more accessible to any layman. "Lloyd's lost his shit," Chuck observed.

Pushing through what was left of the onlookers, Lloyd sprinted for the sign. "House for sale by owner? Sale by owner? *I'm* the owner!"

Uncontained fury and haste impaired his senses. Lloyd must have expected more resistance when he pulled the sign up out of the grass. However, in the early morning darkness, Molly had only taken a few seconds to push the sign's wire prongs into the dewy lawn. Lloyd bent his knees, grabbed the sign in both hands, braced himself, and pulled up with all his might. The sign flew up into his face, and he landed on his butt in the wet grass.

Molly burst out in giggles. "It's a farce, but I do love the theater."

In the span of less than a minute, Lloyd had gone from a foul-mouthed, gun-toting threat to a red-faced fool in wet pants.

That broke the tension. Everyone burst into uncontrolled laughter.

Chuck raised both hands from the steering wheel in exultation. "And the crowd ... goes ... wild!"

For decades, Lloyd Faun had been a person to be feared and respected. In a matter of minutes, he'd become an object of derision. That embarrassment would follow him for the rest of his short life.

19

IRRITATION

In Poeticule Bay, most people knew their neighbors. Old folks were often taken care of. Someone would go out of their way to keep an eye on frail seniors when the power went out, or the weather got too hot or too cold. After any funeral, neighbors would appear to fill the survivors' freezers with casserole dishes, clam chowder, blueberry pies, and apple crumble. But living in a small town also meant that by sundown, everyone would know that Lloyd had graduated from community annoyance to unhinged asshole.

Keith punching and kicking some come-from-away gay kid was one thing. But now, locals had witnessed father and son brandish weapons at *them*. They better understood the threat because, this time, his aggression became a personal affront.

"Consequences," Molly's father said. "The Fauns sure aren't used to that, and they're finally feeling the full sting."

Though Marjorie Faun was given some credit for common sense, locals crowed about the confrontation up and down the coast, from north to The Corners and south to The Forks.

Reputation is currency in a small town. Break your word or act the fool, it's not just that you'll be the object of askance looks. Small-town folks have long memories, and they'll never let you forget any incident where you came up short. Molly had no way of knowing if the Graves family were aware of their tormentors' fresh troubles, but she hoped Barry found out somehow.

However, Chuck didn't really think their play that Saturday morning would be sufficient to curb the Fauns. "Shunning might work with folk who consider themselves pious, but for a man like Lloyd? Shunning won't do the job."

"They acted like lunatics!" Molly said. "How could it not be enough?"

"Look how Lloyd reacted with that little tempest in a teacup he had with the Baptist church. He doubled down. Lloyd likes to think of himself as mayor and king of all he surveys, but he's really an anti-social knob. His laundry chain sponsors the Little League, and he buys drinks and claps backs down at the bowling alley — "

"As if friendship is the same as the price of a beer?" Molly sneered at that.

Chuck nodded. "Getting backs turned on him won't be enough powder behind the bullet."

Molly had been elated at their success with the ad gambit. Now she began to deflate.

"Chin up and don't look down," Chuck said. "The laughter will skewer them mightily. Harassment and gossip will give the family pause, but the whole town laughing at such a pillar of the community? A generational big wheel? I don't know about the boy, but Lloyd will have a hard time with that."

"They'll remember getting laughed at, but I want them to leave town."

Chuck stared off into the distance as if doing math in his head. "Tell me, would you settle for the golden boy bully asking to switch schools? Maybe get sent off to a military academy to learn some respect and discipline?"

"Do you think Barry Graves suffered just a little embarrassment?"

"Yeah," Chuck sighed. "We're not half done, are we?"

20

MISEDUCATION

Lloyd was desperate to find the culprit behind the prank campaign. He and Keith marched down to the sheriff's office immediately to file a complaint against the paper. However, it was father and son who almost got hauled off to the county jail.

Before Lloyd and Keith arrived, Sheriff Hobbs had already received several complaints about the Fauns' antics. When the pair walked in, Hobbs looked up from his desk, his face brightening. "If it ain't the Faun boys, ole Lloyd and his demon seed! You two have saved me some shoe leather. I was just about to get off my duff, put on my hat, and come pay you a visit! What the hell was you thinking? I'm betting you wasn't."

"Someone put a sign on my lawn sayin' I was selling my house."

"The house Big Jim bought you, yeah," Hobbs said dryly.

"A mob showed up, pounding on my door at the crack of the ass of dawn!"

"Uh-huh. From what I've been hearing, this whole situation has got you in quite a twist, Lloyd. I understand that. However," he looked pointedly at Keith, "the rooster woke you up early 'cuz the chickens are coming home to roost."

"We're targets!" Keith whined.

Sheriff Hobbs sat back and stared at Keith for a long moment. "You remember the talk we had at the hospital, boy? After what you did to the Graves kid, what did I encourage you to keep in mind? Did you commit to memory what I told you to remember?"

"You said I had a lot to live down."

Hobbs nodded. "A lot of young fellas with a wee too much testosterone and more muscle than brains are too much like you. Seen it a thousand times."

He shot Lloyd a look. "And when some boys get older, they get their courage from a bottle. Were you up all night drinkin', Lloyd?"

Lloyd's defiant gaze softened and shifted to the floor. "Not so much."

"But more than a little? You have the look."

"I may have been up a chunk of the night watching the woods behind my property, *defending* my property. I thought the hoodlums would come back, but not like this."

Hobbs sucked his teeth a moment before turning his attention back to Keith. "Out of deference to your father — "

"And me supporting you in your next election," Lloyd interrupted.

Sheriff Hobbs put a finger to his lips to silence him and began again. "Out of deference to your father, I gave you a second chance. That wasn't the whole story. I encouraged the Graves family to press the matter, press charges. However, they feared further repercussions for their son. I couldn't promise I could keep you and your friends away. Guarding Barry Graves twenty-four seven isn't in my budget. So, I went with the flow and let it go. I am now regretting that little mercy. I got a lot of calls today, even before my morning coffee."

Lloyd began pacing back and forth like a caged, hungry animal. Hobbs wondered how much alcohol was still careening through the man's system, soaking his brain. The sheriff could smell it on Lloyd's breath. The odor leaked through his pores as he sweated profusely.

"Guns and alcohol, Lloyd. You won't find that mix in any gun safety handbook."

"I'm fine," Lloyd said.

"No one sane would say you look it. This whole experience has put me off my digestion. I gotta say, I don't care for it, boys. Leaves me a bad taste in my mouth. Tastes like shit. You like the taste of shit, Keith? Lloyd? Do you? Me, I don't care for it at all. In short, my mercies for you are at an end."

Lloyd gritted his teeth, holding back the curses he wished he could hurl.

"What does that mean?" Keith asked. "The no more mercies thing?"

"Well, genius, you two have anger management issues. I'm gonna have to confiscate your guns. I'll be talking to several folks this afternoon. We'll see if anyone wants to give an official statement and press charges and so forth."

"What about our statement?" Lloyd protested. "The harassment — "

Sheriff Hobbs smacked his desk with an open palm. "You got a history of running outside with a gun in your hand, Lloyd! Right now, your problems with vandalism are my secondary concern. In short, stop bein' a goddamn nut, *will* you? *Can* you?"

According to several witnesses on the street, Lloyd and Keith exited the sheriff's office "in a tizzy." Father and son loudly proclaimed that they needed their firearms to protect themselves from intruders. The sheriff followed them out, yawned at them, and pointed to his car.

Hobbs was louder than he needed to be, making sure that bystanders heard him ordering the Fauns around. "I'll meet you two at the house. I'll need all your firearms. Keith, you collect them and put them in the trunk of my car. Lloyd, you get out your permits. I'll need to have a look at them. While you get that sorted, I plan to have a sitdown with Marjorie over a cup of tea."

Lloyd demanded, "What are you gonna discuss with my wife?"

Hobbs looked him up and down. "I'm the whip to keep you in line. Marjorie's the chain. Maybe she can save me some paperwork and you some time sittin' in my jail over the weekend. Long as she's willin' to jerk your chain and hold you back from your worst urges. I don't know. You're not impressing me, boys. For public safety, you need to impress me."

With steely defiance, Lloyd asked, "And what if I don't?"

Sheriff Hobbs crossed his arms and rocked back and forth, toes and heels. He pursed his lips in thought as he took Lloyd Faun's measure.

"Lloyd, let me be clear as crystal with you, okay? Keep in mind I'm trying to help you here. Do *not* do stupid shit."

"And what if I do? You really gonna do anything about it?"

Born in Navasota, Texas, Gordon Hobbs got his start in law enforcement working in prisons. The Wallace Pack Unit was just down the road from the house in which he'd been born. With 313 federal prisons in the state, there was plenty of employment for those odd or desperate few who could stand the stultifying work.

Hobbs had run into challenges like Lloyd before, but his attitude didn't make sense to the sheriff. Lloyd Faun was a rich man. Too used to dealing with poor criminals, Hobbs didn't really understand a rich one. He assumed Lloyd would comply because he had too much to lose.

Hobbs looked from Lloyd to Keith. The Faun boy was looking at his dad with pride. Keith respected his father's defiance of authority and maybe thought it was all a joke. Hobbs was sure they'd laugh about this encounter later, giggle about how they'd won something, showing him up as a hick sheriff they could ignore.

When he finally spoke, Hobbs put more bass in his voice, and he spoke slowly, "You ever think about how whales die, Lloyd?"

The sheriff made a vague gesture toward the Atlantic. "I'm told they used to show up out there in the bay sometimes, depending on the time of year. Lost, maybe."

"What about it?"

"Whales are huge, eyes like basketballs. I hear tell of some whales or other capsizing big boats sometimes. Yachts, even! It's a problem not confined to *Moby Dick*. It's real. It happens."

"What's your goddamn point, Gordon?"

Gordon, not Sheriff. Not Sheriff Hobbs. Not sir.

Hobbs shrugged as if unbothered. "Whales are big, is all. And they're animals, like you and me. They breathe air, biggest mammals on the whole damn planet. No matter how big and strong they get, even their time comes. At some point, they're too weak to get back to the surface. This huge thing, born of the sea, born for the sea, drowns. 'Magine, that? Old whales die by drowning."

"And?"

"Dunno, Lloyd. Seems like there should be a lesson in there somewheres, yeah? Something about stayin' humble, maybe. I guess if I were to come at ya other than sideways, I'd ask you to summon the strength to come up for air. Right now, I see a man drownin'. You're drownin' in alcohol, paranoia, and bad decisions. Before you do anything else, I'm tellin' you now, summon the strength not to be an asshole. Take a breath."

Called out, Lloyd looked to his son. His cheeks burned with embarrassment, but his eyes burned, too. Burning with silent fury.

"If you don't summon that strength to take a breather and take it easy, somebody could get hurt. If that happens, with you or your boy, we'll be having a different conversation, and it'll be short. It'll start with me tellin' ya to put your hands behind your back. It's my duty as sheriff to warn you."

Keith looked like he was about to say something. Hobbs shut him down. "Mouth closed. You've got nothing to add to this conversation, you little sadist. Remember when you admitted to me at the hospital that what you did was a prank gone 'a little far.' Just stand there, shut up, and appreciate the irony."

Hobbs turned back to Lloyd. "It's my need as a friend to tell you, summon the strength. *Comprende*?"

Lloyd nodded as if he understood, but he didn't. He learned a different lesson from the sheriff's speech. He'd taken in Hobbs' rambling about drowning whales and shit out the idea that he and Keith were on their own. The law would be of no help. The cop was focused on him, not the people trying to banish him from his birthright, his kingdom.

Lloyd prayed silently. *Give me the strength, Lord, to crush my enemies. Just let me find them, and I'll do the rest.*

Mistaking Lloyd's silence for shame, Hobbs gestured to his vehicle. "C'mon, I'll give you a ride home."

Keith sat in the back of the police car beside his father as they rode back to their house. He sulked and stared at the back of the sheriff's head as Hobbs drove. Pressure was building in his head. He needed to *do* something. The cop would have him do nothing, as if he *were* nothing.

He practiced a speech in his head. "I am more powerful than you can imagine, and I *will* dominate. Fear me, fuckers!"

Keith was too immature and stupid to understand he was only reassuring himself. His threats to everyone and no one in particular were an exercise in self-protection. He was shoring up the damage that had been done to the shaky foundations of his ego.

That done, he moved on to homicidal fantasies about all the people who disgusted him: the cop, whoever was out to get him, the crowd of bargain hunters, and, of course, Barry Graves.

Molly Jergins had embarrassed him, too. With her little lecture at school, she spoke as if she knew him. She pretended she cared, as if she wanted to help him. Molly had made it onto Keith's kill list, too.

21

ADMISSION

The following Friday, the sheriff was quoted in *The Poeticule County Lens*, "I won't comment much on an ongoing investigation, but I will say I hope the situation is cooling down to more civilized levels."

Hobbs allowed that he was reluctant to interfere with anyone's Second Amendment rights but reports of father and son "being sent into a blind rage while brandishing weapons at innocents, that does give one pause."

That was on page one of the news coverage, but the story continued deep into page two and three in breathless and exhaustive detail.

"I was right there on their front walkway, just a few feet from the porch," Mrs. Audrey McGloughlan complained to a reporter from the *Lens*. "You never expect to see something like this around here. Lloyd Faun and his son came out hooting and hollering in front of God and everybody. And they were holding guns. They put on quite a show, I'll tell you! All I did was answer an ad, hoping to get a hockey card for my grandson or something. Maybe find some good yarn."

Mrs. McGloughlan also enthused about her search for celebrity

autographs. "I have quite a collection and am in need of Harry Belafonte's signature. Put that in your paper in case there are any collectors looking to trade a Harry B. for a Sammy Davis, Jr. I got two of
those! Anyway, I was about to go in when Lloyd and his boy lost their
darn minds!"

Given the previous vandalism, the Fauns might have been
forgiven their panic at the sudden invasion of overly enthusiastic
bargain-seekers at dawn. What several witnesses could not abide was
Keith raising a hand against his mother.

Mrs. McGloughlan informed the *Lens* reporter, "Then the wife
comes out and tries to drag both crazies back inside. The young one
— holding a squirrel gun, mind you — points with it at folks in the
crowd. 'Who did it? Who did it?' he says. Who did what, I didn't
know. I'm just a little old lady who loves Harry Belafonte and the Rat
Pack, for pity's sake! Worse was, when the wife tried to tell the boy to
calm down, he pushed her away. She got ahold of him eventually."

Many had something to say about what happened that morning,
but Mrs. McGloughlan's account proved most colorful and indelible.

The story took up most of the third page and the following quote
from the old woman was placed dead center in large type and in bold.
"That poor woman fell sideways against the iron handrail on their
steps and got herself an awful blow. I don't know if it was the railing
or her skull. Whatever it was, rang like a bell! And the husband was
too bent on finding somebody to blame for his perturbations. The
guy barely spared a look at his poor wife draped across the front door
like a floppy welcome mat!"

Some maintained that Lloyd gibbered about a death sentence for
"the ninja spray painter." Others were softer in their relation of
events. They said the Fauns were only holding shotguns — not
pointing them — but everyone agreed Lloyd had a crazed look in
his eye.

As one local put it, "That house for sale sign loosened the lug nuts
on the wheels of that man's little red wagon." That's old guy Maine
talk for going insane.

"There are too many witnesses to let all this nonsense slide," Sheriff Hobbs later confessed to his circle of codgers at the barbershop. "I got an election coming up! Have to be seen as the cooler head prevailing when a couple of hotheads are running around with hard-ons and twelve gauges. I confiscated their weapons. I took them back to the station to file a full report. Mainly, my aim was to give both boy and man some time to simmer down."

The following week, Marjorie Faun was seen around town at the Dollar Mart and the post office. She wore huge sunglasses that failed to hide the shiner under her left eye. A few observant folks noted that when she appeared at the bank on Wednesday morning, her right eye was turning black and blue, too.

Then Marjorie disappeared from Poeticule Bay. Word was, she went to live with her sister in Tampa. Leastwise, Ginny Augustine at the post office noticed that's where Lloyd sent an envelope addressed to his wife.

"I didn't want to break up the family. I want them all gone. That's one-third of the Faun family gone, but the two-thirds that stayed are so much worse."

Chuck was sanguine at the revelation of Marjorie Faun's running away. "If she was willing to abandon ship when the waters looked a little choppy, their boat was sinking long before you and I came along. The Fauns have been bullies since Christ was a carpenter. She's better off. We all are, by a third, and my sense of it is the town is turning on the Faun boys."

"How come they've owned this town for so long?" Molly asked. "How is it that Keith can beat up a kid and get away with it?"

Chuck shrugged. "It's not necessarily all of them. Maybe we've been weak. Bad people take advantage of good people's better natures."

Anger gripped Molly again. She couldn't walk up behind Keith, take him out at the knees with a length of rebar, and get away with it.

"Truth is," Chuck continued, "maybe if I'd settled Lloyd's hash in high school — "

"Then why didn't you? You should have!"

Chuck held up two palms in surrender. "I don't have a time machine. There were ... mitigating factors, but you're right. If I'd taught Lloyd some humility back in the day, maybe we wouldn't be sitting here now. Perhaps his son wouldn't be such a criminal. From what you say, young Keith has the confidence of a serial killer. I figure he's bound for jail or a career in politics."

"Why you didn't push back in high school?"

"Reasons," he said. Seeing that Molly was unsatisfied with his answer, he tried again. "I had some stuff I needed to learn before I could be of some use in that regard," Chuck admitted. "Plus, I was a bit of a coward, scared to get hurt. It would never have occurred to me to risk getting shot to make a point."

"I didn't plan on that," Molly said.

"But you shrugged off the pain like a champ."

"With painkillers and your doctoring, yes."

Molly waited for her pulse to throttle down to a slower pace. Finally, she said, "I did what I did, so now we're committed."

"All in." Her father smiled. "Let's see how these boys do when they have to swallow a bit of their own medicine."

"Didn't we just do that? They're already crazed."

"Gotta up the dosage on their bitter pills."

Molly's father was given to wry, lopsided grins. Sometimes, he allowed the odd chuckle to escape, as if rationing out a short supply for a long, hard life. That morning, his smile was pure, made beatific by the certainty only avenging angels possess. "People like you, Molly, are outliers, but you shouldn't be."

"People like us, Dad. People like *us*."

He reached for her hand and gave a hard squeeze. Molly smiled. The gesture did not feel awkward, and she did not pull away. "Thanks for ... " Words failed her.

After a moment, Molly tried again. "Thanks for understanding me, Dad."

She'd almost said, "helping me," but being who she was and not being alone, being *understood* was a much grander thing.

They didn't know it then, but her father was only the first soldier

Molly would recruit in her war on bullies, assholes, and anyone else who escaped justice and deserved retribution. Her targets would be those whom the law did not touch. Her goal was to protect victims and ensure that there would not be more victims. This was only her first campaign in her war, a conflict that would last the rest of her life.

EARTH

You saw me as your plaything, your convenience,
    your tool.
That's how you made me a weapon.
Soon you'll conclude you were a terrible fool,
when I return to teach you a lesson.

22

PROPAGATION

Lloyd, ever the hothead, managed to turn up the heat on himself. He'd all but forgotten Sheriff Hobbs' whale speech. And once again, the townspeople of Poeticule Bay were watching when he screwed up.

The following Wednesday evening at the elementary school, he got into an argument over a parking space. Lloyd threatened to punch a grandmother who'd come to watch her youngest grandchild pitch.

The grandmother in question had pulled into a parking spot ahead of Lloyd. He wanted that one and no other. Everyone at the ball field heard him shouting curses at the old lady. There was no waffling or delay. Someone called the police.

Deputy Whitey Lime soon appeared. The deputy was born and raised in Poeticule Bay. His real name was Whitford Green, but all through high school, everyone but his mother called him Whitey. An unremarkable but friendly fellow, he graduated from Poeticule Consolidated and immediately enrolled in the police training institute. When he returned, fresh from training in Orono, he informed everyone that he preferred to be called Deputy Green. "It's got less whadayacaller? The racial overtones, you know?"

Sheriff Hobbs found his request amusing. "I've known you since diapers, and now you want us to call you something different?"

"Yes, sir."

"I'm cogitating, Deputy. For your first investigation, I need you to go on a run to the paint store down in the Forks."

"Why so, boss?"

"I need to know. What color do you get when you mix white and green?"

"I dunno ... light green, maybe?"

"Skip the trip to the paint store. Let's call it Lime. That sound okay to you?"

"Yes, boss, but why — "

"And so shall you be rechristened henceforth, Deputy Lime!"

Whitford Green didn't like it, but the Sheriff made sure the name stuck.

The deputy arrived too late to witness Lloyd Faun's hissy fit beside the elementary school's baseball diamond. However, he did take statements, if only to provide Sheriff Hobbs with a fresh story to share with his coffee klatch at the Eric Walter's barbershop. The coffee was nothing fancy, but the chairs were comfortable, the *Playboy* magazines were old, and the car magazines were new. The gossip was always better than the haircuts.

"That Lloyd," Sheriff Hobbs observed later, "is in serious need of a vacation from which he should not return. I swear, my job used to be mostly dealin' with drunks, speeders, ruinin' the fun of young lovers, chasing 'em out from under the Poeticule River bridge. Dealing with Faun family drama is filling my schedule big time! I don't know which is worse, father or son. That young Faun boy is young and fulla blue piss —"

"Lloyd's worse, definitely," the barber put in. "That man's a tick on a boil on the ass of this town. I swear Lloyd's always got the mood of a drinkin' man who's already three sheets to the wind."

"Born mad, is all," Hobbs replied. "And mad about what? That man's got more money than God, the Pope, and all the angels."

Walters bobbed his head in agreement. "Plus, he had Marjorie before she escaped to parts unknown, God bless her. That was some good-looking woman."

Sheriff Hobbs shot Walters a look that informed the proprietor he was interrupting the flow of a good story. Then, the old cop heaved a sigh and plunged back in. "Lloyd's gonna hurt tourism with his antics."

The assembled looked from one to the other, exchanging troubled looks.

"Plus, his thug of a son is so dumb, after he takes a shit, he tries to wipe his ass with his feet. That boy would make a puppet out of himself before he deciphered the correct use of toilet paper."

The assembled men laughed, but there was tension in the room, too. Few had dared to speak about the Fauns with such open contempt before.

"Enough people saw them losing their damn minds, I'm sure the *Lens* will take note," the sheriff added. "Even if they cool it on the Graves clan, I guarantee there'll be incoming fire in the letters to the editor."

The barber stopped cutting Frenchy Symmond's thinning hair to raise his hand. Catching the sheriff's eye in the big mirror, he waited for the cop to give him a nod. Getting the go-ahead, he added, "The school librarian — Mrs. Rainier — I'd bet a boodle she'll write in. My wife says she's still pissed at Lloyd, living next door to the OK Corral and all."

"I took his guns, but he's still shooting his mouth off rapid fire," Hobbs said. "The old lady he got into it with over where to park his precious car? He called out that poor woman. 'You damn come-from-aways! You don't have priority here! I live here year 'round! I'm here when it's cold!'"

The assembled shifted in their seats and rolled their eyes. Since the fish die-off, tourism was all they had left, integral to commerce up and down the bay.

The sheriff himself had his leash pulled taut by the town council. Word was, any driver of an unfamiliar car or a vehicle with out-of-state plates had free rein to speed through town (except for the school zone). Locals might get a speeding ticket to support the town's treasury, but residents of Poeticule *needed* to appear friendly to tourists and their dollars.

"I tell you, boys," Hobbs said, "Lloyd's always been more rotten apple than sweet peach, but since his boy beat up that kid, he's way too much fiend and certainly no friend."

Walters tutted and tsked as he brushed trimmed hair from the back of Frenchy's neck.

"Lloyd really went off." Hobbs stood to retell the next part of the story, flailing his arms in dramatic mockery. "Everyone in the bleachers heard Lloyd declare, 'I need that spot! I gotta keep an eye on my car! I've already been messed with! I need a spot where I can leave easily when the game's over in case I need to rush home! I can't be stuck in a damn parking lot waiting on your fat ass to move your crap wagon!'"

Every man present winced at that.

"If Lime had been johnny-on-the-spot, he could have breathalyzed him. The deputy was too late. Can't arrest Lloyd for being rude."

Frenchy's bushy eyebrows shot high. "We got no anti-asshole laws on the books?"

The sheriff ignored him. "It gets worse but funnier. Lloyd then says to the lady, 'Don't you know who I am?'"

Every man in the barbershop laughed, but the barber downright giggled. "Who does Lloyd think he is? King Shit of the Dung Beetles or somethin'? He a celebrity I don't know about?"

The sheriff settled back into his red leather chair. "Oh, you haven't even heard it all yet. Lloyd's got himself convinced he's got a posse after him. I'm not sayin' he's wrong, but him or his son were at my office whining and complaining more than my deputy. I tell you, Lloyd Faun has been beatin' me over the head with his victimhood so hard, I'm about ready to join the terrorists."

The barber was still chuckling. "Parking for a quick getaway. It's a little league game in a one-horse town. He's not navigating a traffic jam after a Black Bears game up in Orono!"

When the laughter died down, the sheriff told the rest of the story. He spoke quickly, so as not to be interrupted again by Walters.

"To her credit, the old woman — near tears, mind you — stood her ground. Rightly so. There were plenty of other places to park. That's when Lloyd starts screaming, "But I'm a sponsor! I'm a sponsor! Do you know how much those kids' jerseys cost? I raised a mountain of money to fix the community pool! My wife headed up the steering committee to fix up and maintain our lighthouse as a historic site! Jesus, you're stupid!"

By then, the kids on the diamond were on their own. Everyone stood frozen, taking in the scene and not knowing what to do.

"No one was watching the game, not even the ump." The sheriff's face darkened. "No one came out to settle Lloyd's hash, either. They call it the bystander effect. The folks in the bleachers all turned to gawk at the spectacle, but nobody moved."

Effrum Jawbly leaned forward to turn up the knob on his oxygen tank. Taking a long drag from the hose that fed air to his nose, the old man offered, "At least somebody called you, Sheriff." He gasped and took another moment before adding, "Too bad young Lime didn't catch him in the act ... and kick his can. People are fed up with the Fauns."

Hobbs considered the old man for a moment. "You know, I suppose some might object, but things have changed in a way I don't care for. In the old days, somebody would have come to the aid of a lady and kicked Lloyd's ass. People are gettin' soft is all I'm sayin'. Maybe a little ridicule did the job. It was prolly just nervous laughter, but some was laughing enough that Lloyd finally picked up on the fact that the town was watching him lose his shit again."

"His face was as red as a beet," Jawbly offered. "I hear tell. I wasn't there... but the Fauns sure are the talk of the town."

When he realized he had an audience, Lloyd had jumped back in his car, flipped the old lady the bird, and tore off in a cloud of dust.

"I'm gonna cite him for speeding in a school zone," Hobbs said. "Don't know whether it'll cool him off or cook him good, but I'm through coddling that bastard."

It turned out that the woman in the parking lot wasn't really a come-from-way. She'd been born and raised in Millinocket. More importantly, her daughter-in-law was high up in management at the Down East Community Hospital in Machias. That was the same hospital with which Lloyd had a laundering contract.

Within a day, that contract was canceled. No linens from that hospital would be cleaned at Eleanor's Cleaning and Gleaming in Poeticule Bay.

"Lloyd is raging at that fresh injustice," Walters added. "He was in here talking restraint of trade or some shit. Said he'd sue, but nothing will come of that. Maybe Machias hospital has a morals clause ... or an anti-asshole clause."

Alan Danner, a retired Mennonite pastor, surprised everyone by adding to the gossip fest. A pinch-mouthed man with a reputation for being against all forms of fun, Danner finally piped up. "Mr. Faun said the loss of the hospital contract doesn't make any difference to his bottom line. Methinks his laundry franchisees are about to get a raise in fees to cover the shortfall."

The little group nodded sagely.

"Big spirals down to little spirals. That man is throwing himself all the way down the drain," Danner said. "You know, after the fish went away, Lloyd had to let go of that Indian family. They used to work in the back, the dry-cleaning end. I wonder if Lloyd sees himself, and you know, the big picture."

"What do you mean by the big picture, Padre?" Walters asked.

"I'm just wondering, do you think that he and his son even suspect that they are indeed colossal assholes?"

Everyone burst out laughing.

Sheriff Hobbs repeated that anecdote often. "Lloyd had pissed off the Baptists early on, but Pastor Danner wouldn't say shit if his mouth was full of it. When you manage to turn a Mennonite against you? Well, damn! That's a bad day."

Derision had become an essential element in solving the problem of Lloyd and Keith Faun. But they weren't banished yet.

23

AGGRAVATION

The following week, early Sunday morning, Chuck drove Molly to the Fauns' laundromat and dry-cleaning business. The fresh board around the new door at the back of Eleanor's Cleaning and Gleaming hadn't been painted yet. Chuck came prepared with a crowbar, assorted tools, and pre-measured wood. Molly pulled bags of what looked like groceries out of the pickup.

Chuck broke the back door so they could get in. Then he got to work repairing it immediately. Meanwhile, Molly entered the laundromat with the foodstuffs and a sock full of quarters.

"If Keith or Lloyd show up before we're done," Chuck instructed, "I wouldn't object if you hit 'em with the sock of quarters in self-defense. Otherwise, use the coins to get all the machines going."

Heart pounding harder, Molly advanced into the gloom of a hallway. To her right, a bathroom. To her left, a storeroom. To the front of the store, vengeance.

And yet, Molly hesitated. After they'd goaded the Faun men into waving shotguns at a crowd of bargain seekers, she was hesitant about proceeding with their private little war. "Some people might think we're the bad guys in this situation, Dad."

"I understand your trepidations, so one question. Are you one of the people who think we're the bad guys?"

The memory of Barry Graves' face at the school assembly sprang to her mind. Some of the hockey goons had called him "Raccoon" because both his eyes were still black.

And Keith Faun just sat there, handsome and strong and untouchable, not a mark on him. People like Keith seemed destined for a comfortable life, never worrying about money, too confident they could never be hurt.

Despite his injuries, Barry had gazed back at them with a mixture of sullen dignity and helplessness. It was the helplessness that spurred Molly forward.

But characterizing Barry as merely injured didn't feel right. Injuries arise from accidents. What happened to Barry was no accident. Barry's pain rose from Keith's actions, the bully's monstrous, mountainous, incomprehensible malice. Wounded was a better word than injured.

When Molly thought of Barry sustaining wounds in a war of good versus evil, her cause felt pure and moral. Breaking and entering was nothing compared to the monster's assault.

Molly wondered if Barry ever plotted revenge against his oppressors. Probably. Who wouldn't? But she was also sure he wouldn't be back to act on such impulses.

She didn't know the kid, of course. Based on how he acted in the school assembly, he seemed like a good person. He had endured much more than Molly had. He was angry, but he used his words. Maybe he was so good he even managed to forgive his enemies. Or was forgiveness a myth? Just a coping mechanism the helpless use to get on with their lives?

Though Keith's assault on the boy had been her instigating incident, in a strange way, she didn't care so much about Barry anymore. Her anger spawned more from principle now. Barry was far away, out of harm's way.

There were bigots everywhere, but at least he'd escaped the immediate dangers in Poeticule Bay. Molly still lived in the town with the bully. She genuinely felt for Barry as a victim, but her rage was bigger than her compassion.

Seeing her standing in the hall, Chuck asked, "Molly? You okay? Thinkin' of stopping the train before it goes off the tracks?"

"Just thinking. Civilization's really broken, isn't it?"

Chuck bent to remeasure a length of wood for the door frame. "What are you on about?"

"The civilization train is already off the tracks. What we're doing is repair work, trying to stop another derailment."

"Okay, then. Get to it. Philosophical discussions should be confined to before or after the break and enter, doncha think?"

Molly hurried deeper into the store.

The rear rooms of the laundromat were dark and smelled sickly sweet. She had expected the air to be lemon-scented, but that was for the cheap soap sold from the dispensers at the front of the store. The back room smelled of a strong chemical she could not identify.

She entered a large room. Molly could barely discern the outlines of machines that may have been washers, dryers, or perhaps a press. She passed a long table she assumed was used for folding sheets and ironing.

A small office sat in the middle of the store with glass to the front and to the rear. She thought they were windows at first. Backtracking a few steps, Molly realized these were one-way mirrors. From his ratty swivel chair, Lloyd Faun could survey his customers and employees through the one-way mirrors.

The office smelled of cigar smoke. The peeling wallpaper was from another age, yellowed from the smoke of perhaps thousands of cigars. With its cartoonish pictures of daisies, bunny rabbits, and strawberry plants, she guessed the decor would have been better suited to a nursery from the 1950s.

She paused in the office doorway and peered in with no particular aim in mind. She hoped to spot a safe Chuck could drill open. The small room was crammed with boxes marked "Perc" — some kind of solvent — and filing cabinets the color of mustard.

To her right came an open area behind the front counter. A

carousel of clothes hung on a winding track that circled back toward the dry-cleaning machines and large tubs. Shirts, suits, and dresses wrapped in flimsy plastic and tagged with bright yellow slips stood waiting to be claimed by customers.

The laundromat took up one large room in the front. Aside from brown stains in the ceiling tiles from water damage, the front of the store looked well-kept. Coin-operated washers and dryers lined the walls. A large cream-colored laminate countertop stood in the middle, a ready place to sort and fold clothes.

It was the perfect business for Lloyd in that he had very little interaction with customers. Aside from yelling at young people that they were overloading the washers with jeans, she guessed he wouldn't have to talk to many people during his workday.

Her father had mentioned to Molly that Lloyd used to have more employees "back when the town was more of a going concern."

Molly's gaze shifted back to the carousel of clothes. The rack was not full. In fact, it appeared quite sparse. The Faun family money seemed to come mostly from Lloyd's father's lumber legacy and franchising the laundromat and dry-cleaning business across New England. Now that the locals understood that Lloyd was much more than a mere prickly pear, they weren't giving him much business.

We are having an effect, she thought.

Molly would rather have concentrated her campaign on Keith. However, since it would be Lloyd's decision to abandon the Bay, they had to keep the pressure on him. And Eleanor's was his baby. Mess with his business and he might really leave town.

Barry's bully concerned her slightly less of late. Perhaps Sheriff Hobbs' scolding had chastened Keith. The bully had fallen silent and sullen at school. His handsome face had become stony. Even the puckheads had quieted around him, no more jibes, jokes, or rough-housing. It was as if Keith carried a stench from which his friends needed to distance themselves.

Molly's mother often said, "You're judged by the company you keep." It seemed the hockey team — and their parents — had finally received that message.

Molly hefted the bags and made her way toward the washers and dryers.

If Lloyd and Keith are the question, banishment is the answer, she thought. *Go be someone else's reason to hate.*

Molly moved through the gloom of Eleanor's Cleaning and Gleaming. As she got to work, she sang softly to herself as if she were still a small and innocent child, "Fauns, Fauns, go away, don't come back another day!"

It soothed Molly's nerves to pretend to be childlike while she committed her righteous crimes.

24

INVESTIGATION

News of the latest attack on the Faun family came from an unexpected source. Instead of filtering through the town gossips, Molly's campaign made the television news. Bangor News at 5 sent a camera crew all the way from the city.

Chuck called Molly into the living room to watch the report. Aside from the visuals of their clandestine work at Eleanor's, it boiled down to an interview between Lloyd and a reporter named Auddie Bent.

"I spotted the news van go through town," Chuck said. "Thought they were lost. I'm a little surprised they even found us on the map. We're usually invisible, so I guess Lloyd made it sound like a hate crime."

"It is a hate crime," Molly said. "I hate him and Keith both."

Chuck made a cutting gesture at his throat as Kay limped into the room, her back bent. She looked uncomfortable, but her tone was light. "Look at you two, thick as thieves lately."

Chuck pointed to the television screen. As the camera panned Eleanor's interior, a wide grin spread across her face. "Alert the media. We officially have a big blue hullabaloo!"

The reporter's tone sounded serious and sad, as if he were

reporting on mass graves in a war zone, "At this laundromat and dry-cleaning outlet in the tiny seaside village of Poeticule Bay, police are investigating a series of events the owner describes as a harassment campaign. Sometime over the weekend, unseen and unknown hooligans filled washing machines and dryers with bags of rice. The rice swelled and hardened. Worse, investigators say drywall mud was also used, ruining the machines. The owner, Mr. Lloyd Faun, does not yet have an estimate of the total cost of the damage."

Kay did not look surprised. "It takes a lot of labor to make more foes than friends, but Lloyd and his boy sure did put in the work."

Lloyd appeared on camera in a faded T-shirt with a picture of a rock band called the Rustic Overtones. Unshaven and slurring his words, Lloyd said, "There's no sign of forced entry — which I don't understand — but they sure cost me a bundle! It's gonna be some expensive."

"And how many thousands of dollars did it take for the Graves to move?" Molly asked. Her father shot her a censorious look.

Red-faced, Lloyd continued, "I can't figure how the punks got in. These machines are meant for washing, drying, and pressing clothes, not for food. Really gummed up the works."

"He's drunk," Kay said. "That's a shame, out there in front of God and everybody! Should have cleaned himself up for his TV appearance. The whole state will think we're all a bunch of nincompoops."

"Or just poops," Molly added.

Lloyd bobbed side to side so much that the reporter had to move the microphone to keep up.

"Looks like Lloyd has to pee," Chuck jeered.

"They filled up one dryer with popcorn and set it on high heat!" Lloyd ranted. "That's mostly a mess and a nuisance, but rice and gunk in the washers? They're filled to the brim and all! And they put cans of shaving cream under the heat of the press in back! The cans exploded everywhere, all over everything. Lucky they didn't start a fire!"

"Next time, maybe," Kay cackled.

The camera view of the laundromat's interior appeared again, this time focusing on a broad expanse of wall. In bright red paint, Molly's message was broadcast across Maine:

YOUR CLAN WILL BE BANISHED

Lloyd returned to the screen. "Listen! We're a small town! Everybody knows everybody, right? The terrorists are somewhere among us. Somebody knows somethin', for sure."

Chuck and Molly exchanged a look but said nothing.

Lloyd looked directly into the camera. "If you know something, come to me. I'll make it worth your while."

Auddie Bent frowned. "Are you offering a reward, Mr. Faun?"

The man shook his head. "I'm thinkin' more just desserts. This is terrorism."

"Terrorism, sir?" The reporter seemed skeptical. "I understand this mess will shut you down for a time, but vandalism — "

"Terrorists!" Lloyd insisted. "They've messed with my cars! They've come to my home, spraying graffiti! My wife got so scared she had to leave town."

"That's not what I heard why Marjorie left, God bless her," Kay said.

The story shifted to the surveillance recording from the Faun's backyard. The recording was of poor quality, but it did show a tall, burly figure enter the yard from the woods. Molly's eyes widened. There she stood wearing several jackets, spraying graffiti in the name of vengeance for a kid she barely knew.

Chuck caught his wife's eye. "Hey, Kay? Do you recognize that hoodlum with the spray can?"

Kay Jergins leaned forward with a grunt and squinted.

Molly popped a sweat and suppressed the urge to squirm, but her mother shook her head slowly.

"I don't understand it," Kay said. "They can send pretty pictures from the landscape of Mars, but surveillance cameras always look like they're shooting through diarrhea and Vaseline. That's nobody *I* know, do you? Whoever it is, they've got nothing to worry about from that picture."

Molly thought her father's gamble was reckless. However, when Kay declared she couldn't recognize her own daughter from the fuzzy recording, Molly relaxed and felt reassured.

Auddie Bent faced the camera with Poeticule Bay's lighthouse perfectly framed over his left shoulder. "Mr. Faun says his family is the target of organized attacks by an individual or a group but claims he has no enemies."

"So, I guess it's his *friends* who are after him?" Kay crowed.

The reporter continued, "The sheriff's department says they are pursuing several leads but have no further comment at this time. Whatever is happening in this tiny coastal community may be baffling to law enforcement. However, I spoke to several local residents on condition of anonymity who gave a different perspective. Some say a Faun family member may be involved. A recent incident in which a student was assaulted may have kicked off this campaign to oust the Faun family from a town they've lived in for generations. I asked Mr. Faun about that."

Lloyd appeared on camera once more, looking angrier than before. Molly suspected the interview was heavily edited to avoid airing swear words.

"I don't appreciate your questions," Lloyd told Auddie.

"Auddie Bent is really making a meal out of this, isn't he?" Molly's mother said. "Guess they had to make the trip worth the gas. Lotta noise over nothing much, you ask me."

Molly bit back harsh words and shushed her mother.

Lloyd was making familiar excuses. "There was a kerfuffle down to the school, sure. My son and another boy got into it as boys sometimes do, but that other boy is gone. It's over."

Shame is never over, Molly thought. *Someday soon, Lloyd, you'll feel its burn.*

25

IDENTIFICATION

The television reporter kept a smooth and reasonable tone with Lloyd. "I'm told that incident drove that other boy's family out of town, and that didn't sit well with some folks around here. You don't see a possible connection between them leaving and the messages you're getting? By the painted message in your store and on your house, they're literally trying to banish you."

Bent tipped his microphone to Lloyd's mouth. The laundromat proprietor's eyes shifted back and forth as if searching for the answer on a blank cue card.

After a long pregnant pause, Lloyd finally burst out with, "That family moved away! Done is done and spilt milk is spilt! If this is somebody bothering us because they're offended on someone else's behalf, they need to keep their noses to their business and leave my business alone. I don't have time for this — "

Lloyd's mouth moved but the television station censored his string of curses: B*leep this bleep-bleep bleep*ing *bleep!*"

With that, Lloyd spun on his heel and disappeared off-screen.

The journalist turned to the camera, a slight smile tugging at his lips. He'd gotten the drama he'd come for. "For Bangor Live at 5 News, Auddie Bent reporting."

Kay plopped down in her worn recliner. "That whole story stinks. *I* know who the midnight spray painter is."

Molly sat up very straight, doing her best impression of a good girl. That didn't seem enough, so she rearranged her expression, imagining herself mystified by the world, as innocent as a dim infant.

"Don't believe a word coming out of that man's mouth," Molly's mother decreed. "Classic false flag operation."

Mom listened to conspiracy theorists on the A.M. radio frequently, so Molly supposed she shouldn't have been surprised by her mother's use of the term false flag.

"Just look at that surveillance footage!" Kay continued. "No sound. Grainy. Could be the Faun boy himself! And I think that's exactly who it is."

"Lloyd said he shot the bastard as they ran away," Chuck said.

"But no man showed up shot! Smells like shit of the bull to me! I tell you, Lloyd's in for a fall, and this is all going to blow up in that boy's face eventually!"

Molly's right shoulder blade still ached when she tried to sleep on that side. However, she was secretly pleased that, being female, she seemed above suspicion. Being a woman had so few advantages in life. She was glad she didn't fit the profile. Her edge was preconceived notions of which gender was more likely to engage in certain kinds of criminal activities.

In full Sherlock mode, Molly's mother plunged on. "You can even hear it in the reporter's voice. I believe in Auddie, and Auddie doesn't believe him. He didn't say Lloyd 'said' this or that. He said the bone-head 'claimed' no enemies. We all know that's not true, and there's a big difference between 'said' and 'claimed.' That reporter is giving us a wink and a nod there."

Chuck shrugged his agreement. "Lloyd has money and influence in this town, but everyone knows his whole family emerged from the womb pieces of work."

Molly had been fifteen before she realized that when her parents called someone a 'piece of work,' they meant 'piece of shit.'

"Lloyd made a grandma cry at a kid's ball game," Chuck added.

"People remember. Maybe it's about more that than boy who got hurt and the family going away."

Kay turned to Chuck. "He's bad. Even *you* had run-ins with Lloyd way back, babe."

Molly's father shrugged. "Truth. He made high school more awful than it had to be."

"That poor kid got half-murdered," Kay said, "and the Faun boy is getting all the way off!"

"And if you're counting the Fauns' enemies, don't forget the Baptists," Molly teased.

Kay pointed a finger at Molly and booped the tip of her daughter's nose. "You're goofing with me now, but that's enough about the Baptists. Don't you see? I'm right about the culprit on the tape. It has to be Keith Faun. Don't you see the most suspicious thing?"

Chuck and Molly looked at each other again, equally entertained but trying to appear serious.

"No forced entry!" Kay crowed. "Who breaks into the back of a store without breaking the lock?"

"Maybe they picked the lock," Molly suggested.

Her mother shook her head. "Even if what Lloyd is spouting were true — which it damn sure is not — this is the Bay! It's not a jewel heist in Monte Carlo! One way or t'other, the stuff that's happening to the Fauns is of their own making. It's been a long time coming, but when the truth comes out, no one will shed a tear for that bunch!"

"So, you don't think the police will take this seriously?" I asked.

"Please! This isn't high crimes. Misdemeanors, maybe. The pranksters are *petty*. Relentless, maybe, but ultimately fairly harmless and nothing less than what's deserved."

Chuck shook his head. "Destroying all those machines at Eleanor's would put the people who did it in jail for real time. This is a for real problem now."

"You can only push people so far," Kay replied. "Then people push back."

Molly was still concerned the blame game might extend beyond

Poeticule Bay. "You don't think Barry or his family are doing this, do you?"

"Nah! The sheriff's lazy, but he'd be all over that. Lloyd would make him pursue that wild goose all the way to the bottom of the bag. I told you, this is a false flag."

Honestly mystified at her mother's reasoning, Molly asked, "But why would you think that's Keith Faun on the surveillance recording?"

"Lloyd's orchestrating all this as a play for sympathy. After what their thug of a son did? The school and the police covered for Keith, but the whole town isn't as rotten as all that. A lot of people were disgusted with what he did to that boy."

"Disgusted, maybe," Molly said, "but they didn't do anything."

"What did you expect people to do?" Kay shot back. "Run around at night spray painting houses and making more trouble? Anyway, I'm tired and this whole thing gives me the gas."

Her mother did not drop the subject. The following night, she held court at her knitting club meeting. After explaining how the crimes could have been self-inflicted to appeal to community sympathy, her fellow knitters nodded and clucked. The false flag theory spread.

Juicy gossip powered and spun the rumor mill. Eventually, inevitably, the idea that the richest and nastiest man in town was looking for pity got back to the Fauns. Naturally, Lloyd grew even more furious and went around town trying to kill that theory.

When word got back to the Jergins family, oddly, it was Molly's mother who appeared most elated. "One word on the wind and I got Lloyd. When a rabbit is hunted, he runs in circles, and I got him running in circles. Didn't need a single can of paint or do a break and enter! That's how it's done!"

26

FRACTION

You can only push people so far. Kay had said that. At the time, Molly didn't consider how close to the edge some people were — or how close she was to doing to Keith what Keith did to Barry.

When she pondered going after the goon physically, it felt like a bubble of elation rising in the center of her chest, expanding as if she might defy gravity and lift off the ground. Or explode.

She had been dismayed when her mother deemed her missions little more than a prank war. To Molly, the missions were more war than prank. She fantasized about dozens of acts of vicious vengeance night and day.

Sand in a gas tank led her to envision pouring sand down Keith's throat. Kicking him in the knee to deny him a pro hockey career seemed fair. Then she visualized using a tire iron to break more bones. She could even picture the smile on her face as she swung the weapon.

But Molly didn't want to kill Keith or Lloyd Faun. She wanted to punish them. Looking deeper, Molly wished for the impossible. She yearned for them to see the error of their ways, to beg for forgiveness, to repent, and make restitution.

They would never admit they were wrong, though. That was a given, so her mission was merely for the Fauns to suffer the same fate as the Graves family.

"Shunning is an ancient tool that shaped civilization," she told her father. "Banishment was a lathe that shaped all early societies."

"More civilized than hangin' him up by his thumbs, I guess," Chuck mused. "Lookin' at Lloyd, I can't help thinkin' Poeticule Bay needs an enema. You're right, Molly! Gotta flush out those Fauns."

Chuck and Molly went to the Drift Inn to discuss their next steps over a platter of clams and fries. The actual "inn" part of the establishment had burnt down in the late '80s. What remained was a battered seafood restaurant on its way to ruin. There'd been no repairs since the original owner's death, so the structure had deteriorated to little more than a large but a slouching shack hunched against the ocean's wind.

Only summer people called the Drift Inn by its full name. Locals just called it the Driftin'. The restaurant was mostly a summer people place for those who didn't have the good sense or time to drive up the road to a better eatery.

The Driftin' only opened during Maine's warmer months, and sometimes only sporadically, depending on the cook's mood. The locals mostly avoided the place because the mussels were dependably gritty with sand.

"The menu is too short, the prices are too tall, so the place is pretty empty," Chuck said. "We can plot and plan without your mother hearing and telling her knitting club. Your mother's a crafty woman, but we don't want her input on this. She wouldn't approve."

Molly had never hung out to eat with her father at a restaurant in the middle of the day. However, they had more in common now that they were co-conspirators.

Rejecting a table with a view of the water, they took a secluded booth against the wall. A faded sign overhead read: *The fish you eat today slept last night in Poeticule Bay.*

Chuck dipped a French fry into the little hill of ketchup he'd carefully squeezed from a handful of packets. He pointed at the sign with the fry. "That's from before the dead zone. I think all their so-called fresh fish comes down from up north, off Halifax or Newfoundland. Maybe Japanese trawlers way farther northeast. You know what the local old guys say about the dead zone?"

"Tell me."

"They say it's Roddy's curse."

The former owner of the Drift Inn, Roddy Atkinson, went crazy one night. He set fire to the hotel with several jerry cans of gasoline. Some said it was his debts that did him in. Others said he committed arson for the insurance money. That secret died with Roddy because his plan went awry one summer night in 1986.

The coroner reported that Roddy got burned pretty badly in the inferno. Somehow, he managed to stumble to his brand-new Sting Ray, hit the gas, and zoomed right off the cliff behind the Drift Inn. He hit the water, not the rocky beach.

The volunteer fire department did their best. They couldn't save the inn, only the attached restaurant. They didn't know Roddy plunged his car off the Drifting Cliffs until the next morning.

"They found the Sting Ray and Roddy's body when the tide went out," Chuck said. "Maybe it was suicide. Maybe he went over the cliff to get wet, to stop from burning alive."

Molly muttered a soft, "*Jesus!*"

Federal government scientists blamed the algae bloom due to an excess of phosphorous and nitrogen, probably because of agricultural runoff upstream. Fishing yields had plummeted in the region for a long time, but Poeticule Bay wasn't officially declared devoid of all fish until two years after Roddy's death. Still, the locals blamed the dead innkeeper and made him the stuff of legend.

"Around here, bad news sticks like glue," Chuck said. "Your grandfather knew Roddy well. Always said he cursed having to pay taxes. Maybe the tax load was why he killed himself. They say him going over the cliff cursed us, town and ocean both."

"Dad! You don't believe that, do you? Hexes are a little out there."

"Your mom reads the horoscope every day to decide what kind of day she's going to have. I dunno. All I can say about Roddy is people are crazy everywhere. Some people, like Lloyd and Keith, do things that are either silly, stupid, or downright mean. Doesn't leave a lot of room for much else. If they lived somewhere else, they wouldn't get away with all their shit."

"Let's change that," Molly said.

"Nobody's managed to tame those two yet."

"That doesn't matter," Molly assured him. "Everything is unprecedented until it isn't."

27

AFFLICTION

"Why do you think the Fauns are the way they are?"

Chuck stared toward the window as he pondered her question. Apparently, the gray sky and roiling ocean offered no answers. Finally, he shrugged and suggested, "Smooth brains?"

"I don't know about that," Molly replied. "There are kids at school whose eyes cross when they open a textbook, but they seem awfully nice."

"Y'know, whether it's screwed up blood, bad habits, or twisted genes, I do believe in *family* curses. If there was ever a single good person in the Faun family tree, I don't know about it. Maybe Lloyd's great-great-grandfather was a mean drunk. Or maybe he just wasn't enough of a hugger and that's what got us to where we are today."

"I'd like to hang on to the fantasy that people are good, or that bad people can change," Molly said. "I'm not sure I really believe that, though."

Chuck took a pull on the straw of his malt. "Lloyd did have a little sister — Susan, she was. That was a nice girl by all accounts. You'd never know she'd sprung from the same poisoned tree as Lloyd."

"The exceptional Faun who defied her genetics?"

He shrugged. "Guess so. Lloyd and Big Jim bullied that poor girl 'til she ran away. If you can have good and bad kids in the same family, I don't think I have much to say on the subject of nature versus nurture."

"What happened to Susan?"

"Last I heard she was a pharmacist in Newport. Not so far, but she never comes home."

People tracked the Bay's escapees with the intensity of meteorologists watchful for killer storms. The townsfolk kept tabs on where the progeny fled, how well they were doing financially, and the number of grandchildren they did or did not provide. Any interesting weakness was dwelled upon. The frequency of a child's return home to visit their parents was always a variable up for inspection and discussion.

Molly wondered about Susan. How old was she when she escaped her tormentors? How did she pay for her education to become a pharmacist? Lloyd's sister's new life gave her hope for Barry Graves. Maybe he'd be okay, too.

Molly chewed her breaded clams thoughtfully. When she looked up, Chuck had almost demolished his pile of fries.

Her father had an update. "Marjorie's outta here for good. Might even have saved her life."

Marjorie Faun's exit had been surprisingly satisfying. However, it galled Molly a little that she couldn't claim direct responsibility for the woman's flight.

"Somebody spoke to Lloyd's sister-in-law up in Macwahoc. The report from afar was that Marjorie left her husband after he hit her 'in front of the whole town.' By that, she meant the bargain-seekers on that fateful Saturday morning."

"So, was it really the violence or embarrassment at people seeing her husband for what he is?"

"Your mother's sure there were other times that were more serious. Marjorie wore oversized sunglasses on foggy days. It was so folks wouldn't spot she had a black eye. When they noticed anyway, Marjorie claimed to have fallen. Nobody her age falls down that much."

"Sometimes it seems this town is a surveillance state," Molly mused.

"It's not like this in the city. You go urban, you can be lonely in any crowd — "

"Happy lonely! Sounds perfectly peaceful to me. Peace is people minding their own business. I don't care how kind people are, as long as they aren't unkind."

Chuck took a deep breath and let out a long sigh. "It's not all so bad. The upside of knowing your neighbors is people do tend to look out for each other."

"Example?"

"Don't get too cynical. You know the widower up the hill? Earl?"

"The man who used to own the sawmill."

"Right. When the weather's nice, he's out on his scooter a bit. The neighbors to either side of him keep an eye on the old fart. With all the pies and leftovers and casseroles, Old Earl will never go hungry. They look in on him."

"Well, that's nice for him, but nobody looked out for Barry and his family."

"Can't argue there. Weren't around long enough, I guess. The Graveses were still come-from-aways, but you and me, we're catching up on that debt, evening things out, yeah?"

"Are we? What's next?"

"I imagine more pandemonium," her father replied. "Lloyd and Keith won't stop being who they are."

"So, we are just catalysts, showing people what the Fauns are," Molly said. "Ultimately, they'll be the authors of their own destruction."

"What they hate will do them in. The key to a good life is doing what you love until it kills you."

Molly shot him a quizzical look.

"I think that's a universal," Chuck said. "We are all writing our own book. For instance, I'm eating French fries. Love 'em! I got lots of aches and pains, but it's probably a heart attack that will get me."

"Don't talk like that."

"That's just nature at work, doin' its thing. In the meantime, the fries and clams are delicious."

Molly didn't want to discuss her father's mortality. "Let's focus on the bad guys. What should we *do*?"

"What *should* we do? We should stay home, keep out of trouble, forget all this, and get you graduated. But we're beyond shoulds, aren't we? We're deep into doin' the don'ts."

Her father scrubbed his mouth with a crumpled napkin. "Okay, suppose we give Lloyd some time to cool off so he doesn't lose his shit entirely. Hit him too often and he'll get numb or more violent."

"Or we'll get unlucky?" Molly suggested.

"That could happen, too, so I think there's value in turning down the heat so Lloyd doesn't boil over."

"How's that going to get him banished?"

"Don't be overly eager. Too eager, you'll make mistakes, and we'll get caught. When Lloyd thinks we're done and assumes he's safe, we'll be safe enough to make our next move. The idea is to make him feel like our campaign will never end until he leaves town. If he thinks this is a marathon, not a sprint, Lloyd will question his stamina."

"Okay, okay! Not to sound overeager, but what are we going to do next, though?"

"Big Jim was a hard man, but he really spoiled Lloyd with his cars. Jim bought his darling boy a car while he was still in high school. Lloyd *loves* his cars."

"I already went after his cars."

Chuck turned and stared off into the distance. In a wistful tone, he said, "Y'know, it's a funny thing about spray foam insulation. You put the nozzle in a little hole, squirt it in, and it expands and hardens. I wonder if ole Lloyd would be encouraged to hitchhike out of town if we filled up his car, made it into a Boston cream donut? The cream filling would be all polyurethane. I think spray foam insulation in Lloyd's Lincoln would make for a fun daddy/daughter project."

Molly brightened. "I never thought of a hardware store as an armory, but I think you're on to something. That *does* sound like fun!"

They never got the chance to have that fun together.

28

RECOGNITION

There had once been fifty-five stores in Poeticule Bay. Many of the town's entrepreneurial endeavors had long since closed. There wasn't a bank anymore, just an ATM at the Gas 'N Go.

Two stores on Commercial Street sold scented candles, stuffed animals, whirligigs, and touristy geegaws. Molly's mother referred to their inventory as "dustables" since the stuff served no functional purpose. Since both stores were so often empty, it was rumored they were money laundering fronts for the state's busy drug trade.

Sunday mornings, there wasn't much open. Gardeners in town and farmers from the surrounding area patronized the hardware store.

After a long night of insomnia, Kay was having what she called "one of my headache days." All she wanted was sleep. Failing that, she settled for peace and quiet. To that end, she evicted her daughter and husband from the house for a few hours.

Chuck and Molly exited the house just before lunch. Sunday morning services had just ended. When they stopped at the Seaview Bakery, Molly and Chuck stood in line with the church crowd.

Molly whispered her father, "These people, all dressed up and looking so nice, make me feel like a grubby heathen."

"Only because you don't know their secrets," Chuck replied a little too loudly. "Lloyd's a Presbyterian and loud about it. He wears nice suits. Does he make you feel bad about yourself?"

"Only that we're technically the same species."

"There you go."

Emerging into sunshine, father and daughter ate iced cinnamon rolls. The treats were so shiny it was as if they were coated in lacquer. White icing coated the sides of Chuck's mouth. Keys in one hand and a huge container of coffee in the other, he held the bun in his jaws and grinned at Molly. Rendered mute, he handed her the keys to the truck.

Molly's eyes widened in surprise. "You're letting me drive? Is this a special occasion?"

She had learned to drive using her mother's Volvo. Her parents referred to the old Volvo as "the jalopy." They thought the rusty relic was safer for Molly to pilot.

Chuck pulled the cinnamon roll from his mouth and spoke around a large chunk, "You're big enough to get shot and shake it off without shitting yourself. To my mind, that makes you big enough to drive the truck. Besides, this *is* a special occasion. We're on a recon mission. We're gonna measure our success. It's Eleanor's grand reopening today. Let's go check it out."

Molly climbed into the driver's seat and soon they pulled toward the back of the parking lot behind the Baptist church. She backed in among a few cars. With Atlantic waves lapping the rocky shore behind them, they had an unobstructed view of the laundromat.

A few church-goers had apparently lingered. Down the shore, a young family in their Sunday best picked their way down the rocky beach. Two young boys chucked rocks into the water. It appeared the older brother was teaching his younger brother how to skip stones. His efforts were unsuccessful but entertaining.

After the damage done to their washers and dryers, the Fauns were making a big deal of their relaunch. Lloyd stood in the parking lot tending to burgers and hot dogs on two huge barbecue grills. However, the laundromat's parking lot stood empty.

Chuck looked pleased. "His stock around here sure has plummeted. When no one shows up for free food, even Lloyd might begin to suspect he's a piece of crap. That's a big step toward banishment, don't you think?"

"I don't think self-awareness is a thing they do, Dad, but it's a nice idea."

It had been three weeks since they had sabotaged Eleanor's. Chuck speculated, "Between losing that big hospital contract and the business out of commission, their bottom line must be achin' like a bad knee."

Chuck rubbed his left knee. That pain was obviously on his mind. Molly caught the hint and reached into the glove compartment. She pulled out the bottle of aspirin he always kept there and handed it to him.

Chuck thanked her and, tossing his head back twice, dry swallowed two pills.

"I don't know how you do that, swallow pills without a big glass of water."

"Pain and practice," he replied. "What were you thinking about Lloyd?"

"That he's got all that franchise money."

"He's comfortable."

"Beyond comfortable," she said stiffly.

"So, what do you think would make a rich guy feel like living here isn't worth it anymore?"

"I'm not sure what it will take, not yet. Hindsight is twenty-twenty," Molly said, "but I think if no one else knew about all this, maybe we'd have a better shot at getting rid of him. He won't want anyone thinking he's been run out of town."

"Yeah, his pride might make him eat more shit than an ordinary man is prepared to swallow. On the other hand, I'm buying some more spray insulation."

"Enough to fill up his car?"

Chuck shook his head. "Soon. It wouldn't do to get it all at once or from the same place. Folks might notice and the sheriff might get curious. Next time I take a run all the way over to Oubliette, maybe then we'll have enough to deal with Lloyd's Lincoln. Shoppin' too close to home is shittin' too close to the dinner plate."

"I think we have to hit the Lincoln when it's not parked at home or at the laundromat," Molly suggested.

"High risk."

"Yeah, but imagine the psychological impact if we manage to pull off the next mission in a place where he'd least expect it."

"Keep finding pain points and planning attacks there, Hannibal," Chuck replied. "I'll work on acquiring the ordnance."

Lloyd's push to reopen Eleanor's must have been the biggest ad spend the local radio station had enjoyed in decades. Penobscot Valley Radio ran promotions all day for a week.

Eleanor's sign was repainted. Lloyd had even rented an Airdancer. The wavy-armed balloon man flopped around above blowers as if his business was a car dealership, not part of a laundromat chain.

As they watched Lloyd fuss at his grill, Molly came up with another idea. "You're thinking about spray insulation. What about the pink kind?"

"Huh?"

"What if we hit the laundromat again? Some irritant in the dryers, maybe? Make the clothes itchy. Fiberglass could do that, right?"

Chuck nixed that brainwave immediately. "We don't want to punish the wrong people. We're going after Lloyd and Keith, not the town. Let's keep the collateral damage to a minimum, shall we?"

"Sorry."

"Don't be sorry, just give yourself more time. We gotta recognize our limits. When you don't have a good enough idea, keep thinking. Somethin' always comes along."

"Always?"

Her father smirked. "Change always comes. Aren't a lot of guarantees in life, but California will get hit with the big one and slide into the ocean. That big volcano under Yellowstone will erupt and murder the planet someday, too. Just be patient."

"Thanks for those happy predictions, but you've lost me. What are you talking about?"

"Patience, 'specially with yourself. Do that."

29

UNIFICATION

Earl MacAdam buzzed by the laundromat on his Rascal scooter. He paused beneath the balloon man dancing above a fan. Craning his neck to look up at the Airdancer, the old sawyer shook his head in disbelief.

Lloyd strode forward to greet Poeticule Bay's oldest resident. However, MacAdam shot off as fast his scooter could take him. He did not return Lloyd's wave. In a colossal breach of small-town etiquette, he didn't even acknowledge him with a nod.

The old man went up the road and in a little while buzzed back. Turning into the church parking lot, MacAdam steered to the rear edge of the parking lot to look out to sea.

After a brief pause, the old man passed the truck. MacAdam slowed his scooter and shot them a lopsided grin. He tossed his head to indicate Eleanor's. "Hey! You wonder how much all that nonsense cost the bastard? I wonder. Church is out just across the street and not a single member of the congregation will go over to take a free hot dog from the son of a bitch! Lloyd should never have pissed off the Baptists."

"I try not to give Lloyd too much thought," Chuck said.

"Can't hardly believe that!" MacAdam exclaimed. "After all the hullaballoo?"

"The Fauns are not the best of us," Molly said.

MacAdam smile grew wider to expose a couple of missing teeth. "Darn right! But what do you suppose goes on in a cranium like that? My granddaughter's gay, 'queer' so she calls it. What's it to Lloyd's boy? Kid's got the world by the ass on a downhill drag, and he's still mad at everything. You think those Fauns think they run the whole world?"

"I think they think they might," Chuck replied.

"It's a weak man who has to try so hard to look strong," MacAdam muttered. "What a world. Anywho, enjoy the day! Warmer than usual all of a sudden, idn't? Like a sauna, but I still like it hot. The diabetes makes me cold. Gotta get home and light a fire to heat things up! Tally-ho!"

Without waiting for a reply, the old man gave them a cheery salute and buzzed away.

A few minutes later, Keith emerged from the laundromat wearing a huge sandwich board that read: Clean clothes! Clean Spirit! DON'T LET THEM WIN!

Molly rolled her eyes. "We're 'them,' huh?"

Chuck, unperturbed, sipped his coffee. "Feels good, doesn't it?"

Keith turned and revealed the rear side of the sandwich board. It was a picture of a rainbow with a big red slash through it.

"Keith beat up Barry so bad his whole family left town, and somehow it's all the kid's fault!" Molly objected.

"Same shit, different day, higher pile." Chuck sighed. "Once, when I was on leave, Len, an army buddy of mine, wanted to go to Canada. He heard the strippers take everything off up there. I mean *everything*."

"Dad!"

"Relax. We didn't end up a strip club. We got lost in Toronto and ended up in the gay area."

"A gay area? Were there street signs?"

"Well, I don't know if it was that official, exactly. Len and I were walking along, and he kind of freaked out when he realized there were four other men on the street — couples — and he and I were the only ones not holding hands. Anyway, we were thirsty, so we walked into a bar to get a beer. Had my first limoncello spritz there."

"Limoncello — "

"It was recommended."

"You never told me all this!"

"It's kind of obvious I never told you lots of things, but you're old enough now, and it's finally relevant."

"You in a gay bar? Hard to picture."

"It was a bar, Molly! The beer in Canada is a little stronger, and the limoncello was excellent. *Anyway,* turns out they had a problem with homophobia up there, too. There were a couple of bouncers, and they both wore white T-shirts that said Bash Back. That was years ago in another country, but kinda feels like we're full circle, doesn't it? Some folks think we're changin' too fast, but I don't think things are changin' much at all."

"Did you learn anything else during your wild night in Toronto? Does Mom know?"

"It was just a beer or two, and yes, your mother knows. She laughed her ass off about it. If you weren't laughing at me opening up and making wisecracks, we could have had a sweet father-daughter moment."

Molly couldn't suppress a chuckle. "So, nothing more to report from the experience?"

"Yes," he admitted. "I wish women were at least half as forward and flirty as gay guys."

"Dad!"

"Your mother made me work so hard to get her to the altar, I felt like a leper at the wedding. If I were gay, I could have been married much earlier and maybe be better dressed."

Molly put an index finger to his lips and pressed hard. "Stop."

He pulled his head away and beamed a big smile her way. "Hey, all I'm saying is I never understood all the hate. I never felt threatened. I don't freak out over gay marriage. I married your mother.

Somebody else's marriage never had anything to do with me. I mean, what's the fret?"

"The fret is that people like Barry still get beat up. Some get murdered or are driven to suicide. A lot of gay kids are kicked out of the homes they were supposed to grow up in. Those kids end up on the streets, and some charitable organizations make a point of not helping gay homeless people."

Chuck's chin fell to his chest. "I didn't know that last bit, but I don't know who you think you're arguing with. I'm on the right side of the rainbow, but I know we're not done. That's why I'm here with you, doing this."

"I wouldn't call myself an ally, exactly. I just hate bullies. Years from now, if someone found out ... I don't know."

"You lost me, there. Found out what?" her father prompted.

"What if people thought we were the bad guys? For going after the Fauns like this, I mean."

"I don't know the Graves kid, but I'm here for you. I've known Lloyd and his whole damned family too long and too well. More important, I know *my* kid. That's how I know your cause is righteous."

"*Our* cause," Molly corrected.

Chuck smiled. "Ours, yes."

30

RETRIBUTION

A few cars slowed as they passed Eleanor's, but no one entered the laundromat's parking lot. Lloyd stood stubbornly by the grill. Keith made no attempt to hide his displeasure. The bully stood perfectly still and glared at passing motorists.

"He's mean muggin' anybody who comes close. Do a job bad enough, I suppose you won't be asked to do it again," Chuck said.

"It's almost funny," Molly said.

Her father grinned. "I think it's all-the-way funny. Lloyd's a storm cloud, and Keith obviously doesn't want to play sandwich board boy. He should be waving and smiling — "

"That sandwich board?" Molly enthused. "*That* is humiliation."

She checked her watch. They'd been watching for more than twenty minutes. "No one's coming, or at least not enough people to eat up all those hot dogs."

"Lloyd underestimates this town. He had things go his way for so long, he couldn't conceive of failure. We're not all sheep lookin' for a shepherd, after all."

"You think people are scared off after he and Keith went to their door with guns?" Molly speculated. "Or maybe they think something bad will happen if they show up? Are we scaring the bystanders away?"

"It's not us. It's Lloyd."

When she gave him a quizzical look, Chuck dug into his coat pocket and pulled out a piece of paper that had been folded over and over. He handed it to her to read. "This came to the house. You missed it."

Molly unfolded it and smoothed out the paper on her lap. It was a bright yellow pamphlet.

"I'm guessing everyone in town got one in their mailbox," Chuck said. "For Eleanor's grand reopening, the idiot wrote a manifesto. I swear he's turning into the Unabomber."

The flyer held little information about the services offered at his store. Instead, it was a screed detailing Lloyd's feelings about his victimhood.

In part, it read:

Everyone in Poeticule Bay knows by now that terrorists are trying to run me and my family out of town. Generations of Fauns have lived in the Bay. We aren't going anywhere. This is our town. We are *owners*.

This all started after my son Keith got into a fight with another boy at school. My son (and I) have been called bullies and bigots. To those who oppose us, I'll tell you the truth. We are bullies when it comes to doing the right thing. You call it bigotry? We call it self-defense.

We know good people are on our side. We aren't leaving. Instead, we'll drive out the freaks and terrorists.

For all the real Americans we serve, we appreciate your continued patronage. But also recognize, you *owe* us your business because we're fighting for you.

Her father chuckled. "Lloyd's the kind of guy who doesn't let a single thought go unspoken, huh?"

The text went on, and Lloyd's sentiments became increasingly hateful. He did not mention the Graves family by name, but it was clear he was glad he'd run them out of town.

"Run out of town," Molly murmured. "Is this Maine or the Old West?"

Lloyd's bitterness wasn't just reserved for anyone who disagreed with him. He also blamed his wife for abandoning his personal crusade against what he called "the cowardly and wimpy rainbow people."

When Molly came to the part where Lloyd declared Keith "would have been within his rights to kill that boy in self-defense," she crumpled the flyer into a small ball in her fist. She wanted to run, to scream.

"If the so-called rainbow people are so weak, why is he so terrified?"

The oddity of the flyer hit her father differently. "It was the 'owners' and 'owe' line that got me, as if he's king and we're his subjects. Look at that! Lloyd's gone and offended my tender sensibilities again. It's not the first time, but Jesus, if Marjorie had stuck around, maybe she could have reined him in. Like, man, why are you hitting yourself? That owning and owing stuff won't sit well with people 'round here."

Molly went back to scanning the empty parking lot across the street. "There must still be people who agree with him. He wouldn't have gotten this far without them. Where are they?"

Dad shook his head. "Lloyd's not the only one underestimating this town. You wanted everyone to stand up for Barry and his family. They weren't brave enough to stand for somebody they don't know, but folks are willing to sit down for them."

"What do you mean?"

"You've always focused on the downsides of livin' here, but that right there — " Chuck pointed at the empty parking lot — "is shunning in action. They're opting out of Lloyd's war. He's not likeable enough to lead. The town's unwilling to follow. They're voting with their dollars. That means a lot."

"So, homophobia and random violence is over? We solved it?"

Chuck spoke patiently. "There are people who still agree with him, of course. No one wants to look bad by standing with that entitled piece of shit, though. When all you have to do is stay home to let a dick know how you feel, easy choices make for easy protests."

Molly was genuinely surprised. Shitting on her hometown had been easy, but not everyone was evil. Her frustration with the school administration, the town, and the police had blinded her to that possibility.

"Your mom talked to her friends," Chuck said. "I'm sure there are a few guys out there who wouldn't mind the Fauns' homophobia so much. Thing is, most of them have wives or girlfriends who don't appreciate how Lloyd treated his wife. I'm told some people down at the pickle ball club liked Marjorie."

"I only spoke to her the once. She wasn't nice."

Chuck saw the doubt in his daughter's face. "But?"

"It's good she got out. I didn't like her, but no one deserves to live with those two. I'm glad she got away from them."

Chuck bobbed his head. "Ugly divorce ahead. That'll cost Lloyd plenty more. Titanic? Meet iceberg."

31

IRRITATION

Chuck was right. Lloyd's declarations did not sit well with Mainers. The laundromat got bombed with one-star reviews. None of that was Molly's doing. Nothing about the quality of Eleanor's services was mentioned. It was the flyer that did in the Fauns. It seemed all of Poeticule Bay was outraged by Lloyd's tone.

Reviews hammered home how rude, mean, and homophobic the management was. The vitriol spilled down to the chain, and franchisees complained Lloyd was hurting their business.

Lloyd made things worse by replying to every jeer with a comment about how well he'd served customers for years without complaint. After he repeated the same assertion several times, Lloyd changed tactics and blamed the anonymous negative reviews on Barry and his family. Later, those comments were deleted. Lloyd then blamed "that bitch who works at the hospital and her mother."

His obnoxious retorts were all deleted. Chuck suggested they disappeared on the advice of legal counsel. "God knows he doesn't have a friend left in the Bay to hold him back from doing his worst."

Molly wished she'd thought of undermining Lloyd's business that way, but at the time, review-bombing on the internet was not as huge as it would become.

Upon her return from her Wednesday knitting club, Molly's mother reported that Lloyd was "drinking again, and more. He always was one to let his mouth run away with him, but alcohol can lubricate the tongue too much."

"Heard the same," Chuck agreed. "These days, seems he's taking a shit into a megaphone for all to see."

Molly couldn't stop smiling. "That's not how megaphones work."

"Nobody wants any part of his holy war," Kay said. "He's blaming the entire town for failing to stand with him."

Chuck shot Molly a sly look before asking his wife, "Whoever pushed his buttons, where do you think this ends? You think they'll leave town and start over somewhere? How much worse do you think it has to get before the Fauns might exile themselves?"

With a grunt, Kay sat down heavily at the kitchen table. "Exile? I think he'd kill himself first."

Chuck paled and looked to Molly to make sure she was listening.

"Lloyd Faun is too full of himself to ever do away with himself, though. Too prideful for suicide, but you know as well as I, murder isn't off the table. Given his history, I could definitely see him killing somebody."

"No. He's the author of his own destruction," Molly said.

With more force than she could usually muster, Kay erupted. "Blah! Blah! Blah! So much lah-di-da and blah-di-blah!"

Chuck gave her a lopsided grin in an effort to defuse her mood. "What's wrong, my love, my dove, my sex goddess?"

Molly cringed. "Dad! Don't say that!"

Kay's mood did not improve. She looked sourly from Chuck to Molly and back to her husband. "Whoever's harassing the Fauns, I hope they know what they're doing. Elsewise, the harassers could be the authors of their own blah-di-blah."

"Are you still having a headache day, Mom?"

Kay shook her head. "Nah, just having an attack of logic. Instead of pokin' the bear, better to take the Fauns way out in a boat in the dead zone, sink it, and make it more dead."

Chuck said nothing. The sudden silence made the Jergins' living room seem cavernous and cold.

In an effort to lighten the mood, Molly suggested, "It seems a lot of people have come around to thinking the same way about the Fauns. If you're on board with drowning them — "

"Drown 'em both! Drown 'em in a bag like we used to do in the old days when we had too many kittens to feed!" Kay said.

"Okay, first, gross and sick. Kittens are adorable and never deserve that. Second, if you feel that strongly, Mom, the people trying to push the Fauns out must be doing something right."

Kay still looked angry.

Chuck suddenly appeared disquieted.

Molly remained confident in their mission.

Meanwhile, Keith was hiding from his father at his girlfriend's house. Lloyd didn't know where his son had got to and at that moment didn't care. He stood in front of his open refrigerator staring at two dozen cooked and untouched hot dogs.

Lloyd was getting drunk again, soaking his brain with Stoli vodka, outrage at his newfound victimhood, and even more rage.

When someone carries the weight of that much anger, they can set it down or find a place to put it. Like Molly, Lloyd wasn't the kind to let anything go. He would find a place for his rage. Unlike Molly, he didn't care who suffered his wrath, nor how much.

32

IMAGINATION

School would soon be over for the summer. A few weeks before the end of classes, Keith showed up with two black eyes, a pronounced limp, and a hangdog expression. Unusually talkative, he told anyone who would listen that he'd been hit by a car as he jogged along the Shore Road. He said it wasn't an accident, but an attempt on his life. Molly didn't believe it, but the story spread through Poeticule Bay Consolidated like a virus.

She overheard him in the cafeteria at lunch. Everyone listened as he held court with the hockey team, giving his account of the attempt on his life. "I was gearing up for a workout after being cooped up at the laundromat all day. It was dark, but they saw me all right. This car came up behind me fast. I had my headphones in, didn't hear it coming. I was already over on the shoulder as far as I could get. I know because my first clue was the crunch of the gravel under the bastard's tires."

Keith pulled up his shirt to show his left side, black and blue. "All bruised up! If I hadn't jumped to the side at the last second, I'd be dead for sure. I hit a lot of rocks rolling down the embankment. Lucky I didn't crack a rib."

The puckheads were rapt. Molly had never witnessed the hockey team so quiet and attentive. To her dismay, she noticed a senior sitting close to Keith. Her hand was on his shoulder. She seemed to be listening more intently, more sympathetically, than anyone. It was Sarah, Mrs. Rainier's daughter.

Molly hadn't made the connection before. This pretty blonde girl lived in the house next to the Fauns. She hadn't noticed her hanging out with Keith before, but the way she looked up at him adoringly, she looked like she was trying to be girlfriend material.

Molly had to admit that Keith was hunky, but she wondered how the school librarian felt about her daughter setting her sights on the school bully.

There are bad boys, Molly thought, *and then there's just plain mean and evil.*

For his part, Keith seemed oblivious to the girl. Molly had to hand it to him, Keith was a good storyteller. He proceeded to rile his teammates. "So, I'm laying there, dazed — probably got a concussion — when I hear someone coming. I thought it was maybe somebody coming to help at first. It wasn't help. It was three guys in ski masks."

His teammates erupted in sympathetic cries of outrage.

Todd Wentzell's voice rose above the rest. "*Three?* Three on one? With you already down? Major personal foul, man! *Major!*"

Keith waved his hands in a calming gesture so the mob would settle enough to hear the rest. "I'm lying there seein' stars and some of them are real and some of them are movin' around, so I know they're my brain rattling around and throwing up lights. Two of the guys pin my arms down while the fattest one sits on my chest, and you know what he says? He says, 'This is for Barry.' Then he punches me in the face. I don't know how many times, but they stopped before I got ugly." At this, he beamed a big smile to show he still had all his pearly white teeth. His grin reminded Molly of a great white shark.

Painting himself as both hero and victim, the puckheads cheered Keith on. He flinched in pain when one dolt, in sympathy and congratulations on his bravery, clapped him on the back.

As usual, Todd Wentzell's voice carried farthest, obliterating all others. "That wasn't half fair, man! Not even half!"

Sarah looked like she was about to swoon. Molly thought she was the prettiest girl in school. No, more than that. There were several pretty girls at school, but Sarah crossed over that ill-defined border from pretty to sexy. Molly worried for her.

"They probably thought I was mostly dead already and didn't have the guts to push me all the way over the edge," Keith told the crowd.

"Who was it?" someone asked.

"They wore masks!" Keith replied flatly.

"Yeah, but who was it, you think?"

"Some pussy pieces of shit from the rainbow crowd, obviously. If they come back for more, I'll be ready for round two. The fight isn't over until I say it's over."

He added that the sheriff was investigating whether the Graves family was back in town. Keith put on such a brave, determined face, Molly almost believed him.

Hitting Keith with the truck on a deserted section of road was actually one of her fantasies. It beat a face-to-face physical confrontation she knew she would lose. She'd even shared the idea with her father during one of their brainstorming sessions. Chuck rejected that notion out of hand at the time, but she had to wonder. Did her father spot Keith along the Shore Road and turn the wheel his way on impulse? A moment of improvisation, maybe?

Molly dismissed that fleeting suspicion. She suspected Chuck had it in him to contemplate such a thing. She had to admit she adored the idea of running the thug off the road herself. However, with his arthritis, she couldn't see Chuck scrambling down an embankment to beat up Keith on a rocky beach. Her father took a while to bend over to pick up anything he dropped on the floor. He struggled to get his socks on in the morning.

Besides the difficult logistics, Chuck Jergins was a fan of having a plan and what he called, "reasonable response escalation." He'd planned the sabotage of the laundromat as if it were a bank heist. Running his truck into Keith? That would be too brutal, too risky. The plan was to banish the Fauns, not murder them.

But were there other likeminded folks in the Bay who weren't so meticulous and reasonable? Had her campaign combined with the Faun family's antics spurred someone else to take up the torch of vengeance? Had Barry or someone in his family returned for vengeance?

It was possible, but Molly leaped to the most obvious and simple conclusion. Keith's tale of three brutes in ski masks was too much like a movie, but Lloyd Faun had a history of violence. Marjorie Faun had served as his target. With his wife successfully banished, Molly was almost sure Lloyd had turned his abusive nature on his son.

If Lloyd had beaten up Keith, why? When Molly spray painted the Fauns' house, her mother had erroneously suggested it was a play for sympathy. Was this a real attempt to win back the residents of Poeticule Bay? Was it a ploy to rekindle the sheriff's interest in investigating the Graves family? Maybe Sheriff Hobbs hadn't been contacted at all.

For all her questions, Molly was really only concerned with one big question: What would it take to banish Lloyd and Keith for good?

For good. The expression haunted Molly.

She was studying *Julius Caesar* in her English class. In the play, Shakespeare has Brutus and Cassius conspire to assassinate the despot for the good of the republic. She had to write an essay on whether the ends justified the means.

She hadn't decided yet. For Rome, the historical results were mixed. For the good of a tiny town in Maine, though, maybe Molly would have to become more evil.

33

DECEPTION

As Molly left the cafeteria, she glanced back to the gathering around Keith. He was still holding court, but the blonde who appeared so infatuated with Keith was no longer staring at him. Sarah was glaring at her, brows knitted.

They'd been invisible to each other. Molly found her sudden interest unsettling. She hurried out, pretending to be distracted as she fussed with the textbook under her arm.

Sarah lived next to the Fauns. The night she'd crept from the woods to paint graffiti on the Faun house, Molly had thought she'd seen a curtain on the second floor flutter. Or was that just a product of paranoia, her imagination working overtime? An anxious mind could reconfigure a trauma event and become unreliable.

If it happened, was that Sarah? Could Molly have been recognized somehow? Unlikely, but the worry gnawed at her.

The mystery of Keith's assailants was solved later that afternoon, at least, as far as Molly was concerned. As she emerged from History class, she passed Keith in the press of students changing classes in the narrow corridor.

Molly did not meet his eyes. Instead, she looked down. She spotted battered knuckles on Keith's left hand. He had thrown some punches recently. The bully had not mentioned that in his account of the attack by the side of the road. If he had fought back, surely he would have included that detail. His ego could not have held him back from bragging.

You were in a fight, Molly thought, *and you lost.*

She was sure now. The father had taken out his frustrations on his son. It was easy to envision. All the Faun family's troubles had begun with Keith assaulting Barry. If not for Keith's cruel crime going unpunished, Molly would not have embarked on her crusade. Only Lloyd had the power to decide to move the family elsewhere. Molly had focused her energies on Lloyd, his home, and his business. With his wife gone and unable to confront his tormentors, Lloyd had turned on his son. Keith was finally receiving the blame he deserved.

Molly guessed Lloyd had coached Keith in what to say to any inquiry about his injuries. That line about the "rainbow crowd" sounded more like an old man like Lloyd, not a high schooler. That was definitely Lloyd Faun's language.

Striding to chemistry class, Molly cursed softly under her breath. Instead of researching nefarious uses for industrial adhesives, she should have been focusing on homework. She was supposed to have memorized the periodic table by now. An essay about *The Great Gatsby* was due soon, too.

As if we need an old novel to give us a metaphor about the death of the American dream, Molly thought.

Surrounded by derelict fishing boats, the dead zone, poverty, and corrupt authorities, she didn't need further education in such metaphors. She understood her country's mythos firsthand. All she had to do was look around.

Distracted, Molly sat in chemistry class. Her teacher, Alden Finneman, demonstrated the interaction of acetone and polystyrene. Pushing a styrofoam cup into a beaker with a little acetone, the cup dissolved into a tiny puddle of white goop in seconds.

Red-faced and jubilant, Mr. Finneman stirred the remains of the cup with a glass rod. "See? The acetone dissolved the polymer strands!"

After the demonstration was complete, the class assignment was to explain the interactions in terms of molecular structure. Molly stared at the blank sheet on her desk, pen poised. She wasn't contemplating the experiment. Instead, she pictured Lloyd and Keith swallowing acetone. Exposure could cause headaches, nausea, and dizziness, but drinking it could induce coma. It could kill.

She pictured herself in a ski mask standing over Lloyd and Keith, holding power over them the way Keith did to Barry. They were bad people who cast themselves as victims. Maybe it was time they got a taste of the real thing.

Mr. Finneman rapped his knuckles on the Lucite surface of her desk. "Molly? What do you call molecules with uneven distribution of electrons?"

She looked up blankly. The teacher was still wearing his protective glasses. She stared through him as if he were a window.

Finneman chuckled. "Where'd you go to?"

She didn't tell him she'd been wondering if her old baseball equipment was still in the trunk of the jalopy. Molly pictured pitching her softball straight into Lloyd's face as hard as she could. She saw herself standing over Keith, her bat in one hand, a glass of acetone in the other. In her mind's eye, the glass held a tiny paper umbrella, as if it were a cocktail.

Molly had readied a speech about how the Fauns made other people feel. "Unsafe," she would tell the Lloyd and Keith. "This is what unsafe feels like. This is what you've done to everyone. How's it feel to be on the receiving end?"

Acetone can be a dangerous accelerant, too, she thought.

"Earth to Molly! Do you read me?"

"Sorry, Mr. Finneman. I was in my happy place."

Molly should have stopped there, but things in motion tend to stay in motion. Her fantasies were becoming more elaborate, more mean.

Meanwhile, Lloyd Faun was getting worse.

34

ACCELERATION

Molly continued to fantasize about using that baseball bat over the next few days. She imagined herself an avenging angel finally convincing the Fauns to change their ways, curing them with the pure power of her rage and their fear. The trouble was, she didn't know how to get away with it.

Superhero movies provided satisfying but dangerous inspiration. She had dared to disguise herself once with a hood, a hat, and bulky winter coats. However, that was in the dark on empty streets. She felt lucky she had not run into anyone face to face. Traipsing around Poeticule Bay in a cape and cowl wasn't a realistic solution.

Lloyd didn't know who she was, but he *was* on the hunt. Could Molly have stopped? Was their collision inevitable? Of course it was, but she didn't see that then.

One Thursday evening, Lloyd strode up to Molly's father in the Pick-Right's parking lot. Unsteady on his feet, his eyes watering, Lloyd looked like he hadn't slept in a week. The smell of liquor wasn't just on his breath. Saturated, the acrid odor oozed from his pores. Without a word, he handed Chuck a neon yellow flyer that read:

. . .

$1000 REWARD for information leading to the capture and conviction of the terrorists trying to destroy my family and my business. Contact Lloyd Faun at Eleanor's Laundry and Dry Cleaning or call the Poeticule County Sheriff's Office.

AT THE BOTTOM of the page beneath a phone number, Lloyd had scribbled an afterthought:

(Also: Get 10% off your next dry cleaning when you present this flyer at Eleanor's, Poeticule Bay location only!)

"The offer at the bottom is a nice touch," Chuck said. "That might help you more than trawling for snitches."

"You've heard what's going on?"

"Everybody has, sure. There's no other local news."

Lloyd stepped close, his eyes boring into Chuck. "Something's got to be done! I've talked to Gordon so many times about this, I should bring a sleeping bag and camp out at his office."

"Sheriff Hobbs still has no leads?"

Lloyd made a sound of disgust as he shook his head. "Couldn't pour piss out of a boot if the instructions were on the heel."

Chuck gave him an understanding nod but couldn't resist poking the bear. "I hear tell people are talking to Gordon about you, Lloyd."

"How do you figure?"

"This whole thing has gotten out of hand, don't you think? The town's talking about you losing your shit at your garage sale. Quite the spectacle. By all accounts, you should have been arrested. Young Keith should have been arrested, too. Might have been good for him, simmer him down a bit."

"First off, it wasn't *my* garage sale — "

"I know, Lloyd. It was a prank and you overreacted. People are concerned."

"You don't know what I've been dealing with. Marjorie left."

"Sorry about that."

"People are looking at my kid as if he's a monster."

Chuck didn't blink. "Like father, like son?"

Lloyd flushed pink with rage. "What happened with that boy, I've told everyone, *we've* told everyone — "

"I know, I know! Boys will be boys. Thing is, Lloyd, Keith looks like a man, and he beat that Graves boy hard. It's only a fight if you give some and you take some. That was a beating, and not between a couple of kids who are going to make up and forget it. I can relate to that, or have you forgotten our fight in high school? I haven't."

"A spat, ancient history, get over it," Lloyd replied.

"As if that wasn't enough," Chuck continued, "you drove the Graves family out of town. I do understand what you're going through, Lloyd, and I gotta say, the pushback you're getting is not unfair. The Graves kid didn't deserve any of that."

"That wasn't — "

"Listen to me. We go way back. We've seen this kind of bullshit before, you and me. You were born mean. and man! The cheese is sliding off your cracker. Grow up, or at least grow a little. Didn't you hear? It's a new century. Been so, a while."

Lloyd's gaze was a reptilian stare. "New century, huh? You're one to talk, Jergins. You're still stuck on high school. I beat you like a bongo drum. You talk about growing up, but you're still not over that?"

Chuck shrugged. "I remember that being more of a fight. Do you even remember how it started? You've been in so many fights over the years, it's apparent you don't need much of a reason."

Lloyd said nothing.

"And remember my father's chip and clam shack? Used to be next to your shop? We were the Bay's only alternative to dining at the Drift. We sold a lot of soft ice cream in the summer. We served up a lot of clams and chips in cones of rolled-up newsprint, too, remember?"

"Yeah, I recall."

"Your dad wanted our land. My father didn't want to sell. Then the rumors started that we were serving up E. coli with clams and making people sick. It wasn't true, but it hurt enough. Dad had to sell."

"Why're you bringing all this up, Chuck? I remember that was your nickname in school. Upchuck!"

"On behalf of Big Jim, for the land, you started the rumor mill turning."

"That's a lie!"

"I heard it was you from multiple people, Lloyd. It was you."

"Stop rechewing old meat — "

"I remember it like it was yesterday," Chuck said. "That's why I can tell you, physically, the Graves boy will recover, but the scars nobody can see are forever. Nobody is owed redemption who does not seek forgiveness."

"You always had a mouth on ya."

"And you're the only creep in town who ever called me Upchuck. To friends, I'm just Chuck."

Lloyd replied, "We were never friends, and you know why."

35

APPROPRIATION

Chuck held the yellow flyer under Lloyd's nose. "You really expect *my* help? Ya know, I'd lay a wager you haven't really forgotten our fight. After school in the dugout at the old baseball diamond? Your buddies cheering you on, pinning my arms at the end so you could get a few more cheap licks in? I gave you a black eye and you gave me two, but you started with a sucker punch."

Lloyd smirked. "Sucker punches for suckers. After what you did, you shoulda seen it coming."

"Still proud?"

Lloyd shook his head. "Haven't given you or her any thought since." But his smile betrayed him.

"You were always a dick. A lot of people think so. You've never apologized to anyone for anything in your life. You make it hard to feel sorry for you. That's why *this*" — he held out the yellow flyer — "won't work."

Lloyd refused to take the flyer back.

"All that money, but you're still a mutant porcupine, lotsa quills, all asshole. You're at the top of the tree, but nobody really likes you. After your hysterics and waving guns around, you think you have a friend anywhere? Marjorie runnin' away, that an equation you really can't solve? It's not a mystery to anybody else. You and your son, lots of tussle but no hustle, all wrestle and no tassel."

"What do you mean by that?"

"Always looking for a fight, never up to facing the truth. And as for no tassel, I'm hearing rumors. Keith won't get to attend his graduation ceremony. With all he's done, people are afraid of him. For all he's done, for all you've done, seems to me like he's still gettin' off easy."

Lloyd's smug smile disappeared. "That so? Well then, screw you and this whole town! I'll tell you what!"

"You're drunk, man. Your eyes look like two piss holes in a snowbank. Go away."

"You think I'm a prick now? Wait and see what happens if this campaign against me keeps up! Criminals are coming after me. If they aren't caught, maybe I'll take a deer rifle up to the lighthouse! From up there, I'll be able to scope the whole town. Maybe that way someone will take my problems seriously."

Lloyd's brow was a sheen of sweat. As his madness grew, the whites of his eyes were visible all around the pupils. "Maybe with a night scope I'll spot whoever these people are, creeping around at night. What do you think of that? How do you like me now?"

It was only then that Lloyd realized he had an audience greater than one. Several townspeople witnessed his outburst.

Earl MacAdam sat in his scooter by the Pick-Right's entrance with his hand cupped to his good ear. Sully Peddit sat in his restored Delta 88 with the window rolled down, obviously enjoying the show. Janice Bull and her brother Pete lingered by their rusty old Ford pickup. Pretending to fuss over the groceries in the bed of their truck, the siblings were obviously taking it slow to better eavesdrop.

Lloyd lowered his voice. "It's true your dad went out of business and my family got that land for a song."

"Worse," Chuck replied, "you never did anything with it. It's just a parking lot, and it's pretty empty these days, huh?"

Lloyd's smile returned. "That must chap your ass and frost your nuts, huh? After all that, we got the land and let it sit. If your poor daddy — and I mean dirt poor — had kept that shop, would you have had to go off and join the army?"

Molly's father turned to stone. He said nothing.

Lloyd looked Chuck up and down. "If you'd stayed home, would you be messed up like you are now?"

"It mostly worked out. I saw some of the world and served my country. Besides, if I had inherited the shop, we would have been neighbors. No good could come of that. I hope you're happy paying those municipal taxes on an empty lot. The way this town is headed, you'll never unload it for near the price Big Jim paid for it."

"You're a son of a bitch, Upchuck."

Chuck smiled. "If you're trying to suck up to me now, you're a little late, decades late. You've poisoned your own well. You know what you do with a poisoned well, don't ya? You board it up and you move away."

"But it was your father who got exiled out to the county, wadn't it? Lonely out there, you think, dying alone on his farm? And not for nothing, you took from me first, remember?"

"What I took from you wasn't yours to give. She — "

Lloyd talked over him, "*Then* I beat you up! *Then* my family took from yours!"

"Go somewhere else, Lloyd. Cut your losses and start fresh where people don't know what a pile of shit you are."

"Why're you talking to me like this? Why isn't everybody after the terrorists comin' for us? All this 'banished' shit — "

"Let me cut you off at the pass there, Chief. I'll explain it slow so even you get the transmission. Folks around here see you for who you are. They're sick of you. *We're* sick to death of you, you and your shitty son."

Lloyd raised his voice again, not caring who heard. "Folks around here better learn somethin'! Hear me now! Comin' after me and mine is a big mistake! Useless as tits on a bull! Comin' after me, you may as well fart against thunder!"

He was still ranting as Chuck limped back to his truck. Before he got home, word was already spreading about the confrontation. Lloyd had threatened to shoot up the town from the lighthouse's gallery. Soon everyone would know.

When Chuck recounted the incident to Kay, Molly learned another Jergins family secret. She hadn't known why her grandfather closed his chip shop and left town to take up farming way out in the county. That was yet another reason why her father was so sympathetic to her campaign against the Fauns.

Cruelty is never the end of things. Once that ship leaves port, there is no safe harbor.

36

DEVASTATION

Before Molly could take action on an ill-conceived plan, Barry Graves did something stupid in her stead. He returned to Poeticule Bay. To Molly's surprise, he called her up, asking to meet at the Drift Inn.

"What about?"

"Not on the phone," Barry replied. "This has gotta be one of those look-me-in-the-eye conversations."

Molly jumped in the jalopy and headed over to the seaside restaurant right away. She found him sitting alone at the back corner table nursing a plate piled high with French fries. His bandages were gone, and his injuries were healed, but he looked leaner than she remembered. No, not merely lean. Gaunt.

Barry pushed out the chair opposite him with his foot and gave Molly the nod to sit. "I saw your video." His face was unreadable.

"*My* video?"

"Other people's video, at school, with Keith. You were pretty articulate talking him down like that."

"Oh, right. Thanks."

"It wasn't exactly a compliment."

His flat tone mystified her.

"I notice you still have all your teeth. No bandages, huh?"

None that you can see, she thought. Her shoulder had healed from the salt load and the bruise had faded. However, her sleeping habits were off. Her neck ached because she still only slept on her left side, never on her back or right side.

"Am I missing something?" Molly asked.

Barry glowered at her. "You spoke up for me and lived to tell the tale. You saw what happened to me. Why'd you risk that?"

"We all should have said something — "

"People didn't. What makes you so special?"

She wasn't sure what to say. "You mad at me, Barry?"

"The worst day of my life was when Keith Faun beat me up. Watching you defy my bully and defend me like that? Maybe the second-worst."

Shocked, she said nothing. Molly did not — could not — believe him. It wasn't up to her to decide how Barry felt, but she didn't understand his anger.

The boy's frown deepened. "You never talked to me before all this, not once."

Molly could not find words to fill the tense silence between them.

"Do you have a boyfriend, Molly?"

She shook her head. "I held a boy's hand in elementary school once. Then he pulled my hair and called me a poo-poo head. Romantically, it's been downhill from there, but that's okay. I'm not interested in drama."

"Not that kind of drama, anyway." Barry picked at his fries, not looking up. "Can I ask you a personal question? Tell me if you want. This is a friendly question, okay? Are you queer?"

A chuckle burst from her throat before she could rein it in. That was not the best response, but she was taken by surprise. "I'm not gay. Just because I don't have a boyfriend — "

"Then why'd you defend me? What's your investment? Why are you out there fighting my battles? In the video, you made like you were trying to help Keith, but I'm too smart to believe that. I got your message, even if Keith didn't really."

On firmer ground now, Molly found her voice. "It's simple. I don't like bullies. You saw the video. Keith was going after another kid. Even after all he put you through, he hadn't learned a thing."

"Learning?" Barry smirked. "I think he might be allergic to that. All humans are primates, but Keith is simian. It's a permanent condition."

"Then he should be in a cage. Keith still acts like an ape who has escaped the zoo. If someone doesn't stop him, his abuse will go on forever. I don't see the school ever doing anything about him. Look, I'm sorry people can be so shitty. The principal and vice-principal are especially useless — "

"Keith Faun is a bad seed, him and his gang," Barry said. "They act like they own the school. They never shut up, and they never manage to say anything funny or good. You'd think people who talk that much would say something useful once in a while, at least by accident."

"Some people are just no good, all the way down to the toes."

"I don't want to think that way," Barry said. "I don't believe in real evil, but stupid is pretty strong."

"Then you're a better person than me," Molly admitted.

"I wish I'd known you when I lived here."

"The school's small, but did you ever talk to people in other classes, other grades?"

He gave a small nod. She guessed that meant he conceded her point. Friends were made by proximity, and they'd never shared a classroom.

The boy's shoulders fell. "I'm not mad at you, not really."

"I don't think you should be — "

"Please listen!" Barry said sharply. "It feels like no one listens to me."

Silenced, Molly gestured for him to continue.

Perhaps as a peace offering or an easy way to shut her up, Barry pushed his plate of fries halfway across the table. He'd poured vinegar over them. Molly didn't care for that but accepted the conciliatory gesture. She took a few fries and dipped them in ketchup from a little paper cup.

"When I saw the video of you talking to Keith the way you did, I was jealous. When he attacked me, he wasn't worried about any consequences. I wish he worried more. How is it that some people don't seem to worry about anything? I worry about everything, especially since that day. Anyway, what happened to me ... it was like I was nothing. I'm not even a person to that guy. That's why I'm back."

Molly straightened. "You and your family are back to the Bay?"

Barry rolled his eyes. "Here? God, no! We're living in Bar Harbor, for now. My parents both got jobs, but they're looking for something better. My parents think I'm staying with my cousin Kim up in Millinocket. Kim drove me as far as Calais. I hitched the rest of the way here."

"Have you got a plan to deal with him?" Molly had several suggestions prepared using common adhesives and solvents. To her, every revenge fantasy, each act of violent retribution, was as divine as a rich chocolate cake. However, Barry *was* better than her.

He stirred a fry in ketchup but did not eat. "I'm back for a couple of reasons. First, someone is going after the Fauns. Every time they do, a cop comes out to harass me and my parents about it."

Molly felt like she'd swallowed a stone.

"My dad says this one cop from the State Police? He should have worked for the railroad because he's only got one train of thought. We keep telling him we don't know who's bothering the Fauns."

Since the Graves had moved away, Molly had assumed she would cause no collateral damage.

"I'm so sorry," Molly said.

"Not your fault."

But it was.

I've got to finish this thing with the Fauns, and quickly, Molly thought. *I've gotta rip off the Band-Aid. Or burn their lives to the ground.*

Barry had other ideas.

37

DISSERTATION

"**M**y mom told me not to talk to the police," Barry said. "The one time I did, I had a burst of honesty and said Keith deserves whatever he gets. That was enough for them to get tunnel vision. They haven't thought anyone else is responsible ever since."

"Moving away and staying away gives you an alibi though, right?"

"Yeah, though sometimes we wonder if we're being watched."

"So why come back? Being here while you're still under suspicion —"

Barry cut her off with a wave of his hand. "You stole my thunder, Molly. You got to make the speech I didn't. How'd you do that without getting beat up? Has Keith come for you since?"

Besides getting shot with rock salt by Lloyd, a few scary moments, and getting bitched out by Marjorie Faun on the forest path, Molly had gotten away clean.

"The Fauns are sociopaths," she said. "If they didn't run half this town with their money, maybe things would have been different for you. I'm sorry for what Keith did."

"No offense, but a sorry from you doesn't help me."

"What would? If Keith's family were really worth anything, they would have got him to apologize and make restitution. They're terrible people — "

Barry allowed a wry smile. "Apologize? Too much to hope for and too little benefit."

Molly wanted to confess that it was she who'd launched the campaign of terror on the Fauns. Instead, she sent out a feeler. "So, what are your thoughts? Should we break his kneecaps?"

He shook his head. "I really don't think going to jail would make me feel better, do you?"

Unless we get away with it, Molly thought.

Barry pushed back in his seat and tilted his head toward the brown water stains on the restaurant's ceiling tiles. "I need to know how you got away with confronting him. He beat the shit out of me. I mean that literally, Molly. I shit myself. But for you? No bruises. What's your secret?"

Secrets? So many, Barry, so many.

Molly cleared her throat. "When I saw Keith picking on Dylan Caffrey in the hallway, I just plunged in. After the fact, I came up with rationalizations. "

"Which were?"

"I didn't think Keith would risk beating up a girl. I have no doubt he has that capacity, but he wouldn't try it at school. I don't think many people ever thought the Faun family were very nice, but it's more than that, obviously. They're not stable. They have gotten worse since you left."

"Since they've had to face some consequences and minor inconveniences, you mean?"

"I wouldn't put it past Keith to take a swing at me now, but not in front of everybody."

"I've been planning a speech of my own," Barry said. "I lie awake nights rehearsing it in my head."

"Really?" Maybe they weren't so unalike, she thought. "For closure?'

Barry scoffed. "No such thing as closure. When someone treats you bad, especially as bad as the Fauns and this whole town treated me ..." He swallowed hard and went quiet for a moment, choosing his words carefully. "It's still happening." His eyes were wet.

"You're still getting bullied?"

"No, I mean everything Keith did is still fresh. My scalp heats up with the humiliation of it. I couldn't do anything. I didn't fight back, couldn't fight back. I hate that asshole, but I hate myself a little, too. I didn't even try. I just surrendered. Didn't do or even say anything. I just took it. The purple, black, and blue bruises eventually yellowed and faded, but that gave me a lot of time to imagine all the things I could have done or said."

"Keith's a lot bigger than you. You're not to blame. Being a victim doesn't make you wrong or bad in any way."

"That's what my parents say. They're just glad it wasn't worse. Running away from this wasn't easy. I overheard them arguing about whether to sell the house and get away from here a couple of times before we left. They don't know I heard how hard this was for them. To me, they kept up a united front. They love me and all that matters is keeping me safe. I think they may actually be happier in Bar Harbor, so there's that."

"But?"

"But I can't be happy. It's hard to picture what that would look like now. I was at a new school for a while, but I dropped out early. Next September, I'll try again. In the meantime, I watch a lot of TV. I rehearse what I should have said during and after the beating. I can't do much, but I've got a lot to say."

Barry wiped tears away with a crumpled napkin. Giving him a moment, Molly looked away to stare at the gunmetal ocean. After a long silence, she asked, "Are you making new friends in Bar Harbor?"

"How? I'm not at school. Until this trip, I've barely gone outside. I've got no friends, unless you count my therapist. My parents set me up with her."

A therapist the Fauns should be paying for, Molly thought.

"My therapist says lots of kids who are bullied end up taking a break and switching schools. I didn't know that was a thing. I bet there aren't many who had to change towns, too, but that's me."

He looked haunted. She supposed he was. Ghosts haunt, but so do memories. "What do your parents say about all this now?"

"My mom convinced my dad it would be good for me to stay home from school for a while."

There was something more behind Barry's eyes that bothered her. "Is therapy helping?"

"I'm not quite as nervous as I was. I had this thing about checking all the locks on the doors for a while. I couldn't get a wink of sleep without checking the doors again and again. I am better than I was, but still pretty twitchy. If the sheets are too tight on my bed, I panic. It feels like being held down."

"You're back here. That tells me you must be doing better."

"Think so? I don't. I'm still dwelling and wallowing too much. Got some medication, but the doctor says anti-depressants take time to kick in. I guess figuring out the right meds and the correct dosage is a process. In the meantime, I don't have much of an appetite."

Molly took a breath, held it, and let it out slowly. "Tell me exactly what you want to do, Barry. Why'd you call me?"

Except for the boy and girl, the restaurant stood empty of diners. They could hear the Drift Inn's one server in the back talking to the cook. Despite that, Barry scanned the place warily to make sure no one could hear him. Finally, he said, "I keep thinking how I could have poked that asshole's eyes out. I keep having thoughts like that. I don't want to be that way, but you know ..." He gestured to himself and smiled. "Human."

38

SUPPLEMENTATION

"Whoever's going after the Fauns now," Barry continued, "part of me likes that someone's creating problems for them, but this is *my* fight, you know?"

Confused, she asked, "You want to join the campaign to get them banished?"

He gave a derisive laugh. "Shit, no! I just want to have my say and make Keith listen, make him hear me so he understands what he did. I'm exhausted from the way people look at me. Since Keith beat on me I feel like a victim. That's all I feel. I lost something besides blood that day. He stole my pride."

Molly wondered if Barry suspected it was she who waged a secret war on the Fauns. "I still don't understand why you called me."

"Told you, *you* stole *my* thunder. I'm here to steal it back. I need a witness and someone to record my speech to Keith. I don't think he'll do anything if he's being recorded. That's what saved you, right? A camera keeps the bear in his cage. I need you behind the camera. I know you're on the track team, so if you record it and he decides to chase you, I'm sure you can outrun him."

"What's the goal?"

"I'd love an apology, but I'd settle for having my say. My therapist is fine, but it's not like I'm getting a message through to Poeticule Bay's biggest hockey goon, is it? Telling him off could be the best therapy I can get for free."

Her eyebrows shot up. "And if he — "

"If he beats me up again, be sure to record it. At least this time we'll have something to show in a court of law."

"It could work," Molly said, "but it would be dangerous."

"You don't think I know that?"

"Better than anyone, I'm sure."

"My therapist has me journaling, but writing notes to myself seems weak. I'm gay, but I'm not some British girly from the 1800s on her first trip to Paris keeping a diary. Confronting Keith and having my say, how he made me feel like nothing ...." Barry trailed off. His eyes were wet again. "Will you help me?"

Not knowing what to say, Molly looked out to the empty ocean again. The wind was up, and more whitecaps flecked the roiling sea. The sky had turned much the same gray as the ocean. It was difficult to discern the line of the blurred horizon. She lived in a small town that was one big gray area, too, trapped between right and wrong. The boy was still waiting for her answer.

"I assume you want to post your speech to Keith on social media?" she asked.

"Feels right, yeah. Mom says what goes around comes around. Dad tells me karma will get the bullies eventually because they're on the wrong side of history. Screw history. I'm tired of leaving justice to history. Life is short and so am I! My parents say nobody's all bad or all good. People are just people, and some of them have bad brains that allow them to do awful things."

People like Lloyd and Keith ... and maybe like me and Dad, too, Molly thought.

"You know what's exhausting? Waiting for bad people to do the right thing," Barry said. "We could wait forever, or we could do something! Everybody's heard of gay pride. How about some proper gay wrath?

In sudden anger, Barry tapped the table hard with his fingertips.

Punctuating each syllable, he said, "I need my justice *now*. I don't need an ally, Molly. Allies aren't all bad, but too often they're just about words and empty sympathy. I need to *do* something, and for that, I need an accomplice."

Molly took a deep breath. "It'll be dark soon, but there's one big floodlight behind the restaurant. If you're determined to do this, we've got to be smart about it. We've got to come up with a strategy, and I've got to make a phone call."

"For what?"

"Backup in a pickup."

39

ASCENSION

Molly called her father from the Drift Inn. Her plan sounded simple and foolproof. Despite the boy's feelings of urgency, she wasn't going to allow Barry to confront his attacker without help and an escape route.

Chuck was not onboard. "What happened to sneak attacks? Lloyd's on edge, and we agreed on a steady campaign — "

"If we don't help Barry, he'll try to talk to Keith on his own."

"If he does that," Chuck warned, "chances are good he's one dead kid."

"Exactly! How soon can you get here?"

"I'm up in Oubliette repairing a shed. I can be there in a little over an hour and a half."

"When you get here, back the truck behind the rear of the north wall of the Driftin'. There's a floodlight pointed at the rear parking lot."

"The light at the ass end of the building facing the water?"

"Yes, that way I can hide in the truck bed. That's where we'll wait for Keith to arrive. Barry will be waiting for him in the light. He'll be close enough to hear, but all of Keith's focus will be on Barry. The camera focus."

Chuck was unconvinced. "And if you're spotted? What then?"

"Barry runs to the truck, you gun the engine, we go."

"Keith will recognize the truck, and you, for that matter. What about getting the sheriff involved?"

"Sheriff Hobbs isn't going to like that Barry's back in town. Whenever we've done our thing, a state trooper shows up at the Graves' door. Barry has always had an alibi and family to back him up, but they keep coming back."

"Hobbs has made it known the family is in the clear."

"But the Staties keep coming back."

"Shows they've got nothing on us," Chuck said, "but I don't like that our work has come back on the boy's family."

"I thought about that, too. We owe him, Dad. And this will be just like what happened at school. As long as he's being recorded, we don't think Keith will do anything. We're hoping he's had enough."

"Why would you think that?"

"Because I'm sure Keith's dad beat him up." Molly wasn't 100 percent positive, but to save Barry, she had to convince her father.

"So, if Keith gets rough and rowdy, what? You pop out and say, 'Ooga-booga! You're on video!'"

"Basically, but without the ooga-booga. Barry's just coming to talk, Dad. It should go down the same way it went with me and Keith at school. I've gone over it with Barry, what he plans to say, I mean."

"Which is?"

"He's going to tell him right away that he has nothing to do with what we've been doing — "

"You told the kid it's us going after the Fauns?"

"No, no! Barry doesn't know it's us. I just coached him to get that out of the way immediately to keep the meet-up from going off the rails."

After a moment of silent deliberation, her father finally replied, "The kid really wants to have his say, huh?"

"He reminds me of you," she said.

"How's that?"

"Like you wish you had the last word with Lloyd in high school."

Another long silence on the line. For a moment, Molly wondered if she'd pushed her father too far. She'd meant to persuade, but after the words were out of her mouth, Molly suspected she'd slid into emotional manipulation. If so, it worked.

"I'm on my way as quick as I can."

"The laundromat closes at eight."

"And from our surveillance, we know the young Faun will be working this evening. You'll call him?"

"Barry will."

"Make sure the kid tells him to come alone. Actually, what if he doesn't? Suppose the whole hockey team shows up, too?"

Molly had not considered that. "Okay, so we won't have Barry out in the open waiting — "

"Like a sitting duck."

"No, I'll get him to wait by the truck. If Keith calls his buddies, we'll just leave."

"And if they follow?"

"Then we head straight to the sheriff's office."

"Jesus, I'm going to have to take an extra blood pressure pill and another aspirin for the pain in my ass! We'd have a lot of explaining to do, don't you think?"

"People can have their suspicions. Barry may even suspect me, but he hasn't said so. Look, I know this is risky, but all we have to do is stick to the story. Barry saw me confront Keith at school. Barry's family has been harassed by the police. He wanted to talk to Keith and asked for my help. We showed up for Barry's protection, hell, even for Keith's protection. That's how I sold my truth-telling to Keith before."

"Just like at school. You really think it could go down all peaceful?"

Molly answered with a certainty she didn't really feel. "I've spoken to Keith twice, once at school and the time with him and his mother in the woods. I lived to tell the tale. His father is far gone, but Keith must know he'll lose his freedom if he goes after Barry again."

"The sheriff has made no bones about being sick of Keith's nastiness," Chuck conceded. "He seems on the brink of charging Lloyd, too, which wouldn't make me cry. But what about us? Coming to light like this — "

"Like I said, suspicions are fine. We can cool the mischief for a while, but nobody can prove anything. If Sheriff Hobbs really had any clue, he'd have been on our doorstep by now asking questions. We've got plausible deniability."

Her father laughed. "Isn't that what all the bad guys say in movies? Plausible deniability?"

"Translates to real life. That's where the term comes from in the first place."

"And we *will* cool it after this? Promise? Lloyd's already talking about shooting up the town. He should be in jail already, but I'm guessin' Hobbs thinks he's talked him down. Lloyd would use the 'I was just a shit-talking drunk' defense."

"We'll be careful," Molly assured him, "and we'll set up the meeting for after the restaurant's closed. Nobody will be around after eleven. It'll just be Barry talking, me taming the monster, and you as our wheelman."

"If we don't do this, you really think the kid will try it on his lonesome?"

"Barry's determined — mad and determined."

"Can't decide," Chuck said. "Is this stupid or brave?"

"Not sure there's a difference," Molly admitted, "but it feels like the right thing to do."

"Yeah," Chuck said. "The kid's too young to have a death wish or should be. If he's going to do it, anyway, better we're there if things go sideways."

"He needs backup and damage control," she said, "and I don't know about you, but I feel partially responsible. People will say what they will, but our motives were always pure."

"Set it up for midnight," Chuck said, "and for God's sake, stay out of sight until I get there."

Every decision takes us down a different path. On that night, Barry, Molly, and Chuck committed to a road from which there was no return. If they could have seen the future, they'd have understood their choice led to a dead end.

40

DESCENSION

At 11:30 pm, Chuck backed his truck beside the Drift Inn on the blind side of the restaurant. He stepped out of the pickup's cab. He came up behind Molly and Barry crouched at the rear corner of the restaurant.

The parking lot was illuminated while the vigilantes and their charge remained in shadow. The only sound was the crash of the cold waves. It was as if the night, ripe with dark potential, was waiting with them.

Barry stood to shake Chuck's hand and thank him, but the big man waved him off. "Stay low and quiet, kid. Molly? It's not too late to call this off and have a rethink."

But it was too late. Keith arrived early. The Fauns' Lincoln Continental turned off the Shore Road and bumped across the potholed lot. Keith sat in the driver's seat. As agreed, he parked by the pool of white light cast by the restaurant's rear floodlight.

Barry peered around the corner to view his tormentor. He whispered to himself, practicing the speech he'd rehearsed so many times in his head. "Keith, I have nothing to do with the people who are coming after you and your family, but make no mistake, you deserve it...."

Chuck bent to whisper in Molly's ear, "Whatever happens, stay safe, and remember I love you."

"It'll be fine, Dad."

"If not, I have a backup plan."

"Which is?"

"It's going to look risky, but we're all in now. Trust me. And you —
"

"Yessir?" Barry said.

"Have your say. If this is what gets you past what you need to get past, I get it."

"We've got it," Molly said. "Man the getaway car, please."

Chuck retreated to his truck to wait.

Keith remained in the Lincoln, looking around. He had yet to spot them. "Hold back a minute," Molly warned.

"I've already waited too long," Barry replied. "He'll think I chickened out. I have to show him I'm not afraid. I am, but I can't show him that."

The boy stood and marched out of the shadows. Keith climbed out of the Lincoln. Barry looked ever smaller and more frail as he approached his tormentor.

With his hands held up to show them empty, Barry announced, "I have nothing to do with the people going after you and your family!"

A cold gust rushed in off the ocean and took his words away on the wind. Keith said something in reply Molly could not hear.

Deaf to the exchange, she crept closer, clinging to the back wall. She suddenly wished she had her mother's old camcorder rather than relying on her phone's camera microphone.

"Hey!" Barry called louder. "I just came to talk!"

Keith didn't answer. Instead, the Lincoln's rear door popped open, and Lloyd Faun emerged carrying a stick. As he strode forward, Molly realized he held an axe handle.

"Sorry, man. Had to tell my dad. If I hadn't, I'd be the one getting the beating." Keith didn't sound sorry. He was grinning from ear to ear.

Molly stepped forward and screamed, "Barry! Run!"

The boy stubbornly stood his ground. "You did this! You did this to me. And you did it to yourselves!"

"Stay where you are!" Molly yelled. She held her phone high. "You're all on camera and I'm recording! Barry, forget it! Let's go!"

But the boy was too angry to see reason. "When are you gonna —"

Lloyd swung at the boy and barely missed. Only then did Barry seem to understand it was past time for his plan to be abandoned. He stumbled backward, turned, and ran.

"Get 'em, boy!" Lloyd commanded.

Keith did as ordered. He chased Barry and caught him easily. Keith was so strong that as he held Barry by the back of his jean jacket the boy's feet barely touched the ground.

Keith crowed, "Light as a fairy, Dad!"

Chuck had already started the pickup's engine and gunned it. Reversing, he pulled up beside Molly and into the light.

Chuck then hauled himself out of the driver's seat. "Stop! You're in deep enough already, son! Way over your head! Put down the shovel and stop diggin', for God's sake!"

Astonished, it was as if Keith's brain switched gears. He froze, but he still clutched Barry's jacket and didn't let go.

"Well, would you look at that?" Lloyd yelled. "The pansy boy brought a little army of hothouse flowers!"

"And you brought an axe handle to what was supposed to be a civilized meeting," Molly replied evenly. "You must be terrified of words."

Holding her phone high, Molly stepped closer and reached for Barry with her free hand. "C'mon, Barry. Let's go. They didn't come to listen."

"You're right about that," Lloyd said. To his son, he shouted, "Boy! Now!"

In a flash, Keith swatted the phone out of Molly's grasp. Time slowed for a moment. Everyone's gaze tracked the phone's arc through the air. The device spun toward the cliff, out of the light, into darkness.

Both Keith and Lloyd began to laugh, but Keith's laugh was cut short as Molly kicked him squarely in the groin. The bully snorted and gasped. Bent over in pain, he still managed to hold on to Barry's jacket.

Following up on her attack, Barry drove his heel into Keith's shin. The bully yelped and faltered. Panting and wriggling, Barry fought his way out of the jean jacket and leapt to Molly's side.

Brandishing the axe handle, Lloyd continued to laugh heartily. Ignoring his son's pain, he stalked forward.

Chuck stepped in front of his daughter and Barry Graves. "Stop right there, Lloyd. Put down the stick, or I promise you, this'll go worse than you can imagine."

Lloyd appeared unbothered. "You? You're threatening me?"

"Well," Chuck considered, "when I said it, I meant it as a threat. By the stupid look on your face, I'm guessin' it's rapidly developin' into a prediction."

41

NEGOTIATION

Lloyd regarded them all with wild-eyed contempt. "Was it you? Was it you who messed with my car, my home, and my business? It was, wasn't it?"

"Yes," Chuck admitted.

Molly gasped in surprise at his easy admission.

"No use denying it," Chuck said. "We did bad, but you did evil. Simple as that."

"Well, God in heaven!" Lloyd crowed. "Consider my flabber fully and properly gasted!"

Molly could not hold back. "We're not done, either. I promise you, you *will* be banished. Don't you get it? Nobody likes you."

"A girl like you, with all your shit, makes the back of my hand itchy. I wanna slap that hateful look off your face. You want me to leave town? Let's bet on who's more likely successful, huh?"

"Enough!" Chuck yelled.

"You will get your head bashed open," Lloyd replied. "You all will. Let's see what's inside. I'm guessin' your skulls are empty, but we'll see when I start hammerin' and get a hollow sound. I'll keep swingin' past the bone 'til I get to the meat."

The madman stepped beside his son. In the harsh white glare of the spotlight, some of the Fauns' features were washed out. The family resemblance was more than a passing likeness. Molly saw the man Keith would become and the awful boy Lloyd had been. They stood as one monster across two generations.

Lloyd's grin grew ever wider, a joker's face with a rictus grin. "And t'think, all this over a fight between Keith and *that*." He pointed at Barry. "That little nothing."

"I am not nothing," Barry replied. His voice quavered, but his gaze remained steady.

Lloyd shrugged, unbothered. It was how casual he was in his cruelty that terrified Molly most. Her crimes were harassment, trespassing, and property damage. In Lloyd's eyes she saw murder. His careless contempt was as clear as the axe handle in his hands. To him, none of them counted.

"Are you even human?" Molly asked.

Chuck pushed his daughter farther behind him. "Sadly, he is. Takes all kinds. Some just got dropped on their heads as babies, is all."

Molly's father then stepped forward, closer to Lloyd, just outside of the range of his swing.

"You really comin' back for another taste?" Lloyd asked. "With your broke and broke down ass? Really? I can't hardly believe it! You must be feelin' your plums! Feelin' young again, are ya, Chuckles? You and me? Just like in high school all over again. I'm gonna love beatin' you senseless, this time in front of your daughter."

Lloyd tossed the axe handle to his son. "Make sure those two stay put while I put this old man down."

Chuck held his ground. "You say boys quarrel, Lloyd. In my experience, bad men fight. Good men *end* fights. Let's end this."

"What? Is the coward lookin' for a parlay? That's the difference between you and me. You wanna talk and I wanna kill you!"

Lloyd cackled as he put up his fists and bounced on his toes. He threw a couple of practice jabs, his fists less than a foot from Chuck's face.

"Rose?" Chuck called. "You got all this?"

"Here! Yeah!"

Lloyd and Keith looked beyond the defiant trio and froze. Molly and Barry also turned in surprise. As the pickup's engine continued to rumble in idle, the school librarian stood by the passenger door. She held a cell phone in front of her face. "I'm recording, Lloyd!"

Molly was perhaps the most astonished. Rose Rainier had been hiding in the cab all along. Chuck had warned his daughter of a backup plan. She would not have guessed he would bring a stranger into their plots. He'd kept everything from her ailing mother, but he'd brought the Fauns' next-door neighbor into this mess?

Bewildered and suddenly indecisive, Lloyd asked, "What are you doin' out here, Rose?"

"She's another witness," Chuck said. "How many people you willing to kill tonight? The engine's running. She can hop in that cab and get to the sheriff with the video evidence before you can say shit."

"God is watching, too!" Rose added. "Tomorrow, all of Maine will see you for what you are. Maybe the world and everyone in it."

Molly had to smile. Keith hadn't hit her at school because there were too many witnesses. Surely his father would have to demonstrate the same restraint. Her premise for her strategy was right, she'd just needed more people on her side.

"Put down the phone and get out of here!" Lloyd ordered.

Rose came closer, impressive in her defiance. "Why would I ever do what you say?"

"Because no matter what happens, when I get out on bail, I'll still be your neighbor. We got thick history and a thin property line between us. Keith is still dating your daughter. This is just one night," Lloyd said ominously. "You're tied to me for the rest of your life. To my way of thinking, I got lots of leverage over you, bitch!"

Rose heaved a heavy sigh. "Just doing my job like I always do, calming the monkeys at the zoo and shushing the stupid. In the light of day, once the booze wears off, you'll see leaving and going home was the right choice. This feud you folks have got going ends here!"

"My daughter came up with a deal," Chuck said. He nodded to

Molly to continue. "Molly? The fallback plan to your contingency plan is back on. Tell him."

42

DISSOLUTION

Molly cleared her throat and spoke loudly to make sure Rose's phone picked up her words above the noise of the wind and surf. "Here's what you need to know, Mr. Faun. Dad and me ... we *could* confess to our harassment campaign. We were going to stay anonymous, but with Barry coming back, you're too much of a threat. It's stupid and won't work any longer. We could get in a bit of trouble — "

Lloyd trembled with rage. "Damn straight!"

"On the other hand, you just confessed your intent to murder three people with a stick — "

"And make your son an accessory to murder," Barry added.

"So, you pussies brought an extra witness," Lloyd said. "So what?"

Rose Rainier looked at Keith, speaking only to him. "At school, you held back. That was the right thing to do then, and it's the right thing to do now. Step away from your father and throw that axe handle into the ocean. You'll graduate with your class instead of going to jail. You know my daughter likes you. If you keep going, if you stand by your father, you know that all goes away. Any chance at being normal goes away."

Lloyd screamed, "Shut up, you cow!"

Rose Rainier continued as if she hadn't heard him. "We've been neighbors for many years, Keith. I've seen what your father has done to you. I owe you an apology!"

Keith stared at her as if he were lost and confused. "A-apology?" It was as if he'd forgotten he held the axe handle.

"I remember you as a little boy, crying in your backyard over something. Your dad came out and hit you and yelled at you. He kept hitting you until you stopped crying. I'm sorry. I should have said something then. I was scared of him, so I said nothing. Maybe if I had talked to Marjorie, or you, you wouldn't be like this. Maybe you wouldn't be becoming your father."

Keith turned to Lloyd. "I remember that. I think it's one of my earliest memories. You hitting me to stop me from crying." Keith actually let out a giggle. "That was ... that's crazy, isn't it? It seemed normal at the time, but — "

"Your dad isn't right in the head, Keith," Chuck said. "You see that, right? My question is, is it genetic? Can you stop?"

Before Keith could answer, Lloyd ripped the axe handle from his son's grasp.

"Stop!" Molly yelled. "We have a deal for you. You haven't heard the rest!"

"What?" Lloyd shouted.

"Go away." She was supposed to be terrified, but Molly delivered her command in a calm tone.

Lloyd paused in confusion. Smacking the axe handle in his palm, he asked again, "What?"

"You heard me correctly. Go away and the sheriff never needs to know about your death threats."

"Little girl, life is a death threat. You're just too young to get that quite yet. I will teach you."

"No one else needs to know why you left," Molly said. "Get out of town and all the drama stops. If you stay we'll show everyone the recording. We'll show the town what you are. You're a proud man,

Lloyd. Think of the Faun legacy. Think of your son. You won't do the right thing for anybody else. I get that. Do what I say because it's best for you and Keith."

"Banished, right?" Lloyd asked with a chilling smile.

A monster made of teeth, Molly thought.

"I'm gonna cave all your heads in!" Lloyd crowed.

Molly's father charged at him, lumbering forward as fast as he could manage. Lloyd scoffed at first, but his laughter was cut short when Chuck gripped the axe handle.

Lloyd had the weapon, the muscle, and a killer instinct. Chuck had arthritis, sixty pounds on Lloyd, and a father's instinct to protect his child.

Chuck pulled and twisted the axe handle, but he could not wrench it from his enemy's strong grip. Lloyd started to laugh again, but this time his laughter sounded strained.

Lloyd lashed out at Chuck's shin with a vicious kick. Chuck grunted, but refused to let go.

Breathing heavily, Chuck managed to say, "I know pain. Do you?"

Lloyd attempted another kick. Chuck swiveled to one side and, rather than attempt to pull the weapon away, pushed.

Taken by surprise, Lloyd fell back several steps before digging in his heels. The loose gravel under his feet offered little purchase.

Chuck pressed forward, toward the cliff, toward the long drop to the ocean below.

Molly screamed, "Dad!" as she started forward to help.

Too late.

Both men went over the edge, dropping from sight. Without a sound, Lloyd and Chuck fell, disappearing into permanent silence.

The dead zone, Molly thought. *My father has fallen into the dead zone, and he took the monster with him.*

Had the tide been rolling in, the pair might have fallen into deep, cold water. They might have survived that landing, but the tide was not in. The crashing waves masked the sound of their impact on the rocky beach.

Molly and Keith rushed to the cliff's edge. It was so dark it was difficult to see the bodies at first. Then, pulses from Poeticule Bay's lighthouse yielded terrible glimpses as the waves reached for their fathers. The children of the dead gasped together as watery black tendrils of the Atlantic claimed its prize.

Dolls, Molly thought. *They look like broken dolls.*

"Sharp rocks. long drop," Keith said. "No way they made it."

Barry Graves' mouth hung open. As if trying to wake from a nightmare, he scrubbed his face and scalp with both hands. But this wasn't a nightmare. It was real, but his mind was still a few seconds behind reality and struggling to catch up.

Molly refused to look down anymore. Her vision blurred as she stared at the empty space at the cliff's edge. She stood where her father had been only a moment before. She refused to weep and wail in front of her enemy, but silent tears escaped and slid down her cheeks.

Keith's face was unreadable, his eyes dull as black stones. Molly couldn't decide. Was he numb? Did he feel relief? Or was it that he wanted to conceal his thoughts? Perhaps he was devoid of emotions.

Rose charged up between Keith and Molly. She threw herself to the ground to peer down over the edge. "Done. They're done. It'll take a while for the fire department to get to them. Maybe the Coast Guard could get here faster."

"No rush," Keith said.

The woman climbed to her feet slowly. "Are you two satisfied now? Are you proud?"

"Of course not," Molly croaked.

Keith did not answer. Standing mute and expressionless, he made Molly think of an unfinished statue, one without a face.

Rose took Molly's right hand and Keith's left. Pulling them back from the brink, the librarian said, "You did this! You *both* did this."

In that moment, Molly forgot who was predator and who was prey. She only knew that she would always be haunted by the memory of her father's sacrifice on the Drifting Cliffs.

Rose Rainier was right. Her fate would be tied to Keith Faun forever. Trauma has great power. We can get past it, or it can turn us one way or the other. Together, they'd created the worst night of their lives. At least, it was the worst night of their lives at that moment.

The future is patient.

43

VISION

Neither Keith nor Molly could bear to look down, so they both gazed up at the night sky. A few stars emerged from behind the thin veil of cirrus clouds.

Molly was struck by an odd thought. *Thunder should be crashing overhead. Lightning should be electrifying the skies and strobing us in our misery and misdeeds. Something gothic to emphasize how terrible this all is.*

But she'd read too much fiction and seen too many movies. The universe is indifferent to the petty collisions of humans. Her dad would have put it more simply, "There is no God, not that I ever seen, anyway."

"I should call my mom," Keith said finally.

Molly spared her enemy a look. "That all you have to say?"

He shrugged. "Dad's dead. Maybe she'll come back now. Maybe I'll live with her or on my own. There's stuff to figure out."

"I'm going to figure a few things out for you, all of you," Rose said. The librarian pocketed her phone. "Your little war is over. Nobody won! Everybody loses! We're going to call this an accident."

Neither Molly nor Keith could mask their surprise.

"You heard me. This was an accident. Keith, you can walk home from here. If anyone asked, you went straight home from work. Lloyd drove the Lincoln. Chuck just happened to be out here when he saw Lloyd too close the edge. He was drunk and Chuck tried to save him. They fell. End of story. I take pills for insomnia most nights, but they don't always work. I'll say I went out for a night hike for a chance to get fresh air in the hopes of getting sleepy. I'll say I saw it happen. That's the story for Sheriff Hobbs."

"Why?" Molly asked.

"Because this is your second chance. I believe in second chances, especially for a couple of high school kids whose fathers let them stray from sanity and deep into stupid. If I tell the sheriff the truth, you two will have more trouble on your plate. You've already lost your fathers. Surely, that's enough for you. It is, isn't it?"

Barry Graves looked pale. He patted Molly on the shoulder and muttered, "Thanks for trying. I'm so sorry. Do you hate me?"

"I want to," Molly admitted, "but Dad and I ... we walked straight into the propeller blades, didn't we?"

Rose turned to Barry. "The cops were already looking at you for making trouble. You've gone through plenty, and I'm not going to let this grind on for you, either. You were never here. Understand?"

Barry nodded and wrapped his arms around Rose in a spontaneous hug of thanks.

It was Molly who drove Barry in the pickup to a bus station in the next town.

The boy looked worried. "Do you think Keith will leave me alone after all this?"

"If he's determined to hold a grudge, he'll come after me first. If something happens to me, you'll know you're next. I think the recording Rose made will keep us safe, though. Keith's had enough."

"But he won't change," Barry replied. "You do know that, right? Someone that bad isn't suddenly going to turn good."

"He doesn't have to be good. He just has to keep his hands to himself and shut up."

"What about you? Are you really done with him?"

"It's a shaky truce, I guess. I'll keep my hands to myself, too." She didn't sound confident in her words.

"Right now, I feel like I have to focus on taking care of my mom. This is going to freak her out." Molly began to cry again, in earnest this time, in great halting gasps she couldn't control. "I'm freaked out. Dad's still down there."

"Rose said she'd take care of it. If anyone can smooth this over with the cops, she can."

"But I can't tell my mom the truth," Molly said. "She'd never understand."

"We both know he was a hero," Barry said. "The way Rose will describe it, him trying to save Lloyd, the town will still see him as a hero. They'll see Lloyd as the drunken idiot who got him killed, too."

Molly wiped away her tears. "It's not the truth, but it's sort of the truth, isn't it?"

Barry leaned in and hugged her. "Thank you again for trying. Stay safe. I don't trust Keith."

"Rose and her recording are going to keep us, well, if not safe, *safer*. Don't worry about that. Just, I don't know ... get on with your life. That's what people do, right?"

Barry managed an awkward smile. "I don't know. I'm a kid. Haven't got it all figured out yet."

Molly shook her head. "The school, the sheriff, this town ... a bunch of idiots sure is making us grow up fast, aren't they?"

Barry's bus arrived. With nothing more of use to say, he patted Molly's shoulder and stepped out of the truck.

They would not cross paths again for twelve years.

44

REFLECTION

Rose's deception seemed to work. Sheriff Hobbs' initial efforts seemed focused on recovering the bodies. The coroner in Orono confirmed that Lloyd was far over the legal limit of alcohol in his system.

"Both men died when they hit the beach," the sheriff told Molly and her mother. "You needn't worry that they drowned. A fall like that ... I think the town is going to look into putting up some kind of barrier and a warning sign."

"A sign?" Molly's mother asked. "You think that'll make everything okay?"

The sheriff blushed. "That's not fair, Kay. Nothing's gonna bring Chuck back. Just sayin', maybe they'll put up a fence or something so a tragedy like this doesn't happen again. I dunno. That's not up to me."

"I thought public safety was your job," Kay said pointedly. "And all we get is a sign and maybe a fence."

Hobbs gave her a serious look. "I don't know what you want from me — "

"I guess I want you to go back in time and handle the Fauns the way you should have done the first go 'round," Kay replied.

The sheriff shifted from one foot to the other and stared at the kitchen floor. "I'm sure neither of them felt a thing, really. An impact like that, as far as they're concerned, they were flying and never landed. They're still flying. That's how you have to think about it. Flying like angels."

It was a nice thought, but Molly didn't believe him for a second. She'd read somewhere that no death is really instantaneous. For her mother's sake, she said nothing. She never told her mother that Chuck died a hero saving his daughter from a madman swinging an axe handle.

Kay left the cop standing in her kitchen and limped away stiffly. She walked straight to her darkened bedroom, her rumpled bed, and a long stretch of depression.

Before he left, his hand on the doorknob, Hobbs told Molly, "I have an inkling of what really happened, you know. I'm not an idiot. Rose Rainier says she saw them fall, says she just happened to be out there, taking in the view, the lighthouse, the moon on the ocean — "

"But?"

"We don't know why your father was out by the cliffs when Lloyd went on a drunken stroll. Any thoughts on that?"

Molly shook her head.

"An axe handle washed up on the beach. My deputy found it. Looked brand new. Lloyd bought it. The receipt was in his wallet. Mysterious, isn't it?"

"Is it?"

"Not really. I can add two plus two."

"You've done some calculations. And?"

"If Lloyd had bought an axe instead of an axe handle, I wonder, do you think there'd be more casualties? Or if I'd let him keep his guns? How'd that have played out, I wonder? It didn't end in banishment, did it?"

"Not exactly."

"I'm a curious fella, Miss Jergins. I like to solve for X, you know? You got an answer for me?"

"Only one question." Her eyes wet, Molly asked, "Can you keep your math to yourself, Sheriff?"

The cop sighed and shrugged. "Depends. Has justice been served, y'think?"

"No," she said. "Lloyd Faun got off too easy. He and my dad didn't deserve the same fate. If you're right about the flying like angels thing, Lloyd should have drowned. Slowly."

"That may be but move on. That's the healthy thing. I won't make you no trouble over what I can't prove."

Molly could not stop herself. The words she yearned to speak weighed heavily on her heart. "This is partly your fault. You know that, don't you, Sheriff? You didn't do what you were supposed to do from the start. You didn't serve and protect Barry Graves because you didn't care. If it had been your son...."

Hobbs held up a hand to stop her. He ignored her jab and said, "I have a feeling there will be no more acts of vandalism around town. Am I right? I better be."

She felt as if the air had been sucked out of the room, out of the world. A lump tingled in the back of her throat. She thought she might choke.

Molly didn't answer Hobbs, and he did not insist she reply. Instead, he said, "Your mother has troubles, health stuff and now a widow to boot. I hope you'll put your energies into helping her out as much as you can. That would be a good use of your time and talents."

With that, Sheriff Hobbs gave her a curt nod. "Be a good girl, Molly." Hobbs closed the door behind him quietly and left.

The town mourned Chuck Jergins. Poeticule Bay missed Lloyd Faun less, but he still got a plaque on the bleachers by the baseball diamond. Dead men are soon forgotten by most, but it's different for their loved ones. The dead leave holes in the days of the living. Those gaps may lessen but never completely fill in.

Molly was on anti-depressants for a while. Her mother stayed in her room most of the time and ate less and less until her doctor insisted she start consuming protein drinks to up her weight.

Kay occasionally pulled out photograph albums — pictures of

Chuck when he was young, photos of her husband looking hand-some and fresh-faced in his uniform, shots from their wedding. She did not speak his name.

Keith graduated with his class and won a hockey scholarship at a small college in Michigan. Apparently, they were willing to ignore his disciplinary record. Keith moved out of the Faun house and lived with his mother for the rest of that summer.

Molly graduated the following year. The August before Molly went away to university, Chuck's brother Vincent moved in to help Kay.

With her mother cared for by her uncle, Molly left Poeticule Bay on the second of September, bound for Middlebury College in Vermont.

Determined to reinvent herself, Molly resolved to act kindly and be seen as a generous, patient person. Over and over, she repeated the sheriff's admonition as a mantra, "I'm a good girl."

She often told herself, "Even if it's just an act, I'll be a method actor. I'll fake it 'til I make it. I'll pretend to be someone else. I'll be the girl who didn't get her dad killed. I'm a good girl, or at least I can make people think I am."

She never believed it, of course. Molly had suffered a traumatic event and a great loss. That wasn't the same as having a personality transplant.

For the benefit of others, she put up a good front. Molly tried to become the sort who did not yearn to visit vengeance upon the deserving.

Because good girls don't.

Positive affirmations can be helpful. "I'm a good girl" often kept her natural impulses in check. However, when affirmations begin to fail and nature reasserts itself, her mantra became another torture.

Each morning, Molly would look herself in the mirror and repeat, "I am a person worthy of love. I love myself."

But she meant hate.

AIR

Noises drowned our voices
as foes refused to learn.
Their new teacher is Vengeance.
It's Her time and Her turn.

45

REVISION

Molly studied hard, stayed out of trouble, and acted like a responsible adult. The itch to take down bullies remained, but she managed to curb her darker impulses until her second year at university.

A particularly nasty professor was well-known for unkind remarks to her students. Betty-Ann Waddings, a communications professor, made no secret of her contempt for her students. She went too far when she targeted a well-liked classmate and made her criticism personal.

Peggy Craftsman sat up straight and trembled when Betty-Ann called on her in class. "What is Peggy short for? Pegtunia?"

"Margaret." Peggy smiled wanly. "It's short for Margaret."

Molly's ears perked up. Molly was also short for Margaret.

The professor appeared unimpressed. "Words and how we use them have impact. Do you really want to have a future in journalism, kid? If so, change your name, put away the crayons, and grow up! Peggy is a little girl's name. Knock off your bubbly little girl schtick. It's tiresome, you're tiresome."

Peggy's smile collapsed and she looked like she might cry. "It's not a 'schtick,'" Peggy objected. "I'm just a positive person."

"Sad and weak, more likely, *so* desperate for everyone to like you. Do you think your interview subjects will like you if you do your job correctly? Maybe you're better suited to working as a flack for some politician. I don't have time for Pollyannas in my class. The world doesn't need you."

The class plunged into shocked silence.

"Anybody as happy as you seem to be is either pretending, high, or stupid." Waddings persisted with a mocking, sing-song voice. "Which is it, little girl? Are you phony or stupid? Maybe you should change your name to Pollyanna."

Tears appeared in Peggy's eyes. She looked back at her attacker, unsure of how to respond.

"You're really going to cry? What is this? Elementary school?"

Peggy found her voice, "I guess I'm not as mad at the world as you."

"Stupid, it is!" The prof declared. Her glee was evident.

One boy gave a nervous laugh. Molly leaned forward and smacked him hard across the back of the head. He hunched and cringed, and did not laugh again.

Molly stood. "Professor Waddings? Perhaps Peggy's upset because a minute ago she had so much respect for you. You blew it, for all of us."

"Sit down, Ms. Jergins."

"You said it yourself. Words have impact." Molly then stalked to Peggy's desk and pulled her to her feet.

Molly whispered, "Don't give her the satisfaction of seeing you cry. She's jealous of you. You have friends. All she's got is a couple of cats at home. The way she acts, they aren't pets. That's a hostage situation."

Peggy snuffled, then nodded and let out a little chuckle.

Molly squeezed her arm. "Also, you don't have to put up with this. None of us do."

"You're right. I don't."

Together, they walked out. Peggy really was popular, and several other students demonstrated their solidarity by following them out in silent protest.

"Oh, c'mon!" Waddings called after those exiting. "You'll never make it if you can't handle honest feedback! Grow a thicker skin!"

Molly looked back and answered, "I think we'll stay human instead!"

Peggy lodged a formal complaint. Molly had hoped university would be different from her experience at Poeticule Bay Consolidated. She was mistaken.

The dean promised to look into it and have a talk with the professor. A week later, Peggy was informed that this "valued professor" had been reprimanded. That was as far as the discipline went. Peggy did not receive an apology, so she dropped the class.

What lasted was Molly's nickname for Betty-Ann Waddings: BA for Bad Attitude.

But a little name-calling yielded no satisfaction. "That bitch needs an attitude adjustment," Molly vowed, "and if I don't administer the correction, who will?"

A week later, Molly shoplifted a gift card to an expensive restaurant. She put together a fruit basket and left it on Waddings' desk while the professor was at lunch.

"We want peace in our classroom. You have a reservation at La Gloria tonight at 8 pm. Please accept this gift card of $200 for a great and memorable evening," the note read. "Enjoy your night. You deserve this!"

La Gloria was the most expensive restaurant in town. There was no money on the card. At the end of an extravagant evening, the professor had to pay out of her own pocket.

Molly had included a bunch of bananas in the fruit basket. She had carefully needled a message in the banana skins. As they ripened, her messages emerged. In brown script, the words emerged:

You deserved that
Be better
Or else

Your cats will eat you

At the next class, the professor seemed particularly agitated. She shook her head occasionally and muttered about "this generation."

Molly sat in the front row, smiling broadly as if daring the professor to turn on her. Waddings' eyes flicked her way many times throughout her lecture.

She knows, Molly thought. *Good.*

However, Waddings got through the class without harshly criticizing her students. Her behavior improved for rest of the term.

After class, Molly sought out Peggy Craftsman. "If you want back into that class, you could. The cow is cowed."

Peggy shot her a confused look. "What are you talking about?"

Molly told her exactly what she did to intimidate the professor. "I don't think she'll disrespect us again anytime soon."

But Peggy was not pleased. "I don't think that's the sort of thing that makes things better."

"It was a gentle correction," Molly said. "It's not as if I left photos of her asleep in bed or tied her up and shaved her head down the middle. That would be more in line with the honest feedback I'd like to give her. You know, just some honest feedback from a friend who wants her to be better."

"I dropped the class," Peggy said. "I'm not going back. There are other classes. It's no big deal."

"But she humiliated you! She made you cry!"

"She embarrassed herself and my tears dried."

To Molly, this was a prank that hardly counted as vengeance. Seeing Peggy's reaction, she soon understood her miscalculation.

"Please take this as kindly as I mean it, okay?" Peggy asked.

"Okay," Molly replied warily.

"Have you considered therapy?"

"Why? I'm, like, 46.8% certain everything will work out fine."

"I'm serious, Molly!"

"You don't understand. Vengeance is therapeutic, right? For me and for them. I've done things that some people only fantasize about.

I try not to do those things, but the way she treated you was too much!"

"Your smile," Peggy said. "The way you smiled when you said the thing about shaving the professor's head — "

"Well, you wouldn't tell somebody who loves food that they can't enjoy fried chicken and fudge ever again."

"You're not funny!" Peggy insisted.

"I wasn't trying to be funny."

"So, it's an addiction. Please listen! Addicts need therapy."

Molly lowered her gaze to the floor. "I'm not saying you're wrong. I'm just saying it's hard to see bad people get away with stuff, you know?"

"How much are you like Professor Waddings?"

"Not at all!" Molly said.

"Look, Waddings is mad at the world. Sounds like you are, too. So? Do you think I'm a stupid coward? Waddings thinks I'm stupid for being nice."

Molly took a moment to answer, choosing her words carefully, "I think you must be braver and wiser than me. You are how you are, and that sounds pretty healthy. Good for you. Meanwhile, assholes are gonna asshole, you know? I'm from a small town, and it could be rough. I love figuring out ways to deal with nasties like Waddings."

Peggy stared at her a moment. "I'm from a small town, too. There's another way."

"Is it murder? I'm not into murder. Lets the target off too easy."

The woman Molly had meant to help was not amused. "Kill them with kindness. When I was little, I was at a county fair with my parents. This happened at some food venue, lots of people around eating at tables. Some man named Ryerson came after my father. I don't know what the beef was about. I do remember the man holding a knife under my dad's crotch and telling him, 'Up on your toes! Up on your toes!' My father grabbed the man's wrist, and it was about to turn into a wrestling match for the knife when Mrs. Ryerson screamed up behind her husband. 'Ronny!' she says, 'You're drunk! A raft of our chickens died last night, and the bank is gonna take our car! You think you can afford bail? What the hell do you think you're doing?'"

Molly approved. "Good line. Did that take the wind out of his sails?"

"Sure did. Ryerson let go of the knife and turned beet red. But that wasn't the best part. Dad said, 'Ronald! I had no idea you were so hard up. Bad luck and poverty might make me drink too much, too. Let me buy you and Monica lunch.'"

"That was big of him."

"Ronnie Ryerson never bothered Dad after that. He was so embarrassed, he stayed out on his farm. We only saw Mrs. Ryerson in town, and she was always sweet as pie."

"Impressive. Your father didn't kill him with kindness. He murdered him with mercy."

"You might try that," Peggy said, "because right now, you're more like Ryerson than you are like my father. Too much like Waddings, too."

Molly was about to argue but saw there was no point. Peggy was not about to change her mind. Though she still felt no shame for her actions, Molly was embarrassed at her miscalculation.

"To be honest, you scare me," Peggy said. "You've got a mean streak in you. Learn to let things go."

"That sounds good, but I don't know how. How do you do that?"

Peggy shrugged. "You just *do*. Therapy or yoga, maybe? I can't say, Molly. Your story isn't mine. I wouldn't presume to speak to your issues. I appreciated your support in class, and I don't want to sound ungrateful, but stop. I won't tell anyone what you did, but please, for my peace, stay away from me, okay?"

"I promise I'll never bother you again."

"Cool! And good luck, girl."

"Good luck or goof luck, I'll deal."

Good luck was with Molly this time. Though the college administration demonstrated little interest in curbing Waddings' classroom behavior, they were motivated to investigate the fruit basket incident.

The dean of students and the head of the student union sat down with everyone in Waddings' classes individually.

When interviewed, Molly pretended to be as mystified as everyone else. True to her word, Peggy did not implicate Molly. She got away with it.

It seemed the "or else" worried administration the most. The order of the messages on the bunch of bananas caused some confusion. Was it "Or else your cats will eat you"? Or was "your cats will eat you" meant as a separate message? "Or else" seemed to promise further harassment.

In any case, the incident came to be known as The Fruitless Banana Investigation. Within a couple of weeks, security cameras were installed in the halls of the Journalism department.

Peggy's counsel to seek therapy often arose unbidden, but Molly never followed her advice.

Betty-Ann Waddings didn't seek professional help, but she used her colleagues as amateur therapists. Paying the bill at La Gloria wasn't the worst day of the professor's life. However, she spoke of that night with anger long afterward.

Waddings had few friends, so the same people heard her retell the tale and restate her hatred for students often. They grew weary of her constant negativity, and by the end of her short life, she had even fewer friends. Words do indeed have impact.

Perhaps no words have deeper force than a dire diagnosis from a doctor. Betty-Ann Waddings returned home from her appointment and called her sister immediately. Long estranged, Beth Tait was mystified by Betty-Ann's sudden reappearance.

"I need you to come pick up my cats," Waddings said. "I'm not feeling well so I'm putting Woodward and Bernstein up for adoption. Please come take them, Beth. Come take them because I don't want to feed them."

Only six people attended Professor Waddings' funeral — all out of obligation rather than love. The eulogy was delivered by a priest who knew her not at all. Molly did not know of her old professor's passing.

Interestingly, it was Betty-Ann herself who arrived at one last inkling of self-discovery as she lay bald and dying in a hospice bed.

Woodward and Bernstein are probably happier with my sister, she thought. *And I deserve this.*

46

STAGNATION

Molly managed to behave herself until her senior year at Middlebury. Then a sophomore named Ron Chestnut crossed her path. He was a bodybuilder prone to dispensing his vapid pearls of wisdom as if everyone else was an idiot.

Jillian Godfrey, Molly's roommate, was in a kinesiology class with Chestnut. "He's in love with himself and the sound of his own voice," she complained. "His voice carries, so wherever you are, if he's in the room, you know. He bangs on about pea protein powder, weightlifting, and how Communists are about to take over the world and lose to God's plan for America. And he keeps telling me I shouldn't wear bras, you know, for my health."

Molly had overheard Chestnut's pontifications in the cafeteria. His hapless tablemates endured his monologues for a short time and then fled.

"He's relentless," Molly told Jillian. "He has the manner of a manipulator, the self-awareness of a potato, and the eyes of a serial killer."

Chestnut's hungry gaze followed every woman, sizing them up the way a starving animal looks at a piece of meat.

But Molly left him alone.

I'll be a good girl.

I am a good girl.

You've got to learn to let things go.

You just do!

But Chestnut became so fixated on her roommate he activated Molly's mean streak. Jillian worked a part-time job serving at the nearby diner. Chestnut came in several times a week, ordering egg white omelettes every time.

He'd been almost sweet when he asked her out the first time. Jillian knew him by reputation, so she turned him down. Chestnut kept asking, but his tone became more of a demand than a question.

Then came the lewd and rude comments about Jillian's body. Despite her polite refusals, Chestnut whispered promises of what he intended to do to her sexually. "Give me one date, and you'll know you should have said yes the first time. You're really missing out, Jilly!"

"It's as if he thinks I owe him," Jillian said.

"I know the kind," Molly said. "He thinks he owns the world."

"I try to be nice," Jillian said, "but he just won't take a hint!"

It seemed to Molly that abusers got the benefit of the doubt too often. People with kind natures thought everyone was as good as they were, so the abuse continued with impunity.

Others excused terrible behavior simply because they were also terrible, too. The diner's manager, Al Lipton, fell into the latter category. He was of no help. He wouldn't even let Jillian switch tables when Chestnut sat in her section.

"It's not that serious," her boss said. "It's just words. The boy will get tired eventually, and in the meantime, we'll sell him a lot of omelettes. Pretty girls like you get privileges, so you can't complain when you get more attention."

The more insistent Chestnut became, the more Jillian looked to her manager to help her. Instead, Lipton dug in his heels.

"It's a rule of the restaurant business and every other business," he told her. "The customer may not be right, but he's never wrong.

And tits get tips, girl! Enjoy the attention. You're not in high school, anymore. Toughen up, buttercup! Service with a smile, not a snarl, right?"

Lipton sounded too much like Bad Attitude Waddings. "These people," Molly swore, "need a course correction."

While Chestnut aimed at Jillian, Molly's revenge fantasies intruded on her good-girl thoughts: Dangerous allergic reactions, getting locked outside naked, ipecac in his protein shakes, explosive diarrhea, cut brake lines, or maybe even falling from a great height into the sea.

It was some comfort that, though Chestnut fancied himself a stud, every woman on campus seemed to have received the memo: Ron Chestnut is an asshole and a creep. Not one woman at Middlebury voluntarily chose to be in his company.

Molly's resolve to do something about Chestnut solidified the night she returned to her dorm from a late class. She found Jillian on her bed crying.

Chestnut had come back for more egg-whites and harassment. When Jillian placed his plate on the table, he leaned close to say, "Still playing hard to get? Is it because I'm an athlete? You think you're too ugly? Too fat? Is that the problem here?"

Shocked, Jillian said nothing. She went straight to the kitchen to tell her manager. Lipton just laughed, so Jillian headed for the back door.

Lipton followed her. "You can't leave me short-handed! Your shift isn't over. I have you until ten!"

Jillian kept walking. Her anger bloomed later, after her tears dried. She'd said nothing in her own defense, so she was angry at herself, not just Lipton and Chestnut.

Talking it over with Molly, Jillian obsessed over all the things she could have or should have said to her useless boss and the repulsive creep.

"That's it! I quit. I'm not going back."

"I don't blame you," Molly said.

"I don't feel safe there. Am I wrong?"

"You're not wrong and you're not safe."

"Why do they have to be like this?"

"They do it because they can," Molly told her.

Molly's need for retribution could not be denied. *They do it because they feel too safe.*

She felt like she was about to indulge in a feast after a long fast. The pull was as irresistible as a riptide. Once Jillian was asleep, Molly slipped out in search of Al Lipton's car.

The diner's manager lived in an apartment over the diner, so his car was easy to find. It was the only vehicle parked in back of the diner.

Molly used her keys to scratch deep into both sides of his Buick. She drew a large flower on the hood. Molly wasn't sure what a buttercup looked like but did her best.

Toughen up, buttercup!

47

DESTRUCTION

The vandalism was reported to the police the next morning. Her roommate was the prime suspect, but Molly swore Jillian was in her bed the entire night.

When the investigating officer left, Jillian gave Molly a hug and a knowing smile.

Molly put a finger to her lips. "No questions. I wouldn't want to have to fill you up with bullshit. It'd stink up the dorm."

Jillian kissed Molly's cheek. "You are *feral*! I love it!"

Ron Chestnut's red Miata was next. The act that had served as a warning and an inconvenience to the diner owner became more serious in Chestnut's case.

Molly waited a week before she struck. His license plate was ANoi. A Number One. Molly wrote the word "stalker" all over the car using shaving cream. She painted the license plate so it read: ANUS.

The shaving cream destroyed the paint so thoroughly overnight that the car had to be repainted. Chestnut couldn't afford the paint job, so the damage remained for the rest of the semester. He became a campus joke, and much to Molly's satisfaction, even more of a pariah.

Ron Chestnut did not return to Middlebury the following

semester. The banishment plan that had failed her in Poeticule Bay worked at Molly's college with relative ease.

Perhaps the mocking was more than he could bear. Molly thought the note she wrote in grease pencil across his windshield did the trick:

Every night every woman on campus fantasizes about blowing up your car with you in it. Not a single person on Earth would miss you.

The night nurtured her vengeful urges. Writing on Chestnut's windshield, acting on the vendetta, eased her mind.

Reading that message marked the third worst day of Ron Chestnut's life. The second worst arrived three years after leaving Middlebury.

Students remembered the vandalism done to his car. It became the stuff of campus legend. Molly's note sparked several conversations among Chestnut's other targets. Three years later, several young women came forward alleging he had committed sexual assault.

His worst day was his last. Chestnut flipped that same red Miata on Route 133 at the Canadian border in Highgate. Officially, he was speeding when he hit some black ice. Maybe he was just driving too fast on a November night trying to escape to Canada. The family suspected that, in anticipation of arrest, he'd committed suicide.

Molly had moved on to another school by then, so she didn't hear how Chestnut died. Had she known, she would not have grieved his exit from Earth. She'd meant what she wrote.

The attacks on Lipton and Chestnut lessened the pressure she'd felt in her gut and in her head. The urge to take action when no one else would or could was enormous, as powerful and inevitable as the tides. She considered the damage she'd done to those cars two of her better days.

Her need for vengeance sated, Molly went back to playing nice. She stayed off law enforcement's radar. She put her head down and studied and worked on getting her next degree.

Fortunately, few people crossed her path whose assholery rose to the level of needful retribution.

Most people are doing their best, and they're fine, she thought. *I'm doing my best. I'm a good girl doing my best.*

As time passed, Molly was almost sure she could leave her old self behind. She surrounded herself with people who valued positivity. Nice people with good manners decreased social friction. That peace was what Molly needed.

In gray times, those days when she retreated to the dark well of memory, she felt like she stood on the edge of a cliff again. Looking down, she felt the death drive: aggression, repetition, a compulsion toward self-destruction.

On dark days, she would retreat to her bed to escape into sleep. Sometimes, when her dreams turned into the same nightmare: Over and over, she saw her father fall, only this time, he fell backwards into darkness. Lloyd Faun wasn't there. It was just her dad, staring up at her as he fell.

On waking, her heart would pound at the false memory. In the light of day, after she calmed down, Molly was more rational. Chuck Jergins would not have wanted for her the things she so desperately wanted to do. Her father's ghost pulled her back from jumping into the abyss.

It's a struggle, but sometimes the best thing to do is nothing, she reminded herself. *Keep pretending!*

Restraining herself didn't feel brave, but Molly's effort to appear normal certainly was heroic.

And she knew it couldn't last.

48

TENSION

Eleven years after the Drifting Cliffs, Molly had earned a PhD in English. Job loss is a stressful process, so she was about to endure one of the worst days of her life. What was about to transpire would have repercussions that echoed until Molly's last breath.

An evening cocktail party swirled around her. A guest among strangers in the dean's residence of Greenbriar College, she felt like a rock in a babbling stream. The party swirled around her as she stood stone still, silent amid the jabbering throng of academics.

Molly had hoped teaching communications in the backwaters of Indiana would be a way forward to greater opportunities. Instead, she felt as if she'd missed an on-ramp and arrived at a dead end. Though she'd only recently been hired, her job was already on the chopping block. She had failed to navigate the petty politics of academia. Were she to be let go, her savings would run out in a few months.

Until recently, Molly had been consistent. She'd isolated herself from conflict, pretending to be someone she wasn't. She tried to do socially acceptable things or at least shut up and mind her business.

However, a particularly nasty student had come to her attention. The familiar urges prodded her, pushing Molly to be her old self.

This time, she had not operated in darkness. There'd been witnesses, and her job was in jeopardy.

Surveying the party, feeling like an outsider, Molly nursed her glass of cheap sherry and stared down at the worn and faded area rug.

Dr. Helen Benhaven, an associate professor of molecular biology, came to her rescue. Molly had been hired on with the lowly title of lecturer, but Helen had given her a warm welcome to Greenbriar College.

Helen gestured with her glass. "Look at those two. You hearing this?"

In the middle of the room, two senior professors, Barnes and Collins, were at odds over the difference between prejudice and racism.

"It's more than semantics," Helen observed, "but these blowhards argue over the minutiae of issues that don't touch their privileged lives in the slightest."

"You missed their discussion of the difference between sex and gender," Molly said.

"Yeah? How'd they do?"

"Got it wrong, but at least they agreed with each other in their wrongness."

Helen chuckled. "Their natter and chatter may as well be geese honking. God forbid they ask the opinion of the only black woman in the room. I could let 'em know. Feels like I'm only visible when they want to sleep with me."

"That's not true," Molly teased. "When next year's syllabus comes out, pictures of you will be all over the college website."

Helen laughed. "Right! I was so focused on their sexism and misogyny, I forgot about the tokenization."

The biologist had become a fast friend. She and Molly did laps in Greenbriar's Olympic-sized pool three times a week at six-thirty in the morning. They both hated the experience because the water was always too cold.

"I want that pool as hot as a bathtub!" Helen said. "I'd rather start the day with a big coffee and an apple strudel as big as your head. For our stupid health, I'll keep going if you will."

Helen and Molly were alike in other ways. Both were saddled with huge student debt. They lived in tiny one-room apartments, hardly bigger than the dorms in which their students lived.

Watching the faculty's festivities, Helen leaned in and whispered, "I've been hearing more badass things about you. How goes the struggle, comrade?"

Molly shrugged. "Still waiting for the axe to fall."

"Bureaucracy is so slow, maybe it'll take so long, tempers will cool, and it'll all blow over. Wait it out. Smile and nod, that's my motto."

"That works?"

"Keeps me out of the kind of trouble you're into."

"Fair," Molly replied.

The women watched as the professors' argument grew more heated.

"It's like we're on safari watching from the bushes as the males of the species go through their ritual dances," Molly said.

"Not mating dances, I hope!" Helen quipped.

"To mark territory. That seems to be what it's all about around here. Big egos at war."

Helen grinned. "Those two pedants have been here since Jesus was a carpenter, still teaching out of the same text they started with in a long-ago eon. The dinosaurs didn't go extinct. They disappeared into academia and became tenured professors."

"And here I stand," Molly replied, "bored and praying for an asteroid strike. Who knows? If their debate escalates to blows, maybe one of them will keel over and we'd have a shot at employment everlasting."

"Molly! Don't wish death upon our colleagues. It's not wrong, but it's bad form to say out loud."

"Sorry. I'm not *very* serious. I just envy the power of tenure. There is no tenure track anymore. We're stuck."

"Up Shit Creek without a canoe, sure, never mind the paddle," Helen agreed. "Academic job security is a thing of the past. Meanwhile, we're told to be grateful. My TAs are starving and sleeping in my lab. That's why I go out of my way to make nice with Whelan."

She meant Greenbriar's dean, Richard Whelan. Molly raised her eyebrows. "Make nice? What does that entail?"

"You know ... flirt."

"I don't have that skill set."

"Hey, I'm not happy about it. He's a lech who looks like a bridge troll's infected feet. I had a meeting with him about my curriculum this afternoon. He talked to my chest the entire time."

"That sucks."

Helen gave a tired sigh. "Oh, it gets worse. You don't know the half of it!"

49

HYPERTENSION

"Crystal, one of the custodial staff, visited my office yesterday. She wanted me to know she'd scrubbed some graffiti off a bathroom wall. Crystal comes to me — all embarrassed, you know — and says, 'Dr. Benhaven? On the wall of a toilet stall, someone drew a raunchy sketch of you and wrote under it Dr. Breast Haver. Got rid of it, but I thought you should know, I think it was one of your colleagues.'"

Molly gaped at her friend. "Nah! Had to be a disgruntled student, right? Some kid unhappy with a grade on his paper?"

Helen shook her head. "It was a *faculty* bathroom, Molly! At least the perv called me by my title. *Dr.* Breast Haver!"

Molly went into target-seeking mode. "Who do you think did that?"

"My prime suspect is the one who laughs loudest at sexist jokes. Today, Richard asked me if a student failed the mid-term orals, would I be open to doing supplementary anals."

"Gross, not funny, and lazy," Molly said.

Helen gave a dismissive wave. "He's putting out feelers, sniffing around to see if I'll respond with playfulness, checking if I'm open to degrading myself. Next thing I know, he'd be closing his office door and chasing me around the desk."

"I'm pretty sure you could take him, put him down hard," Molly said.

"I gave up my evening karate classes for swimming with you at stupid o'clock in the morning!" Helen replied.

She seemed much less bothered about the dean's sexual harassment than Molly felt.

"Anyway, it's all such foolishness," Helen declared. "Whelan acts ridiculous because he's untouchable."

"Untouchable *so far*," Molly replied.

"Well, *I* don't want to touch him. I'd write Dean Dickless on a wall for all to see, but that would just mean more scrubbing for poor Crystal. I don't want to make more work for anybody."

"I'm so sorry!" Molly said.

Helen laughed it off. "It's too childish to engage with."

Molly remained incensed. "I didn't realize Whelan was that much of a creep. He doesn't do that with me, but maybe I'm too flat-chested for him."

Helen eyed her friend. "It's not that. It's just that you have a vibe."

"What vibe?"

"The only time I ever see you truly happy is when you're talking about your work. You're crazy for literature."

"I am! I love it!" Molly agreed. "But as Francis Bacon said, 'It is impossible to love and be wise.'"

"Yeah, yeah, nerd!"

"Nerd?"

Helen shot her a grin. "Molly, the other day you couldn't shut the hell up about gender trends in authorship. I don't give you a dissertation on the chemicals in your food over lunch, do I?"

"I do go on sometimes, don't I?"

"Yes, you do. I don't really mind because you manage to be interesting. However, my point is about the *other* times, when you're not in Molly Word Mode."

"Molly Word Mode?"

"When that's turned off, you've got this don't-mess-with-me thing going on."

"I think you're telling me in a kind, roundabout way that I have resting bitch face."

"No, it's not that, at least not exactly. Something about the way you carry yourself, I guess? Can't quite put my finger on it. All I know is when we go to the pool, the boys don't dare stare your way for too long."

"They're staring at you."

"No — well, yes, but no. It's your vibe, like you probably wouldn't cut them, but you might. I'll let you know next time I feel it."

I let my mask slip, Molly thought. *She saw me.*

After a beat, Molly said, "Yeah, I'm weird. Must be the social anxiety. I've been called weird before."

Helen shook her head. "Don't indulge that. When people say something is weird, what they really mean is the object of their derision is outside their previous experience. When someone's world is narrow and they don't do shit, everything seems weird. You're not weird, friend. You just have a vibe. It's powerful."

"Lotta good that does me," Molly said. "Using that power is why I'm going to be pulled before the disciplinary committee."

"The cafeteria thing? Don't write yourself off quite yet," Helen advised.

"I don't understand your optimism," Molly said, "or optimism in general. Wish I could."

"I wouldn't say I'm blindly optimistic," Helen objected, "just patient and confident things will work out. Meanwhile, I'm trying to endure the dean until he's gone. Greenbriar's captain will steer the ship into an iceberg, eventually. Then the fearless pervert will be shoved out."

Fearless? thought Molly. *Richard Whelan should not be fearless. Someone should teach him about fear. He should know how deep and dark it is, how it feels like falling. It tastes like pennies under your tongue as icy fingers paw at your racing heart. I could make his palms sweat as his bladder tightens and his bowels turn to water. I could teach Richard about fear, to feel the screaming inevitability of pain and doom. Slipping behind him and yanking a plastic bag down over his empty head and tight around his worthless neck would be simple but effective.*

Oblivious to Molly's savage reverie, Helen continued, "After my shitty meeting with Richard, I talked it over with Gilda."

Gilda Milner was the school's professor emerita in economics. She the oldest faculty member and had retired only briefly a couple of years previously. The old prof had collected shells on a Florida beach for a month before deciding she was ill-suited to the joys of a leisurely retirement. Bereft of the knack for idle pleasures, she had returned to teaching. Gilda Milner was the crown jewel of Greenbriar's faculty. Molly had met her several times but had been too introverted to go out of her way to befriend the old woman.

Helen, ever the extrovert, was friendly with everyone. Molly envied her friend's ease and ability dealing with people. *She still thinks most people are good,* Molly thought. *How lovely it would be to be so trusting.*

"Gilda wasn't surprised about the leering and the stupid bathroom thing," Helen said. "When Whelan goes, she might be slotted to be the next dean. I hope so. I love her. She's got sweet, funny grandma energy."

"Does she think the dean's exit is imminent?" Molly asked hopefully.

"I asked. Not imminent, but inevitable, according to Gilda. The rumor mill says Whelan got a freshman pregnant last year, but he covered it up. That should have been it for him, but here we are."

"Covered up? How?"

"Money," Helen replied. "Same as ever. When they have what we don't, they get away with more shit and for longer."

"How much longer? My hearing is in the next week or two."

Helen leaned in and rubbed Molly's back. "Don't worry so much. I hyped you up to Gilda. She's on that committee."

"Thanks. In the meantime, I stew in my own juices. I literally cannot wait for him to go before the axe falls. We can slay our enemies or wait for them to die. You know ... Whelan is a man of a certain age and carriage." A small smile came to Molly's lips.

"He's old and heavy, sure." Helen's eyes narrowed with suspicion. "What are you thinking?"

Molly smile widened. "Balance issues. I wonder if the steps outside the dean's residence are salted regularly. It would be a shame if they were icy or doused in cooking oil. Slips and falls are one of the most common causes of fractures and death in the home."

Her friend chuckled. "There's that vibe I was talking about. And when you talk like that? That's when you look happiest. That's not resting bitch face. That's a Joker's smile!"

"Sorry."

"No, no! You're good. Mean is bad, but funny and mean kind of make it okay."

As long as you keep thinking I'm not serious, Molly thought, *I am good. A good girl.*

Helen hoisted her glass and drank. "While we wait, lubrication with alcohol helps ease our feelings of powerlessness and self-hatred."

"Does it?" Molly asked doubtfully.

"Shut up and drink! Also, to clarify and amplify, I would *never* sleep with him. However, the sexy go further in life. It's just a biological and anthropological fact. We all use what we've got to cope."

Molly's only coping mechanisms were all revenge fantasies. She wondered what her parents would think of her coping skills. Her true self had resurfaced lately. As a result, the career she'd only begun to build was in jeopardy.

Stress made her urges stronger, and Molly was certainly stressed.

50

REPUDIATION

"You've heard the rumors about more budget cuts?" Molly asked Helen.

"It's going to go much deeper than the hiring freeze the board announced."

At that moment, Dean Whelan emerged from a gaggle of educators where he'd been holding court.

"Don't talk to him about it now," Helen whispered. "Why poke the bear and rush to the end? Enjoy the mystery of whether we're doomed to homelessness while being chased by debt collectors."

"What will change if we don't confront him?"

"You first," Helen said. "I'll hang back and guard the booze."

Molly eyed the dean, a smile creeping up at the edge of her mouth. "I was born a couple of centuries too late. I wanted to be a poet. I think that was lucrative once."

Helen shook her head. "Only sort of. Back then, you lived in a hut, crapped in a bucket, and the pay was in eggs and chickens, maybe a goat. Now? Unless you're the sort of poet who writes lyrics for hit songs about buxom chicks in bikinis, forget it."

Molly sighed. "Very well. I'll tackle Whelan. When the cops haul me away, my crime will be that I believed I could make a better world."

"To a better world!" Helen toasted. "Until that happy day, stay drunk! Maybe poetry will make a comeback after the apocalypse."

The women clinked glasses and finished the rest of their drinks in one gulp. Empty, both moved to get refills.

"This sherry is terrible," Helen said, "but the aspect of its flavor which I find most charming is that it is free."

"That wasn't a perk listed in my contract," Molly replied.

Helen, quite tipsy and failing to hide it, giggled. "I'm good at math. I should have been a banker. Instead of counting money, I'm badgering students to clean test tubes."

"When I applied here, Richard told me I was the top pickle in Greenbriar's pickle barrel," Molly said.

"He tells everyone that."

"That's deflating, but I should have known. No wonder Richard's nickname is Dick."

Helen watched Molly over her refilled glass. "I think you're the only one who calls him that. Look, I'm not up for a rumpus. Just keep your head down, teach the little ingrates and know-it-alls, and hope for the best. Don't make waves with Richard. He could capsize your boat."

Molly shook her head. "I'll fight for us both, but I'll keep your name out of it."

The dean suddenly appeared at Helen's elbow. "Fight for what now?"

"The climate emergency," Helen blurted. "We're against kids dying in floods, at least in principle. I'm flexible on this point, of course."

"Bold choice." Whelan gave an appreciative laugh, but it sounded hollow. His lifeless eyes looked like two black buttons. The dean took his time looking up and down her body.

Molly looked away. The argument between Barnes and Collins had devolved further. The professors were repeating themselves, but louder.

"Flooding's bad, but" — Molly gestured toward the men — "we're still for the extinction of the dinosaurs."

Helen quickly turned back to the bottles on the table for another refill.

"How's the sherry, Molly?" Richard asked.

Pretentious, Molly thought. *This isn't Oxford.*

He caught her look. "If it's not to your liking, there are other choices at the bar. I brewed the beer myself. It's the soda pop of beers, or should I say the beer of soda pops?"

"Actually, I was wondering if you had more news about the budget for next semester. I hear it's been decided for weeks, but no one has told me anything official."

She'd said, "No one," but it was the dean who had shirked his duty.

"Our budgetary priorities are being reevaluated, true. Don't worry about that for now."

"But I am worried, Richard. It's a small community. I'm hearing the phrase 'last hired, first fired,' so it feels like there's a target on my back. If so, I'd like to know ahead of time."

He grinned and made a helpless gesture. "The committee and I have concerns. There will be some fallout as we work toward our targets."

Molly looked at him coldly. "There is a target on my back and you're the sniper. Given recent events, I feel like you're stringing me along."

"Our budget cuts are a secondary concern in your case, Molly."

"What I said in the cafeteria?"

"Let's not get dramatic here — "

"I corrected a student. Meanwhile, you're messing with my life. I think I will be a little dramatic about it."

Whelan's empty smile did not fade. "I've always sensed anger in you, Molly."

"You do inspire me, Richard."

The dean made her miss who she'd been in Poeticule Bay, the

kind of person who did not endure injustice, the kind of woman who would not tolerate disrespect.

Remember who you are, and the nice person you're pretending to be, she thought.

Her life would have been easier had the vindictive part of her followed her father's fall into the dead zone. She'd resolved to be better, to be kinder. Mostly, she'd stuck to that resolution.

Sometimes, though, upon reading a news report or spotting a social media post that inspired her nastier nature, Molly would stride to a mirror. With her face inches from its surface, she'd stare into her eyes and say sternly, "Don't. Do not! Do not risk it again."

The aching need remained. Molly understood hunger. Had Richard Whelan understood who he was dealing with, he, too, would strive to be kinder.

51

EXFILTRATION

The dean gripped Molly by one elbow and steered her away from the milling crowd. Once they were alone in a hallway, any trace of his chummy facade dropped. "You are right to be concerned about your employment status. Frankly, I'm surprised if you're surprised. Perhaps you're not as smart as I thought."

"I'm not stupid. This is about sanity and fairness. I'm hoping cooler heads will prevail."

He gave a derisive laugh. "Reality is a bitter pill. I did warn you this was a short-term contract."

"No, you said you'd fight to turn it into something much more. Your exact words were, 'I'll make sure you have a home at Greenbriar.'"

"No home is forever, Molly. You're a big girl — "

"*Woman*," she corrected. "I'm a woman, and you're pissing me off — "

He spoke over her. "Your naivete charmed me at first. I was prepared to write you a recommendation letter. I see now you're not a good fit for Greenbriar. Maybe you'd do better as a guard in a women's prison."

"Right now, it feels like I'm in a women's prison."

Whelan ignored that and continued, "I was desperate to fill the position, but circumstances have changed. With the new board coming in the fall, we are rearranging our priorities for our machine."

"I'm such a new cog. I can't possibly be rusty already."

"Not rusty," he replied evenly, "but too squeaky by half. To my way of thinking, you're simply not Greenbriar caliber. I wouldn't be doing you a favor by keeping you on."

"You're worried about doing me favors now?"

"I'm pushing you on to find your mission. I only want oiled cogs in my machine. Your niche must be elsewhere. To be honest, very soon, I plan to send you packing back where you came from."

I don't want to go back to Poeticule Bay, she thought. *Home is where the ghosts live.*

Unless she hid in her room and barred the window, the view from home would always be the Drifting Cliffs, the dead zone, and her father's face.

Molly felt sudden heat in her cheeks and hated that she was showing him the depth of her anger involuntarily. How great it would be not to need him, not to need anyone.

"When did you decide you'd made a mistake hiring me?" A pleading, wheedling tone had crept into her tone, and she hated herself for it. Still, she carried on, "I'm curious. How quick you were to go back on your word? I've made a difference here. I've taught these kids critical thinking. I've got them making arguments instead of simply making assertions. If you look at my class evaluations, the students love me — "

"Your students may enjoy you, but you were truculent and disrespectful to your peers out of the gate. Your students don't have the power to hire and fire. I do."

And I don't flirt with you, she thought. *I don't smile and nod.* Part of her wished she had or at least been smarter and more strategic.

"In your next position, perhaps you'll give more thought to where the power lies."

"Power lies. That sounds right."

When he hired her, Richard had spewed a lot of gas about valuing her input as an educator. One misstep was all it took to piss off the dean. Worse, it was only words. She hadn't really done anything, had not acted on her baser instincts. Still, a joke and a few words of warning to a creepy student were enough to get her in deep trouble.

Texas, she thought. *That's what started my fall. For a guy who thinks he's so strong, Whelan sure can't take a joke.*

Her spiral had really begun at a welcome party very similar to this one. The previous September, she'd been new to Greenbriar's faculty. A political science professor had argued with a visiting Russian historian, and she'd made the mistake of chiming in.

The history prof suggested that if Russia genuinely wanted a return to the past in which they owned an empire, "Why not go further back to when the Mongols owned everything? Why not go further back and let those with ancestors among the Huns run Russia?"

The political science prof rolled his eyes impatiently. "I am no apologist for the Russian government — "

The historian put up a palm as if he were a cop at a traffic stop. "Don't say but! Don't even finish that sentence!"

Molly, who'd been watching the exchange, blurted a laugh which drew an annoyed glance from the poly sci prof.

"I was about to say," the prof continued, "I'd be more sympathetic to Ukraine, but there's the problem of Nazis in the their army. That drains all moral superiority from their cause."

"All this talk of Nazis in Ukraine," the historian replied. "After the war, the Ukrainians can have their democracy and proceed with denazification. That's all a red herring, anyway. There are probably just as many Nazis in Texas as there are in Ukraine."

Molly added, "So you're saying, to get rid of our Nazis, we should bring democracy to Texas? When do we invade?"

The historian chuckled, but his smile dutifully faded when the dean spoke up. "That's quite enough slander of my home state, Dr. Jergins! I'm from Houston!" Whelan had glared at Molly as if she were a particularly monstrous insect.

That's all it took to doom her budding career at Greenbriar. The dean was so fragile, Molly's mind turned to ways of breaking him. How delicious that would be.

But she'd stopped herself from acting on such fantasies. She'd been good. She'd occupied herself with books and exercise. Keeping her mind on distractions instead of violent plots on people who richly deserved comeuppance required discipline.

I'm a good person now, she thought. *I haven't acted on those impulses in years.*

To honor her father's sacrifice, she'd held back. But all restrictive diets fail, and redemption would always elude her.

And now, only a few months later, the dean stared at her with that same look of disdain. Molly downed what was left of her drink and handed him the glass. Molly wished she'd put off the inevitable and stayed quiet and drunk with Helen.

"I doubt that pursuing this conversation further can lead anywhere constructive," Whelan said. "Be mad if you must. I am not responsible for your poor vocational choices. Haven't you heard? English is a dead language. Literature is all nasty comments sections and emojis now. Try to keep up."

"Goodnight, Dick!"

"*Richard,* you mean."

"I said what I said, you dick!"

52

FRICTION

The following week, Molly sat before Greenbriar's disciplinary committee. Five men and two women stared at her glumly as Richard Whelan put her on trial. "I called this hearing because we have something serious to discuss with you, Dr. Jergins."

"The last time I thought we were having a serious discussion, you hired me. I have since lost faith in your gravitas."

"No one ever taught you how to speak to your superiors, did they? Or to anyone else, from what I've heard. It's almost as if you have zero sense of self-preservation. Introversion is no excuse to act like an asshole, you know."

"Nor should extroversion be," Molly countered. "I've played nice for a long time, and now I see where it's gotten me: here, with you."

His head snapped up. "What did you say to me?" It wasn't really a question. It was a dare.

Molly took a deep breath and let it out slowly. *Don't say it,* she thought. *But I've already lost the job, so why not? He heard me. This is a test to see if I'll be cowed.*

"I will not be cowed. I don't moo," she said.

"What?"

"Cowed? Cow? Moo? Get it? Wordplay?"

With the exception of the dean, the committee members smiled or chuckled.

That encouraged Molly. "When you say 'superiors,' it's clear you really mean 'betters.' You're definitely not that."

Several of the disciplinary board members looked to each other, smirked, but remained mute.

"Do you not recognize the authority of this committee?" the dean asked.

"Depends on how many vote with you. Do you know what all those sycophants at your parties call you behind your back? The Mad King."

She took a moment to look each committee member in the eyes. "Not sure how many of our colleagues here share that opinion."

Richard looked to his fellow board members and tried to make a joke of Molly's challenge. "As long as they call me king and bow their heads as I pass." He smiled wider but communicated no warmth. "If nothing else, it seems you need an education about how the real world works."

She threw him a glare. "I've heard that before. When someone talks down to others about how the so-called real world works, I have to wonder. What other world you think we come from? You're using condescending language in a transparent attempt to control me. Stop. When it comes to manipulating bullies with words, I'm better at it than you. After all, that's why I'm sitting here right now, isn't it? I gave a bullying student a verbal smackdown, a bully you proved yourself impotent to control."

Whelan winced and Molly grinned. "Sorry if I made you especially uncomfortable with my use of the word *impotent*."

Every woman on the committee smiled.

Whelan flushed a bright red. "Molly, such truculence — "

"Oh, this isn't truculence. I'm just warming up! So far, this is petulance. Are you sure you want to keep going? You won't like it."

The dean straightened his tie, taking a beat to regain his composure. "I'm very concerned with the level of respect you accord our faculty and students."

"Where I come from, what I've done suggests I have character. You calling this meeting suggests something else."

Whelan took a deep breath and let it hiss out through his teeth. "The tragedy is you actually could have been a minor asset to the English department. However, your words and actions ensure I can't save you."

Gilda Milner cleared her throat. As she leaned forward, her long gray curls spilled over half her face. Her manicured nails were immaculate French tips. That detail was somewhat incongruous with the rest of her persona. Milner's shapeless black frock made her look like she'd be at home teaching magical botany at a wizard school. The old woman's eyes, however, shone with intelligence and warmth.

"Dean Whelan? If I may? Perhaps before we build a gallows, we should hear the specifics of the complaint you've brought against Dr. Jergins? You are the chair, but the disciplinary committee does not speak with only one voice, at least until we've rendered judgment. Let's not speed the proceedings willy nilly. Besides, Dr. Jergins seems to be enjoying herself. She might adopt a more respectful tone if she thought you were keeping an open mind."

Molly shot the woman a grateful smile. Richard Whelan was determined to get rid of her, but Milner knew the man from long experience.

The old woman eyed the other members of the committee. "I'm sure we'd *all* be interested to hear Dr. Jergins' account or perhaps provide more context for this situation."

"What context would exonerate her? She did it!" Whelan decreed. "I know because I had to deal with the parents, both of whom are alumni and contributors — "

Milner interrupted him. "Dr. Jergins? If you please? The dean seems certain but elucidate the conflict for the rest of us."

53

ELUCIDATION

Molly plunged in. "A second-year was making predatory remarks about girls in the cafeteria."

"Tanner Renault!" the dean interjected. "The name of the student she threatened was Tanner Renault."

"Uh-huh, the offender. I was at the next table when he started in. 'Fresh meat,' he called the freshmen girls, along with several more offensive remarks."

"None of the girls made a formal complaint," Whelan put in. "And you didn't lodge a complaint against young Tanner, either."

"Such remarks would be against Greenbriar's code of conduct," Milner said stiffly. "Please continue, Dr. Jergins."

Molly didn't tell them all of it, of course. She didn't reveal to the committee what she'd whispered in Tanner's ear. She'd said several things only the kid could hear.

Molly addressed the committee. "You know what I loved about my father? My dad was a protector. He made me want to be like him. He was a friend, too, but possibly the best thing about my dad was that people who were different from him didn't bother him. He didn't judge people for what they were or how much they could do for him. He did what I'm doing now. He judged bad people by the things they did. I said some things to young Tanner to get him to stop being an asshole."

Had it ended there, she might not have been sitting before the disciplinary committee. However, once Molly had whispered a plot in Tanner's ear, she saw the looks on the faces of his target that day. That's when Molly had got up from her chair. She had raised her voice to make sure she had the attention of the entire cafeteria.

Molly knew from experience, bullies hate to be mocked, especially for all to see. "When I was done with him, the girls were laughing at him. Everyone did. I suppose they felt no need to make a formal complaint after the scolding and the scalding."

"Scalding?" Milner looked worried.

"I speak metaphorically, Professor, of course," Molly assured her.

"Of course." But Milner appeared unsure.

"I teach English, so I used fiction to burn him with words."

"I see," Milner said in that vague way people use when they don't understand at all.

"I had to tame the animal in him, go around the frontal lobe to hit him where he lives, torch his lizard brain. Like a good girl, I used my words instead of slapping the shit out of him."

Milner laughed. "I've taught for many years. To be perfectly honest, there have been a few students with whom I wish I'd had a whip and a chair handy. Or, in my younger days, my field hockey stick."

"I enjoy your honesty, Professor Milner," Molly said, glad to see someone on the disciplinary committee seemed sympathetic. "It is irrational to expect an irrational person to be rational. We can, however, curb their noxious behavior."

"Ah! I like that!" Milner enthused.

Whelan did not — would not — understand. He couldn't even conceal his irritation. He raised his voice. "Get back to the point! The code of conduct applies to *faculty* as well as students. You threatened a student! What happens when you encounter another difficult student? Will you burn them in effigy in the quad as an example to the others?"

"I take on bullies on a case-by-case basis," Molly said. She'd tried to sound light in that moment but failed. Surveying the group, the line of faces looked dour. Whelan was against her, of course. Only Milner seemed to lend a sympathetic ear.

"It would have been well if the students defended themselves from the drunk horny baboon," Molly added. "I don't blame them for staying quiet, though. They were no doubt scared or in shock at the vile things Renault said. My main concern was the young lady to whom he was particularly vile. All she did was exist. She was just trying to have a meal undisturbed. She'd said nothing to him, but he spoke loudly, embarrassing her, shaming her for her body."

"He called her fat," Whelan said dismissively. "*I'm* fat. So what?"

"You are fat, sir, but your estimation of the situation in the cafeteria that day is less than accurate. Tanner Renault called his target a heifer. He compared her to a moose, a whale, and a pig. He made oinking sounds at the poor girl."

At this, several of the committee members looked ashen. The dean looked amused. Milner caught the dean's expression and muttered, "Ball bag."

Molly wasn't sure if the old prof's comment was aimed at Tanner Renault or Richard Whelan.

The dean threw up his hands. "The crux, which is not in dispute, is that you decided to defend the fat girl with physical threats — "

"Kelsey! The victim's name is Kelsey Chang. You seem very concerned for the offender without a thought of the young woman he bullied. She's a nice kid, wants to be a lawyer someday."

"How ironic!" Whelan scoffed. "If she fulfills her ambitions, you may need her services in the future. You threatened Tanner instead of reporting him for a proper disciplinary hearing. That's the long and short of it." His head swiveled left and right to the members of the committee. "Why are we still talking?"

Before he could call for a vote on Molly's future — her life — Milner intervened again. "Bureaucracy takes time, but let's not lose sight of the bullied. The young ladies of Greenbriar, their value and their sense of humanity is worth our time. It's what we do here, correct?"

The dean pointed at Molly. "The English department can do without an instructor like that! She admits she threatened Tanner."

Molly rocked her head back and forth slightly as she weighed the word 'threatened.' At last, she said, "I had words with him."

"What words precisely?" Milner probed.

"I asked if he'd been drinking. He admitted he had been up drinking beer all night."

"Hardly surprising," Whelan said. "Things get a little wild. He was a drunk college student. What was your excuse? Were *you* chemically impaired?"

"No, but I reject the premise. I didn't need an excuse to intervene in a situation where one student was attacking another. Anyway, Tanner said he liked beer. He needed to be squashed like a gnat, so I told him about my favorite cocktail."

That's it, Molly thought. *I've said too much. We're really going to get into it before they show me the door.*

54

FICTION

Professor Milner gave Molly a quizzical look. "Pardon me? Your favorite cocktail, did you say? I don't understand."

"I told him I enjoyed an Irish slammer from time to time. That's the new name. It's not politically correct now, but the drink used to be called an Irish car bomb. Then I asked him — casually — if he owned a car on campus."

Several on the committee allowed a small smile. Whelan scowled. Gilda Milner grinned broadly, clearly amused. She reminded Molly of a dotty old neighbor she'd loved so much as a child, an aunt who wasn't really an aunt.

"Did you think you were being subtle with your threats?" the dean asked.

"Tanner is too stupid to appreciate the subtle approach. Anyway, I'm an educator, so I gave him a short history lesson about the suffragettes. In 1908, the length of hatpins was regulated so they would be less effective as weapons against men who groped them on the street. Before then, sticking mashers with long hatpins was a common defense."

Whelan wiped his brow dramatically. "Tanner's parents shit kittens over that remark."

"Considering that Tanner should face expulsion, I'm surprised he couldn't keep his mouth shut about our interaction. I suggested that he pretend to be mute from now on, but perhaps I was too nuanced for him to understand the hint."

"Was that the end of it, Dr. Jergins?" Milner asked.

"My factoid about hatpins naturally led to a concise lecture on a tragic bit of medical history. I suggested that, theoretically, a knitting needle could be used in place of a hatpin to perform a lobotomy. I explained to Mr. Renault in some detail the effects of a lobotomy — you know, because I'm helpful. Then, apropos of nothing, I asked Kelsey if she knitted."

Milner laughed out loud. Though some of the committee tried to remain stoic, the rest followed Milner's lead and let out a chuckle.

Molly shot them a serious look. "Please don't lose sight of Tanner Renault's target. Kelsey Chang was holding back tears, not very successfully. She'd been humiliated. I acted on impulse in real time, immediately. Perhaps I could have been more diplomatic. On the other hand, to Kelsey's credit, when I was done, she burst out laughing."

"Like we did just now," Milner added.

"A lot of students laughed, but that's not remotely the point," Whelan said. "Tanner did not laugh. The entire cafeteria laughed at the boy, right? I thought laughing at people was bad, according to you."

Before Molly could answer, Milner put up a hand. "The boy was the aggressor. Let's not get mired in false equivalencies."

"Even when the proposed weapons are hatpins and knitting needles?"

"I don't knit," Molly said. "And words were my weapons. Ridicule can be a fast and effective weapon against bullies. I never thought there would be a need to progress to actual hat pins and knitting needles."

"So, one could say, it was more of a pointed joke," Milner suggested.

Whelan was so flushed, his ears were pink. Molly predicted a stroke lay in his near future if he didn't get his blood pressure under control. "You, the adult and faculty member on the spot, don't see that you bullied the boy?"

Molly remained defiant. "With all the respect you are due, Tanner's not a boy. He's a man of age to go to war. He's no innocent child. I was not the bully in this situation. I was the defender. If Kelsey were your daughter, would we be having this conversation? Would I be at risk of getting fired, or on the tenure track?"

Whelan slumped in his chair. "I guess it's fortunate for you that he refused to make an *official* complaint."

"That was our agreement. As long as he kept his thoughts to himself, he was safe from me bringing him to you for further disciplinary action. Then he blabbed to his parents, they called you, so here we are, anyway. I swear, I try to control my temper. I try so hard to be g— " Molly caught herself, slowed down, and cleared her throat. "I try to be patient."

I've been patient, for years, she thought.

Whelan had said something more, but Molly had lost his useless words to her tormented thoughts. "Pardon?"

"I said, you try to be patient, but? But what?"

"Some people wind me up. People like you who make excuses for … " Molly looked to Professor Milner. "People who make excuses for ball bags."

Milner smiled and addressed the dean as if Molly were not in the room. "Dean Whelan, you said something earlier that confused me. Mr. Renault still has not made an official complaint against Dr. Jergins?"

"He was coerced not to."

"Mm-hm, but he did complain to his parents?"

Whelan nodded. "I had to spend a half hour on the phone talking them down from legal action!"

"And you were successful? The parents were sufficiently mollified?"

Whelan straightened with pride. "I was successful and the

parents are calm. They said they will have a talk with their son, as well."

Milner let out a long sigh. "I know your time is valuable, Richard. You spent a half hour on this issue. Is not our time also valuable? I've got papers to mark."

Before Whelan could answer, Milner pressed him. "Regarding this girl, Kelsey, who plans to be a lawyer. She has no apparent plans to sue the boy for harassment? And no plans to sue Greenbriar for failing to provide a safe learning environment?"

The dean looked down at the tabletop, as if consulting his notes. "Um ... no, not to my knowledge."

Milner brightened. "Well, let's go have some tea while we get the vote out of the way. This afternoon won't be a total waste. I have new pictures of my grandchildren to show everyone."

The dean scowled at the old woman. "Professor Milner, you are awfully sanguine about these violent threats to students. Why is that?"

Milner rolled her eyes. "Oh, c'mon! These threats were of the idle variety, surely. I've looked at the online reviews. Dr. Jergins is, by all accounts, a sweet person, caring and kind."

"To those she deems deserve it, I suppose."

"Richard," Milner said, "you seem desperate to defend this young man. Why is that?"

"It's my job."

"Your pearl-clutching seems very selective," Milner replied. "Dr. Jergins gets higher ratings with her students than I do mine! Can we put this teapot tempest to rest, please?"

Whelan did not look at Molly as he gathered his papers to leave. Milner gave her a wink as the committee filed out of the room. "Thank you for your service."

The old woman tittered as she left, shaking her head and muttering, "Ball bag! *Hee-hee!* Delightful!"

Over the dean's objections, the disciplinary committee voted by a slim majority to take no serious disciplinary action. Molly received the mildest of reprimands for her personnel file, but no suspension of pay or job loss.

Molly found it ironic that she'd come closer to punishment in academia than she ever had with law enforcement back home.

She'd slipped again, but Molly was confident Tanner Renault would curb his worst impulses around female classmates. He hadn't told anyone what else she'd whispered before she raised her voice to get everyone's attention in the cafeteria.

Renault would play nice around Greenbriar girls from now on, she was sure. Molly was so confident because of their secret conversation, the notions she whispered to him. What Renault was too scared to divulge would have gotten her fired immediately.

55

FACTION

Targeting cars was safer and easier than home invasions and physical confrontations. That's why vehicles were her first choice when dealing with bullies. However, Molly thought her secret conversation with Tanner Renault was some of her best use of words as weapons.

A casual observer might guess they were lovers; she in her early thirties, he a young college student. Such an observer might have made that mistake unless they saw the haunted look on the harasser's face.

"Sh! Sh! Listen a moment," she'd told him. "Do you have strong teeth?"

Her target looked at her, mystified by the question. "Yeah?"

"I bet I could make you eat a lot of cherries." Their heads just inches apart, Tanner had stared at her in a woozy trance. Mesmerized, he sensed her commitment to doing whatever it took to correct his bad behavior.

He looks as if he's falling, Molly thought. *Silent and helpless to gravity. And he knows it. I own him.*

"I'd make you eat copious amounts of cherries, crunching down, pits and all," she whispered.

"Yeah? So?" he replied dully.

"Cherry pits are usually only a danger to dogs, but you're a very bad dog. With enough time and patience, it would work with a human."

He shook his head. "I don't get you."

"The pits are full of prussic acid, also known as cyanide. Cyanide is an ugly way to die. Well, ugly for you, beautiful for me to watch. Most murders are brutal, but they can be clever. You're a piece of shit, but I bet I could transform your death into a piece of art."

Tanner's big Adam's apple bobbled up and down as his alcohol-soaked brain struggled to process her words. It was a funny thing. Since Molly whispered to him, he whispered back. "Why would I eat all those cherries like that?"

"Because if you refused, I'd peel your carrot, make it a baby carrot."

His eyes widened in fear, but Molly wasn't done. "There are other persuasive tactics. The IRA used to kneecap their enemies. That was the Irish trademark. Later they just shot into the soft tissue, you know, for better public relations."

"You're crazy, aren't you?"

"Crazy and deadly serious. That's the point, moron. No one will believe you, so just shut your mouth and listen."

The girls watched her whisper in his ear. Curious and talking among themselves animatedly, the women around Kelsey Chang grew even more agitated.

Furious and tearful, Kelsey got up to leave. Molly shot her a look and gestured for her to sit. "Wait," she commanded. "You won't want to miss this. We'll get to you in a second."

She turned back to the bully. "Another alternative is to force feed you castor oil. If I decided to let you live, it's just the worst case of diarrhea. Mix it with gasoline, it's much worse than that."

Tanner Renault turned white. "What? You're nuts! How ...?"

"Shut up, stupid. I'm educating you. My major was English Lit, but my minor was history. History is full of assholes like you, bashing at each other across the years. The future is assholes like me, open to using the tools of the past. History is a sadist's delight. Trust me, I would know."

Tanner raised his voice for the first time. "Okay, okay! Sorry! I was just teasing. I didn't mean anything! It was a joke!"

She reached for his hand and squeezed hard to quiet him. He winced and began to pull away. She held him fast.

"If you don't cooperate and keep your voice low, I'll make this so much worse for you. Do you believe me?"

He gave a slow nod.

"You think you're funny, huh? I'm not joking. Here's what's going to happen. You'll apologize, but before you do, I will embarrass you in front of everyone. You're going to sit there and take it. *Then* you're going to apologize to your fellow students for your behavior."

She squeezed his hand until her knuckles went white. "Understand?"

Renault nodded, faster this time.

"Whatever I say, know that it's a much better alternative than me coming through your window some night with a Sig Sauer P226, ropes, a carrot scraper, and big bags of cherries."

Was the threat real or fiction? Tanner Renault had no idea. In that moment, she looked like she meant every word. Molly certainly *seemed* eager.

He did not know that Molly was not the owner of a Sig Sauer pistol. However, when intimidating a target, she thought it best to speak in specifics.

She whispered, "There are people who deserve to die, Tanner. Ask yourself, are you one of them?"

He shook his head. "For fat shaming a girl?"

Molly's eyes sparkled with malice. "I was speaking more generally."

Renault's mouth went dry. His bottom lip quivered, unsure how to respond and afraid to provoke her. Finally, he managed, "Y-you're crazy!"

"Careful with the name-calling. That's how you got my attention in the first place. I'm a popular teacher of English," she whispered.

"But sometimes — just sometimes when I burst out of the dark — I'm a monster made of teeth."

To her credit, in that moment, Molly thought she was lying, just spinning a tale to curb yet another bully. She thought she had her nature under control, but she still had much more to learn.

Molly let go of his hand. "What I've said to you privately will stay between us. Now, I'm going to say a few things for all to hear. You're going to keep your mouth shut. If I take you to a disciplinary committee, you're out. What I'm about to do will sound mean, but it's the better option for you. Then you'll apologize and make sure you look like you mean it. That's very important, right?"

Delight washed over Molly when Renault agreed to her terms.

She had played out many vendettas in her mind, more so lately. With the talk of budget cuts at Greenbriar, her preoccupation had again become a daily obsession.

The plots she envisioned were vivid and detailed. Molly imagined herself showing up at four in the morning to surprise some deserving monster. She reviewed what more she could have done — or should have done — to Lloyd and Keith Faun. Richard Whelan needed some minor punishment, too. (He was a dick, but he was no Lloyd Faun.)

Molly had many fantasy targets. She made lists of the deserving in a notebook. She sorted the names of her targets, their offence, and what might be their appropriate punishment.

Nasty people on the internet needed a little reality check — something proportionate, yet adequate to make them reconsider all their life choices.

She considered learning more about hacking computers. Anonymity often made assholes on the internet feel safe. Learning about cyber security, she thought it would be useful to know more about how to rip away that anonymity.

Then there were the stalkers, the users, and the abusers of the world. Various terrorists and evil-doers deserved more violent ends.

Spinning various scenarios, Molly came up with things she could say to the deserving. She made notes in the margins of her notebook.

The chuckles about her escapades were only for her, but those fantasies soothed her.

She wouldn't simply declare, "I'm here to kill you." That would be too obvious, lacking elegance. Instead, Molly would say, "I'm here to reduce your carbon footprint permanently." She might say, "I'm an avenging angel, and you're the sort of moron who thinks Hollywood should remake *The Princess Bride!*"

In darker moments, she considered the line, "I want you to meet my father."

Occasionally, as she practiced her lines, self-assured and looking cool, she caught herself in the mirror. Sometimes she saw her father.

Dad meant well, she thought, *it just didn't work out right.*

Other times, she saw Keith Faun in her reflection.

But I'm not Keith, she told herself. *I'm sure. Almost sure.*

Practiced or not, real or not, she'd convinced Renault of her utter sincerity. Molly didn't think she was evil, at least, not yet.

Some well-chosen words were how Kelsey Chang got her apology. Tanner had given up the minor details to his parents but had divulged nothing about her threats of grisly torture and ugly death.

In the end, her triumphant success did not matter. Despite all her machinations, Dr. Molly Jergins lost her job at Greenbriar College.

The reprieve, largely thanks to Professor Milner's intervention, allowed her to continue to teach until the end of the semester. Whelan couldn't get rid of her using the disciplinary committee, so he used Greenbriar's budget against her instead.

Molly had so loved teaching literature. She'd had great moments with her classes discussing Tolkien's lore and Shakespeare's inventive use of language. She'd championed Ernest Hemingway's short stories while casting aspersions on his longer prose. In writing workshops, she engaged her students in earnest discussions about whether artists needed a touch of madness and talent, or was discipline and luck more important?

The life of the mind had been so stimulating, far from the red tides and black waters of the dead zone. Isolated from conflict behind ivy-covered walls and running from her past, Molly had thought herself safe at Greenbriar.

She'd long known conflict was her trigger. Molly thought she and everyone else would be safe if she simply stayed away from bullies. But she'd failed to learn a lesson from Shakespeare, a favorite line from *The Tempest* she'd taught her students: "Hell is empty and all the devils are here."

Conflict can be found everywhere, so no matter how deep Molly buried them, her urges would always rise to the surface. *Can't run from the devil,* she thought, *not when the devil's in you.*

56

REINVENTION

Molly was clearing out her tiny office when Richard Whelan came by to gloat. "Just wanted to say goodbye, Molly. How are you doing?"

"How you'd expect."

"Good."

"Tell me, do you value what we do at all? Or is it just about using your position to push us around? Or lech on students and faculty?"

Whelan stepped into the office and closed the door behind him. Molly stepped behind her desk, feeling wary.

"You think you know me? Let me tell you a little about you," the dean said. "You take illiterate children to semi-literate. The next generation of Americans needs real skills. Our students *already* speak English, so you're quite redundant. Artificial Intelligence will write the next century's sonnets. Humans will carry heavy things and install the pipes and grommets."

"When I first met you, you called yourself a guardian of education," Molly replied. "I guess that's true in the same way that buffalo wings come from buffaloes."

"Good luck in your future endeavors. You'll get no recommendation from me."

"I didn't ask. Before I go, I wanted to share a theory. I think people who go around crushing innocent people's spirits haven't known enough fear. If they had a few more worries, they'd be more careful around strangers."

"Uh-huh. Well, you're packing up. I'm playing golf this afternoon. By the fifth hole, I hope to forget your name."

"Do you ever wonder if any of your golf buddies really like you? Are they just sucking up and letting you win? How many women on the faculty feel they have to tolerate your creepiness and grab-assing to get ahead?"

Whelan was about to leave when she added in a low voice, "I've been to your house."

He stopped. "So?"

"The dean's residence is a fine old Victorian design. I noticed your staircase is long and steep. Have you ever watched movies where an intruder breaks into a house at night? They turn on the TV to lure the homeowner downstairs. That wouldn't work, though. I've given this some thought."

"Are you going to threaten me like you threatened that kid in the cafeteria?"

Molly continued smoothly, "If I were to turn on your television at, say, three in the morning, you'd hear voices. You might not rush downstairs to investigate. You'd go straight to your phone to call the campus police."

"Where are you going with this?"

"Your office is in the dean's residence. People come in and out of there all the time, and the front door is always unlocked throughout the day. If I took advantage of that unlocked door and waited until the wee hours — "

"Stop!" Whelan demanded.

"I'd set off the smoke detector in the kitchen," Molly continued. "That would get you up and running, wouldn't it? That would work. Groggy from a deep sleep, you wake up in sudden fear that you must have left the stove on, and the fire is spreading. The question you have to ask yourself is, do I tie the tripwire at the top of your staircase? Would I secure it closer to the bottom? Depends on how much I hate you, doesn't it? You're a little dung beetle, but I could give you wings. I could make you fly!"

Whelan's mouth hung open a moment before he found the words to try to reassert his authority. "If you aren't out by noon, I'll have the custodians come in to throw your belongings to the curb."

Molly ignored him. "But about that wire placement? What do you think? A fishing line stretched across the bottom of the banister would do. Up top, you snap your neck. Closer to the bottom step, maybe you break an arm or get a concussion. Look in my eyes, Dick. How angry am I?"

Searching for words and finding none, he stared back.

"You *will* remember my name, Dick. You'll be worrying about that staircase as long as you live in that house. The tripwire would be easy to set up anytime, and not just by me."

Sweat beaded on the dean's forehead.

"I think about this sort of thing a lot. Now, you will, too. In the meantime, stop being such a colossal asshole and start treating the students and faculty with more respect. It's not just me thinking these sorts of thoughts. Maybe I've shared this idea with the people you've most offended and preyed upon. You think I'm the only one who hates your guts?"

His eyes widened in fear. She had scored a direct hit. He believed her every word.

"The way you talk makes people feel like they don't matter," Molly said. "You talk more than you listen. Listen to this: I'm a human being. I *matter*."

Whelan finally recovered. "Not here you don't, not anymore. You really missed out on an opportunity at Greenbriar. You'll be gone today and here I am, waving goodbye. When I retire, they'll put up a portrait in my honor in the Convocation Hall. What will you do? Go back to nowhere? I predict I'll be golfing and vacationing somewhere with palm trees while you're still scrambling to make a living out of two or three jobs."

He brightened suddenly. "What do you call a wage slave trapped in the gig economy? You know what that makes you? You're a gigger!"

Without thought or hesitation, Molly strode up to the dean and slapped him across the face, hard and fast. The office was so small, the sound of the loud smack rang off the walls.

"If you call me a gigger, I wonder what you call Helen when you're in the company of others like you? We know your condescending little jokes, the way you treat female staff. Drop that shit, man. Seriously, if Greenbriar's Human Resources department was more than just you, you'd already be out in the cold. You'd lose your job, just like me. It's almost funny that you're on your way out, and you're too blind and arrogant to see it."

Whelan was still reeling in shock from the slap. "I don't — uh ..."

"We see the racism in your eyes, the misogyny oozing out of your stupid mouth. The faculty is sick of it. Don't count on a plaque or a portrait. Guys like you are not bound for the love of a grateful nation. There will be no shrine to your supposed greatness. You're already hated and you don't even know it."

Whelan backed toward the door. He wanted the last word, but the sting of Molly's slap had temporarily wiped his mind.

Speaking slowly, Molly warned in a low voice, "*Run*. If you stay, you are in danger."

Struggling to retain his dignity, he squeaked, "Why do you say such things? You are not normal."

"You're too normal," she shot back. "That's the problem. *You* are the problem."

Molly's smile faltered, and despite herself, her eyes teared. "You don't understand the Newtonian physics of social interaction. You push me, I push back. You're not used to dealing with someone more vicious than you."

He swayed back and forth, shifting his weight anxiously. "Like I said, good luck in your future endeavors, hopefully far from here. Goodbye, Dr. Jergins."

For more than a decade, Molly really only used words as

weapons. She'd never hit anyone before. It wasn't much consolation for losing her job but slapping him had felt good. Great, even.

The euphoria faded quickly. As she packed up her books, the prospect of returning home loomed. When she moved away from home, she'd managed to focus on the future. Stepping into the past frightened her.

Back in Poeticule Bay, history was inescapable. There, ghosts and monsters waited.

57

CONTENTION

After twelve years, Molly was back in her childhood bedroom. Her first days back, she'd been filled with nostalgia for the good times. She had to search for them, but those memories were there.

Despite the blistering cold February weather, she had ventured out. Poeticule Bay had surprised her with how it had changed for the better. The fishery was coming back. The dead zone was alive with cod, lobster, and haddock again.

It was the curious stares of the townspeople that drove her back to her house. Molly had escaped her small town, worked hard, and failed. She told herself it was her imagination, but that didn't stop her from feeling all eyes were upon her.

Depressed, she'd spent many hours retreating into sleep. Her eyes were still closed against the invading dawn, but she couldn't hide out anymore. Straining to detect some sound, the house was quiet.

I have an eidetic memory for every pornographic image I've ever seen, every minor slight, and each insult, but it's time to get going again. Restart the engine!

It was only Molly's eighth day back home. Cataloguing her life, she calculated that this was the forty-second worst day of her existence.

Begrudgingly, she opened her eyes to stare at the cracked ceiling. Molly contemplated her mother's condition. Kay Jergins had recently returned from another stay at the hospital in Orono. Molly suspected it was a recurrence of cancer, but her mother stubbornly refused to discuss her ailments.

Kay had had a rough night, having to get up several times. She was superstitious in a strange way. To acknowledge disease was to open the door to capital-D Doom. To discuss her diagnosis would accelerate the ravaging. She would only talk about her problems with her doctor.

Perhaps it was not superstition, but pride. When Molly's uncle was sure Kay could not overhear him, Vincent confided, "Your mother feels weak. To a woman like Kay, weakness is unacceptable. Right or wrong, she's ashamed."

"Ashamed of being human?"

Vincent smiled. "Of not being immortal and all-powerful, I think."

But mortal she was. She'd become so weak, sometimes she was unable to get up in the night to go to the bathroom on her own. She kept a walker by her bed.

Kay rarely went outside, but Vincent had built a ramp to the front porch since Molly's last visit. An electric wheelchair stood in a corner of the front room, ready and waiting when needed for her rare outings.

Kay was not even really elderly, but she looked old. Her mother had never been to New York or Paris. She would never travel to exotic places. Kay had lived a small life, and it was becoming smaller and smaller.

Molly was not ready to become an orphan, but if Kay lived too long, she pictured her mother continuing to shrink until Molly could hold her in the palm of her hand. Soon, she would become so small that she would disappear into an urn. Shrinking and dying were two competing forces in a race to kill Molly's mother.

"Kay's never been what you call an open person. Since Chuck passed over, your mother keeps herself to herself more than ever," Vincent told Molly. "With her conditions, she's got no time or temperament for courtin' a new beau. Too tired to bother to begin again and too sick for nonsense."

Once so vital, Kay now used a little bell by her bed when she needed help. When she rang, Molly or Vincent would come to her aid. Kay always rang the bell with purpose. It was never for company, but for practical tasks: a refill of distilled water for her CPAP machine, her pills, a change of towels or sheets, a drink of water, or help to and from her bathroom. When Molly tried to chat with her mother for more than a few minutes, Kay tapped the remote to increase the volume on her TV.

Kay opened up a little only the night before. Molly suspected an extra pain killer had loosened her tongue. "Everything is so much more fragile than we are led to believe," her mother told her. "It's all falling apart. I'm breaking into rusty, crusty pieces. No big deal, happens to everybody."

She'd stayed in the hospital a couple of days and undergone a battery of tests. When Molly pressed her again about the results, Kay did not share her diagnosis. She just shook her head and muttered, "Same old, same old. My bones are thinner and I'm getting fatter. I'm supposed to avoid falling down, as if there's any danger I'd go hang gliding.

"Pity you weren't around," Kay added. "You could have talked to the doctor. He was cute, but I s'pose specialists are a weird bunch. He had lots of bedside manner, but most of it was pretty bad."

Molly had learned from her Uncle Vincent that Kay had suffered a mini-stroke. Chuck's big brother let slip that it happened while Molly was working on her master's degree in Boston. Molly had known nothing about that.

"Her problems are coming to a head, but you know Kay," Vincent said. "Ask after her health, and if she's in a decent mood, she'll say, 'Kay-a-okay.' Never is true, o'course. That's fine. On just about any topic, we're all fulla shit, anyway."

Molly could not conceal her frustration. "Why is all that so private, even from me, though?"

"It's different with our generation. We don't talk everything to death. Admittin' anything medical makes mortality real. You don't get it cuz you're young and healthy. Also, she doesn't want to be grist for the gossip mill around here, for one thing. You get to a certain age, stage, or condition, and that's all people want to talk about. Can't blame her."

"Can't I?"

"Give her a break, Molly! My first bender was on a school field trip to Hill House in Bangor. I threw up out the bus window on the way back. Somebody around here is still yakkin' about it, I'm sure."

"She's my mom! I feel like I need to know," she said.

"Can you keep a secret?" Vincent asked.

"Yes."

"So can I. If she wanted you to know, she'd tell you. Not my stuff to tell."

"Sorry, I had no idea you and Mom worked at the Pentagon. I just want to help, that's all."

"You're not that kinda doctor. You're back and you're helpin'. More info doesn't do anything. Just clutters your head with more bad stuff to think about." Her uncle had put on his headphones and went back to reading the news on his phone. Discussion over.

The Prodigal Daughter was home after a long absence, but she still felt shut out.

58

DEPRESSION

Molly got up to peer out the window. The cold floor under her bare feet made her want to dive back under the covers.

The bed pulled at her like gravity. She desperately wanted to climb in and pull the covers over her head. Molly resisted the urge. She measured the weight of her untreated depression in tonnage, so she considered her achievement mildly heroic.

Through the window, she watched the weak winter sun crack over the Atlantic's horizon. Soon it would bathe the Appalachians in pale yellow light. The little town would be stirring, sluggish and reluctant.

The sun has no power here, she thought.

After Greenbriar, Molly had stayed away as long as she could afford. That wasn't long. Her job search had been a dead end, and there were still bills to pay. Her choices seemed to be living a life without shelter or coming home in defeat.

Robert Frost's poem "The Death of the Hired Man" sprung to her mind. She recited the relevant line aloud, "Home is the place where, when you have to go there, they have to take you in."

Over a century old, that poem, she thought. *Still true. Winds shift, we get blown off course, people die, but Robert Frost's words are forever.*

Poeticule Bay days were mostly interchangeable for her, but not so today. Molly was about to meet a stranger from the past who would change her course again.

Molly dressed quickly in the morning chill. To ease the fuel bill, her uncle insisted the thermostat to be set to a wicked cold temperature he referred to as "witch's tit."

If Molly complained, Vincent told her to put on a heavier sweater. "Besides, the cold makes it easier on your mother. With her troubles, she's too hot all the time."

Vincent could be blunt and crude. His pronouncements sometimes seemed calculated to make Molly cringe. Her mother often said, "I don't know which to get Vince for Christmas, a filter or a muzzle."

He was good with her mother, though. It seemed only he could cajole her into eating and drinking when she didn't feel like it. He encouraged her to knock back protein drinks she didn't care for.

Lately, she had become prone to choking. Instead of water, she had to drink thickened liquids. The mixtures looked disgusting, but didn't trigger Kay's gag reflex.

When she tried to wave the drinks away, Vince persisted. "I know you hate it, but who cares what you hate?"

"I care and I hate you now."

"I know, but I'm bigger than you, so I'm not too worried. Just another sip? Be okay, okay, Kay?"

"Fine. Still hating you, though."

"Yeah, yeah, but I get the house when you die. You gonna give me that satisfaction, or are you gonna stay fed and hydrated?"

"Fine," Molly's mother replied. "I'll drink that awful stuff, as long as you know I'm only doing it for spite."

Kay's moods often required her caregivers to be patient. Vincent took her orders well. A retired steelworker, Molly's uncle seemed an unlikely nurse. However, when he had come to Maine for his brother's funeral, he saw his sister-in-law's need. He sold his house in Pittsburgh immediately and moved in.

His generosity allowed Molly to go away to university. Vincent often tested Molly's patience. However, given his kindness, she adopted the motto, "Go along to get along."

Or smile and nod. That's what Helen would do, and she was better than me at being a person.

Molly descended the creaky stairs and headed straight for the closet in the front hall. Passing the living room door, she found Vincent already awake.

He looked up from his spot on the couch where he was reading a thin local newspaper. The *Lens* was now called *The Bay Monitor*.

Vincent called after his niece, "You skippin' breakfast? I can't do that. If I miss a meal, I feel so starvin' I could eat the ass right out of skunk!"

"I'm okay."

"And you're headed out? Again?"

"I haven't been outside for days, Vince."

"That's what I mean. You were out a while ago. Stay home and I'll make you a hunter's breakfast: eggs and bacon, sausage and toast — "

"I was up a couple of times in the night with Mom."

"Small bladder on that woman, but too stubborn to wear the diapers. I'd wear the diapers. When you pee, I bet it feels nice and warm, at least at first."

"I just need a bit of fresh air."

"When will you be back?"

"I don't know."

"Don't know?"

"I'm not a teenager. I think I'm a bit beyond having a curfew, don't you?"

"But not beyond getting an allowance." His guttural laugh held little humor.

Upon her return to the Bay, her uncle had offered to help with her expenses. He was retired but still made what he called "a boodle" off of various rental properties in Pittsburgh.

Molly appreciated the help but also resented how often he reminded her of the debt. Vincent was generous and good with her mother. However, he never tired of dwelling on her poverty. Vincent let her know on several occasions that her father would be disappointed at her wasted potential. He thought he was being subtle, but he made it clear she should leave the Bay "at her earliest inconvenience."

On her first night back, he'd prodded her over dinner. "All that education, and you're back? If all else fails, start thinkin' about marrying your way out, before it's too late."

It was enough to start a fire in Molly's eyes. "You're sitting in a comfortable chair," she'd told him. "Say that again, and you'll be sitting on your fork."

He'd laughed, and her mother had chuckled. But, noting her glare, Vincent hadn't pushed that particular button again.

Her uncle had a knack for pushing smaller buttons, though. Allowing her to get out of the house without question was his habit. "We have coffee right here in the kitchen," he said, "so why buy?"

"It's not the same."

"Free is too cheap for you?"

"No lattes in your kitchen."

Your kitchen, not ours, she thought. *Dad wouldn't approve of that.*

For the most part, Chuck Jergins went unmentioned. Only one picture of Chuck and Kay remained on the mantle — their wedding day.

59

LAMENTATION

When Molly looked at that picture of her parents, she was flooded with the memories that cursed her into a confessional mood.

What plagued her now was actually a false memory. She had not seen her father's face as he fell from the Drifting Cliffs. He had not fallen alone nor had it happened in slow motion. Chuck Jergins was not sucked down to the depths never to be recovered. He had died on the rocky beach. Yet when she looked at that picture, bundles of neurons misfired, and her treacherous mind unspooled a scene that never happened.

Most important, Molly did not push him off the edge. But she saw that, too.

My brain is trying to deceive itself. Dad didn't die that way.

Though she knew the truth, it didn't matter. Just as placebos sometimes work even when the patient knows the injection or pill is fake, her body reacted and her mind reeled. Tears welled in Molly's eyes as hot guilt washed over her.

The night before, at midnight, Kay called her to help her sit up in bed. Plumping her pillows, Molly propped her mother up.

Her mother didn't have the TV remote close to hand. With no

retreat and a captive audience, Molly admitted, "I think of Dad several times a day."

"I think of him all the time. If he were here, he'd be plumping my pillows."

"Do you believe in heaven, Mom? Some kind of afterlife?"

Kay took in a breath, gathered some spit, and swallowed. "I don't know about heaven. My husband's dead. That's hell."

Molly reached out to touch her hand. Kay allowed that for a moment, then withdrew her hand.

"Just like you, I used to run. I was on the track team, just like you. If I'm honest, I am jealous of you. Be grateful for your youth and health. Are you?"

Molly thought the question was rhetorical, so she didn't answer.

With sudden anger, Kay demanded again, "Well? Are you?"

"I am."

"Now I'm in pain and aging like a prune under a heat lamp. I will never run again. That's a little slice of hell, too."

"I'm sorry."

"No use being sorry. That's life. Irrelevance and pain can be a gift. Makes it easier to let go when your time comes. I can do and say things now I never would have before. I can say, for instance, that your father died too young for it to ever be okay. See? Irrelevance and pain let the honesty in."

"You're not irrelevant to me, Mom. I love you."

"You have to, I'm your mother. Thing is, we both know if I died tonight, you'd be moving on with your life right quick."

"That's not true! I — "

"Take the worst tragedies we've ever faced, somewhere people are making jokes about it. War, 9/11, the pandemic, whatever you can name — "

"I'm not over Dad's passing," Molly countered.

Kay slumped. "Yeah, about that, me neither, obviously. I think him dyin' got me on the same track, going over the cliff, just a bunch slower."

"Mom!"

Kay waved her off, bidding Molly to be silent. "I don't know if this will make sense to you, but to me, your father's absence feels like a presence."

"Like a ghost, you mean?"

"If so, he's too quiet and lazy with his haunting. He's not even leaving the toilet seat up just to mess with me anymore. You ask about heaven and hell. Heaven was when Chuck was alive." Molly's mother tapped her own sternum, over her heart. "Hell's right here."

"I feel that," Molly admitted. "I feel that a lot. What keeps you going?"

Her mother smiled. "Pain pills, videos of cute dumb dogs, and videos of people getting wax excavated out of their ears."

Despite herself, Molly stifled a laugh.

But Kay suddenly gave her a serious look. "Okay, okay, honestly? You want some mother-to-daughter wisdom? What keeps me going is the idea that someday I can feel like things left undone are finished."

"What things?"

"I dunno, things left unsaid, for instance. Chuck knew I loved him, but my last words to your father were to close the shed door and lock it up. Raccoons were getting in."

Molly found she could not meet her mother's eyes. "So, do and say what needs to be done and said. I understand. Then you can sleep better at night?"

"Then I can die," Kay said flatly. "Close loops, Molly. Finish what you start. That's how you get to peace, maybe. I suspect so, but I'm not there yet myself."

"I appreciate you taking me in and Vincent's financial support, but I will move out as soon as I can. I promise — "

Kay waved her off. "I'm just telling you to fulfill your purpose in life before you end up like me, held together by pain pills and spite."

Molly patted her mother's hand. "I'm sorry you're having such a hard time."

"People say they're sorry I'm sick. You won't realize how little that means until you're sick, too. Stuff like that just reminds me how powerless we all are."

"Mom, I said I'm sorry about your troubles because I don't know what else to say. I — "

"This isn't a pity party. Get out of here and go do what you were meant to do. I can say you can still accomplish what you need to do from a wheelchair, but it is harder. You're *young*, Molly. Young doesn't last. It certainly evaporated much quicker for me than I expected."

Molly was sure her mother was advising her to move out, find another university job, and get a life. She was mistaken.

60

DISCONNECTION

"**M**olly?"

The Drift Inn. The Drifting Cliffs. I am drifting. Somewhere far below me, I see my father's face. He looks ... worried.

The faraway voice sounded louder this time. "Molly!" It was her uncle.

She stood frozen in the entrance to the living room, her eyes unfocused, looking at nothing.

Then she was back.

"You change your mind? You still headed out?" her uncle asked.

Molly snapped to attention. As she hurried to put on her coat and scarf, she bit back harsh words. "Got a lot of university websites to scope out. I need the atmosphere at the coffee place."

She called it the coffee place or the Drift Inn Diner. The new owners had rechristened it The DID. She could get coffee at the gas station, but only her old haunt had hot food, good coffee, and a warm place to sit indefinitely that smelled like bacon.

With some difficulty, Vincent rose from the couch, limped over, and glared at her from the end of the hallway. "I guess I just don't understand how it is that an unemployed adult thinks payin' for — "

"Their internet connection is better."

That wasn't a lie. It was also the only answer that might come close to shutting him up.

"I'll be back when my laptop runs out of juice, or when my butt gets sore from sitting too long, whichever comes first." Molly grabbed her briefcase and slung the strap over her shoulder.

"Whatever pulls your pud, I guess."

Molly made a face. "Don't be gross."

"Sorry, kiddo!" Vincent said cheerfully. "I find my joints ache bad first thing in the morning. I'm about as stiff as a shit after three days' constipation."

Molly muttered a curse under her breath.

"Just come home before you run out of money, yeah? And before the hemorrhoids set in. Good luck with the job search."

Vincent's words were delivered in a jocular tone but sounded like a jinx and a threat. The home in which she'd grown up felt so much smaller than she remembered, claustrophobic even. Sometimes Molly felt claustrophobic in her own skin.

Vincent called after her, "Your mom will prolly sleep to noon now. I'll let her. I'll make sure she takes her pills with lunch. Gotta stay ahead of the pain, y'know?"

That isn't information, she thought. *It's passive aggression, a reminder that he's a saint. I'm the prodigal daughter, the one who left after Dad died and rarely came back to visit. A reminder that I'm back because I need to be.*

Molly stepped out onto the porch, strode across the yard, and turned left on Pine Street toward Shoreline Road. As she muttered soft curses, each exhale was a cloud of steam.

Though the winter had been mild through Christmas, the February air now carried a ferocious bite. Still, that first slap of Atlantic wind was life-giving. Getting outside felt like surfacing after being held under hot water a long time.

Our house is no longer my home, Molly thought. *But where can I live?* All the worldly possessions she'd deemed worthy of shipping from Greenbriar sat in six boxes and a trunk in the garage.

She wondered what the neighbors thought of her unceremonious return. Would a better daughter have found a better job and sent money home? Or should she have always stayed home to take care of her sick mother, their lives entwined and tangled until one of them perished?

Knotty and naughty, Molly thought. *Staying home all these years would not have ended well. It might not have even ended. Mom is the slowest-dying person I've ever known.*

Molly found herself on some twisted middle path, neither eager to return to the snake pit of academia nor enthusiastic about working as her mother's nurse.

Worse, her uncle wanted her to achieve some grand destiny she couldn't envision. Worse than that, Molly didn't feel her mother was happy to have her home, either. If anything, mother and daughter appeared resigned to their fates.

Molly had become just one more adult among many who'd come home to live in her parents' house because better options lay beyond her grasp. She spent hours scrolling Academic Careers Online. She applied for academic jobs and expanded her network on LinkedIn. Most of her most likely wells came up dry.

She'd explored the potential of several non-academic positions. She'd even had a couple of interviews over Zoom. That was how Molly discovered the utter wretchedness of being upset about failing to win a job she didn't want anyway.

I'm living small, settling for less, and I'm a loser, she thought.

Molly wasn't sure how she could ever feel like a winner. She was reminded of an obscure word. Not nevertheless, but *evertheless.* Evertheless was the sensation that she had peaked, things would never get better, and her little life would slowly fade away into inconsequentiality.

Molly was mistaken. Her situation was about to get much worse, and quickly.

61

RECONNECTION

Her uncle was fond of saying, "It's not *what* you know. It's *who* you know." She found his adage demeaning and depressing, but probably true.

Filling out job applications was drudgery. Inevitably, the electronic forms required her to upload her curriculum vita. Even so, she then had to answer pages of questions that were all readily answered by a glance at the academic resume she'd already provided.

Molly had little patience for filling out forms, but endless forms were the only path to job talks and in-person interviews. Employers all seemed to want more for less.

She'd attended a decent university for her undergrad, received a master's, and a PhD in record time. However, she'd only taught at Greenbriar College for a year. She'd had a responsible position, and her students learned in her class. However, Richard Whelan had saddled her with the lowly title of lecturer, and her brief stint there furrowed the brow of prospective employers.

Were she a teenager or in her early twenties, she might have gone for some of the worse jobs in earnest. However, she'd already paid her dues in academia. The terms her potential employers set ranged from abysmally low salaries to unrealistic expectations and usury.

Not that her standards mattered much when she received so few nibbles of interest. Most potential employers didn't even acknowledge the receipt of her application.

She wasn't totally ready to give up hope of working at another university. She'd toyed with the idea of working abroad, maybe teaching English in Japan. However, what would have felt like a low-paying yet exciting adventure when she was younger now seemed like an opportunity whose time had passed.

Her uncle had called her spoiled and entitled for her self-pity, but he didn't approve of going to Japan, either. "Lateral move," he counseled. "Don't zero out all you've worked for."

Molly thanked him, but she hadn't meant it. *I've missed the on-ramp, and there's no looping back. Damned if I do, screwed if I don't.*

"And now this," Molly whispered to herself as she took in the flat gray ocean. "Full circle to when I didn't have any degrees at all and was running around at night sabotaging cars and spraying paint."

Molly told herself what happened at Greenbriar had been one small relapse. She hadn't killed anybody. She'd done what every elementary school teacher asks of snot-nosed kids. She'd used her words.

And I don't regret what I did to Tanner Renault. I regret that there were witnesses. With more time, torture, and privacy, I could have evolved that primordial slime into a human being!

As she walked toward the shore, unwanted memories of childhood arrived unbidden. Her gaze shifted from the expanse of water to her right and Poet's Mountain to her left. She remembered being told that people who lived within sight of mountains or the sea tended to be happier. Poeticule Bay had both vistas. Molly had concluded long ago that her experience negated that theory. In fact, she struggled to remember a time when she wasn't angry.

As long as she could remember, Molly wanted to leave the Bay and see the world. Now she was out of work, travel was too expensive, and she was back living with her mother and uncle.

And Dad's still dead.

With the weight of her pack's shoulder straps jouncing against her back, it was almost as if she was a kid again, long before what happened at the Drifting Cliffs. As her stride grew longer and stronger, she indulged the fantasy that she was very young, still innocent, and running away.

She picked up speed as she passed the rest area by the lighthouse. The lighthouse was freshly painted, and the parking lot's edges were neatly accented with white boulders. A few picnic tables and a children's playground sat beside the tower. Apparently, the town had invested in getting ready for the return of the tourist trade and the summer people.

Such cosmetic improvements did not impress Molly. When she spied the lighthouse gallery, Lloyd Faun came to mind. He'd threatened to snipe the town from its high vantage point.

Perhaps her father's sacrifice had saved many others. Molly explored that idea in search of some small solace and found precious little. She would have preferred to have her father, alive and well.

In warmer weather, people came there to stare at the waves. She wondered about the thoughts of strangers. When no one else was around, did they swear as much as she did? What were their secrets? Were their fantasy worlds like movies where they righted wrongs and always won? Were there many others who shared her proclivities?

Walking faster to burn off stress, Molly's trot intensified, really on the brink of a run. She steamed down Shoreline Road and up the hill toward the Drifting Cliffs. As the road rose, she scanned the rocky shore.

Nostalgia is the wistful longing to relive or regain something of the past. Molly's walk through the bitter cold to the Drifting Cliffs was not born of yearning for a better past. It was a morbid fascination with the dreadful memories that pulled her back like a magnet to a blade.

In her absence, the bacterial bloom that had long turned the Bay into a dead zone had ebbed. The mussel population had cleaned and oxygenated the water. The cloudy water was now clear, and the air was fresh again, devoid of the stench that used to leach from the Bay.

Like me, the fish have returned. Good for them. Now they'll get caught on a hook or in a net.

The beach was more interesting than it had been when she left. Low tide pools now trapped urchins, barnacles, and the blue-black shells of periwinkles. The wharves, once abandoned and dilapidated, had been repaired.

Squinting, Molly made out the dim shapes of colorful fishing boats out for the day. In the summer, the tourist trade would be back, dead zone history forgotten as if it never happened.

Keith Faun still lived here. Vincent had mentioned it in passing. "That Faun boy lives up the mountain, built the biggest house around. Once you got more shitters in the house than people, I don't fathom why you'd keep on building! More dollars than sense, you ask me."

Molly hadn't asked. She didn't want to think about Keith Faun at all. But she glanced toward Poet Mountain.

When she was little, Molly had assumed she was born to be a writer or a poet because she was born under Poet's Mountain. Then her mother informed her, sourly, that she was born in a hospital in Orono.

Now the mountain was just a reminder that Keith Faun was here, living above her and apparently living well.

She looked away, her eyes to the ocean, as if to avoid a hex. In her favorite Shakespeare course at Wellesley College, she'd studied *King Lear*.

To avoid falling into insanity, Lear says, "O, that way madness lies. Let me shun that."

Feeling witchy, Molly riffed off The Bard and Emily Dickinson to compose a poem in her head to ward off her peculiar curse. The resulting fusion:

> That way madness lies.
> If I don't look Fate in the eyes,
> maybe Fate will pass me by.

. . .

STILL, her gaze crept back toward the mountain. Molly felt as if she were being watched, maybe through a telescope, maybe through a rifle scope. But it wasn't fear that rekindled old embers. Her yearning for vengeance gave them air. Suddenly, Molly felt she could burst into flame.

The top floor of one big house with two huge windows rose above the trees.

That must be Keith's lair, Molly thought. *Not a house or a home. A lair. My need to get justice done led to my father's death, but your bigotry started it. Which of us is worse? There's a wrong answer.*

Cruelty is never the end of things. Once that ship leaves port, there is no safe harbor. For Molly, Poeticule Bay would always be the dead zone.

Despite being bogged down with her briefcase, Molly began to run.

62

PRECAUTION

Molly was panting as she arrived at the Drifting Cliffs. The restaurant had had a facelift and was now open twenty-four hours. A huge sign elevated on a tall pole blinked on and off in garish pink neon day and night:

The DID! Below that: Feeding Great Fish Since 1964!

She'd been back here a couple of times since her return, but that sign still gave her pause. Whoever commissioned the sign didn't care much for truth or accuracy. The wording was ridiculous.

"Feeding great fish" made it sound like an aquarium, not a diner feeding seafood to people. Besides, no one had ever called the Drift Inn Diner by the ridiculous name of The DID. Not while she'd lived in Poeticule Bay anyway.

At night, the sign presented an asynchronous signal with the long, bright beam of the lighthouse. To ships that cut close enough to the coast, it looked as if some massive creature was winking, one eye dim and pink, the other bright white.

A couple of eighteen-wheelers were parked beside the restaurant. The building had new siding, and the parking lot was no longer the rutted dirt patch. The paving looked quite new.

Erosion had made the rear of the lot smaller than she remembered. Everything in Poeticule Bay seemed smaller than she remembered. Contrary to Sheriff Hobbs' promises, there was still no barrier along the cliff's edge, not even a warning sign.

The word "claustrophobic" boiled up in her mind again. She took a deep breath and let it out slowly through her teeth. That claustrophobic feeling didn't disappear but lessened enough that it was tolerable.

Sometimes that discomfort escalated, visiting her at night. It felt like someone holding her down, and she had to kick off the bed covers.

Through her darkest hours, Molly's skin felt too tight. There was no escaping that feeling. Most mornings, her bedcovers looked like someone had fought them through the night.

Add post-traumatic stress disorder to my list of neuroses, she thought. *Who can I tell?*

Molly had sworn she'd never return to the scene of the crime. Circumstances conspired against her. A half dozen crying seagulls hung above the restaurant, their wings spread, almost motionless in the rising wind. Surely a bad omen, but there was nowhere else to go. Shivering, Molly stepped into the restaurant to escape February's icy grip and her mother's cold stares.

The restaurant's layout was the same, but the decor had received a facelift. The worn wooden floors had been replaced with a checkerboard black and white tile. Molly suspected the detail was meant to harken back to a 1950s diner.

Incongruously, a fishing net with urchins and buoys in its webbing hung from the ceiling. The booths were separated by high plexiglass dividers, surely a remnant from the pandemic.

When she'd set out, all Molly really cared about was escaping the house for a few hours. The diner's strong wifi signal and strong coffee were merely pluses. However, the aromas emanating from the kitchen and the sound of sizzling bacon changed her mind. She salivated at the thought of breakfast.

Food is the answer to my anxiety problems, she thought. *That's it! I'll get fat! Fat and happy!*

Scanning the restaurant, several tables close to the door were occupied. A pretty young brunette in a server's uniform handed her a menu. Her name tag read Debbie.

"Sit wherever you like, hon. I'll be right along to take your order. And here, got your hot bean juice right away."

She handed Molly a cup of coffee. Molly took the hot cup awkwardly as her briefcase strap began to slip from her shoulder. She hitched that up and stuffed the menu into her armpit to accept the steaming mug.

Had Molly not worn gloves, it would have burned her hands. As it was, she was grateful to feel the heat seep from the ceramic and through her cold leather gloves.

As Debbie retreated to the kitchen, Molly went to the same spot where she'd once sat with Barry Graves. The wooden seats had been taken away to wherever old restaurant seats go. The chairs were now green vinyl, and the spot was now a booth, not just a table.

She had to wonder where Barry Graves had gotten to. Where did exiles from Poeticule Bay go? What happened to his family. Putting aside why they left, did they end up happier to have moved away?

How often was Barry haunted by memories of his high school trauma? In anxious moments, did he still look over his shoulder for Keith Faun?

Scanning the menu, Molly hoped the dopamine rush of a short stack of blueberry and chocolate chip pancakes would settle her stomach. The server soon returned to take her order. Molly requested their lighthouse stack, the highest number of pancakes she could get without ordering for two.

Debbie squinted at her as if she were hard to see. "You new? I've seen you a couple of times in here with your computer."

"I'm ...uh ... visiting."

"Well, welcome back. I'm glad you're here. Really glad." The server gave Molly a smile and stood still, staring.

Unsure what more Debbie needed, Molly added awkwardly, "This place is busier than I remember."

"The fish came back, so the people are back. Huge news around here!" Debbie surveyed Molly through narrowed eyes again. "Folks say the curse is lifted, but I'm not so sure."

"Oh?"

"I know who you are now," Debbie said.

"I don't — um, what?"

"I called my boss. He wants to talk to you. Don't tell him I told you, but I thought you should get a heads up."

"A heads up about what?"

The server ignored her question. "You helped my cousin back in the day. I was a coupla grades behind you."

Debbie leaned a little closer to inspect Molly's hair. "Little gray coming in, eh? I think maybe more grades than a coupla, huh? Anyway, everybody in the family heard him sing your praises."

"Sorry, who's your cousin?"

"Dylan? Dylan Caffrey? Remember him?"

One of Keith's targets, the one Molly was shamed into helping after she failed Barry. She'd ended up lecturing Keith. It had worked that first time she depended on witnesses for her safety. Nobody died that first time.

63

CAUTION

"I wanted to say something when I saw you before," Debbie said, "but you left before I figured out for sure it was you. Had to ask around a little. The boss brought in an old yearbook. I saw your picture, and I said, 'That's her!'"

"Uh-huh. Um, what does your boss want to talk to me about exactly?"

"Dunno. Pancakes! Comin' up!"

Debbie hurried away and Molly watched the door, fidgeting as she waited. She'd been recognized. That was hardly a surprise in such a small town. She'd grown up here. A lot of people would have known her on sight.

Molly missed the anonymity afforded by large numbers of people in crowded spaces. Statistically, cities were more dangerous. Molly preferred them for the privacy of being just another blurred face in the crowd.

In Boston, she'd ridden an elevator with a fellow apartment dweller whose door was next to hers. They'd never once even said good morning to each other. In Poeticule Bay, it seemed everyone knew each other's business.

How many knew about her history of vandalism? Her penchant

for sabotaging cars? How many people knew the truth behind her father's death?

Her mind tumbled back to what had happened at the edge of that cliff. She could see it from where she sat. Dwelling on her failures, she chose instead to stare into her mug of coffee as if it contained all the answers to all the questions in the world.

Molly looked up in surprise as a young man appeared beside her table. He held a steaming pot of coffee, but he wore no name tag. He had thinning blond hair and an unremarkable face. The only thing truly remarkable about him was his very short stature.

The man nodded to her mug. "Can I top that up and hot it up for you?"

"Uh ... sure."

He poured. "Tough day." A statement, not a question.

"Is it written on my face?"

The man smirked. "Like permanent marker. But you've had lots of tough days around here, huh?"

She looked up at him quizzically.

"Nothing much going on around here, but maybe I'm wrong. You'd be a better judge since you've been away so long. You know how you don't notice something when you're constantly exposed to it? Like when the furnace shuts off and you never realized it was on until the noise stops? The Bay is like that. I'm always here so I don't notice the changes much. So? Is Poeticule Bay how you remember it? I know! I know! They're fishing again and all that, but has it really changed that much? Has it changed *enough*?"

His last question seemed particularly pointed.

"Seems a bit busier than I remember," Molly answered vaguely.

"Yeah, the recovery certainly is on. Some things are still a mess, but I think we can make it right — "

She gawked up at him, trying to place his face. "Sorry, should I know you?"

"Don't you?"

"You must be Debbie's boss. That's all I know."

"Her manager. I hope she didn't spoil any surprises."

"She didn't," Molly replied. "I don't know your name. Kind of ironic, actually. I was just thinking that around town, everybody knows everybody, and everybody knows everything."

"Almost everything, maybe," he said.

"I sure hope *that's* not true." *Shields up!* Molly thought.

"I'm going to tell you something, but don't take it like I mean it in a creepy way, okay? I don't mean it creepy, but I've been watching you, from afar, I mean. Monitoring your progress, you know?"

"I do not."

"Your uncle comes in sometimes, keeps us up to date. He's very proud of you."

That surprised her, but she did not comment.

"Search engines and social media are all-seeing — "

"All-stalking?"

"Caring. You helped Debbie's cousin Dylan. He went out west a few years ago, looking for work. Came back. Now he's a truck driver. These days, his regular run is Bangor to Chicago and back. You helped a bunch of people back in the day, before you escaped."

"That's a weird way to put it. I grew up, graduated, and left. Most people did, didn't they? Everybody leaves."

The young man tilted his head back and forth. "Most everybody. Some of us stayed. I got a wonderment about you."

"A wonderment?"

"You escaped, but did you escape for good? I mean, you ran away to accomplish great things, right?"

Her face darkened. "Ran away?

She looked him up and down more carefully, her gaze slowing at his thin sandy hair and bright blue eyes. "I don't recall your name or — wait! Are you wearing contacts? Did you dye your hair maybe?"

He played coy. "Maybe."

She shook her head, unwilling to admit defeat. "You do look familiar."

The man put on a hurt look, but his tone was cheerful. "I was a child, so I was even shorter when you lived here. When you left town, I still would have been the same size as a lot of other little kids. My growth spurt seems to be late. Still waiting for it to arrive! Musta gotten lost in the mail. Or someone else got the height I was supposed to get!"

He gave her a toothy grin that he might have thought charming. However, with the odd angles his teeth had grown in, it looked like they'd had a fight and were trying to get away from each other.

The DID's manager continued, "I'm a little freak of nature, you see? Puberty is like money. It doesn't get distributed to everybody equally."

To his credit, there was no note of self-pity in his tone, only stating facts.

Molly gazed blankly, reluctant to hazard a guess as to his identity and increasingly annoyed.

"No? Still don't remember? Maybe you blocked me out. High school wasn't such a good time, especially back then."

"If you were in a younger grade — "

He let her off the hook. "What's in a name, really? A name's just a label. Labels lose their glue, curl up, and fall off, right? A name is just another box we're put in. But no hurry or worry! I kinda enjoy being a mystery. Everyone loves a mystery."

"Do they? I'm more a fan of thrillers."

The man reached out and touched her wrist lightly. "It's okay. I'm a friend, or at least a friend of a friend! You're here and there are a lot of people around. Outside those doors, you're not safe. No one in this town is safe, really. *I* sure am not! But you're safe in here, at least until Keith shows up."

Molly's expression seemed impassive. Inside, she'd gone cold and still. She went away for a moment then, everything blurred by a foundational memory. Suddenly, she was a little girl standing in warm sand on a beach in Florida. Her ninth birthday.

The sun was bright that day, but she encountered a darkness that eclipsed all the happiness she'd known. She'd entered the water a child innocent of the world's dangers. Then, ever so briefly, she met the monster made of teeth. Any child knows fear, but none should be acquainted with terror.

The shark did not attack. Molly got back to the beach, whole but harmed, nonetheless. She emerged from that baptism with a new understanding. Our very existence is a mortal threat that always delivers on its calamitous promise. Everyone eventually faces the same realization. That fact is no less tragic for its ubiquity.

Unaware she was speaking aloud, Molly whispered, "You meet the monster, you're never free after that. The monster always returns, and it comes for everyone."

64

INITIATION

The DID's manager was unaware Molly had fallen out of their shared reality for a few seconds. Chattering on, he missed her warning about monsters.

When she came back to the present, the mysterious young man was saying, "It's been what? Ten years since you moved away?"

Molly cleared her throat. "A little more. You said Keith is coming?"

"Yeah, says he wants to see you. I know he can be scary. He sure can scare the shit out of me, and I know you got history. And Dylan? Hell, Dylan won't even park his rig here after a long haul. Debbie has to walk down the hill if she wants to get a ride from her cousin."

"Dylan's right."

"Hey, hey! Keith won't do anything with all these people around. He told me, he just wants to talk — "

"Then you don't know him," Molly said. "And you don't know me. *I* might do something."

"No, no! I remember you well," he continued breezily. "You were the tallest girl in school. Debate club champ and cross-country star Molly Jergins. So? You gonna stay, or should I box up those pancakes for you to take home."

She didn't want to see Keith, but she didn't want to go home, either. It wasn't her home anymore. Perhaps, she told herself, seeing her old nemesis could be productive, or at least interesting. She didn't really believe Keith could change. He was too hard a case. On the other hand, some villains found therapy, Jesus, or transformed themselves with ayahuasca or ketamine. Maybe, just maybe, Keith Faun had meditated his way out of being a piece of shit.

This could be a useful test of her cynicism. Could the worst person she ever met (who was still alive) actually change?

"I'll stay," Molly decided. "Too curious not to."

Her host looked relieved. "Good. I think it will be helpful for you to see him eye-to-eye. After you do that, I want to talk to you more about something. It's important!"

Molly took a sip of her coffee. For all his conviviality, this guy was annoying. "What is it? I'm here now."

"Later," he replied. "You still haven't remembered my name."

"It's very possible I never knew it."

"I even remember your nickname in high school. Jergins, like the lotion."

He sounded so jubilant she wanted to punch him in the face. "Don't remind me. 'Jergins like the lotion' plagued me all through school. I got teased a lot. I don't like to be teased."

"My sister told me Troy Daniels went on and on about that, didn't he?"

She deduced that he must have had an older sister closer to her own age, but Molly still could not place him. And she'd grown tired of his game.

"Troy," he continued, "never was one to let go of a tired joke or a turd joke. He said he wanted to rub you all over him. Announced it to the whole hockey team, didn't he?"

"Everyone heard that one. Not exactly sophisticated humor." She sighed. "The name on my birth certificate is Margaret. I've always gone by Molly. My middle name is Edwina. I always hated it, but on the first day of sixth grade, I had a home room teacher who called out our full names — first, middle, last."

"Mr. Morris? I had him, too, for math."

"That's him," Molly confirmed. "I felt like he was trying to make me miserable, like it was personal."

"Seems like high schools never have a shortage of people trying to make others miserable."

"You could say that. I once made the rookie mistake of eating a hot dog in the school cafeteria. For the rest of that term, Troy called me Edwiener." She gave her voice a sing-song lilt. "Ed-*wiener*! Ed-*wiener*! She loves eating *wieners*!"

"I don't remember *that*," the young man admitted. "I would have still been in elementary school then, I guess. My sister didn't mention that bit."

"I didn't eat a hot dog in a public place again until I was in my twenties. Troy was the classic Schroedinger's douchebag. He'd be mean and then when I got my back up, he'd say he was just joking, and 'Where's your sense of humor?' As if he was innocent of all charges, and his victim was the one being a dink."

What Molly didn't mention was the tiny vengeance she'd perpetrated on Troy Daniels. She'd decided Troy's leash needed yanking. It was in her early days of going after bullies with worrisome notes. Brush back pitches, she called them, the sort of pitch used in baseball to make the batter nervous and back off the plate.

Molly had telephoned a psychologist in Orono. Posing as Troy's mother, she told the doctor that she didn't like her son, that no one did. Molly said she suspected Troy was capable of shooting up his school one day. Troy never knew about the appointment, of course. When he failed to show up, Maine State police got involved.

That single phone call resulted in a satisfying domino effect. Troy got a scare when the Staties showed up at his door to question him and the family. Sheriff Hobbs — gossip that he was — informed his barbershop boys that he and the school administration were keeping a wary eye on the young Daniels boy, too.

The kid was still an asshole, but Molly noticed he was a little quieter at school after that. His parents got worried and kept him home more. Even his grades improved. In Troy's case, she considered her gambit somewhat successful.

"You didn't like being called Winnie, either, did you?" the young man continued.

She startled from her reverie and shot him a hard look. "This is all ancient history. Call me Molly, please."

"Sure, Molly." His face suddenly darkened. "Troy was one of Keith's sidekicks then, wasn't he?"

"One of his teammates and sycophants, yeah." Despite her history with Keith and the Faun family, Molly hoped her face betrayed nothing at the mention of his name.

"Keith and Troy were a couple of the worst of the puckheads." She waved away that ugly bit of high school nostalgia. "Nothing to be done now about history and bad jokes."

"But it wasn't a joke, was it? It was mean. You were harassed, bullied, intimidated."

Molly stiffened. "People tried to bully me, but I was never intimidated. There's a difference."

"Good for you!" He nodded his approval. "I understand the difference, but I wish I were that brave. Being the shortest kid in school with terrible acne and asthma wasn't fun, either. Some guys acted as if my height was my whole identity, so they made being assholes to me their whole personality. High school memories sure can burn, can't they?"

"Is high school really good for anyone?"

"Some enjoy it."

"Better adjusted people who desperately want to know how to calculate the area of a triangle, maybe."

He laughed and tipped an imaginary hat in salute.

"Whatever happened to Troy, anyway? Do you know?"

"I know where all the bodies are buried."

She looked up from her plate sharply, but he barrelled on. "Troy got a job working at a little inn down in Kittery. Married a girl who works at a gallery down there."

"Kittery? That's about as far from here as a person can get and still claim Maine."

"He's got a couple of kids. Came in here last summer. The kids were a little wild, but he wasn't the ass I remembered him to be. He didn't say anything to me about my height anyway."

"If dickheads can change, maybe there's even hope for Keith Faun," Molly replied.

Perhaps there's hope for me, too, Molly thought.

She was mistaken.

65

EXPECTATION

"Don't you want to know what happened to Keith?"

Molly let out an impatient sigh. "My uncle said he's got a big house on the mountain."

"You don't want more of an update than that?"

"You are a *talker*, aren't you?"

"Sorry! We can save that for Keith to brag about. I know he will! Anyway, it's just so nice to chat with someone who's different."

"Different?"

"You know how it is. Most people around here keep their conversation to the changes in the weather. The old guys who wander in here are *obsessed* with the weather. So many of these old folks used to be fishermen, so they're still fixated on clouds, winds, and waves. Since the fish started to come back, they're getting their old dories out on the water. The small talk has gotten worse. I'm no good at small talk."

"I see that."

Debbie arrived with a stack of pancakes with a side of hash browns. "Lookin' cozy. You taking care of the lady?"

"I got it, Debbie. Thank you."

Molly assured the server, "The tip will still be for you."

Debbie flashed a smile and turned on her heel before Molly could ask her the manager's name.

The young man continued smoothly, "Pardon my missionary zeal. It's just nice to see you back home, Molly."

The muscles in her jaw tightened at the insinuation that Poeticule Bay was still her home. He caught her look, and to soothe her, added, "A lot of people didn't care for how things were around here back in the day. It's not all better. Not yet."

He wanted something from her. Molly wasn't sure she wanted to know more.

"If I ask for blunt honesty, can you manage that?" he asked.

"No guarantees."

"Tell me," he asked cheerfully, "do you still contemplate raining down righteous vengeance upon your enemies?"

He knew what she'd done. There was no point in trying to deceive him. And Molly already had an inkling of what he might want. It was the only thing she had to offer. He wanted her vigilante skills.

"I used to think I wanted justice," she said. "That made me feel like I was a good person. In my experience, justice is too rare and too slow. Often, it never comes."

"It happened quick out on the cliff that night, didn't it?"

She waved an empty bottle of syrup at him. "Could I have some more maple syrup, please? Then I'll tell you about something that happened in town. Something fun."

He was only gone a moment. Upon his return, she accepted the bottle with thanks and gestured for him to sit opposite her again.

"You know what happened on the cliff, but I can tell you don't understand it. I don't want to talk about that, okay?"

He nodded his agreement.

"Bad people still bring out my natural tendencies. I can't pinpoint exactly when my hatred of bullies began — "

He grinned mischievously. "Leave that stuff to philosophers and the court-ordered psychotherapist you'll have someday."

Her eyes narrowed. "Funny. Anyway, I do remember the spark."

"Your origin story?"

Molly cleared her throat. The air suddenly felt heavy and hot, as sticky as a mean summer night. When it was humid, her mother would always say, "The air feels close." It felt close now.

Molly had to cool that heat, ease that pressure. It wasn't in her nature to expose herself. Despite his warning that she wasn't safe in town, nothing about him worried her. If he were dangerous, he wouldn't need her.

"Okay, I'll confess, Padre," she said. "Let's talk about how it started."

He leaned forward, eager and smiling that awful grin. *Toothy* was insufficient to describe all that chipped chaos of yellowed enamel.

The word *toothful* meant a small measure of something. Molly thought the definition should be expanded to having too many fangs and snaggle teeth crammed into one small mouth.

"You gonna tell me about the Faun family?" he asked.

"No. You already seem to know that. My spark wasn't the Fauns. It was the Jaguar Woman."

"Jaguar Woman? I'm intrigued!"

"I'll tell you the story if you tell me your name and who the hell your sister was. I hate mysteries."

"I accept," he said. "My name is Anthony, but everybody calls me Ant. Please don't pronounce it hoity-toity, like 'aunt.'" The little man chuckled as he added, "To say my name right, you gotta wrinkle your nose when you say it."

Molly did as he asked and emphasized wrinkling her nose. "Ant!"

"You got it! Last name's Rainier," he added. "My sister is Sarah Rainier. You knew my mother."

"Rosemary Rainier, the school librarian." That explained how he knew so much.

"Mom goes by Rose, not Rosemary."

"So, we all have aliases," Molly said, "like spies."

"Truth," Ant said. "I spied on you the night my neighbor shot at you. Saw it all from my bedroom window. Didn't know it was you at the time but found out from my mom when I got older."

Like a cloud racing over the sun, a look of surprise passed over

Molly's face for a second. However, she regained her self-possession quickly. To show any shock was to give up power. "Fine. A deal's a deal."

Molly told Ant Rainier about her first foray into vigilantism, sharing how one small event at the Pick-Right defined how she saw herself. Every villain and every hero has an origin story. At the time, Molly thought she would always play the hero.

Again, she was mistaken.

66

JUBILATION

As part of her track and field training in junior high, Molly ran each morning and evening. She'd tried out young, but she was already tall for her age. The coach took one look at Molly's lean frame and long legs and pegged her as a long-distance runner.

Molly didn't really like it at first, but she did as she was bid. During the long, dark Maine winters, she wore a ski mask against the cold. Besides slightly warming the frigid air before it hit her lungs, the black mask made her feel like a ninja.

"Since then," Molly told Ant, "I've discovered everyone wears a mask. The retail clerk is not glad to help you, but her smile looks real. The cashier at Walmart does not care when she asks if you found everything you were looking for. The plumber may give you a cheerful grin when you call on a Saturday afternoon, but he hates you for taking him away from a quiet afternoon in front of his television."

"What did you do as a ninja?" Ant asked.

Between bites of pancake, Molly told her story. "That first spark ignited on a cold morning outside the Pick-Right. Someone parked a bright green Jaguar across the two handicapped spots. There was no handicapped sticker on the dash. Presumably the driver had left the vehicle that way to get in and out quickly and so no one would scratch her fancy car. As soon as I saw it, I wanted to key that car."

"Did you?"

"That's not a job you do in broad daylight. I was still thinking about it, jogging in place, when a woman in a puffy vest came out of the store with sacks of groceries. She loaded up and abandoned the cart beside her car."

In her mind's eye, Molly could still see her target in detail. The woman wore her long bleached blonde hair in elaborate braids. The cords in her neck and bare forearms made Molly think of long blue snakes wriggling beneath a thin, taut sheet. She looked very buff in her yoga pants. Surveying the plunging V-neck of her T-shirt, her huge boobs had to be fake.

But it wasn't her looks that irritated Molly, not exactly. What bothered her was that this was a person who had never heard the word no.

"Her selfishness stirred something strong in me," Molly explained. "There are studies about this sort of thing. People who don't return their buggy to the grocery cart corral are more self-centered than people who do. Owners of luxury cars are less likely to stop for pedestrians at crosswalks. The odds that they stop decrease by three percent for every thousand dollar increase in the value of their car. Something like that."

"She bothered you a lot."

"A lot, a lot, yeah."

But Molly's irritation wasn't ephemeral in the moment. Her anger was visceral. Her mother's pain spurred her to take action. On the rare occasions Kay Jergins made brave forays out to the Pick-Right, she used that handicapped spot. If the lot was full and she couldn't park close, her mother refused to get out of the car.

"You and Dad go shop and I'll wait here," she'd say in a martyr's tone. "I'm just too beat to bother today. It wasn't meant to be. Leave the window a crack so I don't die of the heat like a dog. Have fun moving around in society and whatnot."

"Mom's pain broke my heart," Molly told Ant, "but sometimes a little gentle vengeance can slap a happy patch on the hurt."

Most critical to what was about to happen, the woman was not a local. Her license plate told Molly that the woman was from Delaware. Molly didn't have to worry about getting recognized. Better, there wasn't another soul in sight and Pick-Right's parking lot didn't have surveillance cameras.

With her mask on, Molly felt free to be someone different. Anonymity gave her power. She could be the girl who spoke up. "Hey! Those spots are reserved for people who need to be close to the door!"

Jaguar Woman sneered and gave Molly a dismissive wave. "There are plenty of other spots!"

"So why didn't you take one of them instead of stealing energy from disabled people who can't spare it? Have you heard? There are other people in the world besides you!"

The stranger shrugged, laughed, and waved cheerfully as she climbed into her car. Before she slammed the Jag's door, she rolled down her window to raise one gloved hand above the roof to give Molly the finger.

Her anger spiking, Molly raced forward. On a sudden impulse, she grabbed the abandoned shopping cart and rolled it behind the car's rear bumper.

Despite parking at an angle, the Jag was boxed in. The driver gave her horn two long blasts.

"Ooh!" Molly called. "Hear that? It's the mating call of the terminally selfish!"

Exasperated, the driver burst from her car. However, she made no move toward the cart. She gestured impatiently — a silent command — expecting Molly to clear the buggy out of her way.

"She couldn't see my smile behind my mask, but I was smiling wide," Molly said. "I bounced on my toes like a boxer. I'd never felt so much energy. I felt like Tigger!"

"Move it!" Jaguar Woman ordered.

"Fuck, no," Molly replied.

She'd never sworn at an adult before. That was how Molly discovered defiance was delicious.

67

CONCEPTION

Molly kept jogging in place. Each exhaled breath was a cloud of steam in the frigid air.

"What do you think you're doing?"

"The right thing. You should try it. It feels good. The rest of us are trying to have a society, caring about others."

"Move that cart out of the way and apologize! Right now!"

"I have to wonder how someone so pretty can be so ugly."

The woman cursed, long and loud.

Undeterred, Molly pressed, "My mother would advise you that gravity will do a number on those tits. You're going to have to develop a pleasant personality. By then it might be too late, though."

The louder her target yelled, the more amused Molly became. Standing by the cart corral, she mimed that the woman should put her cart back where it belonged.

Finally, the stranger shoved the cart aside. She made for the driver's seat, but Molly was faster. By the time she climbed back behind the wheel, Molly placed the cart at her back bumper again.

The woman got back out, screaming, more vowels than actual words at that point. Grabbing the buggy, she chased Molly, trying to hit her with it.

"I was in sneakers. She was in high heels. No contest. I led her back toward the cart corral and thanked her for being a good citizen. She gave up and went to her car wailing about how I'd wasted her time."

"Woulda been faster to do the right thing in the first place, huh?" Ant added.

"Yeah, I told her, 'Next time, park where you're supposed to park and put your cart back where it's supposed to go!' She told me she was only in the store a minute, but she was a liar. Her cart had been overloaded. That many groceries would have taken much more than a few minutes."

Ant nodded. "Disabled folks are inconvenienced for much more than a minute. Some, their entire lives."

"And she was whining," Molly said. "I'll never forget how she looked at me."

The woman whirled and looked Molly up and down over her sunglasses, lip curled, oozing contempt.

"I was nothing to her," Molly said. "I didn't matter at all. Nobody did. That's what really got to me. Her balloon needed popping."

"And you were the needle."

"That was my first taste of playing the part of an avenger."

"What's that taste like?"

Molly smiled. "Like freedom and chocolate fudge." What started out as a lesson to a selfish narcissist had become so much more.

The woman at the grocery store shook under the pressure of her escalating rage. Molly had stayed dead still. Her tone low and threatening, Molly warned, "This is the scary part for you. I might be the waitress at your next restaurant. I could be the daughter of the woman who cleans your vacation house. I might be friends with people you know, people you think are your friends. But maybe they're really *my* friends."

The woman had scoffed, but doubt crept into her eyes.

Molly spoke slowly, her voice flat and sure. "I could be anyone, anywhere. I *am* anyone. I *am* everywhere, *and I do not like you.* Makes you wonder what could happen next, doesn't it?"

The woman's full collagen-filled lips formed a small *o* as her eyes grew wide. She paled as she hurried to get into the driver's seat.

"That woman thought no rules applied to her," Molly said. "It was freeing to step outside those bounds with her and tell her off, introduce a little worry to someone who didn't worry enough. Tigger beats Jaguar Woman!"

Ant laughed. "And how old were you when this happened? When you found your calling?"

Molly shrugged. "I dunno. Fourteen? Maybe fifteen? My mother didn't bring me up to be like that. Mom would have been appalled. She taught me to tolerate others when they were impolite.

"When I was little, I complained about some girl at school who wouldn't leave me alone. I said I wanted to slap her face with fingerpaint. Mom told me two wrongs don't make a right. But Dad said, 'Try three.'"

"And, best of all, you didn't get caught," Ant observed. "That's the trick. Not getting caught is the tough part. It's what scares me from doing things."

"What kind of things do you want to do?"

"Like you, vengeful things."

"Whoever you want to go after, do they deserve vengeance?"

"Yes." Ant's tone suggested his strong conviction.

"That doesn't mean it will work out the way you hope. Whatever you're thinking, probably don't."

"Even if it's Keith I want gone?"

Molly's irritation rose. She was back at the same place she and her father had planned, where she and Barry Graves had plotted. And now she was talking to another person trying to pull her into a quest against Keith Faun.

"I still want you to get a fresh dose of Keith," Ant said, "but that was kind of what I wanted to talk to you about. As my sister says, if ever there was a douchebag in need of holy retribution, it's her husband."

"Or unholy retribution?"

Ant grinned. "That's where we're hoping you'd come in, yeah. We don't think we can do anything about him without you."

"Why's that?"

"My sister is scared of her hubby. She'll tell you herself."

"And you?"

"I'm more scared of him. Lots of people hate Keith, but you're the one with the most experience. Sarah says, because of your dad, your hate for him is bigger than our fear. That's a quote, pretty much."

Molly eyed the man. She weighed the benefit of telling Ant he should get his teeth fixed or refrain from smiling so much. It was not his array of teeth that bothered her now. She had the distinct impression Ant was a worm impersonating a snake oil salesman. His assumptions about her and his smooth, careless way made her want to get up and leave.

Staring into his bewildered eyes, she quoted a few lines from a poem she used to teach:

> Life's riptides pull us down spirals.
> There is no escape from the past.
> Scream your prayers and pound your Bibles.
> Fears of eternal torments are the only morals that last.

"What's that mean?" he asked.

"Ant, if you're too scared to go to war, maybe you both should call the sheriff. Leave Keith Faun to Man's law and God's plan," Molly suggested. "It's what people do, what they're supposed to do, I guess."

Deep down, of course, Molly didn't mean it. It was in her nature to swim with sharks, too confident she would make it back to shore in one piece.

68

EXPRESSION

"Have you noticed some people seem to get away with anything?" Ant asked.

She nodded as she chewed her cooling pancakes. "Go ahead and tell me."

Ant went into salesmanship mode. "About Keith, is he a big problem or something best ignored? He's big. People say forgive and forget — "

"I'm sure that's healthier and less trouble," Molly interrupted. "Have you considered forgiving and forgetting?"

"Can't."

"You sure? I carry my grudges around my neck and in a bucket. It's a heavy burden."

"Can't forgive and forget when the sins are ongoing."

Ant made a vague gesture toward the window which seemed to encompass the world. "Plenty of examples of bad people out there, but my brother-in-law is the worst."

"Injustice abounds."

"I've felt powerless all my life," Ant admitted. "You hear about the banks in the news lately?"

"No, what?"

"There is this bank that double-charged fees to their customers. They even opened bank accounts for unwitting people, started credit cards for them without asking. The banks got fined, but they made much more than they lost. Nobody's going to jail. Real punishment isn't even discussed. That's that Man's law you were talking about."

Molly nodded her agreement. "Meanwhile, rob those same banks of twenty bucks, and you're headed to prison. I understand the frustration."

She pushed a piece of pancake around her plate to soak up the last of the maple syrup. "During the pandemic, a friend of mine was protesting at the Supreme Court. When the cops pushed her into the back of a van to be locked up for the weekend, one cop taunted her with, 'The jail's gonna be packed cheek by jowl. Enjoy getting COVID!' A police officer said that.'"

"A death sentence for exercising her first amendment, right?"

"One of her fellow protesters had cancer. She was already immunocompromised. The judge let the cancer patient off with a fine. He ordered her to apologize to the court first, though."

Ant looked astonished. "As if she was supposed to be grateful for his mercy? She get through okay?"

Molly shook her head. "COVID killed her before the cancer could. And the Earth spins on, oblivious. It amazes me how easily people forget the worst things."

"Because there are too many worst things." With a shaking hand, Ant poured himself a cup of black coffee. "Polite society's sure got lots of rules, doesn't it?"

"Impolite society, too. For instance, you want to do something to your brother-in-law, but you fear getting caught. You're looking to me for help. Has Keith got a Jaguar that needs a deep scratch down the fender? I think you probably want me to do something more, uh, *proactive* than that. Do you want him hurt or killed? I'm not a hitman. There are no hitmen. That's a myth. Tell Sarah, if she finds one, she's talking to an FBI agent."

"That's another good reason we want to talk to you," Ant replied.

"So, which is it you want?"

Ant looked around nervously to make sure they couldn't be overheard. "Doing something bad to people who deserve it ... it feels good, right?"

He had ignored her question, but she let that slide. It was obvious he was building up to something. She gave him time, more runway for takeoff. He needed more reassurance before he'd really open up.

"Ant, there are two tricks to righteous vengeance. The first trick, as you've mentioned, is to not get caught. To do that, you have to plan ahead, see around corners, and have backup plans for your backup plans. It will probably all go to shit, but you have to have it all rehearsed in your head, anyway."

"What's the second trick?"

"Get inside the target's head. I don't mean just seeing how they see things. I mean haunt their dreams and play on their worst fears."

His grin returned. "Teach me, sensei!"

Molly considered that he was stalling her until Keith arrived. This could easily be a trap. Maybe he was even recording her. No matter. So far, she'd turned him down.

"Buy my breakfast and refill my coffee. Then I'll teach you something," she said.

"It's already comped."

"Fine, just so long as you understand. and for the record, I am not agreeing to anything. A sheriff, a priest, and a lawyer walk into a bar. It's not a joke. It's who you should be talking to. That's my advice on the subject of your brother-in-law, okay?"

"TBD," Ant replied.

Molly sighed. *Bad teeth, spineless, and a thick skull. Evolution of the human species is not distributed evenly.*

"Just shut up and listen," she said.

69

INSTRUCTION

"You want to learn the ways of the ninja? Here's an easy one that's surprisingly effective. Suppose some stranger says something really rude to you. The less they know about you, the better. Say some guy in a grocery store questions your intelligence, says something mean about your mom, tells you you're ugly, whatever — "

"Or says I'm short. I get that a lot, as if I didn't know already. Fighting words. What's your prescription, Dr. Clapback?"

"For this, you'll need to whip a notebook out of your pocket."

"What about just using my phone?"

"You could record them that way, sure, but they'll either escalate to violence or call the cops faster if you do that. I prefer using a notebook. It's something that will feel more tangible and lasting to them. It can really freak the target."

"Okay, notepad. Check! Then what?"

"Pummel them with questions, not your fists. Start with their name. Doesn't matter much if they answer all your questions. Just keep taking notes as you fire questions at them. Name, age, where they grew up, family, pets, license plate number, marital status, where they work. Ask if they're on social media. Make a note of what they're wearing and say it out loud as you do so. Ask when they saw their doctor last. Estimate their height and weight and mutter it just loud enough for them to hear. Any personal details you can think of will do the job. Don't give them any time to think, either. Just keep firing and take notes until they shut down. Refuse to answer any of their questions."

"What's all that supposed to do?"

"If you work it right, your last few questions will stick with them forever. Ask, 'What or whom do you love most? What is your greatest fear? A terrible diagnosis, dying in a fire, drowning, or being buried alive?'"

"They'll say I'm threatening them."

"Of course you are, but tell them it's for the record, for science, for your buddies, whatever. They won't answer, but that doesn't matter. You're in their heads, see?"

"Screwing with them."

"Yeah, but keep it cool and clinical. If you sound hysterical, it won't work. Loud and crazy can be dangerous, but it also suggests powerlessness."

"I feel powerless all the time," Ant admitted.

"Don't let them know that. You're not running for office, here. Power isn't given. Dealing with bullies, power is taken. Be the locus of control. Speaking low and emotionless is much more disturbing in the long run. You're going for the cold and calculated serial killer feel."

"I guess so." Ant still appeared doubtful.

Molly pressed her point. "Look, you're dealing with a hunk of shit, so you're furious, but keep it on the inside. You have to seem like nothing they can say or do could hurt you. Convey that you don't see them as a person, just an annoying math problem to solve."

"Okay, what then?"

"Nothing. You're done."

"What?"

"Job done. You snap notebook shut. Tell them you've got all the information you need and walk away."

"That's all? Really?"

"Well, you could end with, 'You've made an enemy for life today.' Being vague is the key. You could leave them with, 'I'll be watching,' or just shoot 'em a psycho grin. I like to say, 'Could be today, could be a year from now, maybe five years, but when it happens, only you will know for sure it was me.'"

"You've done this?"

"A few times."

Astonished, Ant burst out laughing.

"You don't have to actually do anything," Molly said. "They'll be waiting years for the other shoe to drop on their empty heads. In the meantime, maybe they will have learned it's not wise to be rude. You never know which strangers are dangerous."

"Haunting."

Molly grinned. "They will lose sleep. I hear that can be lethal."

"I want to try it!"

"Share it with anyone you know who works retail. They could use this strategy maybe a half-dozen times a week, or at least once until they get fired."

They both laughed, but she cut him off. "Now it's your turn to tell me more about Keith. What do you and Sarah want from me exactly? Keep in mind, I'm saying no. I'm just a curious person."

Ant shifted in his seat uncomfortably. "You sure? I've learned my lesson. What if *I'm* a dangerous stranger?"

He was trying to turn the tables on her. She smiled at his feeble attempt. "I don't think I have cause to worry."

"Oh? Why's that?"

"I don't consider you dangerous. You know what I did in high school. You won't cross me. Am I right?"

His eyes widened. "I won't say anything to anyone. You're a hero as far as I'm concerned. Can we talk about that?"

"What more do you need to know?"

70

SUSPICION

"Your battle with Lloyd Faun was a long time ago," Ant began, "but if you could help us with Keith — "

"Based on what Rose told you, you're hoping I'm still in the righteous wrath business. I've tried my best to keep my fury in check, but it's difficult. Contrary to what we've been told, the meek don't inherit the Earth. The meek get dirt."

"That is bad news for me," Ant said.

"How many others did your mother tell about my history? I'm not talking about running cross-country and the debate team."

"Only me. Well, okay, there are a couple other people, but I guarantee they're not talking. And Keith would be too embarrassed to admit the truth."

She wasn't sure Ant was being honest. "I hope other graduates of Poeticule Bay Consolidated don't have such clear memories."

When he looked away, she was almost sure he was taking the time to formulate a lie.

Molly stared at her empty plate. "Coming home was a mistake."

"I hope you don't mean that. You're still the girl in the ski mask, Molly. I need Tigger! I need your help. *We* need your help. Maybe that's why you're back to the Bay. Maybe ... I'm not sure, anymore."

He could be baiting her, but she saw doubt in his eyes. "What?"

"The notebook trick and all that. It's just all mind tricks and words. It's all so ...."

"Verbal?"

"Yeah! Are you still willing to actually *do* things? Things the sheriff wouldn't approve of?"

"Already said no." She ticked off his options on her fingers. "Sheriff, priest, lawyer, remember?"

"Look, I'm desperate. Sarah is desperate and I think you *want* to help us."

In this, Ant was not wrong, so she said, "I'll entertain a hypothetical. You asked if I'm still willing to take action. Suppose for a minute that I got fired from a job I loved. I was good at it. A guy who shouldn't be dean of a college exercised power over me, so I did something. Yeah, I can take what you might call kinetic action."

Ant looked skeptical. "What'd you do? Hypothetically."

"I suppose, first, I'd play mind games with him, threaten him in some way."

"That's my point. If it's all just a sternly worded email — "

"Hypothetically, suppose I was very angry, and this person messed with a friend of mine. After I packed up and left my job, I could have gone back to the dean's residence that night. Technically, it was break and enter, but the key was under the mat. Maybe the law would call it criminal trespass. He was out, so I would have time to wreak a nasty vengeance."

"Well, don't keep me in suspense!"

Her smile was back. "Theoretically — "

"Like we were talking before, with the notebook?"

"Sure. You want to get somebody good? Take two spray bottles and fill them with milk. Don't just dump the milk everywhere. Make it a fine mist and then go to town on the bedding, the carpet, the clothes in the closet, every piece of fabric. Be on a train out of the state before it all begins to stink. Your target will still be wandering around trying to identify where the stench is coming from."

"Why?"

"Because it'll seem like it's coming from everywhere."

Ant was still laughing when she reached out and gripped the little finger of his right hand. She squeezed hard. "I'm sincerely not all talk."

He gasped in pain and hunched forward as Molly twisted his little finger back and to one side.

"If Keith Faun is the target, I'm willing to listen. What's he done lately? If you want me to trust you, stop being a coy bitch and open the fuck up!"

Ant blurted it all out in a rush. "He's terrorizing my sister. She's tried to leave and he's punished her. Sarah lives in fear."

"Too terrified to go to the police?"

"Way too terrified. Worse, my mother has early-onset Alzheimer's."

"Rose?" She released his finger. "I am sorry to hear that."

Ant shook his hand to get the blood flow back and massaged his little finger absently. "Yeah, Mom was so smart. She's not anymore. It's as if she's getting erased. Some days, on her good days, she still thinks she should get dressed for work. She talks about going into the school once in a while, as if ... well, you know."

"My mom's sick, too," Molly said. "In a different way, but it's all hard."

"Yeah, but having Keith in the family and ruling the roost is much worse than holes in the brain."

"Say more."

"Mom lives with them. Sarah has to do as she's told, or Keith will smack Mom around."

"Some son-in-law. Call the police."

"I called once. They did a wellness check. Keith talked them out the door. Then he punched Sarah and Mom in the stomach. My sister begged me never to complain again. If they leave, he's promised to track them down and kill them both. I'm sure he'd kill me first."

A car roared up to the front of the building. Ant leaned to one side to peer out the window. "Molly, whatever happens in the next few minutes, please believe me, I need your help. *We* need your help."

Keith Faun burst through the front door. He looked around the restaurant, spotted Molly, and headed straight for her booth.

Ant leaned forward. "Don't say anything about — "

"Shut up. I get it."

But Ant spoke in a hurried whisper. "I'm just the manager. Keith's the boss. Just so you know, Debbie called him. I didn't!"

"I figured," Molly sighed. "Now it's his turn to bend my ear. Can't wait to catch up."

71

ADDITION

As Keith approached, he slowed to a swagger. A peacock, too sure of himself, he hadn't changed much. Except for a touch of gray at his temples, and a little more full in the middle, he was still handsome.

But since she'd seen him last, he looked a little harder. It was not the kind of hard one gets from too much time in the sun. It was the kind of hard a man gets from a lot of smoking and drinking.

Molly's stomach fluttered with revulsion at his resemblance to Lloyd Faun. Keith still thought he was the center of the universe. Molly thought someone should teach him more about the realities of astrophysics.

Debbie popped her head out of the kitchen and gave a jaunty salute. "Hey, boss!"

"Thanks for the call, kid!" Keith bobbed his head and flashed the server a wolfish grin.

My, what big teeth you have, Molly thought. *But I'm not Little Red Riding Hood. I am not fooled by your smile.*

Molly clenched her jaw to bite back a curse. Debbie had been friendly. She wondered if Dylan Caffrey knew his cousin stood on the side of his tormentor. Surely the skinny little kid she'd saved from a beating would not approve of his cousin's treachery.

As he arrived at her booth, Keith shot Ant a sour look. "Deb's a good girl for dialing me in. Shoulda been you who called me, shouldn't it? I guess she understands who signs the checks around here."

Ant said nothing in reply, and with just a flick of one finger, Keith signalled the young man to vacate his seat. Ant rose quickly and scurried back to the kitchen.

Without invitation, Keith slid into the seat opposite her. "So, Jergins! You're back to the ole Bay, huh?"

"And here I thought Debbie liked me."

"How long you back for?" he asked, as if they were old friends. Keith stared into her eyes as if he could read her thoughts.

Her heart pounded harder as she stared back defiantly. His wolfish grin was back and did not falter.

A monster made of teeth.

"How long am I back? We'll see," she replied vaguely.

"Never saw you around, not even on Christmases. Never even came back to see to your mom?"

Molly struggled with her rising irritation but was sure she'd failed already to conceal that emotion. "I came back for Christmases here and there. I stuck to the house and didn't stay long enough for your spies to tip you off."

Keith's laugh was a sharp bark. "Given your history, it's good to know when you're around. If anybody breaks into any of my businesses, I'll know where to send the sheriff."

"I have no *immediate* plans for B&Es," Molly replied.

"Reassuring. Heard you teach English now. How's that going?"

"Great."

"Really? Always thought of that as kind of a dead-end job."

Molly refused to take the bait. She did not aspire to be a great conversationalist with Keith Faun. Silence stretched out between them.

Keith broke first. "D'jou get married? Divorced? Or what?"

"A what," she said and left it at that. Even if they were both immortal, eons could pass, and Molly would never share any personal information with Keith Faun.

Molly had had a bunch of bad dates, one exceptionally terrible date, a couple of serious relationships, and a situationship, not in that order. And she had one great romance.

Soon after Molly received her PhD, Molly got her first and only marriage proposal. A master's student had become obsessed with her and dead Canadian writers, possibly in equal measure. "Let's live in libraries and exist in books," he said. It was a tempting offer. Buddy Gott was the only person to whom she'd confessed everything she had done.

Buddy wanted to pursue his doctorate in Montreal and write his thesis on the works of Mordecai Richler. Buddy claimed that Richler had changed the course of his life with one quote about how pure artists were "the unacknowledged legislators of the world."

He was a good man, and for a time, Molly felt safe in his goodness. She also thought they were too different from each other. She feared she might fall back into old habits one day. Not with him, never with him. Buddy was the kind of person she wanted to protect.

"I've got the job lined up at Greenbriar," she told him. "That's too far from Montreal, isn't it? I can't do that to you."

"What if I want you to do that to me?"

"Everything is too fragile."

"Not me. Not love."

"Me, then," she said. "I'm made of glass and afraid of falling. You know why."

"They call it falling in love, but it's really a leap of faith."

"I worry I might be too damaged to be with someone so nice."

"From all you've told me, I know you are brave, but not enough for a chance for us?"

"Not enough for someone so important," she told him.

"You're a complex kaleidoscope of chaos, Molly."

"You are sweetness," she replied.

"And you are a sweet mess."

At that, she smiled and wept at the same time.

Buddy held her close and whispered, "L.P. Hartley wrote, 'The past is a foreign country.' Not for you, Molly. You live there, all the way back there in the dark."

As she stared at Keith across the table now, it was as if Buddy had just spoken those words.

It may be cold and lonely, she thought, *but down here in the darkness is where sea creatures live. This is where we feed.*

Buddy had been right. Molly was back in Poeticule Bay, trapped in the past, her mind a broken time machine. Since Boston, Buddy had moved on, forward into a future to find the greatest love of his life. He did go to Montreal to work on his doctorate. That's where he met his future wife. In the end, Buddy's leap of faith had landed him, softly and happily, in Wilmington, Delaware. Molly knew all this because she listened to his podcast, Pop and Prose, in which he interviewed writers and discussed pop culture. He wasn't teaching English for a living in Montreal, so he must have loved his wife even more than dead Canadian writers.

When her silence made it clear Molly had nothing to say about her personal life, Keith tried another stab at her. "The romance department is out of stock, huh?"

The first rule of warfare: Do not give information to the enemy. He knew her name, and she had no rank or serial number. That left insults. "Fournier gangrene."

"What?"

"Fournier gangrene. It's a life-threatening infection of the genitals and taint."

He stared back blankly. "Why...what?"

"Because when I look at your face, I think of an infection of the taint."

Seemingly undeterred, Keith probed again. "Staying out of trouble? Kill anybody by accident? Kill anyone on purpose? Not running from the law, are you?"

"Nope. You?"

He shrugged. "As my dad used to say, livin' large and in charge!

Life is good. Closed the laundromat business in town. Still making bank off of the franchises, though. Sold the old house, built a mansion — ”

“And bought out the Driftin’, too, I see.”

Keith looked around his restaurant. “The fish! The tourists! My good fortune came back, all after you left. Seems like it’s bad luck when you’re around, doesn’t it?”

Molly said nothing, merely watched him, same as she’d keep a careful eye on a venomous snake.

“Know what, Jergins? You remind me of someone I saw up in Oubliette last fall. See, I was driving in a rainstorm, lotsa water, bad day. The car ahead of me plowed through a puddle and splashed this old lady at the side of the road. Just soaked her, and boy, was she mad! She’s standing there, wet to the bone and screaming at the car that sped through the puddle.”

“And how does that apply to me?”

He showed her both his palms in a gesture that told her to wait for the punchline. “So anyway, I’m coming up to that huge puddle, and I’m going faster than the first guy.”

Keith broke into a high giggle, almost too giddy to relate his anecdote. “The wall of water from my wheels hits her square in the face while she’s still screaming at the injustice of the world. Caught her mid-scream. Got a mouthful of dirt water, for sure! Mighta drowned! After I stopped laughing about it, I wondered if I should feel bad for the woman, maybe apologize, and offer her a ride, right?”

“But you didn’t.” It was not a question nor a guess.

“Damn right, I didn’t! You know why? She was the one out in a storm standing beside a puddle with her gob hanging open! She had only herself to blame!”

“And you think that’s like me somehow?”

Keith’s smile vanished. “It’s you, comin’ back for more. For the good of the town, you’ll be moving on soon, won’t you?”

He made it sound more like an order than a suggestion and Molly burst out laughing. “Is this an old western? Are you expecting me to be on the noon stage out of town?”

"Whatever."

"Whatever? Well, you sure do make a trenchant argument."

"I wasn't in the debate club in high school. Too busy playing hockey."

"How'd that work out?"

Keith scanned the restaurant, perhaps to make sure no one was listening. "Didn't go pro. I came home, and ... like I said, livin' large. Dad owned the town in a spiritual kind of way. I'm buying it up, owning it for real."

Molly raised her voice slightly, hoping other customers would listen. "If you're done hyping yourself up, serious question: Do you believe people can change?"

"Don't care."

Debbie appeared at the table. Ignoring Molly, her gaze was fixed on her boss. She placed a tall glass of what looked like chocolate milk in front of Keith. "Your usual, sir!"

He took a sip and dismissed Debbie with a nod toward the front of the diner. "I think the guy in the front corner booth is ready to pay his bill."

Debbie reddened and hurried away.

"Protein powder smoothie with berries," Keith explained. "Pre-workout or post-workout, it's all good."

Keith Faun was an idiot who only valued physical strength and idolized power. He still clung to the illusion that he could always be the one in control. That delusion was more fragile than glass and the easiest to shatter.

"We were talking about whether you can change," Molly said. "The official term is metanoia. It means changing your mind, specifically after a breakdown. It's the catharsis you get after you realize you're a worm who dreams of being a human. I paraphrase, but when I look at you, I think that explanation comes close."

Keith looked away. "I don't even know what you're talking about. Do you? I doubt it."

"It's not really a complicated question, Keith. This is a test. Do you believe people can change? It's been twelve years. The last time we saw each other was the night our fathers went over the cliff — "

"The night your dad killed mine, you mean."

"I have my answer. Sad. You haven't changed."

Keith leaned forward. "Have *you*?"

Molly stared at him a moment. "No and that should scare you."

He rolled his eyes and was about to say more, but Molly stopped him. "You won't change on your own. I see that, but I could change something about you. Not your mind, of course. Your brain is a little blob of ground chuck rotted through so bad I can smell it. I bet I could change your behavior, though."

Keith's smile faded. "That's not very friendly."

"Whose breakfast did you think you were intruding on? Have you forgotten who I am?"

"I remember what you did, and this isn't meant to be a friendly visit. This is me saying life would be better for you somewhere else."

"Let's put a pin in that." Molly slid her empty plate to one side and leaned both elbows on the table. In doing so, she palmed the knife, tucking the blade out of sight behind her forearm.

It was only a butter knife, and the sticky maple syrup stained her sleeve. Despite its blunt edge, holding the secret weapon steadied her nerves. She would not dare to show this man any weakness. His eyes were as empty of empathy as a shark's eyes.

To him, she was nothing. To her, he was a predator who needed to be reminded what it felt like to be prey.

Monsters made of teeth come in all shapes and sizes.

72

SUBTRACTION

"Do you have kids?" Molly asked.

"Not yet."

"So, you probably don't own a bouncy castle."

"A what?"

"A bouncy castle. A bounce house! You know, the things kids bounce around on at birthday parties. Kind of like an enclosed trampoline — "

"I know what they are! I just — "

"Every year, on average, twenty-eight people die in bouncy castles. I collect factoids like this. Death statistics spark the imagination."

He did not appear impressed.

"Unusual deaths are much more interesting than the cold actuarial tables insurance companies use. They catalog the big numbers. It's the outliers that are interesting. The odder the demise, the more intrigued I am."

Keith shrugged. "So?"

"For instance, last I heard, three people a year die from swallowing toothbrushes. Over six-hundred thousand die from falls."

Put off by this tangent, Keith Faun looked annoyed. "So, what's this about the bouncy castles?"

"You're probably thinking that kids bounce around, and a few die because they smash their skulls together. That happens, but what's more useful to know is the danger in not securing bouncy castles to the ground."

Molly was beginning to enjoy the perplexed look on her enemy's face. "See, before the pandemic, bouncy castles were something that professional party planners traditionally provided. A pro would come set it up in your backyard and make sure the castle was tied down properly, roped to a tree so it wouldn't blow away."

Keith muttered a curse. "You want to bounce around with me, Jergins? You flirting with me?"

Molly shook her head and continued. "It turns out, it only takes as little as fifteen miles per hour of wind to make a bouncy castle into a kite. You don't tie it down right, it flies. Remember that big windstorm we had here when we were kids? The gulls all blew out to sea and didn't come back for weeks. There were fishing boats all the way up in the woods and the Shore Road was washed out."

Keith's eyes were heavy-lidded, making a show of his boredom.

"Hypothetically, suppose someone blended castor beans into your usual." She indicated his protein smoothie with a glance.

"Castor beans?"

"Makes ricin. It's the easiest poison to make. I mean, rat poison tastes like peanut butter, so that's also a possibility. Anyway, as you get sick and weak, it's fun to think about taking you out back to the cliff and tossing you in a bouncy castle. Under the correct meteorological conditions, you could get carried pretty far out over the sea before you fell out dead. Or you could fall out near-dead and drown."

Keith Faun put down his protein smoothie as if touching the glass could poison him.

Molly cradled her chin in the hand that did not conceal the knife. "For a moment, as you shot up into the air, you'd scream with the wind. There would be a few seconds there where I bet it would feel exhilarating. When I look at you, I see so many interesting possibilities. How's your mom, by the way? She was a peach, wasn't she? Be sure to tell her I wish her a long life! I hope she outlives her son."

Keith looked around the restaurant as if to make sure he was still sitting in the Drift Inn Diner. "You're threatening me again."

"Me? Nah, just sharing a funny anecdote about bouncy castles."

"You fantasize about me."

Keith's smarmy grin disappeared when Molly explained, "Yes, but my fantasies aren't sexual."

"No? I think they might be. You're obsessed with me."

"Don't flatter yourself. I spend a lot of time thinking about how to make the world a better place. The world would be better without you in it."

Keith didn't really feel physically threatened, but he was offended. "While you've been away, I've done a lot of good for this town. My father did a lot of good for this town. People are coming back around to my way of thinking. Despite all you've done, losing your father and all, the Faun name doesn't have the stink on it that you wanted."

"Then you're a fool who underestimates people. For instance, you should be nicer to Debbie. She's infatuated with you now, anybody can see that. Once she gets past the lust and understands what you really are? I'd be mixing up my own smoothies if I were you."

Molly got up to leave.

"See you around, Jergins, but I hope for not too much longer."

"I'll stay in Poeticule Bay as long as I want. You can take over the whole town. You'll never own me."

Keith turned in his seat to call after her. "Keep fantasizing about me, Jergins! Jergins! Like the lotion! I could rub you all over me and you'd love it!"

Several patrons laughed at this remark as Molly walked for the door. Her cheeks flushed. Whirling on Keith, she shouted, "I lied about the fantasies. The things I rehearse in my mind *are* sexual!"

The truckers laughed harder and then clapped to show their approval. A guy in a John Deere hat raised his coffee cup to toast her.

"It's true!" Molly continued. "I see myself drowning you in your bathtub! Then I revive you with the kiss of life just so I can drown you again! You're begging me to kill you, but I keep drowning you until I can't bring you back anymore. That really turns me on!"

The laughter died. The entire restaurant plunged to an awkward silence. Ant and a couple of kitchen staff came out to see what was going on. Everyone stared at Molly.

For the first time, Keith Faun lost his self-possession. It wasn't fear, not yet. But Molly saw self-doubt in the big man's wide, wondering eyes.

Ant stood behind the cash register, unable to meet her gaze. As she passed him, she said, "I'm going to have to meet Sarah and her mother. Can you arrange that?"

Ant gave a subtle nod and whispered, "If you plan to help us, are you going to be more subtle than that?"

"Set up the meeting and get back to me. What happens next depends on what the tyrant's wife has to say."

As she made for the door, Molly passed by Debbie, stock still, holding a tray of eggs over easy, white toast, bacon, and sausages. As the server stared at her, Molly grabbed the sausages and shoved one into her mouth.

Between chews, she said to the shocked server, "You were really friendly when I walked in here. Then you called *him*. Dylan must be so disappointed in you."

Debbie glowered. "The boss wanted to talk to you, is all. He says you're a terrorist and the daughter of a terrorist."

She stiffened as Molly wiped the grease from the sausage on her shoulder. From the other hand, she dropped the butter knife on the plate with a clatter.

"I know he's cute and rich," Molly warned, "but that's not enough in Keith's case. Talk to Dylan more about your boss. Dylan knows."

Debbie didn't look convinced.

Molly tried again, "The guy's an abuser. You may as sharp as a balloon, but you're too pretty to be this hard up! For your sake, take the only tip I'll ever give you. *Run!*"

73

JURISDICTION

The following day, Sheriff Gordon Hobbs rapped sharply on Molly's front door. He didn't ring the doorbell. Instead, he sent a message with loud, insistent pounding. "Sheriff here!" Hobbs bellowed. "Open up!"

As Molly headed to the door, Vincent got up from the kitchen table. "I'll go up and keep your mother company."

"I'll take care of it. Tell her not to worry," Molly said.

Vincent lumbered up the stairs. "Kay don't worry. She only causes that unfortunate condition in others."

When she opened the front door, Molly found Sheriff Hobbs waiting for her with a bearded deputy she vaguely remembered. Hobbs had lost hair since she saw him last, and his broad shoulders now sloped. He was sliding into old age and not gracefully. "Sheriff. Long time."

"Not long enough maybe," he replied sourly.

"You sound angry. If this isn't going to be a nice chat, you can tell my lawyer all about it. I don't have a lawyer, so you'll have to wait until I find one."

The deputy smirked a little, but Hobbs remained dead serious. "It's cold out here on your stoop. Can we come in?"

Molly stood in the door, unmoving. "Not a good idea. Just had the floors waxed. I wouldn't want you to fall down and break a hip."

He looked irked. "Your mom around? I'd like to speak with Kay, too."

"My mom's getting into the bath," she lied.

"How is she? The doctors ever figure out what all is wrong with her? Is it female troubles?"

"My mother keeps herself to herself, Sheriff. Now, the water's running, so if you could not mind her business and state yours — "

"This won't necessarily be a nice chat, Molly, but I'll endeavor to make it quick. You had words with Mr. Faun yesterday. He has witnesses, says you threatened him."

"Our conversation got heated, but no reasonable person would take any of it seriously."

"He took it seriously, says you're a danger."

The deputy piped up. "Don't forget, Sheriff, the waitress says she stole a couple of sausages. They had to remake that plate."

Hobbs rolled his eyes miserably. "*Thank* you, Deputy Lime."

Molly grinned. "Well, isn't that silly? Truth be told, I felt threatened by him. Do you want to head back to your office? Prep some paperwork for a report? I'll be over to sign a complaint after I've taken care of Mom."

"Molly — "

"I notice that, to you, he's Mr. Faun, and I'm just Molly? That's sweet. I didn't realize we were such good friends! My friends call me Molly. You can call me Dr. Jergins."

"Dr. Jergins — "

"So, how does this complaint process work? Does his concern take precedence because he ran to whine to Police Daddy first? I ask because you have a history of giving the Faun men enough rope to hang themselves. You never tighten the damn rope and let 'em swing! Weird, isn't it?"

The deputy covered his mouth and turned around to conceal his smile. The sheriff noticed his amusement. "Deputy? No sense us both freezing our asses off out here. How about you head back to the car and monitor the radio? Keep the heater going on high. I'll be there directly."

Lime tipped his hat to Molly and hurried back down the walk to the police cruiser.

Hobbs stepped closer and spoke low, as if someone besides Molly could hear. "Tell me, you still going on runs late at night?"

"Not so much in the winter. Too slippery. Why?"

"You've been away, but not so long that I've forgotten the bad old days. Let's keep this simple. Stay clear of Keith Faun. Read me?"

"Are you giving him a stern talking-to as well? Telling him to stay away from me?"

"I can do that. Whatever it takes to keep the peace."

"Like staying out of his restaurant? That won't be a problem. Now that I know he owns it, I don't want to give that place any more money."

"All right then, long as we understand each other." Hobbs stepped back but paused. "Just so you know, I've been making inquiries."

"About what?"

The cop looked like he was about to say more but thought better of it. "Making sure you aren't on the warpath again. We don't want a repeat of history is all I'm sayin', and that's more than I should need to say."

"Keith and I only had one dad each," Molly replied. "Can't kill them twice."

"That a confession of something?"

"Bad joke."

Hobbs crossed his arms and studied her. "What you say and the look in your eyes don't match up. Have I made myself clear enough with you, Dr. Jergins? I fear I have not."

"Sure," Molly replied. "No need to come back. It's tub time now."

Hobbs chuckled. "You think you hear your mother calling?"

Molly shut the door in the sheriff's face. She turned to find Vincent standing on the stairs. Her uncle stared at her with a questioning look.

"It's fine," Molly said. "Lost dog in the neighborhood."

"You the lost puppy they're looking for?"

"It's nothing."

"A second ago, it was fine. Now it's just nothing?"

"I had words with Keith Faun. Old high school grudge match."

"The kingpin of the town, huh? I'm friendly with his manager at the DID. Ant says he's an asshole."

"Yeah, about that. I hear you go to the diner a bunch."

"Only sometimes. I'm not good at poaching my own eggs."

"I'll poach eggs for you. Don't go there anymore, okay? You knew Keith Faun owns it now?"

"Surely. He owns a lot these days."

"Please do not go to the diner. The last thing anyone in this family should do is give money to the Faun empire. He's a thug."

Vincent grabbed the banister to steady himself as he lowered his bulk to perch on a step. "The cops keeping an eye on you 'cuz of this grudge?"

"It's not a problem. Hobbs told me to stay away from Keith. That's what I want, anyway."

Vincent sucked his teeth. "Uh-huh."

"Don't believe me?"

"Not what I was going to say. Hobbs might be keeping an eye on you for a while, so conduct yourself accordingly. Attract a cop's attention once, and any state can be a police state. Get what I'm sayin'?"

"So, I should stay home and hide? Maybe dig a hole in the basement?"

Vincent struggled to pull himself to stand. "Hobbs is getting on in years. If he's like me, he doesn't like driving at night. Were I you and wanted to take the air, I'd leave by the gap in the back fence. I'd do it at night."

Kay called from upstairs. "Vince! Molly? What's going on down there?"

"Sheriff Hobbs came by with his deputy!" Vincent answered. "The stupid one with the beard. Never used to see cops with beards in my day."

"What'd he want?"

"Sayin' hi!" Vincent answered.

"Just being cordial?" Kay asked doubtfully.

"No frets! Comes to nothin'!"

"Makes sense," Kay shouted. "Doing nothing is their specialty."

Molly headed up the stairs. As she passed her uncle, he whispered, "Don't talk to Kay about Hobbs more than you have to. It'll rile her up."

Molly put a finger to her lips. "You know me, Uncle Vincent. I'm not a problem. I'm a problem solver."

"Yeah, yeah, sure! And butter wouldn't melt in your mouth."

Molly batted her eyelashes and put on a heavy Southern accent. "Why, I do declare, Uncle! How dare you? I don't know how you dare! I'm as innocent as the day is long."

"It's winter. The days are dark like your moods and short like your patience."

Now is the winter of our discontent, Molly thought. She had taken a class on *Richard III* in her undergraduate years. As she continued up the stairs, more lines from the play sprang to mind:

AND ALL THE *clouds that lour'd upon our house,*
   In the deep bosom of the ocean buried.

"YOU JERGINS WOMEN give me the squirts," Vincent said. "You're like your mother, born sassy and cranky!"

"To fright the souls of fearful adversaries!"

Vincent straightened. "*Whut? Come again?*"

"Shakespeare."

"Well, *la-di-da!*"

"And I'm not cranky. Neither am I sassy. House cats are sassy. I'm furious."

"You gonna do somethin' you shouldn't?" her uncle asked.

"I don't know what I'm going to do yet," Molly admitted.

"Fine, fine," Vincent muttered as he headed to the kitchen. "I'll shut up like always, tend to my knittin', and make a baloney sandwich. Jergins gals! Always spoilin' for a fight."

74

CONCOCTION

Four days later, Molly found an envelope addressed to her in the mailbox. There was no postmark, just a white envelope with her name. It was marked confidential.

The note, written in a hasty scrawl, read:

The Overlook, 3 pm today.

The note was unsigned, but Molly assumed it was Ant arranging a meet-up with Sarah Faun. It was also possible Keith was setting her up to corner her in an isolated place. She would have to plan for that possibility, too.

Ant Rainier had begged for her help, and she believed he'd asked in earnest. However, she wasn't sure he could keep a secret from his boss.

When Ant looked at Keith, she'd seen the fear in the little man's face. If Keith pressed him for details of their long conversation, Molly thought Ant might pop like a balloon. Anyone who would accept an insect for a nickname couldn't have a lot of self-esteem.

What worried Molly more was the site for the meet-up. Had she chosen where to speak with Sarah, it would have been a less isolated place.

The Overlook stood on Poet's Mountain, a high point at the end of Correction Road. The Appalachians were nowhere near as imposing as the Rockies, of course, but the Overlook yielded a commanding view of all of Poeticule Bay and the town. There were benches up there, a popular spot with locals and tourists alike in spring, summer, and fall.

At dawn, it was the best place to watch the sun boiling up out of the ocean. After dark, the parking lot was a popular spot for teenagers to steam up their parents' car windows. In the depths of an icy February afternoon, the Overlook would be deserted.

If Keith planned to ambush Molly, he could hardly pick a better place. On the other hand, the Poet's Overlook was close to the Faun's mansion. If Sarah was indeed the abused wife Ant described, getting out of the house for long might be difficult.

The last time Molly saw Sarah Rainier, she was a cheerleader giving Keith worshipful looks. Despite living next to the Fauns throughout her entire childhood, Sarah had married Keith.

It was unimaginable that Rose Rainier would have approved Sarah's marriage to Keith Faun. And now they both lived under his roof.

Ant's news about Rose bothered Molly very much. "Erased." That was the word Ant had used to describe his mother. The disease made Rose even more vulnerable.

When the law failed to protect Barry, Rose had gone out of her way to protect him. She'd even shielded Molly and Keith from further harm. Knowing that Rose had fallen victim to dementia seemed to demonstrate there was no cosmic justice, either.

If there is no justice, Molly thought, *I guess it's up to me to do what I can to even things out a little.*

She was confident she would be meeting Sarah for a conversation about Keith. But what if he showed up instead? Molly slipped a kitchen knife into the sleeve of her winter coat.

The underrated joys of paranoia, Molly thought. *It's not pathological if it keeps me alive. In my case, paranoia is logical.*

For a moment, Molly indulged in the fantasy of using the knife, backing Keith up to the edge of the lookout. He could choose the blade or tumble off the Overlook. It wasn't as sharp a drop as the Drifting Cliffs. However, there were a lot of rocks and trees. In a few places, the drop-off was almost an eighty-degree angle.

Keith falling down and breaking his head open like an egg. Molly smiled. *What a beautiful irony that would be, but twelve years too late.*

Next, Molly trudged out through deep snow to the shed. The padlock was rusty but still functional. With some difficulty, she got it open, and shoving the door past the resistance of a snow drift, she squeezed inside.

Tiny windows and vents leaked little light into the interior, but the light switch still worked. For his work, Chuck Jergins had spent a lot of time here. She sniffed the air, but there was no trace left of the aftershave he'd favored.

Lime, she remembered. *When I was really little, I liked it because it smelled like those sodas we used to drink at Christmas. Lime Rickey soda pop! Her uncle would bring a case from the Pop Shoppe up in Canada.*

Her father had laughed, not unkindly, when she tried to read the label on the bottles and pronounced it, "Pop Shop-pee."

"Your father's absence feels like a presence," Kay had said. In his workshop, that feeling was stronger than ever.

To light up the shed to its dark corners, Molly flicked the light switch by the workbench. Despite the cobwebs, things were very much as Chuck had left them.

Everything was as she expected except for the shotguns. They weren't hanging on the rack by the back wall. They weren't in their padded leather cases, either. The cases had also disappeared.

Molly bent to open likely cabinets, but they weren't there, either. Her parents had both owned a pair of Remington Model 870 twelve gauges. Each Thanksgiving, they shot clay pigeons on Molly's grandfather's farm.

"Back when we were courtin'," Chuck once told Molly, "we

hunted rabbits and pheasants. When I found out Kay was a better shot than me, I told a buddy, 'I'm gonna marry that girl!'"

Had Kay sold the guns after her father's passing? Molly had no idea. Maybe they were tucked away in the basement somewhere.

Molly wasn't disappointed. It was more a matter of curiosity than preparedness. She couldn't very well walk through town with a twelve gauge over her shoulder and then claim total innocence if the meeting at the Overlook went sour. She didn't plan to kill Keith, but such a display would certainly connote intent to commit murder.

Molly's search continued. Molly didn't know what she was looking for, but she'd find a suitable defensive weapon. In her war against Lloyd Faun, this shed had been her armory. It was a little like browsing a bookstore. She would only know her heart's desire when she laid eyes upon it.

Her father had been so meticulous there was never any sawdust left under the jigsaw. He cleaned up after each job, and when Molly was barely old enough, he'd handed her the broom. She loved the smell of fresh sawdust, too.

Every spot for each tool on the pegboard was outlined for quick and easy placement and retrieval. The shed and its contents were hardly disturbed since Molly had left home.

Vince rarely entered the shed except to pull out the lawnmower and put it back. Their shovels were now by the front porch. As soon as winter lifted, the snow shovels would again be stored here.

Molly scanned the shelves, eyeing the bottles of screws and boxes of nails. Everything was labeled. As a teen, Molly once asked her father if he had OCD.

"Sure!" Chuck replied. "Not before I was in the Army. Before that, I never made my bed. First week of boot camp, they hammer that OCD into you so deep it gets in the bones. Orders, organization, and trying not to puke after long runs. That was the life! It sucked, but it stuck!"

And the duty to protect, Molly thought. *They hammered that into him, too, and that must have gone deeper than the bones. It was in the genes.*

Speaking of hammers, she considered a ball peen for her meeting up at the Overlook. She already had the knife in case Keith had laid a trap. A couple of the screwdrivers might be a useful weapon, as well.

However, Keith was a big guy. She didn't want to have to do battle with him up close. Within arm's reach of a hockey goon? He would crush her. Choreographed hand-to-hand combat looked pretty in the movies, but she needed a weapon to even out the odds.

Tucked away at the rear of a cabinet, she found a canister. It was long past its best-before date, but the seal was unbroken. She shook it. Full and heavy.

Molly read the label. "Shoots twenty feet."

Wasp spray, she thought. *Legal to carry and might even be better than mace.*

75

NAVIGATION

The rusty old Volvo still sat in the garage, battery dead and tires flat. Molly started walking toward the edge of town but soon hitched a ride with an old farmer headed inland after a shopping trip to the Pick-Right. Dropped off at the mouth of Correction Road, Molly began the hike toward the Overlook.

As a girl, she'd often biked up the mountain with her mother. It had been their ritual on Sunday mornings in the summertime. Her father stayed home from those forays. By the time his wife and daughter returned, he had a stack of pancakes, eggs, and bacon ready and waiting.

Molly had such fond memories of her first bicycle. Her father had salvaged the antique from the back of some dead neighbor's shed. He'd repainted it and fixed it up so nicely, she barely noticed it wasn't brand new. For as long as she owned it, that bike was her most prized possession. It was pink, with a banana seat. Puffs of silver tinsel had once hung from both ends of the handlebars. When her father gave her the bike, only a few strands had remained sprouting from the rubber end of the right handlebar. When she rode fast, the tinsel lay flat, straightened by the wind.

Kay had been quite an athlete before time and disease took their toll. Her mother's old bike now hung from a rafter in the garage, with brakes so locked up and broken that the wheels didn't even spin. But as a child, Molly had struggled to keep up with Kay as they climbed Poet's Mountain together.

Her mom wouldn't coddle her by slowing or waiting for her to catch up. Instead, she would call over her shoulder, "Stand on the pedals if you have to! Push, Molly! This is only the hard part! Take care of the hard part first. It's like eating Brussels sprouts. Nobody sane likes 'em, but we do the ugly up front so we earn dessert! Later, on the way back down, we'll just coast and fly! You'll see! The ride back down is gonna be like banana cream pie!"

Her mother was right. The thrill of coasting back down made all the sweat worth it. Once she made it to the top, she could ride for miles, barely pumping the pedals, never touching the brakes, free.

And it *was* like flying. It was warmer up the mountain, so when they were almost back to town, they'd speed into a wall of cold air coming off the Atlantic. They could have closed their eyes and still known they were almost home, welcomed by the ocean air.

Molly couldn't remember what had happened to her pink bike. Had her parents given it away to another little girl when Molly outgrew it? Donated to some charity? Was her old bicycle buried in the town dump or recycled? Maybe the metal was now part of a toaster or made into wire, no longer recognizable from what it had once been.

What was once a joy had become a milestone marker. About the time our first two-wheelers disappear, Molly thought, *life gets harder.*

It seemed that people could generally coast for a while. Then life got harder and harder, no coasting. Kay still refused to discuss her afflictions, but Molly was sure she was getting worse. When asked, her mother insisted her diagnosis was "aching of the everything."

Kay's world seemed to be getting ever smaller by the day now. It seemed the same was true of Sarah's mother. Molly was confident she wouldn't understand Sarah's motivation to marry the high school bully. However, when she met Sarah — if she did — perhaps they could bond over their mothers' health problems.

As Molly headed up Correction Road, wind whipped the tree-tops, making a shushing sound. The erection of the Poet Mountain Correction Institute for Juveniles had accompanied the road's name change. The narrow ribbon cutting through the mountain's green face used to be called the Overlook Road.

Why the county decided to change the name, she could not fathom. Maybe it was meant to scare the kids who attended the institute. If so, that was flimsy, but a lot of people did many things, and their reasoning was frequently opaque to Molly.

The road's surface had been gray macadam when she was a girl. It was now well-paved with dark asphalt and freshly plowed of snow. Tall pines rose on either side, as tight as a phalanx. The trees cut off any view of the town and the ocean below. Thick tangles of buckthorn lined the road, hemming Molly in.

There was no sidewalk, barely a shoulder. The narrow way reminded her of Keith splashing the screaming woman. Molly scanned the woods for deer paths but saw none. If a car or truck came along, any pedestrian would have to depend on the skill, kindness, and mercy of strangers. Molly couldn't imagine ever being so trusting.

After a few minutes, she came upon a few houses on the west side of the road. She was struck by how much had changed here in twelve years.

Correction Road felt very different. Though Poeticule Bay was no longer on the edge of the dead zone, the town was more recognizable.

The difference is rich people live up here, she thought. *I don't smell sulfur and brimstone, but Keith must be close.*

76

PROFUSION

Molly preferred the old slouching houses in town, buildings that seemed to huddle with each other, resentful of the weather. Battered by Atlantic winds, the exposed houses looked worn and tired, but they'd endured. Even the trees along the shore turned their branches away from the ocean's salty cold, but those houses looked like forever.

Old houses had nooks and crannies. Sometimes, they hid secret charms, like a hatch in the floor to a well or a jam and jelly preserve in a tiny, chilly room.

Molly imagined those were happy homes where — when everything went right — people lived a long time. Grandfathers trimmed bushes in the front yard, grandmothers baked biscuits, and grandchildren were spoiled. Those homes offered perfect places for children to play hide and seek.

Her own parents' house had a hidden closet beneath the back stairs. That back staircase was irregular, twisting up at a steep angle.

When she was a toddler, Molly used to hide in that closet. Kay and Chuck had recounted the same anecdote many times. Playing hide and seek, her grandfather would pretend to struggle to find her. When he finally opened the little closet door, she would leap out of the dark. He would shout in mock terror as Molly dissolved into his arms in gleeful laughter.

Molly didn't remember that. She didn't remember her grandfather at all.

Memories are funny that way, how empty they are until the brain readies itself to record everything. The day we start to remember things is another milestone, another marker signifying that life is about to get more complicated.

Her grandfather died alone on his farm sometime before she started school. She wasn't sure when. Cause of death: a broken heart. At least, that's what her father said.

Too new for such oddities, the houses on Correction Road held no such nooks or crannies. Any living architect would deem such deviations from the norm wastes of space and too costly.

"I'm a deviation from the norm," Molly told the trees. "We're underrated!"

These new builds on the mountain were in the Cape and Victorian styles but nestled amongst the pines. Molly breathed in the smell of the sweet cedar chips from flower beds that poked up above the snow. The pleasant mixture of pine and cedar scents made her want to pause in her journey, but she pushed on. She had an appointment to keep.

In town, family names were easy to see. Names were displayed on their mailboxes.

On Correction Road, each home sported a little sign or white stones at the end of each driveway. There were no mailboxes or family names. Instead, each property had a name or a slogan: Halcyon 2, Work's End, Poet Place, Tired and Retired, Plato's Retreat, The Place, Room at the Top, and Narnia.

Molly wondered about the people who lived in those houses. There were no strangers in town. Even if you didn't know someone's name, sheer close proximity and a small population at least made every face recognizable. But the come-from-aways who lived up the mountain were mysteries.

Who could afford to build these places? What did they do before they came here? Could there really be that many orthodontists in the world, all moving to Maine? What did they do with all that leisure time? Was it all jigsaw puzzles, crosswords, and cross-stitch? What was it like to have enough to hide away from the world? Were the people nice? Were they happy?

Molly told herself that the twinge she felt in her gut was not jealousy, not exactly. It was envy. Molly couldn't be sure, but hideaways like this suggested safety. Wealth insulates the fortunate from a thousand minor troubles. With enough money, you could build a home, snuggle up with a good book, and glide through easy days with only your health to worry about.

Molly knew it wasn't their fault, but she had to admit, she was a little mad at strangers she'd never met — people she never would meet. She had advanced degrees but no job and little leverage. She would never have access to their social circles. Molly was angry because the people on Correction Road knew safety. Molly didn't believe she ever would achieve that privilege.

Molly didn't like herself when she was like this. She aspired to be more like her mother. As Vince would say, "Not a whiner."

Still, as she walked Correction Road, she groused, "Underrated and always on the outside looking in."

Her father had been loving but somewhat detached until they discovered each other's secrets. Molly loved her mother, too, but Kay's criticism had always been harsh. She wasn't easy to talk to and rarely seemed satisfied.

When his wife was in her moods, Chuck would say, "The Admiral's slingin' orders again. Musta used sandpaper instead of soap this mornin'. Kay doesn't know sad, but she always has mad in her pocket."

Molly sighed. *I'm not like Mom yet.*

She kept on, trudging through the small drifts at the side of the road until the fancy retreats were behind her. It was not within her power to make the world a safe place. Every media headline was a reminder of her powerlessness. She couldn't cure cancer or solve world hunger. But she needed to do something about Keith Faun.

Safe isn't achievable, but a little better? I'll aim for a little better.

Finally, she came upon the monster's lair. Before she came even with the house, she pulled up the hood of her parka. She had no doubt there would be surveillance cameras monitoring the driveway. Given their shared history, Keith would be security conscious.

Molly knew this was his place because the words "Faun Manor" were woven into the design of the iron gate — ornate yet formidable. His was the largest home on Correction Road.

Of course it is, she thought. *If I wasn't jealous before, I am now. Evil pays well. Or is it worse than that? What if you can get so wealthy, no one cares whether you're evil?*

Suddenly, Molly wanted the chance to launch herself out of the darkness at Keith. She could make him scream, make her revenge fantasies real. Surely, she would be too scared to laugh in glee, but this time, she would definitely remember.

77

COMPENSATION

U p the long driveway of white concrete stood a huge four-car garage. She deduced the driveway was heated because none of last night's fresh snow held to the driveway.

More imposing than impressive, more ugly than not, the Faun house stretched upward three stories. Two massive bay windows on the top floor looked over the trees to command the view of the town and the ocean.

No, not the town, Molly corrected herself. *His kingdom. Like his dad, Keith thinks he owns everything he sees.*

The other homes on Correction Road were fairly grand, but this house dwarfed all others. Those abodes had humble yards. This place was surrounded by vast grounds. A shrine to conspicuous consumption, Keith Faun's mansion was as out of place as a missing tooth in a pretty starlet's smile.

There was no one in sight, but Molly tried to take in the Faun residence in furtive glances, as if she were merely on a nature hike and the house was only an idle curiosity. The possibility that her nemesis might be watching from behind glass made her heart race and the air colder. The wind through the trees whispered *danger*.

Despite her misgivings, Molly stole a longer look. The house looked more like a fortress than a place where anyone would live comfortably. All-angles modern with a massive copper roof, the mansion's dimensions suggested that instead of rooms it held vast, chilly caverns.

A small smile played on Molly's lips. She wondered if Vince ever took her mother up here. If Kay Jergins saw it, she would have huffed and declared, "That's not a house. It's a chore."

Or a symptom, Molly thought. *And that gate! Faun Manor! What a pretentious douchebag. Does he think he's Batman? If anything, I'm Batman.*

Stewing, her head hot, she no longer minded the cold. Heedless of the dangers ahead, she trudged on.

After another deserted stretch, the Correctional Institute for Juveniles appeared on her left. It was a large building with small windows. The layout was simple, as if a child had placed toy blocks together to make a rectangle. The Institute had absorbed the old Scout Camp and was fenced in.

The Correctional Institute hadn't existed twelve years before. In a better world, Keith Faun would have spent some time in a similar place.

Was it a better world now? How often were kids rehabilitated? What was the recidivism rate for violent youths? Was the world more or less homophobic? Could a therapist have convinced Keith that his cruelty was not heroic? That fear and respect were not the same thing?

There were people who said the world was getting better, certainly much better than it once was. Optimists pointed to history's various ills and said, "At least we aren't dealing with that anymore."

But Molly was too focused on the chasm between how much better things could be and not what they no longer were. The optimists encouraged gratitude for what was, but Molly noticed those wise thinkers already had a lot to be thankful for. Those insisting everything was pretty great already had a pretty great life.

Meanwhile, her mother's illness had gone on for years. Kay still stubbornly refused to discuss her ailments with her daughter.

However, it was clear she was getting worse as surely as an eroding coastline. One day soon, Kay, too, would collapse into the dead zone.

Whatever the incarceration statistics of success and failure, her brief encounter with Keith at the diner made it clear he had not changed.

Evil pays and maybe it keeps you young, too, she thought.

Keith may as well have been a clone of the man responsible for her father's death. She had not forgotten her part in the death of Chuck Jergins, but there was a hierarchy of guilt. Molly was certain she bore less responsibility than the Fauns.

Time had not soothed her pain. The heavy grieving was long over, but the consequences of that night out on the Drifting Cliffs remained. Her mother was a widow. Vincent had moved in to help. Her uncle was a loyal nurse and assistant, but no replacement for her father.

And then there was Keith's cocksure grin. When Molly thought of that confident, condescending smile and how he'd poisoned her life, she felt a familiar ache. Her yearning for vengeance was as real as pangs of hunger.

Correction Road rose farther. She was beginning to regret bringing the can of wasp spray. Though it felt necessary, it was too big for her pockets. She'd tucked it under her coat. As she walked, the sharp nozzle dug into her ribs with every second step.

Where can a nice girl like me find a range weapon? What does a trebuchet cost these days, anyway?

Finally, she came to the end of Correction Road. The Overlook's small parking lot was also newly paved and plowed. It used to be rutted dirt. She walked to the edge of the lookout to take in the view of the town far below.

Few whitecaps speckled the Atlantic's waves. The slate sky merged with the gray water so the horizon became a barely visible line. It was as if the ocean just kept going up and up to swallow the atmosphere in a dull ash-colored blanket.

A couple of small boats were making their way back to the harbor, probably from trapping lobster. Far to the north and east,

Molly squinted to make out the shape of a container ship treading toward Halifax.

Before her stood an ornate silver plaque with raised lettering. It read:

OVERLOOK PARK, *established 1895, has been refurbished by generous donations courtesy of the Faun family in fond memory of Poeticule Bay's favorite son, the late Lloyd Faun.*

MOLLY BRUSHED the snow from a concrete bench, sat down, and stared at the plaque. Keith used his money to rehabilitate his father's memory, to lionize the bastard.

Hot tears slid from Molly's eyes and down her cold cheeks. *My father is forgotten,* she thought. *Erasure. That's what this is.*

Fish had come back to the Bay. Tourists would be back when the weather warmed in the spring. In the autumn, they'd swarm in to see the leaves change to the color of flames. The summer people would return in full force, back to their cozy cottages and fabulous second homes. Bold Coast visitors Molly had once thought of as an invasive species near extinction would rise again to clog the coastal roads and make long lines at the Pick-Right.

Even Molly had returned, but to her, Poeticule Bay would always be a grave. Her father's fall into the dead zone had made it so. For her, home meant memories of how her family came undone and regrets for the tasks she had failed to complete.

After Lloyd's death, Keith had thrived. Her dad's awful demise left Molly with a grudge and a burden. Wherever she went, she carried a dead zone in her heart.

FIRE

She once made a man
swallow a key
because forgetting is never easy,
and forgiveness ain't free.

78

RECEPTION

"Hello?"

Molly's hand went to the knife in her sleeve. She swiveled, ready and wary. There was no need for the knife or the wasp spray. Sarah Faun stood in the snow at the edge of the parking lot. She'd come alone.

The pretty young cheerleader from high school now looked like a faded imitation of the memory Molly held in her mind's eye.

Sarah's blonde hair was cut short, and her face was red and puffy. Keith's wife wore high boots and an oversized knit sweater. She crossed her arms across her chest. Perhaps she was hugging herself against the cold. Maybe it was a defensive posture.

She showed no bruises, but Sarah Faun looked beaten. Molly recognized the look. She'd seen that look before.

Maybe it was love in the beginning, Molly thought. *Sarah in love with Keith and Keith in love with Keith.*

Perhaps Sarah thought she could rescue or change him. Molly was sure lust was the most potent ingredient in clouding a young person's judgment.

Molly was shy, cautious, and suspicious of people, but she could relate to Sarah's mistake. Molly had made a similar mistake, but she'd remedied the problem faster.

Many addicts have lapses, but Molly didn't think of that episode of her life as a failure. In fact, she considered her exceptionally terrible date a success. She'd done the necessary thing and had remained (technically, essentially) good.

That ordeal had begun as a whirlwind romance. They matched on a dating app. Her date had been with a stunningly handsome hedge fund manager named Mark Gillaspy. At first, he seemed promising. He said all the right things. That lasted only one Saturday.

By Saturday night, Mark turned out to be an abusive pig. When she tried to leave, he announced, "I claim you."

"You're odd," she told him.

Mark slapped her right cheek hard. Then he slapped her left cheek, but harder. "Never talk back to me, and we'll get along fine. You're going to stay until I say you can go. And you *will* be grateful."

Of course, Molly's nature and guile didn't allow that to go far. She began by dulling his senses with too much alcohol from the bar in his living room. It ended with Molly leaving him handcuffed to his bed. The pig found himself naked, screaming, and pleading for mercy.

His mistake was that he started struggling too late. She'd found two handcuffs in his nightstand. Molly bound his ankles to the iron bed frame using his neckties.

She left a nasty message on his boss's voicemail to say he had quit. She added that Mark was taking all his clients with him to a competing firm. That detail made Mark scream, curse, and beg louder.

She waited for him to stop yelling. He didn't.

"Am I going to have to shove something in your mouth to get you to listen? Your socks? Your underwear? Roast pigs get apples stuffed in their mouths, don't they? I warn you, that's dangerous. You might choke to death."

He settled down after that. "I'll listen."

She pulled up a chair beside his bed. "Have you ever read *The Girl with the Dragon Tattoo?* Great book! You probably saw the movie. I really related to the main character, Lisbeth Salander. Did you know the story was based on real events?"

Mark shook his head.

"The original title in Swedish was *Men Who Hate Women.* I think you might relate to some of the characters, too."

"I'm only going to say this once more," the pig said. "Unlock these handcuffs, and I will let you go."

"Didn't you say your thesis was game theory?"

"Aspects of economic game theory, yes," he said archly. Then he added, "At Yale."

"Uh-huh. That should have been my first clue. You work the word Yale into your conversation an awful lot. That's a fret. That, and you made sure I knew you only bought silk ties that cost more than five hundred dollars each. Anyway, using game theory, which of us is in a stronger negotiation position?"

"Money, then! Let me go and I'll pay!"

"I don't want your money. I hope that underlines how upset I am with you. The thing is, I need money, but I need other things more. Memories last longer than money."

Molly dug around in her purse, found her red lipstick, and reapplied it to her lips. "Remember that scene where the abuser gets tattooed?"

His eyes widened in fear, but wisely, he kept quiet.

"I don't have a tattoo gun. Maybe I could find needles somewhere, get ink from a pen. You know, a jail tattoo job. Bet that'd hurt, but you'd have a lasting reminder to be a better person."

"Why are you like this?"

"I grew up in Maine," she said, as if that explained everything.

He stared at her, reaching for comprehension and not finding it.

"I called you odd, and you hit me."

"A little slap."

"Mark, look at me."

"Two little slaps," he amended.

"Do you think minimizing your actions will placate me?"

He took a moment to clear his throat. Tears began to form in his eyes. "No."

"Good, Mark. It's good you understand that. Now stay very still."

79

PERCEPTION

olly bent to smear her captive's lips with the red lipstick. Then she wrote in block letters on his naked flesh. She wrote on his chest, his arms, legs, and down his torso.

"Some people are not blessed with enough inhibitory neurons. Those are the neurons that stop us from saying undiplomatic things. Maybe that's you. Or maybe you're just an asshole."

"Could you just — "

She cut him off. "This isn't a conversation, Mark. We're past that now. I was about to say, I don't care about your biology or whatever your shitty reasons are. If I were bigger than you and looked scarier, you wouldn't have dared to hit me in the first place. Bullies blame their control issues on their mommies but are suddenly in fine control of themselves when they meet a bigger threat. All I care about is how you treat people."

The muscles in his neck stood out as he lifted his head, straining to see what she was writing.

"ODD also stands for Oppositional Defiant Disorder. I'm no psychiatrist, but I wonder if you have it."

Finished, she stepped back to survey her work. "I got this lipstick from M-A-C because I liked the name as well as the color. It's called

Lady Danger. Picked it up for about eleven bucks. See? You don't have to have a lot of money to have fun, Mark."

He twisted and turned to try to see down his naked body. Gently, she pushed his head back down. Then she picked up a pillow. She stood by the bed a moment, thinking it through, making sure she'd done enough.

"Don't!" Mark said. His eyes were on the pillow.

"Oh! I'm not going to smother you! I wouldn't let you off that easy! Are you grateful?"

He didn't answer.

Louder this time, "I asked, are you grateful?"

"Yes," he squeaked.

"Good!" she said. "Then it's agreed. I'm helpful!" Molly lifted his head by a fistful of hair. Gently, she slipped the pillow under his head.

"I need to take care of one more thing, and then I'll get out of your hair. For insurance and for the fond memories."

Molly pulled out her phone and took pictures of the pig in his vulnerable state. "Should you survive somehow, don't come after me. I am Lady Danger. Come for me in any way, and these pics will be everywhere."

By the look in her eyes, Mark Gillaspy did not doubt her. He would have said anything to placate her. He would have asked her to marry him if he thought that would free him. But he was sure nothing he could say would satisfy her.

"To sate your curiosity, I wrote 'Undiagnosed Oppositional Defiant Disorder.' Like I said, I'm no psychiatrist, but I think you could have it. Well ... one of us probably has it, anyway."

Molly did not take her eyes off his as she put her bra and blouse back on. "You are not a fun date, Mark, but I'm glad we found a way to make it fun in the end ... in *your* end."

She leaned down and, with some difficulty, left one last present for him to remember her by.

As she made for the door, he whined, "You can't leave me like this!"

"I don't need your permission, not for anything. No one does."

She locked the front door behind her. She paused outside his townhouse, straining to hear him calling for help. Even when the Boston street was empty of traffic, her target's screams were inaudible.

"*Hmph*! Nice house, well-built," she said to herself. "He's going to scream himself hoarse."

After twenty-four hours, Molly decided he'd had sufficient time to reconsider how to treat his people. Molly then called his mother.

"The key to Mark's front door is under the potted plant to the right of the living room window," she informed his mother. "The last I saw the key to his handcuffs, it was tucked in your son's anus. You'll find it's located north of a tube of lipstick. Pro tip: Bring latex gloves."

Mark Gillaspy's mom discovered her son in his bedroom just as Molly had left him. That's how he found out he wasn't going to die of thirst, handcuffed and tied to his bed.

He thought he would die of embarrassment. However, he survived. Even the worst humiliation rarely leads to cardiac events in men under the age of fifty.

Molly still had the pictures on her phone, but she never looked at them. She thought that kind of gloating would be wrong, ghoulish, and hilarious.

Mark Gillaspy was too terrified and embarrassed to contact the police. What lasted longest was the disappointed look in his mother's eyes.

Mark misread his mother. The image of her son handcuffed to the bed was indelible. She did not feel mere disappointment. She felt disgust and revulsion.

Molly, on the other hand, felt elation at how she'd roasted that pig.

Two weeks later, Mark received a package in the mail. There was no return address. He knew who'd sent it before he opened it. Mark began to sweat.

He tore the brown paper to find his gift. It was a paperback copy of *The Girl With the Dragon Tattoo*.

A note in black ink was tucked in the book. It read:

You're going to act nicer from now on. I have no illusions. It will be an act, but you will behave better. I don't care about your inner thoughts, but I will check in from time to time on what you're doing. Just like Lisbeth Salander, I'll be watching. Fail me and you fail yourself. I'm done giving you free therapy. If you force me to come for you, I'll come as a surprise, out of the dark. Remember me and get professional help. Mental health improves physical health. You will be grateful.

X

THE *X* as signed with red Lady Danger Lipstick.

As she sat on the cold bench staring out over the town at an indifferent sea, that memory warmed her. She'd gotten inside his head, and he would remain haunted.

Ignoring the lethal dangers of certainty, Molly was sure she wasn't wrong. She had targets. Keith Faun only had victims.

As she studied Sarah Faun at the Overlook, Molly recognized what Sarah was by the look in her eyes. Keith's wife was a victim. Molly didn't know what she was going to do. However, if Sarah said the right things, she had no doubt Keith would be Molly's next target.

80

AMBITION

"We never spoke in school. I'm Molly Jergins."

"I know who you are. Keith told me you were back in town. Ant sent me. My brother thinks you can help."

"And you're going to tell me why I should." Molly brushed off more snow from the bench to make space for her. "It's miserably cold, and this bench is super uncomfortable. Have a seat. Where's your mom?"

"With the housekeeper. I don't get out much, and if Mom gets outside, she tends to wander. The housekeeper gives me a break from time to time."

"Then let's not waste it."

Sarah came forward with a pronounced limp. Her mouth twisted in the combination of effort and pain as she made her way through the snow.

"You okay?"

"Maybe I'll tell you about that. First, I need to know something. Is what Keith says about you true?"

"If it was bad, probably."

"He says you terrorized his family, made his mom leave town, and your father killed his dad."

"Yes."

Sarah's eyes widened. "I gotta say, I thought you'd say more, explain, or put up some defense, make apologies and excuses, maybe?"

Molly shrugged. "I don't feel bad about going after them. No apologies or excuses needed. Better question: Why did you marry Keith?"

Sarah sat on the bench and stared out at the ocean. "It seemed like a good idea at the time?"

"Dig deeper."

"Mom told me not to. If I'm honest, defying Mom was part of the allure. Keith was awfully good-looking. Still is."

"They say the devil is sexy, too."

Sarah smiled. "It was a mistake, but don't judge me too hard. I was a virgin, and I was a kid. Didn't we all do some wild things when we were teenagers?"

"I'm not judging," Molly said. "I'm just trying to understand the mystery. He was a big bully then."

"He's a big bully now." Sarah pulled off her beanie and ran a hand through her short hair. "Keith hates my new haircut. I cut it short so it wouldn't be so easy for him to yank my hair."

"Keith hurts you." Molly was not at all surprised. "Does he hurt your mother?"

"He threatens to hurt her like he hurts me. Ant told you about her, right?"

"The Alzheimer's? Yes."

"Early-onset. Keith could do mean things to her at breakfast, and she could forget everything but the pain by lunch."

"You are being abused." Molly pulled her phone from her pocket. "I'll wait with you until the cops get here."

Sarah reached out gently, grasped Molly's cell, and pushed it back into her coat pocket. "A restraining order is just a piece of paper."

"You don't trust the police to protect you?"

"How did that work out for your dad?"

"It didn't."

"Well, here's the small-town bullshit," Sarah said. "Sheriffs get elected. Keith funds Hobbs' campaigns. Even if the police did help, it would be worse in the end."

History repeats itself, Molly thought, *but never the good parts.*

"Do you know why Keith didn't go pro?"

Molly shook her head.

"Hockey teams want goons, but Keith took it too far. You ever see a stick fight on the ice? Keith didn't drop his gloves or his stick. What he did to that kid … well, he got banned from his college team. He did community service instead of jail time."

"He should have been in jail in high school."

"I didn't think so then. I do now. Funny that the correctional institute for boys is just down the road from the house. He should have had a bed there. Instead, he's next to me each night."

Sarah reached inside her sweater and pulled out a half-empty pack of cigarettes. Her hands shook as she cupped her hand around the tiny flame to light one.

Molly didn't think it was the cold that made her shake. It was nerves.

Sarah pulled in a long drag before expelling a stream of white smoke. "I tried to leave him last April. It didn't work out. I'm afraid of what he'll do if I try again and fail. He'd find me eventually. Then it's the stick all over again."

"So, he has threatened your life?"

Sarah chuckled ruefully. "I wish it were that simple." She stuck her cigarette in the corner of her mouth and bent forward. Moving gingerly, she pulled her left boot from her foot. "Can you get my sock for me, please? Take it easy when you do it, okay?"

Molly did as she was asked and pulled down her sock. The skin on top of Sarah's left foot was cherry red. "That's a burn."

"Scalding hot tea."

Molly rolled the sock back up as gently and as slowly as she could. Then she helped get Sarah's boot back on. "You're in a bad situation. You've got to get yourself and your mom out of it."

Sarah gave an exasperated look. "You see my foot, right?"

"I know, there's no justice in the world. We'll have to settle for the homemade kind."

"You still don't get it. Keith did this to me last week, but it's not because I pissed him off last week. I'm as sweet as can be. I do all I can to placate him."

"What are you saying?"

"I'm saying my loving husband burns me once in a while. It's always a surprise. There's no schedule. He'll do it again, just his little reminder to stay put. The burns are an *ongoing* punishment for trying to escape last April."

Molly's jaw tightened. "I think that might be the worst thing I've ever heard."

"I'm in hell. Finite sin, infinite punishment." Sarah wept quietly for a long time. She needed time to lament the fact that she married a monster. Molly didn't try to stop her. Grieving should never be interrupted.

When she was done crying, Sarah sniffled and said in a small voice, "I don't see how, but Ant says you can help us."

"He can't?"

"Ant has a big heart. I know he can come across goofy and giddy, but he has a gentle soul. He doesn't get burned, but Ant is as afraid of Keith as I am."

Keith employed Sarah's brother. Molly suspected that had something to do with Ant's reluctance to act. Ant had been bullied in high school, too, but had never been pushed to critical mass. He knew the pain of derision, but the little man wasn't broken in the same way she had been.

"Pushing back isn't for everyone," Molly observed, "but your life is in danger."

Molly wondered if they had reached out to her because they thought she had less to lose. Or, based on past events, is it that they knew she'd want to bring Keith down?

Molly stared at the plaque for some time before she spoke again. "Sarah? What are you asking me to do? You want Keith dead?"

"I can't ask that. We're strangers. We weren't even friends at school."

"But?"

"I want him to stop the torture. I don't know what to do, but maybe you can throw a big enough scare into him. After his father died, he wasn't all bad, you know. He was better for a while. The first few years of our marriage, he was good — well, not really good, but not so bad — "

Molly made a chopping gesture to cut her off. "He's gone sour, so let's not dwell on the high points. He doesn't value you. The key question is, what does he value?"

"What do you mean?"

Molly looked around at the Overlook's upgrades. "Keith paid for this plaque and all the paving and cleanup, right?"

"Yes, point of pride."

"Where'd all the money come from? It's gotta be more than the laundromat franchises."

"The ATM business."

"Come again?"

"Private ATMs, not the usual kind at the bank."

"That makes good money? I haven't taken out physical currency since the beginning of the pandemic. Don't people just use cards for everything now?"

Sarah shook her head. "Keith's ATMs typically have a five-dollar service fee."

"That's high."

"Like I said, it's his ATM, not a regular bank. He says the key is location, location, location. His ATMs outside of cash businesses like casinos and dog tracks do well. He even put ATMs inside a couple of strip clubs. The service fee for withdrawals from those machines is twenty bucks. Location, location, location, just like real estate. That's a lot of cash business."

Molly grinned. "I'm guessing drunk guys at strip clubs at two in the morning don't make great financial choices."

Sarah allowed a small smile for the first time. "They do not."

Molly pursed her lips in thought. "How much cash does he keep on hand?"

"I don't know, but it's a lot. Keith brags about stealing a little from the business every day. He says taxation is theft. I thought about reporting him to the IRS, but he'd kill me while waiting for his trial."

Molly shook her head. "While the rest of us are trying to have a society, he's opted out. I just *knew* Keith would be one of those guys."

"He calls his stash his Thailand fund. He says that after my mom dies, we'll move to Thailand. I doubt we'll ever go, though. He likes piling up the money too much. There's one safe for his guns, one safe for money."

Molly gave Sarah a hard look. "Serious question, so give me a real answer. Are you willing to leave Keith before he kills you and Rose? Because what you describe is your escape fund."

Sarah hung her head. "Despite marrying Keith against my better judgment and my mother's wishes, I'm not a complete idiot. I've already thought of that, of course. Can't get at it, though. Both safes are in the panic room."

"He has a panic room?"

"Oh, yeah. Keith talks as if the Faun name is synonymous with the Kennedys. He's Maine royalty, don't you know? Besides, the stuff you did in high school made him really paranoid. He wouldn't have built the house without a panic room in it."

"It isn't paranoia if I'm really coming after him," Molly said.

"I don't have the codes for the safes, though! I don't even have the passcode or the keys to the panic room."

"He has a panic room, but *you* don't have a way to get into it?"

Sarah's eyes were wet. "After I tried to run away with Mom, he took the keys and changed the code. The panic room is just for him. Everything is just for him."

"We'll have to disabuse him of that notion."

"So, you'll help?"

Molly stood. "Is Keith out right now?"

Sarah glanced at her watch. "Out talking with his accountant and making rounds with employees at ATMs. He won't be back for a few hours."

"Let's hurry. I need the grand tour of your house if I'm to come up with a plan."

Together, they walked back to Faun Manor. Sarah limped toward home in growing dread. Molly felt fear, too, but also mounting anticipation.

81

CONFUSION

Molly arrived home in time for dinner. Standing on the porch, she stomped the snow from her boots. Her uncle ripped open the front door before she could reach for the knob.

"Were you followed?" Vincent asked.

She shook her head.

"You sure? I warned you about the sheriff."

"I'm plenty paranoid, but no one's following me. The police have much more to do than keep me under twenty-four-hour surveillance. Hobbs was just blowing smoke, trying to scare me into being a good girl."

"S'pose so, just fretting, I guess."

"Good."

"But are you? For real?"

Molly shot him a quizzical look. "Am I what?"

"Are you really a good girl?"

"Sure."

Her uncle did not look convinced.

"I'm not going to be a prisoner in my own home," Molly huffed. "I had something I had to do in daylight, so I did it. I'm not going to live like a vampire. Speaking of vampires, is the Halloween stuff and Dad's old sports equipment still in the closet under the back stairs?"

"I don't know, maybe, but never mind that." Vincent checked behind him before adding in a whisper, "You have a visitor. Your mother's not feeling tiptop tonight. Kay's taking her supper in bed. All the better for it. Your guest might upset her. She doesn't like strangers in the house. I'll take care of Kay. You have the place to yourselves for a kitchen convo. Okay-fine?"

"Who is it?"

Without answering, he turned to climb the stairs. "There's a pot on the stove. I already ate. Fill your boots."

For a moment, Molly worried that her uninvited guest could be Sheriff Hobbs or worse — much worse — Keith Faun. Still wearing her coat, scarf, and hat, Molly hurried down the hall.

Barry Graves sat at the kitchen table. He appeared to be in deep contemplation of the steaming cup of tea that sat before him on the flowery tablecloth.

Molly stood still a moment, stunned at this unexpected reunion. She hadn't seen Barry since that night on the Drifting Cliffs. He still had a baby face, but his shoulders were broader. Molly had frozen him in her memory as a scrawny kid, but he had filled out, a full-grown man.

Barry looked up, his expression serious. "Long time."

"Yeah," she said. "It was one father ago."

"Two fathers," Barry said, "but I wouldn't count Lloyd the Hemorrhoid, either."

He rose from the table and got a plate from the kitchen counter. "Your uncle told me to help myself. Didn't know when you'd be back, but I figured I'd wait for you. Hungry?"

Molly had left the can of wasp spray under the porch, so she pulled off her parka and draped it over a chair. Then she stuffed her woolen hat and scarf in one of the coat sleeves.

She put the knife on the kitchen table.

Barry eyed the blade. "Prepped for Keith?"

"Not yet, but maybe," she answered cautiously.

"Anyway, supper? It'll warm you up, and it doesn't smell very burnt."

"Vince only makes four things: Mac and cheese, meatloaf, lasagna, and beans and wieners. What is this evening's egregious sin?"

As Barry pulled back the foil, she peered around him to see a pan of lasagna sitting on the stove.

"Too bad for you," Molly said. "The mac and cheese is out of the box, and the beans come from a can, so he can't hurt them much. The only thing worse than his lasagna is his meatloaf. Vince's meatloaf requires *all* the ketchup."

"The lasagna looks edible, still hot enough."

"You have to be careful with it. The dry sheets of cheese around the edges can crack your teeth."

Barry bobbed his head in agreement. "Not enough sauce makes it dry out around the edges. But you know what they say: hunger is the best spice, and I'm starving. Haven't eaten since yesterday."

"You broke?"

He waved that suggestion away. "Nah, just fussy. Don't like much road food. Been on a bus."

"From where?"

"Norfolk."

"I hear Virginia's nice."

"I like it. Got any garlic butter? Some toast would help this."

"Only regular butter."

"Just butter butter, huh? What are we, peasants? Are we animals?" he joked.

"S'all we got."

"Whatever, I'll take it. Want some?"

Barry opened the breadbox and pulled forks and knives out of a drawer as if he lived there.

From Barry, his actions felt like confidence instead of presumption. Molly followed his lead and retrieved the butter dish from the refrigerator.

He lifted the lid, dipped in a knife, and spread a generous smear of butter on two slices of bread. After placing them in the toaster oven, he turned to take her in. "It's good to see you, Molly. You're looking well."

"I'm okay."

"Oh, I'm pretty sure you're not."

"Why do you say that? What did my uncle tell you?"

"He said you lost your job at some college I've never heard of. Says your mom is feeling poorly. Told me Hobbs paid you a visit the other day, but I knew that already."

"How'd you know about that?"

"Because he called me before he came to see you. Old Hobbs wanted to make sure you hadn't 'recruited' me, as he put it."

Molly stepped beside him to grab another plate and a spatula. "What did the sheriff say?"

"He said you had a run-in with Keith. He wondered if you were on the warpath."

"And you said?"

"That I hadn't spoken to you since high school."

Molly finished putting her serving of lasagna on her plate and retreated to the kitchen table. He served himself and took the seat across from her.

"Twelve years with no words between us," she said, "yet you jumped on a bus for a day to get here?"

"More than a day. Rented a car in Bangor for the drive up the coast. Took a week off work."

"Maine in February. Heck of a vacation choice."

"I didn't come for fun, Molly."

To do what she did best, enjoying her vengeful acts made her more effective. Molly thought so, anyway. However, she wasn't yet ready to share her opinions on how to torture monsters for fun and profit.

82

COLLUSION

"The town's changed some," Molly said. "Have you noticed?"

"Oh, yeah! Poeticule's looking a little more prosperous since I was here last. Commercial Street doesn't have as many empty storefronts, for one thing."

"Keith and I sacrificed our fathers' lives to the ocean," Molly said evenly. "Maybe we did break the dead zone curse, but Keith's life got better. Mine got worse."

Barry didn't look up, as if concentrating on his meal. He steered clear of the hard, dry edges and ate his lasagna. Molly left her food untouched. "It's a little weird, you being here. You were never in this house when you lived here."

"We barely knew each other, except for that night," Barry admitted. "It's true we haven't talked since then, but I kept in touch with Rose. I had a lot of support from her after what happened."

"You were tight with the school librarian?"

"Well, she saved me twice, once in the library, once on the cliff. Family and friends were kind, but who else was I going to talk to? Only Rose knew the whole story."

"Your therapist?"

"I got some professional help, sure, but Rose listened longest. She would have made a good therapist. I kept her up-to-date on my schoolwork, my jobs, how I was getting on, moving on, dealing — or trying to, at least."

"My understanding is Rose Rainier has dementia now."

He nodded. "Too young! Too young!"

"There's never a good age for that," Molly said.

"She couldn't talk on the phone with Keith around, so she wrote me letters. I could see the degradation over time. Her handwriting got messier, started misspelling words more and more. Rose typed for a while until she started losing words. It became word salad."

Molly paled. "Entropy. It's the only universal, and it sucks."

"I didn't hear from her for a while. Then I got a letter from her daughter. Sarah wrote to say there would be no more letters, and I shouldn't send anything, not even a card. Keith found her stash of correspondence. Actually, Rose showed him my letters in a fuzzy moment. Sarah didn't exactly say he punished Rose, but I read between the lines."

"When was this?"

He looked up at the ceiling as if to retrieve the answer there. "Her last letter was probably a couple of years ago now. Last she knew, I was still in the Air Force."

"You served?"

"Got out last year. I'd planned to bounce around a bit, but a cousin of mine needed help managing his solar panel business. That's what I'm doing now. Norfolk's working out okay. Moved in with my boyfriend last Christmas. Life is pretty good."

"Life can't be that good. You came back here."

Back to where the ghosts and monsters live, she thought.

Molly tapped her plate with her fork sharply. "Why are you here, Barry?"

"Because of the phone call from the sheriff. Funny, he tried to sound all big and bad, but I remember what a wuss he was. All his bluster reminded me of how he harassed my family after we left the Bay. I lost track of how many times he got the Staties to knock on our door. I thought my mom was going to have a heart attack. She got so strung out worrying that I'd get strung up."

"Sorry that happened. Hobbs did not handle your situation well. If it's any consolation, he knows he messed up from the beginning."

She'd meant to soothe him, but Barry gave his head a short shake in dismissal. "No consolation. Hobbs tried to scare me, but the best he could do was piss me off."

Molly had to smile in recognition. "I get that."

"Thought you would. Anyway, from his little lecture, I got the feeling that you are on the warpath again. Am I right?"

"What if I am? What makes it your business?"

"I want to help. We both have unfinished business with Keith Faun. It's not all just about you, you know."

The toaster oven's button popped up with a sharp *ding!*

"So...?" Barry asked. "Toast?"

"Two questions," Molly said, "Why? Really?"

"I should be with you. It was me he sinned against in the first place. You lost your dad. I owe you and I owe your dad. It's *our* battle, Molly."

"Second question, why now?"

"The kid he assaulted and humiliated was just a kid. I'm not a kid anymore. Time's passed."

Barry took her silence for a refusal. "Look, I gave karma a chance. If karma works, I'm not seeing it. If a comeuppance is en route, it's way too slow."

"I'm working on a plan," Molly admitted. "It's dangerous."

"How could it not be? I know the risks, just like your dad knew. Rose told me enough before her mind floated away. Rose and her daughter are in a prison — "

"I met with Sarah today. You're right. They are in a prison, and Keith is their sadistic warden. Hobbs is useless — "

Barry rolled his eyes. "At this point, getting the law involved wouldn't be very satisfying, would it? If you're going to do this, I've gotta be there. Every Batman needs a Robin. Let's work together to spring Sarah and Rose, okay?"

"Okay."

"But our first priority," Barry said, "is to have some toast with this incredibly substandard lasagna. Then tell me your devious plots and plans. What are we going to do?"

"Two things off the top. First, it's not just going to be you and me. Sarah has a couple of other recruits in mind."

"Okay, and second?"

"We're going to scare the evil out of Keith and spring Sarah and Rose at the same time."

Barry looked skeptical. "If I were at my old job, I'd just call in a drone strike on the bastard. You really think you can scare evil all the way out of the devil?"

Molly showed him her Joker's smile. "I have some experience in this regard."

83

INTRUSION

Two days later, Keith Faun sat in his massage chair sipping a Moosehead Lager. He had no idea this was to be the worst night of his life.

The housekeeper had gone home after dinner. His mother-in-law was locked away in her bedroom. He'd sent Sarah off to bed hours before. Aside from the ticking of the grandfather clock and the commentators on his big screen TV voicing a rundown of hockey highlights, the house was quiet.

Breaking glass.

The noise came from the back of the house. Keith leaped to his feet and headed toward the kitchen. He got to the door before thinking better of it. He doubled back and grabbed a poker from the fireplace.

The kitchen was dark. Keith stood in the doorway, listening intently. All he could hear was his own heavy breathing, nothing more, as if the house itself was listening.

He leaned in, reached for the wall switch, and flipped on the light. A small pane of glass by the back door had been shattered beside the lock. Glass littered the floor. Scanning the room, Keith found nothing else disturbed.

"Anybody there?" he called. "If you're here, you better hope you find your way out before I find you. I'll turn your ass inside out!"

Still nothing.

Keith bent to look out the broken window and stepped back in shock and surprise. Someone wearing a Donald Trump mask stood on the back deck and stared back at him through the broken windowpane.

"Jergins? That you?"

The person in the mask said nothing.

"You're trespassin' and tryin' to break in! Legally, I can beat the snot out of you. Don't worry! If you live, I'll call the sheriff eventually. He'll take some time gettin' here. He can call the ambulance, and they can haul you to the hospital in a bucket!"

The person in the mask said nothing and did not move.

Enraged, Keith lunged to grab the door handle to fling it open. He was surprised to find it was still locked, just as it always was after dark.

The intruder jackrabbited as Keith fumbled the deadbolt and the lock in the knob. He dropped the poker in the process.

Leaping over the deck railing to the patio below, the burglar sprinted around the pool and headed toward the woods.

Hurling curses, Keith scooped up the poker, opened the door, and ran out on the deck. In his rush, he'd stepped on broken glass. He only wore socks, and blood was already soaking through the cotton. Though the wooden deck was cold, the bottoms of his feet stung with each step.

His prey was already halfway to the woods. Leaning heavily on the desk railing, Keith let out another string of curses.

At the edge of the forest, the intruder turned and paused to give Keith the finger with an enthusiastic pumping motion. The figure then disappeared into the darkness beyond the trees.

Keith whirled, wincing at the pain that emanated from his feet with each step. There was no glass on the deck outside the door. He was sure the intruder had to have been Molly Jergins, but apparently, the years away had made her rusty. She'd proved herself an inept burglar.

Opening the back door, Keith leaned in with trembling fingers, trying to reach the paper towel roll on the counter. It was just out of reach. He'd hoped to throw it on the floor so he could use it as a stepping stone over the broken glass.

"Sarah!" Keith bellowed. "Sarah! Come here! I need you!"

Sarah did not come.

"Fuck it!" Keith stepped back into the kitchen. He avoided stepping on the big pieces of glass, but tiny shards bit into his feet once more. Still calling for his wife, he rushed back to the great room, leaving a trail of bloody footprints.

The commentators on the big screen had moved on to talking about basketball. Annoyed, Keith muted the television and called for Sarah again. Still, no response.

He looked for his cell phone but did not see it. Keith paused a moment, patting down his pants pockets and searching the room.

I had my phone with me, didn't I?

Keith was almost sure he'd left the device on the arm of the massage chair. That was his custom, yet he couldn't find it. He hurriedly pressed his hands around the corners of the seat cushion. No luck. His phone was missing, and his wife still had not responded to his shouts.

Keith rushed for the phone in the front hall. He didn't allow Sarah to own a cell phone, but he'd kept a landline. Keith never used that phone, but he kept it for Sarah to call him. It was another way he'd found to control her.

She'd tried to run away to a sympathetic second cousin in Kentucky the previous year. Keith had since successfully isolated his wife from those faraway relatives. If any long-distance calls showed up on the bill, she'd have to explain the charge.

Given his mother-in-law's mental deterioration, it was even harder for Sarah to leave. He'd blocked her family's numbers. Sarah couldn't call them and had no one she could turn to.

Or did she?

The thought worried Keith, but not for long. Worry was for ordinary mortals with complicated feelings. He had anger and that made him strong. When he played college hockey, Keith's teammates called him the Hulk. The angrier he got, the stronger he became.

He called anger Level One.

Rage was Level Two.

When he lifted the receiver to call the police, the coiled wire hung in the air, cut and swinging.

That was the moment he reached Level Three: *Fury*.

84

COLLECTION

"Sarah? Sarah! What the hell is going on?" Despite his pain, he ran for the stairs, taking two steps at a time.

Breathing heavily at the top of the stairs, his first thought was to check his mother-in-law's room. If Rose was still in the house, Sarah was still here. She would never leave without her mother.

The deadbolt on the outside of his mother-in-law's door was still locked in place. He heard his mother-in-law pacing around in there. Rose was typically worse after sundown, sometimes walking in circles in her room for hours.

Where was his wife? Had she heard the breaking glass? She didn't have the code to the panic room. He had to wonder if his stupid, weak wife was hiding under a bed. Was she hoping the intruder got him? Killed him?

"Where are you, you cow?" Keith slammed a fist into his mother-in-law's door before heading down the hall.

Agitated, Rose called out, "Mouses? Is that you? I hear you scurrying behind the walls. Cheese? Cheese slices? Cheesecake?"

If Keith had paused a moment longer, he would have heard his mother-in-law giggle girlishly and say, "Mr. Obama? I can never remember how to spell your first name."

But Keith was otherwise occupied and screaming for his wife. Taking the steps two at a time, he ran upstairs.

He burst through the door to the main bedroom door. Flipping on the light, he spotted her still form under the bedcovers.

"What is wrong with you? I've been screaming my ass off! Somebody tried to break in!"

Receiving no answer, Keith advanced on their bed, yanked back the duvet, and discovered a pile of pillows. Sarah was gone.

"Oh, no. She has *not* taken off and left me with the stupid old bat! Sarah? I will burn both your feet this time! You earned it! I tried to warn you!"

He whirled toward the double doors of their walk-in closet. His suits, jackets, and collection of dress shirts hung to his immediate right. In the gloom cast by the bedroom light, his clothes were just a dark shape.

He gasped as he glanced to his left. Sarah's clothes weren't where they were supposed to be. Only empty hangers hung on her closet rail. *The bitch is on the run.*

Keith's brain slipped a gear, trying to catch up and process what he was seeing. "You're gonna *learn*, Sarah!"

Stepping to the rear of the closet, he headed to the glowing keypad. Keith bent to punch in the code. After five soft beeps, he was rewarded with a loud metallic click as the lock's mechanism disengaged. He slid the heavy pocket door to the panic room to one side.

Despite the pain in his feet and the fury that engulfed him, Keith Faun smiled. His father had tried to deal with bad people with just an axe handle and muscle. That was his mistake.

Keith kept a pump shotgun, a Colt AR-15, and a handgun in the gun safe. The revolver was his favorite weapon. A Taurus Judge, it could fire .45 cartridges and .410 shotshells.

At close range, this double-action shotgun/revolver hybrid's .410 shot pattern would leave a donut-shaped hole in his target.

"You need a donut in your gut, Jergins."

Keith couldn't swear it was Jergins in the Trump mask. However, he was certain she had to be in on the attempted home invasion. Her recent reappearance in Poeticule Bay could not be a coincidence.

He wasn't thinking about the attempted break-in, the cut phone line, or even his missing cell phone. Keith was out for blood.

The only question in his mind was whether he should shoot his addled mother-in-law before he went after Molly and Sarah.

No, he thought. *I'm mad, not stupid. Better to tell the housekeeper not to come in tomorrow. I can let Rose get thirsty and starve, locked away in her room until I get back. Holding her mother's life over her will get Sarah running home quick!*

"Gonna get my answers from you, Jergins. You'll know where Sarah went. Then I'm gonna give you a nice big donut, toss you in the Bay, and get Sarah back ... maybe before the old lady dies of thirst."

He chuckled as he yanked on a pull chain to illuminate the small space. The panic room contained two safes, a shelf with boxes of ammunition, a hunting knife in a sheath, and another landline phone on the wall.

Keith went to the gun safe first. He bent to enter the safe's four-digit code when he heard something behind him.

It was the sound of cloth against cloth and the subtle scrape of metal on metal as hangers were pushed aside. He straightened and turned before completing the access code to the gun safe.

Stepping lightly, a tall, thin figure in a Guy Fawkes mask was coming at him out of the dark, close enough to kill with his bare hands. Someone was behind Guy Fawkes. They stood in the doorway to his panic room wearing a hockey goalie's mask.

He grabbed for Guy Fawke's throat with his left hand and cocked his right fist. Keith had begun to squeeze, but Guy Fawkes was quick. The intruder struck, hitting his ear with something heavy. The world erupted in a high, ringing whine.

Keith reeled and his grip weakened, but he did not let go.

Guy Fawkes struck again and again in the same spot. The last blow caught him just in front of the ear. Savage pain shot through

Keith's head like a high-voltage jolt of electricity. Something in the hinge of his jaw gave a little.

The intruder in the goalie mask came at him, and Keith braced himself, ready for the tackle. At the last second, though, his attacker dove for his legs, grabbing him around the knees.

In such a small space, the big man had nowhere to retreat. His head knocked the hanging lightbulb. As the light and shadows swung around him wildly, Keith let out a garbled cry.

In the kaleidoscope of confusion, Keith clawed at the air with one hand. With the other, he managed to yank off the Guy Fawkes mask.

His right temple smacked the gun safe on his way to the floor. Twisting as he fell, Keith's right arm was trapped under the combined weight of his body and the man on his back. Keith's right wrist bent in a vicious twist that made him gasp.

That pain kept him from succumbing to unconsciousness, but not for long. Keith's field of vision became watery, narrowing to a small circle. Everything else was dark, as if he were in a hot tunnel.

Level Three ... searing fury going away.

Level Two ... rage leaking away.

Level One ... only anger.

Then, only the pain.

Keith craned his neck to try to see his attackers, to look for a weapon, to find a way out. He was really looking for hope. All he had was the Guy Fawkes mask, gripped in his left hand.

When the room steadied from its wild rocking, he looked up. Molly Jergins stood over him. In her gloved hand, she held a long Maglite.

A final thought floated up past his pain: *I've been knocked to hell by a woman with a flashlight full of batteries. Shit, D-Cells are heavy.*

Molly grinned as she watched her target's bloodied face. Keith lay at her feet, embarrassed. Maybe, in the short-term, that was the worst of it for him. His headache pain would probably go away eventually, by healing or by drugs. But to be beaten by a woman? By *this* woman! He would carry that secret for the rest of his life.

Dimly, he understood how she'd suddenly appeared in his inner sanctum. She'd been hiding in the walk-in closet, standing behind Keith's jackets with the man in the goalie mask.

She'd heard his plans for her, even his weird utterance about giving her a donut before tossing away her body. But Keith Faun's plans didn't matter anymore and he knew it.

Staring into his eyes, Molly watched him downshift from homicidal mania to pure fear. Only Molly's plans mattered. *She* mattered.

Keith felt himself beginning to fall into the void. He fought to stay awake. In his hockey career, he'd been concussed a couple of times. Darkness was coming. Soon, he would sleep, at least for a minute or two.

As he blacked out, he heard Molly say, "Dude! You were supposed to hit him with the wasp spray!"

"I would have, but you were doing fine without me," the other voice replied. "Frankly, I was enjoying the show. That was overdue."

A damp, heavy curtain covered Keith's awareness. He was grateful to pass out. Unconsciousness was his only escape.

That, or death.

85

DEMONSTRATION

Rousing slowly, Keith kept his eyes closed and took inventory. His hands were pinned behind his back by zip ties. The wide plastic straps bit at his flesh, and his sprained wrist throbbed. His left ear was plugged, and his temple felt like it was sliding down the side of his face.

Mostly, Keith's head ached. Someone was pounding nails nearby, and that made the pounding in his head worse.

Keith opened his eyes. It wasn't nails that were getting hammered. The man in the goalie mask was going at the panic room's interior keypad with a chisel and hammer. The intruder popped the panel away from the wall. He then began cutting the wires to the door's locking mechanism.

Keith tasted blood. It turned his stomach and made him cough. "What are you doing?"

Goalie Mask Man didn't look up from his sabotage. "You weren't out long. That's good. We wouldn't want you to miss anything."

The man in a Trump mask appeared in the doorway. "Truck's backed up and ready."

Goalie Mask Man rose to get out of his way and assist him. Trump wheeled in a bright red dolly and angled it toward the money safe.

Keith gasped in surprise when he realized his gun safe was gone already. "Hey!" he screeched. "What do you two dumbasses think you're doing?"

"Whatever we want," Trump replied.

Goalie Mask Man gave Keith a jaunty salute. "Feels like shit, doesn't it?"

Together, the intruders tipped the front of the safe up an inch to slide the dolly's blade beneath it. That done, they cinched the dolly's wide belt around the safe to secure it. They then tipped the safe backward onto the dolly. With a little back and forth, the pair maneuvered the safe out the door.

Alone for a moment, Keith struggled against his bonds. He tried to push up against the wall to get to his feet. The zip ties that bound his wrists cut into his skin. The pain was too sharp. He had to stop.

Molly poked her head in the panic room's doorway. "Hello, again."

He tried to spit at her, but something was wrong with his jaw. He only managed to drool blood and saliva down his chin.

Molly leaned up against the doorframe and crossed her arms. "In the movies, we'd have a safecracker on the crew. How many expert safecrackers does Hollywood think there are in the world? I wouldn't even know where to begin to find somebody with those skills. Craigslist? Put an ad up on the bulletin board at the Pick-Right, maybe?"

Keith cursed at her at length.

Molly waited patiently for him to run out of energy. "Have you got all those bad words out of your system? If you go on being nasty, you might eventually hurt my feelings, but we don't have all night. Anyway, the question about where to find a crack safecracker was rhetorical."

Keith took a deep breath. When he spoke again, his voice was shaky. "What are you doing with my stuff?"

"Your guns and big honkin' stash of cash? You know the problem with safes like these, right? They are portable. You really have to go old school, cementing a safe into the wall. Hang a painting over it to hide it. You know, a wall safe, like in the movies."

"Like in the movies," Keith echoed.

"We're taking the safes someplace far away. That way, we can take our time cutting into them. I don't know what it will take. Drills? Cutting torches? We'll figure it out in private."

"That'd be a lot of work. How about we work out a deal? Cut me free, and I'll give you the codes to both safes."

"Back at the cafe, you told me my life's work is a dead-end job? I love the English language. Funny how the word safe and safe mean two different things in this context. Your weapons and money are in the safes. And then there's me."

He looked up at her with a bewildered look.

"I don't feel safe when you're on the loose. I haven't really felt safe for a very long time, but your existence puts a lot of people in danger. You and people like you ... the world has too much of you in it."

"Fuck you."

She shrugged. "Can't tie up everybody, but at least I have you. You are the top pickle in my pickle barrel, Keith."

Her calm, flat delivery irked him. The hunting knife around her waist worried him more. It was *his* hunting knife.

She followed his gaze and drew the long knife from its sheath. "It's nice. I used to adore flick knives, stilettos, and switchblades. I'd see them at flea markets and pawnshops. They always looked cool to me, something a spy might use."

"Like in the movies," Keith said hoarsely. The taste of blood in the back of his throat nauseated him. It tasted like pennies, but he kept his gorge down.

Molly crouched so she was level with her captive, eye-to-eye across the small space. His gaze followed the blade as she waved it slowly between them.

"Hypnotic, isn't it? Not pretty, but it's got a good heft to it. There's a problem with the kinds I like, the stylish ones. For the first stab, it's fine, but there's no decent guard at the top of the handle."

Molly pointed to the knife's large finger guard. "After that first stab, you want a guard because the handle will get slick with blood. Several killers have been caught because they cut themselves while attacking their victims. I bet this is the reason they accidentally cut themselves. Their stabbing hand slips forward on the blade, et voila! Murderer DNA all over the crime scene."

"How many people have you killed, Molly?" he asked.

"You usually call me Jergins."

"Like the lotion," he said, managing a lopsided smile. "You didn't answer my question. How many?"

"Killed? Just one good man and one bad one. You were there. You saw it. Why do you ask?"

"Just wondering how an unemployed English teacher knows shit like that."

"They conceal all kinds of information in books. You should try reading sometime."

"Details like that?" he said incredulously. "Like how slippery a knife gets when you're stabbing somebody?"

Molly's smile was back. "I think a lot about these kinds of issues."

"Thinkin' of me?"

"For more than twelve years, dingus. Every day."

86

TRANSFORMATION

Keith's arms and legs began to shiver and shake.

"You're coming down from your adrenaline dump," Molly said. "It's time to talk of many things: of shoes — and ships — and sealing wax — of cabbages — and kings."

He stared back at her without comprehension.

"No? Lewis Carroll? *The Walrus and the Carpenter*? I took a course in Carroll. It's subtle, but the poem is about greed and abusing your power. I thought you could relate."

"You are *so* crazy," Keith said.

Good, Molly thought. *For this gamble to work, I need him to believe all the cheese has slid off my cracker.*

"You're in pain," Molly said. "No doubt you've got a concussion. If I allow it, and if you're very good, you will probably live through this experience. Just realize the position you're in. Perhaps that understanding will encourage you to be more rational."

He cursed at her again.

"Be more polite, Keith. I can let you live and still make this a lot harder for you."

Keith opened his aching mouth to curse her out again, then

thought better of it. When he spoke again, his tone was more restrained. "Everybody wants something. What do you want?"

"This is not about what I want. Someone else wants to speak with you. *Be nice!*" Molly stood and gave someone he couldn't see a nod to enter the panic room.

Sarah appeared in the doorway holding a silver key. Her eyes were wet, and her face was flushed.

His wife had been crying, but Keith's sole focus was on the key. He recognized it. Were his hands unbound, he would have patted his pants pockets. But he already knew. The intruders had taken his key ring while he was unconscious. Sarah held the key to the panic room door.

She handed it to Molly. The guy in the goalie mask leaned in from the doorway to hand Sarah a tray of muffins and an extra-large travel mug.

The masked man disappeared for a moment but soon returned with a bucket and a couple of water bottles. Molly took those items from him and put the bucket and water bottles where Keith's money safe had stood.

Sarah knelt to place the mug and the tray of muffins on the floor. "I baked these this afternoon," his wife told him. "Bran muffins. I added raisins because you hate raisins."

Keith ignored her to survey the collection of items on the floor. "You're planning to lock me in here. That's a bad idea. Forced confinement ... or maybe it's kidnapping —

Sarah made a face. "Forced confinement like you've done to me and Mom for years? That's rich."

Keith looked into Sarah's eyes. "Your mother's marbles roll all over the place. Locking her in was a good thing."

"And terrorizing and controlling me? Burning me? Was that a good thing, too?"

"Shut up, Sarah. You're not the shot caller here." He ignored his wife and focused on Molly. "You destroyed the keypad, and you've got the key to that door. How long do you plan to lock me in here?"

"That's going to depend on you," Sarah said. "Just so you know, the muffins were my idea."

"Is there anything you want to say to him before you go?" Molly asked.

Sarah brightened. "I want you to know it was me. I cut the landline phone's cord. I stole your cell. I let them in."

Keith nodded toward Molly. "This is all really Jergins, though, isn't it? Call the police when you get out of here, and I will forgive you, Sarah. I can do that for you. I don't want my wife in jail. Everybody in town would laugh their asses off if I allowed that."

His wife shook her head emphatically. "You think I'm so weak. You know what? Enduring what you've done to me and Mom took almost as much strength as doing this. And it's not all about Molly! *I* let them in the back door while you were in the bathroom. You spend *so* much time on the toilet, I knew all I had to do was wait for you to sit on your throne. The almighty Keith Faun, King Shit! King Shit Keith!"

Keith struggled to sort out the details. Hobbs, he knew, would want all the details for the coming manhunt. "Who are the guys in the masks? I saw the one in the Trump mask at the back door. He smashed the glass in the back door, but I chased him away."

"You still don't understand!" Sarah said. "The others were already inside. I did that. The smashed glass was a distraction to get you out the back so they could get upstairs!"

"And now these guys are running off with my guns and my money. You're a goddamn traitor, Sarah."

"Go ahead and think of me that way. In my head, your name is King Shit. I've been thinking of you as King Shit for years. Couldn't tell you that until now, but I thought you should know."

He sneered. "I didn't think you actually had thoughts."

"This isn't what I saw in you the day we were married. Remember? Was this what you thought would happen? I sure didn't. Not then, but I need you to know, you *deserve* this, King Shit."

Sarah walked out.

Keith called after her, "Where you goin'?"

"Sarah and Rose are headed to freedom," Molly told him. "That's all you need to know about that. And you're going to let them go."

"Why would I do that?"

"Because as bad as all this feels, I could come back and make everything worse for you."

Still defiant, Keith muttered, "Yeah, yeah! Just *go*, Jergins."

He craned his neck to eye the landline phone on the wall above his head. "How about this? I'll give you time to get going before I call for an ambulance. Leave the keys outside the door so they don't have to call the fire department to get me out."

"Negotiating? You still don't understand your position. You're not in control here. I know that's new for you but figure it out. I'm in kind of a rush. I'm out of here before first light."

Steel crept back into Keith's voice. "You should be thinking of getting to other countries by dawn. Mind you, there's no place you can go that I won't find you. Be careful what you do next, bitch. Think of the future. You plan on taking your mom and your uncle with you?" His lips drew up on one side. Keith couldn't manage a smile. He could only show his bloody teeth. "Jergins, like the lotion, you shoulda kept that mask on. I've *seen* you now."

She shrugged as if she didn't care. "No great endeavor goes exactly according to plan. That's why you're in such danger. You could still die tonight. Maybe you've got a brain bleed."

She waved that away. "The mask doesn't really matter, does it? You'd know it was me. Hobbs would know, too, but you're not just dealing with me. My friends and I will be each other's alibis."

"Alibi for all this?"

"Doesn't matter what the sheriff thinks. All that matters is what he can prove. You've funded his reelection, but he's really not good or even motivated to be a good lawman, is he? If he were, we wouldn't have to be here in the first place."

"You won't get away with this."

"Maybe, but we're all committed to the cause. We'll claim to have been elsewhere together. Seriously, you've got to stop thinking of this as a crime."

"What is it, then?"

"This is an intervention, Keith. I'm here to change your life for the better."

"Well, you're off to a helluva start."

87

MICTURITION

Molly held up the key to the panic room door. She pointed to items on the floor. "Bran muffins, a big black coffee, a bucket, and the key to that door. The keypad is broken, but the manual lock will work."

Frustrated, Keith struggled against the zip ties. "What is this shit?"

"This is how I'm hoping to change your character."

Molly held up another key identical to the first. "You kept *both* keys to your panic room on your key ring? You didn't give one to your wife to keep her safe? You didn't even hide the spare key somewhere."

"If I had, Sarah might have found it."

"Somewhere on Earth, there could be a more selfish person, but it's hard to imagine."

Choosing his next words, Keith bobbed his head back and forth. He stopped immediately. Moving that way intensified his headache.

"I was thinking I'd put my massage chair up in here, make it a man cave. Wish I had that chair right now. Anyway, are you done? You're fuckin' talkin' me to death. Last chance! Get out. Call an ambulance. Save us all some time and grief."

"Listen carefully," Molly instructed. "I'm going to ask you to do something. If you don't cooperate, I'll bring my guys in here, and we'll do this the hard way."

Keith struggled again to sit up. With great effort and some wriggling, he managed to rest his back against the wall. He winced as he tested his bonds again. The skin of his wrists had been raw before, but now he was bleeding.

He thought about Molly's lecture about blood making blades slick. Maybe if he bled enough, he'd be able to slip out of the zip ties. Just maybe, but it hurt an awful lot to even try.

Molly held up one of the silver keys again. "I'm going to give you the key to the door to your cell."

"Finally!"

"You want it?

"Of course!"

"If you want it, you're going to have to swallow it first."

"Swallow it?" His voice was suddenly high and squeaky. "I can't swallow that!"

"You can. My mom takes pills that are almost this big. Do that, have a couple of muffins to chase it down, and you'll get out of here."

Keith eyed the bucket in the corner. "I'll get the key after I — "

"After you pass it, yeah."

"How long will *that* take?"

"I have not taken the speed of your bowel habits into account. Like I said, how fast you get out of here depends on you."

"Fine."

"You agreed too quickly. You think you can puke it back up as soon as I lock the door behind me. We will wait around a bit to make sure you don't do that. Some processing time, right? If the sharp edges of the key don't tear up your intestines, you'll be out after your next big poop."

"Don't do this."

"This is happening, Keith. You're used to doing things to others. This is happening to you."

His Adams apple bobbed up and down, and he began to pant.

Molly made a calming gesture. "I imagine this would be a logical time for you to panic in your panic room. Let's skip past that stage. After all, I'm not a sadist."

"You sure about that?"

"I'm not a sadist, Keith. I'm an altruist with a temper."

"All this is because of Barry Graves," Keith said.

"It's because of what you did to Barry," she corrected. "And my dad."

"My dad died, too."

"That's something for you to care about, not me. Now, let's talk about you a minute. Your secret was your money. My secret is that you and I are kindred spirits, two sides of the same coin. You and your dad taught me that."

Despite everything, he had doubted her resolve to follow through with her crazy plan. Her steady, calm voice left no room for doubt now. If Jergins was stupid enough to take him on, she was probably crazy enough to finish.

He tipped his head back and opened his mouth. "*Do it, bitch!*"

She stepped closer and dropped the silver key into his open mouth and held the travel mug to his lips.

He sputtered and drooled, "It's too hot!"

"Hot coffee was Sarah's idea. I would have given it to you cold, but I saw how you scalded her. You did that several times to teach her a lesson. What lesson do you suppose you're learning right now? Remember, this is about changing your life. You're going to have some alone time. I encourage you to think about that. *Learn*, Keith."

The panic room key did not go down the first time, nor did he get it down his esophagus on the fifth attempt. He choked, spit, and coughed through the ordeal. Finally overcoming his gag reflex, he succeeded on the sixth try.

Eyes watering, nose running, Keith said in a hoarse whisper, "If it doesn't tear my guts out, expect to see me soon. If it does tear me up, keep looking over your shoulder. I'll get over it. I won't help the cops, either. It'll be me coming after you."

"I'll have your guns."

"I can get more."

"Your father said something like that to my dad. Do I look worried?"

He refused to answer.

"The way I'm feeling tonight? I feel so light, Keith. Light!" She tapped her chest. "Right over my heart. Reminds me of puncturing your dad's tires — "

"My tongue's burned," Keith complained. "How's this for a new deal? I'll shut up if you will."

She nodded. "Sorry. We'll just wait in silence a while until we're sure you won't vomit up the key. Have a muffin, Muffin?"

She waited two hours just to be sure. At the end of that time, Molly told her captive, "The internet was surprisingly specific. It can take between ten and fifty-nine hours before your payload becomes a pantsload. That's how long until you'll be able to retrieve the key and open that door. You can try to break out, but it's pretty sturdy."

"I get it."

"Not quite yet, you don't. Hockey Man! Stage Two! It's hammer time!"

The man in the goalie mask must have been awaiting orders nearby. He appeared in the doorway holding a hammer. Keith recognized it from his own toolbox.

"Molly?" the intruder said. "Sarah's packed up, but Rose is agitated. I think they need help gathering the last of her things."

"Obama and Trump haven't done that by now?" Molly asked, sounding annoyed.

Hockey Man shrugged. "They're getting the safes on the truck, but they need some extra help with Rose. You go, I got this."

Molly paused, but then the man in the goalie mask added, "You promised I'd have a moment of one-on-one time with him."

Molly bobbed her head in agreement. She handed him the big hunting knife. He tucked the sheathed blade under his belt at the small of his back.

"The meal is served. Play nice," Molly told him.

"Play nice?" her co-conspirator asked. "What's that supposed to mean?"

Molly ignored his question. "Keith? If you know what's good for you, you'll leave me alone. You'll leave Sarah and Rose alone. You do not want to see me again. Do *not* give me any more reasons to come after you. I've got a million ideas of how to get back at you, and each one is worse than what's happening here tonight."

Keith gritted his teeth, biting back words.

"If you're smarter than you look," Molly added, "this really is goodbye. Do the right thing by me, and you will never see me again. You do *not* want to see me again."

With that, she walked out of the room. Her friend waited a moment to peer after her, making sure she was gone. When he turned back to Keith, he hefted the hammer.

"At last," he said with relish, "it's just you and me."

Keith pissed his pants.

88

POSSESSION

Hockey Mask Man stepped closer to Keith with purpose, the hammer gripped tight.

Defenseless, Keith shouted, "No!" and turned his head, squeezing his eyes shut.

But the invader did not kneecap him or break his head. Instead, he smashed the phone on the wall. It shattered into several pieces that showered down on Keith's head.

Cowering, the captive looked up at the man in the mask. "Bastard!"

The man paused, then crouched, straddling Keith's legs. With one gloved hand, he raised his mask to reveal his face.

Keith stared in disbelief. It was Barry Graves.

"Molly's trying to scare you into changing your ways," Barry said. "All I've ever wanted was to make you feel as weak as you made me feel. You treated me very badly in school."

"We were just kids."

Barry placed the cold steel of the hammer's head beneath Keith's jaw, forcing him to raise his head. "Are you going to try to excuse your behavior? Are you going to dare to write off the pain and humiliation you caused me?"

"No."

"Good answer. Maybe you will learn something tonight, after all. Molly thinks it's not likely, but possible."

"What do you want from me?"

"Just speak honestly. If I think you're lying, something bad could happen."

"Worse than *this*?"

Barry used the hammer to add a little pressure under Keith's jaw. Keith winced.

"Tell me what you would do if I let you out of this room?"

"I'd have to let it go."

"Because?"

"Sarah doesn't want me. It would be pathetic to chase after a woman who doesn't want me. I don't know why I hung on so long, anyway. Rose is a burden — "

"You're a terrible liar." Barry placed the hammer head over Keith's crotch and leaned his weight on it.

Keith let out a gasp and yelped in pain. Barry eased the pressure but didn't stop entirely. "Secondly, Rose is a saint. She helped me until she couldn't anymore. She's a thousand times a better person than you ever were or could be."

"Okay! Okay! I'll leave them alone! I'll leave you and Jergins alone!"

"Why?" Barry persisted.

"Because *this*! This is bad enough! I'm scared, okay? You win! You scared me!"

Barry gave a slow, almost imperceptible nod. "Fine, if true. Too bad all that doesn't matter, anyway."

"What do you mean it doesn't matter?"

Barry rose and stepped toward the door. Then he stood still as a statue, staring at Keith, taking in the moment.

"What do you mean it doesn't matter?" Keith asked again. "Jergins is a shitty bitch, but she gave me a way out! I get a second chance!"

"*Second* chance? How many chances do you think you've had? It's a lot more than two, Keith. You know, it's really sad how much you're like your dad. You're a loner with no friends. The only love you've ever known is the love you have for yourself."

"Maybe it's a sickness. Ever think of that? Can't blame a person for a disease — "

"If so, you enjoyed your disease too much. You *loved* torturing me. I remember every second of what you did to me. I wonder how much you remember? I bet you've forgotten half of it. Mean people are built different. When you're mean all the time, every sin you commit is just another day in your life. One act of evil is no more significant than any other because it's all you do."

"But you're doing this to me now," Keith said. "You're no better than me."

"I don't love this, but I do feel it's necessary. You're a rabid dog, man. I will remember every minute of this for the rest of my life, too. This isn't just another day for me. I'm not casually cruel. Cruelty is not my life's work."

Keith spit blood on the floor. "Says the torturer."

"Molly asked me about ranking the days of my life. I hadn't thought about it that way. The day you decided to beat and humiliate a gay kid for daring to look your way a second too long was the worst day of my life. Today is my second worst."

"For a guy who's sweet as pie, you sure know how to carry a grudge."

"Oh, I didn't come here to hurt you, Keith, not really. I just wanted you to understand. I don't know if you have that capacity, but I had to try for your sake. Before this night is through, I think you might repent."

Keith straightened and pulled at the zip ties. He kept trying, grunting as much from the effort as from the pain.

"Hockey Guy?" Molly called from far away. "We're ready to go."

"Yup! Just a sec!" Barry yelled back.

"We're done here, Keith. I've said all I need to say. I'm supposed to tell you that Sarah will be in touch, but only through lawyers, but that's not going to happen. You know that, right?"

The zip tie around his right wrist would not break, but Keith thought he'd managed to stretch the plastic slightly. He was strong and his head had begun to clear. Given a little more time, he might get his hands free.

Barry stood over by the door and was about to leave and lock him in. Were he to leave, Keith's only way out was to shit out the key he'd swallowed.

89

CONTRITION

In desperation, Keith pleaded, "Wait!"

Barry hesitated.

"I'm sorry. I just wanted to say I'm sorry!"

"That's nice," Barry said. "But I think I'll choose to think you're lying. Believing you're truly repentant makes all this worse for me."

"You don't forgive me?"

Barry considered Keith's request for what seemed a long time. Finally, he said, "Yes. I do."

Hope bloomed. "Yes? You forgive me?"

"Sure, it's the right thing to do. I forgive you, Keith. Maybe you're right. You had a bad dad. Maybe it is bad genetics. Whatever."

"Then you can't do this! When you're all gone, slip away and call the cops! Call Sheriff Hobbs! Get me out of here!"

"No can do, Chief." Barry tossed the knife to the floor beside the muffins. "While you digest, you can spend the first while wriggling around to get that knife. Cut the ties around your wrists."

"There's another way! Don't lock the door! Just leave the knife and don't lock the door! It will take me a while to get free."

"Can't do that. See, what I want or think doesn't matter. If it means anything to you, you do have my forgiveness, but I can't help you, man."

"Barry Graves! Ha! Your name is like a prediction, idn't it? I will bury you in a shallow grave. When I get out, I will find you."

"True colors," Barry replied. "There they are. We've really thrown gas on your fire here tonight, haven't we? Despite my best efforts, no saints here. You're a hateful son of a bitch, Keith, and it's not my forgiveness you should be begging for. You've done damage to more people than just my family and yours."

"Like who?"

Barry ignored the question. He pulled the goalie mask down over his face. "I forgave you, and you ruined it. You never even saw me as a human being. Just to prove I am human, I'm going to add a level of difficulty to your task. What you have to do, you can do in the dark."

Barry lifted the hammer, grabbed the hanging lightbulb, and smashed the glass. They plunged into darkness together.

A very dim light cast from the bedroom yielded nothing but a gloomy suggestion as to the location of the exit.

"Find the knife," Barry said. "You'll have to go by feel now. Careful not to cut yourself. That would be tragic."

"I take it all back!" Keith wheedled.

"Some things you can never take back. Don't you know that by now? It's all too late."

Keith thought he detected real sorrow in Barry's voice. Being the person he was, Keith took this emotion for weakness.

"You don't want to do this to me, so don't!"

"It's not me, man. You and I are done. Molly and Sarah and Rose? We're all done. There's someone else you have barely given a thought to because you don't care about people. That's your whole life. Your cause of death will be arrogance, and you never saw it coming."

Keith's eyes were adjusting to the dim light. Barry hovered by the open door. He didn't believe it was too late until Barry said, "When the time comes, you'll know what to do with the knife. I'm showing you mercy you never showed me."

Keith drummed his heels on the floor in frustration. "What does that mean?"

"You sure got Molly-whopped tonight, but it gets worse."

Barry's dim silhouette retreated. The metallic click of the heavy lock seemed loud in the small, bare room.

Keith's enemies possessed the spare key on the other side of that door. The only other key was somewhere in his small intestine. He could not exit until the key did.

Or ...? Had Barry been suggesting he use the knife to perform surgery on himself? Dig out the key out somehow? No, that wouldn't work. He couldn't do that to himself, and he'd bleed to death first.

In the depths of darkness, Keith wept. He contemplated the choices that had brought him to this place. He hated Barry, Sarah, Rose, Molly Jergins, and whoever else was on her crew.

Keith screamed for help, but it was as if he were dead, yet not dead. This small room was his tomb. There was no one left to intimidate, no bargains left.

He cursed the unfairness of it all, and he was not sorry. Despite everything, Keith never came close to the human emotion of regret. He had committed violence. Violence had been committed upon him. All he wanted was to murder them all.

Keith Faun had learned nothing.

90

MOTION

The school librarian Molly had known was erased. In her stead was a woman who did not recognize her. Rose could walk on her own, but Sarah had to guide her mother from her front door to the car.

Barry, now without his mask, opened his rental car's door. With a big, friendly smile, he waved Rose and Sarah forward. "Right this way! We're going for a nice, long car ride, somewhere safe. All your luggage is in the trunk. No worries. You're going to love Virginia, Rose!"

Molly's two remaining soldiers, Obama and Trump, still wore their masks. They were busy loading the heavy money safe onto the lift on the back of a moving van.

Rose pointed at the pair with a trembling hand. "Presidents? Why presidents? I voted for ... I voted for ... "

"It's as if the answer is on the tip of your tongue, isn't it, Mom? Don't worry about it." Sarah patted Rose's shoulder, then slid her hand down her arm to gently take her mother's hand.

Molly strode over to the men. "You took care of all the security cams and recordings, right?"

The one in the Obama mask nodded emphatically.

"So, take off your masks. You're freaking out Mrs. Rainier."

Dylan Caffrey — Ant's recruit to the mission — removed his Trump mask and tossed it in the back of his truck.

"I was in her room with her the whole time packing. Mom was okay with the mask, then," Ant complained.

"Doesn't matter," Molly chided. "She's agitated now. Did you take care of the cameras or not?"

"Fine." Ant lifted his Obama mask so it sat on top of his head. Then, with some difficulty, he climbed on the truck's hydraulic lift.

Dylan stepped up, too, one hand balancing the dolly, the other pulling the lever to activate the hoist. As the lift rose, he congratulated Molly. "Solid work tonight."

"Thanks."

"I warned my cousin. Keith always was a piece of shit. Debbie wouldn't listen. Said her boss was the best-looking piece of shit in the diner on any given night. Didn't matter to Debbie he was married, neither. Debbie's kind of a piece of shit, too, come to think of it."

"How long until you're on the road?" Molly asked the trucker.

Dylan contemplated this a moment. "I got a pickup waiting for me at a furniture warehouse in Bangor. If I can load up there at nine? Prolly be on the road by eleven, eleven-thirty at the latest."

"Ant, when do you usually open the diner?"

The little man checked his watch. "Seven, usually."

"Then be there on the dot, like nothing's happened. As far as you're concerned, it's just another day. When the cops come calling, it wouldn't hurt to look a little distraught at the burglary."

Dylan chuckled. "Don't try to go for an Oscar or anything. He's just your asshole brother-in-law with a fat key down his gullet. No big deal."

"Been a long night," Ant complained. "Maybe I'll have time for a short nap before I head in — "

"Long night of hiding in your mom's room and packing her and Sarah's bags?" Dylan smirked. "Sure, man. You had the toughest job of all. Now grab the blankets. Cover up the safes, and I'll wrap belts around these big buggers. I don't want the load shifting around in transit."

Suddenly, they were all blinded by the glare of high beams as a vehicle turned up the driveway.

"Oh, shit!" Ant exclaimed. "Is it the cops? I knew it! It's the cops, isn't it?"

"Nah," Barry said in a weary voice. "We took too long. They're early."

The driver extinguished the headlights and sat there a moment. All Molly could make out in the dim light was the silhouette of a pickup truck.

"Take it easy," Dylan said. "It's a friendly."

"A friendly?" Mystified, Molly strained against the darkness. She couldn't make out the driver who exited the vehicle as he disappeared behind the truck. However, she had heard the door squeak as he opened and closed it.

"Oh, no." The realization had already dawned on Molly, even as her mind reeled, striving to reject the obvious.

The passenger side door opened slowly. The occupant stepped out gingerly. The driver emerged from behind the vehicle pushing a wheelchair. It was Molly's uncle. Wobbly on her legs, Kay stood by the truck's door, clinging to it so she wouldn't fall.

Molly whispered, "What is going on?"

"Secret squirrel stuff," Ant said. The short man then leaned out from the back of the truck and waved enthusiastically. "Hi, Mrs. Jergins! We did it! We got him! He's up there!"

"Holler louder!" Kay called back. "Maybe somebody down the mountain didn't hear ya!"

Ant retreated into the back of the van without another word. Molly could hear Dylan chuckling as they began to cover and secure the safes.

Molly walked forward, but it was as if she were on an escalator carrying her forward, rising to a dead drop.

Barry jogged ahead of her to greet the newcomers. While Vincent held the wheelchair, Barry took Kay's hand to steady her as she plopped down into her chair.

He bent beside Kay, whispering animatedly, but Molly's mother pushed him away. In the clear, still air, she heard Kay bark, "All right! All right! I got it! Let me see Rose!"

Ignoring Molly, Vincent rolled Kay over to Barry's rental until she was beside Rose in the back seat. Sarah, already in the car beside her mother, leaned over and opened the door. The dome light popped so Kay could see Rose clearly.

Kay reached out to Rose, who accepted her hand. They just looked at each other a moment, saying nothing.

"These men," Kay muttered finally. "These fucking men."

91

NOTION

Molly put a hand on Kay's shoulder. "Mom? You shouldn't be here. You've got to go."

Kay kept her eyes on Rose. "Don't mind my daughter. She's a worrier. You take care, dear. We've both been through the wringer, haven't we? I see that in you. You've had to carry too much. It'll be better for you from now on, I promise."

Rose's look of bewilderment cleared. "Kayla?"

"Bingo and on the money, dear! Just Kay, now. Nobody's called me Kayla in years."

"Kayla Donnegal? You wore that yellow dress I liked."

"Kay Jergins, since I was twenty-one, Rose. You were at my wedding. Remember? We were young and perfect, you and I."

By her faraway look, it was apparent Rose existed in two worlds. Physically, she was in the present. Mentally, she had a tentative foothold in the distant past.

"You were always the bad girl in school," Rose told Kay.

"Good at being bad, you mean. You wrote it in my yearbook. I still have it. You signed your name as Rosemary back then."

"Yellow dress!" Rose enthused. "You ran around with all the boys!"

Sarah leaned over and pulled her mother's hand from Kay's grasp. "Sorry, we really have to get going, Mom."

Kay nodded her agreement. "Time to escape the dragon's keep." Kay glanced at Barry. "You got the dragon's gold ready to go?"

"Yes, ma'am! In the truck, all thanks to your daughter."

"Then haul ass," Kay said. "Don't keep in touch. You and me, we're done. You're paid up, in full."

Barry bent to kiss Kay's cheek. "Thanks again, Mrs. Jergins, for everything. I'm sorry — "

Kay waved Barry away. "Don't be bothersome. I've heard your apologies so many times, you sound like a damned Canadian! Stop saying you're sorry and *do!* Be useful and take these ladies to safety. Go far, go fast, don't look back or come back."

But Molly stopped him. "Et tu, Brute?"

"At the risk of apologizing too much, sorry I didn't tell you everything," Barry said.

Her tone hard, Molly demanded, "Then tell me *something.*"

He sighed. "After Rose couldn't communicate anymore, I reached out to Kay. She thought if you knew everything, you might not ... you know — "

"Join the caper?" Molly suggested.

Vincent spoke for the first time. "Do Kay's dirty work, you mean." The bass in his voice signaled his impatience.

"We've got this, Barry," Vincent said. "You should be far from here. Run away. That's what you do best. Do as Kay says, make yourself useful and go. Give Ant a ride into town on the way, would you?"

Overhearing this and eager to escape, Ant jumped down from the truck. He hurried to get into the rental's front passenger seat.

Molly caught Ant by the elbow before he got to the car and grabbed the Obama mask off his head. "No souvenirs from the crime scene, genius."

Molly tossed Ant's Obama mask to Dylan, who threw it in the back of the van.

If there was a weak link in the crew, it was Ant. He was perhaps only slightly more useful to the project than Rose. At least Rose probably wouldn't remember anything she'd witnessed.

Ant climbed into the car and rolled down his window. "Thanks for saving my mom and sister. By my build, Keith would have known it was me in a heartbeat. I appreciate you getting involved and leading the expedition."

"Did you know my mom was going to show up?"

Ant shrugged. "Our moms were friends from way back."

Sarah piped up from the back seat. "Ant wanted to bring you in, but after all Mom told us, I got him to talk to Kay first."

"We didn't know how to move forward," Ant said, "but when you came home — "

"You and the others figured out how to use me," Molly said, "and I'm the monkey in the middle."

"Your mom's idea," Sarah said.

"Don't pout, Molly," Kay said. "I needed your arms and legs. Last chance to finish the long dance."

Barry spoke to Molly rapid-fire, giving her no opening to respond. "You've got the number for my lawyer friend. Call him once you've retrieved the money for Sarah. And thanks! We couldn't have done this without you. You are really good at being the bad girl."

Barry kissed Molly's cheek, then hurried to climb into the driver's seat.

Tears ran down Sarah's face as she waved to Molly through the rear window. "Thank you!" she called.

As Barry started the engine, Vincent closed Rose's door. He did so gently, but the woman still looked startled.

"Poor thing," Vincent muttered. "We're watching the movie, but she's takin' in what she can like it's in a foreign language, no subtitles. Slo-mo speed intake in a fast-forward output world."

I feel like I'm living that way, too, Molly thought.

The car's headlights cut through the darkness. Barry's rental accelerated down the long driveway. He weaved around Vincent's truck and wheeled onto Correction Road.

Barry, Ant, Sarah, and Rose disappeared into the night. The sudden quiet could almost be mistaken for peace.

Job done, Molly thought. *I'm a good bad girl. And the bad boy living on Correction Road is finally corrected.*

But the job wasn't quite finished because Kay Jergins wasn't done.

92

LOTION

"Sarah's going to live," Kay said. "They both will. The difference is, Rose will have the peace that comes with a Swiss cheese memory. She won't even see the reaper coming for her. How nice that would be. That bastard has been coming for me for years and can't seem to close the deal."

"You kept in touch with Barry and never told me," Molly said.

"You never told me lots of things," Kay countered, "like how my husband really died. Rose couldn't keep the truth from me. It ate away at her that I didn't know."

There was acid in Kay's tone when she added, "No such compunction from you."

"I thought you'd be happier not knowing."

"For your sake or mine?"

"Steady, Kay," Vincent said. "Be okay — "

"Vince, if you want the house when I'm dead, please shut the fuck up. I'm having a moment with Molly now, hear?"

Vincent did indeed shut the fuck up.

"Rose was a strong woman with a sweet soul," Kay continued. "She encouraged me to bury the hatchet. Couldn't abide my need to bury said hatchet in young Faun's head. She told me I should forgive. So much talk, talk, talk! It's just words. Words are empty."

It was too dark to see her face clearly, but Molly could imagine her mother's disgusted expression, feel her disdain.

"The way you started out, I thought you'd end up in law enforcement," Kay said. "That's what your father thought, too, God bless his fool soul."

"Don't talk about Dad like that."

"Don't tell me how to talk about your father. You and your damn quest to evict the Fauns got him killed. It started off righteous, but you've got a problem with follow-through."

"I'm standing here!" Molly said. "I took down Keith Faun! How have I not followed through?"

"Lloyd Faun was a monster and a danger to everyone. Your *father* followed through. His lousy son is a monster, and you were standing right next to him on the cliffs. You could have pushed him over right then."

"You would have wanted me to be a killer?"

"I wanted you to stop messing around with your little pranks and petty vandalism. People like the Fauns don't get scared. You don't win by giving them more chances to hurt you. You win by winning. You were satisfied with a tie."

Every bitter word was a blow to Molly's heart. Hot tears slipped down her cold cheeks. "He was my father. He sacrificed his life to protect me and Barry and Rose."

"Don't glaze the donut too much," Kay replied. "Chuck lost a fight. You played at pranks and word games. You think you're so smart, doctor of words and all. It never occurred to you that Chuck would tell me everything about your hijinks?"

"He did?"

"Of course, he did. He was my husband! Chuck and I didn't keep secrets from each other. He didn't tell me right away, but he got around to it."

"Why didn't you say so then?"

"He wanted me to stay out of it. He did it your way, said I'd take it too far. I curse myself every day for tolerating your goddamned half-measures! I'm mad at him for dying to leave me to die alone. I'm mad at you — "

"I'm sorry, Mom."

"Oh, please! You only came home because you lost your job. You came back to a place you always thought you were too good for and you mope. I'm exhausted, Molly!"

Vincent put a hand on his sister-in-law's shoulder. "Easy, Kay. She's still your daughter."

"Always more Chuck's than mine, a real daddy's girl. I'd have taken care of this all myself if I hadn't become a toothless house cat. Soon I'll be a worm city! Past time we evened things out, for once and forever."

In the dim light, Kay Jergins was a small angular silhouette, but her voice still had the honed edge of a knife. "Chuck was worth five Lloyds. I am glad you're here for the big finale, Molly. Thanks to you setting things up, this old house cat still has claws."

Vincent intervened again, his tone hard this time. "That's enough. The night's a-wastin'. Be okay, Kay, okay?"

"Fine, fine! I'd rather let the boy stew, but the sun'll be up soon. This will make for a better display in the dark. Let's show Molly how it's done."

Vincent headed back to the truck.

"You sound like you hate me, but I loved Dad, and I love you, Mom."

"Of course, you do! For one thing, I'm a delight. For another, you have to love me. I'm your mother and you don't know any better. Parents and their kids are just accidents by birth. That's circumstance. Chuck and I *chose* each other. It's different."

Molly stood in stunned silence.

"You should get going," Kay said. "Vince and I can close this loop without you and your tender sensibilities."

Vincent loomed out of the darkness carrying something in each hand. His tone was conciliatory. "Don't feel too bad, Molly. Your dad loved you very much."

"Of course, he did!" Kay said bitterly. "After he joined your little crusade, you looked at him differently. He wasn't just some old, broken-down dad anymore. The night you two broke into the laundromat, he called it prime daddy/daughter time. He wanted to spend as much time with you as he could before you grew up. He worried about it. 'Losing you to the world,' he called it. In the end, Chuck loved you to death. He didn't lose you, did he? You lost him for me."

Molly was unprepared for the searing heat in her mother's words. Kay had harbored many secrets, but more shocking was the black depth of her mother's resentment. She really had kept herself to herself.

"I wish you'd kept that ..." Molly choked up. "I wish you'd kept these thoughts unexpressed."

"You mean you don't want any blame."

"Not from you. Dad sacrificed himself for me. He's a hero."

"I'd rather have a living saint than a dead hero for a husband. He never should have been in that position. He killed for you. He died for you. All I wanted was for Chuck to live for me. When he took Lloyd over that cliff ..." For a moment, Kay's voice failed her.

Rose Rainier was blessed with forgetting. Molly and her mother were cursed with excellent memories. Those primal visions had set them to war with Keith Faun and with each other.

"When your life blows up, there's only one balm for that burn," Kay said. "And we brought along a couple of big cans of aloe."

93

IGNITION

Dylan appeared by Molly's side and set a suitcase and a backpack on the ground beside her. "We ride at dawn," Dylan said. "It'll be light soon. Past time we got going."

"Yep! Skedaddle! Vincent, get me over there, closer to the steps."

Confused, Molly left the luggage behind and pushed her mother in the wheelchair toward the pale glow of the mansion's exterior lights. She needed to see her mother, *to understand*.

As they followed Vincent toward the front door of the house, Molly realized her uncle carried a large jerry can in each hand.

Kay barked orders at her brother-in-law. "One can in front of the panic room door, Vince. Poke a hole in it. Then poke a hole in the second can and bring it back out here. Like a trail of bread crumbs in reverse, that's the most efficient way."

Molly stopped. "Gas?"

"Gas."

"You're going to burn Keith alive?"

"Pushing the bastard off the cliff would have been quicker and nicer, wouldn't it?"

"Mom, this is too much!"

"Nah, it's just right. Ant told Vince everything about what he did to Sarah, the repeated scalding and all. Ant filled us in on your heist. He's got a knife in there, right? He's got options."

"I won't be a part of this. All I wanted to do was get Rose and Sarah out — "

"And convince a monster not to be a monster anymore? Doesn't work. A thing like him? None of you will ever be safe as long as Keith Faun is alive. The only cure for him is deletion."

Kay flicked open a Zippo under her chin. The flame cast disturbing shadows over the topography of her mother's lined face. Molly barely recognized her.

"I guess it's true," Molly said. "Nobody really knows anyone."

"Vince packed your things. Ride west with Dylan and make sure Sarah gets her money so she can start over. I'm sure she'll spare you some so you can start over, too."

"What about the law?"

Kay clicked the lighter shut. "What about it? Vince is my alibi, and I'm his. Hobbs couldn't find his ass with both hands, but if they get me, what do I have to fear? I'm already dying. I'll never live to see a trial."

"I didn't know it was that far along."

Kay shrugged and clicked her lighter open. "You live." She snapped the Zippo shut to extinguish the flame. "You die."

"Simple as that?"

Kay shrugged. "Everybody's on the same railway tracks, and the death train's always a-comin'. You just haven't been hit yet. Makes me smile to think that train is bearin' down on Lloyd's demon son tonight. I'm very sick, but he won't outlive me. I won't stand for it."

"You can do this?"

"You're a bad good girl," Kay said. "I'm good at being bad. Fact: I'm excellent at it. Chuck and I were so much alike. He understood me. He only held back for your sake. Mercy for the Fauns was no kindness in the end, was it?"

"I was trying to take the high road — "

"The high road killed Chuck. I warned him a couple of shotgun shells would have solved all our problems. Better than all that runnin' around with spray paint and a poison pen! If I see Chuck in the next life, I can't hardly wait to tell him, 'I told you so.' If you're not going full tilt at a problem, you may as well give up. 'Let's not and say we did' woulda avoided all this in the first place, but you had to go for revenge. For the sake of a stranger, you lost your father, and me my husband."

Vincent emerged from the house splashing a thin trail of fuel behind him. He jiggled the jerry can to gauge how much gas was left in the container. When it was almost empty, he walked back toward Kay and Molly.

"Any word from the condemned?" Kay asked.

"I heard mostly curse words," Vincent said. "I gave him your message, the who and the why."

"And?"

"The gentleman informed me of his intent to kill us all."

"Well!" Kay chortled as she gave her daughter a pointed glance. "That boils all the moral objections down to math, doesn't it? This isn't murder. It's self-defence in advance. What is it you people say? Welcome to the Resistance!"

"Burning a man alive is too much!"

"You had your chance, girl. Let me tell you something. Back in high school, Lloyd and I were boyfriend and girlfriend. I cheated on Lloyd with your father. That was the real beginning of Lloyd's beef with Chuck."

Molly went wide-eyed and had the sudden urge to sit down. "You and Lloyd Faun? Why?"

"Hormones, probably," she answered dryly. "He was attractive. Believe it or not, so was I. I suspect I understand poor Sarah better than you do. Anyway, after much research and close-up inspection of Lloyd, I discovered his company was best enjoyed at a distance, say, through a rifle scope. Chuck and I shoulda tossed him over the cliff back in the day. Lord knows, I thought about some such things quite a bit. If I had the strength, I woulda used one of their own presses at the laundry, flatten their fat heads. Didn't mean to leave this chore to my daughter, but finally, here we are, goin' whole hog."

"Why are you telling me this now, Mom?"

Kay made a *tsk* sound. "To make the point that if things had fallen a different way, who knows? I might have even made the mistake of marrying Lloyd. If I had, and that was my son in there, I'd *still* burn him down. Some people just need to go to make room for brighter days and better people."

"B-but Hobbs will b-blame me for this!"

"It's fine," Kay said coldly, "or it will be."

"Apparently, you're okay with burning me down, just, you know, not literally. Prison, instead."

Kay stared up at her. "You'll be fine."

My mother is a dangerous stranger, some fierce and feral thing, Molly thought. *A monster made of teeth.*

Dylan had retrieved the suitcase and backpack. He set them down again at Molly's feet. "I'm your alibi, but we've got to go. I don't want to be here for this. We gotta get on the road."

South, then west, then parts unknown, Molly thought, *but what happens here will be with me no matter where I run.*

"Hobbs can have his suspicions," Kay told her. "What matters is what he can't prove. Leaving is all you've thought about since you been back, anyway. Get going, Molly."

"Hope I packed all your essentials," Vincent said. Her uncle stepped forward. He smelled of gas. Vincent gave Molly a big bear hug, lifting her off the ground for a moment. "Don't sweat this. We got it. This isn't on you."

To Dylan, her uncle added, "Safe travels. Keep it on the pavement. Remember, for every mile of road, there's two miles of ditches."

Molly did not move. Her father's words from the night she was shot came back to her. He'd said of Kay, "People think she's the nice one."

Molly straightened and cleared her throat. "Mom! Don't do this."

"Half-measures is what got Chuck killed. One perfectly good 12 gauge and all this could have been solved with two shots years ago."

Kay flicked her lighter. "I told you, Molly." With her free hand, she tapped the center of her chest. "Hell is right here."

She snapped the lighter shut. "You know the difference between a destructive fire and a cleansing fire, Molly? The one who holds the match. Go. You basically ran away once. Do it again. Sail new seas."

Molly started forward, reaching for her mother. "You can't — "

"Too late fer talkin'!" Kay flicked the Zippo open and tossed it to the ground. With a whoosh, the trail of gasoline blazed over the walk, up the steps, and into the house.

Appalled, Molly froze. Uncounted seconds later, she screamed, "No!" but her voice was swallowed by the explosion. A couple of upstairs windows burst out in a rain of glass, sound, and fire.

Molly felt as if she were looked down upon by two flaming eyes. It would be dawn very soon, but for now, Faun Manor became a bright, smaller sun burning above a dark land and an empty sea.

94

EVACUATION

As the moving van descended Poet's Mountain, snow began to fall. Sweating until she glowed, Molly shivered. Her arms and legs trembled. Dylan activated the truck's heater but to no effect.

"I'm cold, but it's not the winter. It's me," Molly gulped. "Shock reroutes the blood."

Dylan nodded, said nothing, and kept his eyes on the road. Offering a distraction, he reached for the radio.

In the middle of a report, the newsreader said, "All capabilities from land, sea, and air will be deployed."

Molly assumed at first that the mobilization was a response from FEMA. The US Virgin Islands had recently been pounded by a freak storm. However, it became clear the report was not about mounting a rescue effort. The response from land, sea, and air was about mobilizing armed forces across Middle East borders.

"Syria, Israel, Lebanon, Beirut — seems all those places are on fire all the time," Dylan said. "I couldn't point any of 'em out on a map if my dick depended on it."

Molly turned off the radio. "When I was a kid, I thought troubles were for other places, but ...." She waved a hand, gesticulating at nothing in particular and at everything. "It's everywhere, even in Nowhere, Maine."

"Trouble turns up wherever people are," Dylan said. "Think there might be a connection to be found in there somewheres?"

Molly did not reply. Uncomfortable with silence, Dylan asked, "Quite a night, huh?"

Feeling her enraged stare boring into him, he glanced her way and flashed a conciliatory grin. "Sorry! Captain Obvious, here. Just, um, I was wondering what's next for you? Do you know?"

"I've known for a while," she answered. "I loved teaching English and history, but somebody once said to forget following your passion. Follow your talent. I'm going to rescue more people, people like Sarah and Rose. That's where I'm needed if I can find a way to do it right ... you know, with less burning and death."

The truck driver merely nodded. He wanted his dangerous passenger to remain calm. It was apparent to Dylan that Molly Jergins had learned nothing.

"Did you know my real name is Margaret?"

He seesawed his head and shrugged. "Sure, Margaret is Molly, Molly is Margaret. Can't say I gave it any thought, but that's a common thing, right?"

"When I was very little, I liked having a secret name. I thought it was like being a spy. Mom and Dad were the ones with the big secrets all along. Your parents are your parents. We don't think of them as humans until we see how they aren't strong. Mom got sick. Dad got arthritis. One day, you start thinking about how they won't be around forever, but we all act like we have forever."

"My parents are still pretty young," Dylan said. "I don't like to think about that stuff."

"You know what else?" Molly blurted. "I didn't say goodbye to Mom! I just ran for the truck." She was quiet for a moment, then asked, "How long did you know? You weren't at all surprised when my family showed up."

Dylan shrugged. "Ant's got diarrhea of the mouth. When he told me the terrible shit Keith was doing to Sarah, I considered the path of righteousness."

"And?"

"Forgive is in the Bible. Forget is not. The way Keith came at me back in the day, you don't forget a thing like that. You don't appreciate bullies. Me, neither. Ant would be useless, so I decided I owed you some backup."

"It was that easy for you?"

"Easy?" Dylan allowed a small smile. "Nah, I thought about what your mother wanted, gave it full and serious consideration."

"How long did it take you to decide to back her plan?"

"Maybe four or five minutes. If it makes you feel better, when I heard your play, I didn't hesitate more than a minute or two."

"You're joking, right?"

"Well, *I* thought I was jokin', but if you didn't catch that, maybe I was wrong about that."

"Ha."

"Nobody's wrong to get rid of that bastard. Like your mom said, it's math. I saw the writing on the wall. Way I see it, I saved my cousin tonight."

"Oh?"

"Sure. Given a little time, Debbie would have ended up like Sarah, beaten and burned. Keith had his chances. His family was rich and he got richer. Married the prettiest girl in school, a cheerleader! I didn't even know hockey even had cheerleaders. Always thought that was just a football or basketball thing. I was on the basketball team, but I never got so much as a long look from any cheerleaders."

Molly wondered how much of Dylan's motivations to help came from his brief history with Keith. Was it that he was another furious and frustrated victim? Or was it jealousy? Would he admit to lethal envy? Would she ever know with certainty?

"When the cheerleaders went for the hockey players, they weren't really cheerleaders. I think the official term was puck bunnies," Molly said.

"Yeah? Well, anyway, no tears for assholes. The stuff you pulled on him, getting the safes and all, was genius. Sarah will have decent seed money, I'm sure. The Sheriff's department will look hard at her, but Hobbs is no Sherlock. He's not stupid, but when you're that lazy, smart don't matter. We'll all alibi each other, so eventually it'll all come out in the wash."

Molly almost laughed. "You *believed* that?"

Dylan looked confused. "Whaddayamean?"

"Oh, c'mon, man! Keith Faun dies in a fire and I flee? Hobbs will have the FBI after me. Explosions can't be undone. I'm collateral damage. Like it or not, you're aiding and abetting a fugitive right now."

"Well, technically, I'm a fugitive, too. But you really think your mom won't take the fall for you?"

"Didn't you hear how she talked? She blames me for Dad's death, maybe almost as much as she blamed the Fauns! I can't go back, not ever."

95

CONCLUSION

Dylan was quiet for a moment, slowly digesting Molly's revelation. Finally, he muttered, "So, you're banished? Damn, that's ironic *and* cold, idn't it? That mother of yours, *whoo!* Kay is one hard woman. Kinda puts one in mind of Darth Vader. He was disabled, too, with a CPAP machine on his chest and all, but powerful."

"She is ...."

A monster made of teeth.

Molly slammed her fist into her door. "If I'd known Mom was going to kill him — "

"You would have done what? Stopped her? You did a good job scaring the bejesus out of Keith and scooping his stuff, but this thing was never going to end in a pillow fight."

Molly swallowed hard. "I guess the torture wasn't necessary."

"The torture was the icing on the cake," Dylan said. "Cakes need frosting. Your mom said punishment was necessary."

Molly's breath came too fast. She had to concentrate to slow her respiration. "You know what Nietzsche said about hunting monsters?"

Dylan raised a hand from the steering wheel as if about to answer a question in class. "No idea!"

"If you're going to hunt monsters, you have to be sure not to become one."

"That so?" Dylan fished a pack of gum out of his pocket and offered it to Molly.

She refused and stared out the window as they passed through Poeticule Bay one last time. The sky to the east lightened with the coming sun.

As they turned right on Shore Road to head south, Molly turned in her seat, craning her neck to look back up the mountain. It was still too dark to the east to spot the column of smoke from the burning house. However, amongst the trees, the high, blown-out windows were visible. The eyes of fire still followed her.

Fishermen would be up early. They would be the first to point and shout and raise the alarm. The fire hall's siren would rise and fall. Volunteer firefighters would swarm. They would be far too late. Keith Faun was erased to nothing but memory, burnt meat, ash, and bone.

Shifting into higher gear, they exited Poeticule Bay. A blur of trees shot by on their right. To their left lay the Atlantic, vast and deep and cold.

The ocean is a living thing that swallows all history — everything but her father falling from the Drifting Cliffs. No amount of blood could bring her father back or erase the memory of her failure.

She wondered, does trauma have to last? Did time really heal all wounds, or do people simply get tired of telling themselves the same story over and over? Years in the future, would she feel better? Could she get to a place where she rationalized and justified her actions? She didn't know.

Molly was startled from her reverie as Dylan cleared his throat. He'd said something, but she hadn't heard him. "What was that?"

"I was sayin' about that thing you said about not becoming a monster. I don't think that's right. Keith was a monster, but your mom is Godzilla."

"Your point?"

"If you're in the monster-hunting business, it's okay to be one, too. For safety, I suspect maybe you gotta be a bigger, better monster."

A good bad girl? More like Mom, she thought.

"I guess we all have it in us," Molly said.

"Have what?"

"The potential to become a monster. It's a strange thing to realize you don't really know somebody you thought you knew. Maybe you *can't* ever really know anybody. I learned that lesson with my father, but I got to know him better just before he died."

Dylan turned his head to shoot her a questioning look.

"I didn't understand what a warrior Dad was at heart. I had to learn that again with Mom today. I didn't know she had it in her to murder anyone. Especially like that."

"I still can't believe she dated Lloyd Faun!" Dylan crowed.

"Yeah ... but the murdering thing is worse, right?"

Needing to placate her, Dylan said, "Oh, sure, hideous, but Chuck is avenged. Maybe you can focus on the future now. Everybody's got a past, Molly, and unless you're crazy like the Fauns, everybody's got regrets. Just think about the people Keith can't hurt anymore."

"Right now, I'm just thinking about my mom. We're so ... disconnected. We all are. One night, back when all this began, Lloyd shot me with rock salt ... *hmph!*"

Molly's emotions and thoughts were a tangled jumble, twisted knots impossible to pull apart.

"I think I see it now, what my dad was trying to tell me. Just trying to be a person, surviving, can be a lonely chore."

"Sometimes, that's so, but you had friends on your side today. I like to think there's more cherry than there is pit, you know?"

Molly sighed. "Yeah, it's a beautiful world full of beautiful people doing beautiful things, as long as you don't look too closely."

Dylan perked up. "That's why we shouldn't think about it that hard. Life's too short to ponder big questions. I stick to the little ones I can maybe deal with."

"Is Keith Faun dying in a fire one of those easy little problems?"

"Not for nothin', Molly, but that key coulda tore him up and killed him, too."

"Maybe, but my way, I gave him a chance."

"After Ant pulled me in, your mom had a chat with me. Kay said something to me about how he'd probably die of suffocation before he burned. If the explosion didn't do him, maybe the fire would burn up all the oxygen. Or smoke inhalation, maybe? I dunno. Whatever it was, it would be quicker than all the tortures he put people through."

"So, it's all okay?"

"Nothing is okay, Molly, but some states execute people. They dress it up with a bunch of ceremony, but what we did was quicker."

Molly sensed that wasn't really Dylan talking, anymore. She'd never heard her mother utter those words, but she could easily imagine Kay saying them now. Dylan was parroting what she'd taught him.

"I would never have guessed my family's morality was so complex," Molly said.

"You're overthinking it," Dylan said. "It's simpler than all that. Give your mom a break, or at least try to understand her. The Fauns killed her husband."

"She blames me for Dad's death, too." Molly searched her mind for solace but found none. Her stomach still roiled.

"And you blame yourself?"

"Complications ensued. Whom the gods would destroy, they first make mad."

"Huh?"

"It's an ancient saying that's been quoted through the ages, and fuck me, it never gets any less relevant."

Dylan shrugged and left her to her thoughts. He kept his eyes on the road and hummed to himself.

Finally, she said, "My punishment is banishment. That's what I wanted for the Fauns from the beginning. I've kind of come full circle, but I guess I'm pretty lucky."

"Pretty lucky or ugly lucky?" Dylan asked. "Shine a light, cuz I can't follow ya in the dark."

"You ever apply for a job you don't want? Then, when you don't get it, you're still pissed and sad? It's kind of like that, but now I see it for what it is. I lived in Poeticule Bay all my life, even when I didn't live there. Forced to move on, I can finally leave because I have to. I'll try, anyway. Mom and Dad had different ways of getting me up on my feet and out the door, but it worked both times. It turns out, coming-of-age can come at any age. I've decided something or maybe finally decoded something: I don't have to be so angry about the past, anymore."

"Really?" Dylan's doubt was evident.

"Oh, yeah! It's time to get angry about the future."

She'd existed in two worlds and lost both. She would have to design a new one for herself and live there. Molly would begin again. She would continue forward, partly because she was stubborn, mostly because she had no choice.

Snow began to fall, thicker than it had before. Soon, it would become a deep blanket upon the landscape, making everything quieter and more peaceful.

When Molly spoke again, they were miles from Poeticule Bay. "I was so sure I knew everything there was to know about my mom. She could be okay but also not a little cantankerous."

"A bitch, you mean?"

"Well, yeah, a raging, raving bitch on wheels, sure. Also, she was often boring, but she was wearing a mask my whole life. We're so alike. Mom came at me to slide the blade between my ribs and twist the knife on the way out. I never saw it coming, but she got me. She wins. Mom's the best good bad girl. We should have been friends."

To her surprise, her words held not a single note of bitterness. Molly's tears dried, and she actually began to chuckle. "Tigger tricked Jaguar Woman, but Tiger Mom ate Tigger!"

The trucker glanced away from the icy road to look into her eyes. Her laughter was bewildering, but Molly Jergins no longer frightened him.

"All along, I thought vengeance was mine," she said. "I was wrong. Vengeance is hers."

DISCUSSION

Book Club Questions

1. Despite her father's death, Molly can't seem to stop her quest for vengeance. Does this qualify as addiction?
2. Do you believe people can fundamentally change? If so, how do they accomplish that?
3. Do you forgive and forget? If so, how?
4. Do you consider Molly a hero, anti-hero, or villain?
5. At the end of the story, Molly is unsure of the precise moment she went too far. Can you identify that moment?
6. What is your revenge fantasy?
7. Have you ever perpetrated an act of vengeance or a prank on anyone? What were the results of your action?
8. Are you confident societal systems will bring justice to those who deserve it? Do you believe in karma?
9. Molly deals with challenges in socially unacceptable ways. What regret do you wish you'd handled differently? How do you believe you could have done better?

10. Can you share a time you were wronged and took the high road? How did that choice and its outcome make you feel?

11. Discuss the connections between the choices of chapter titles and the text.

12. Molly ranks the best and worst days of her life. What are your top five best days so far (not including wedding days and the births of children)?

PROPOSITION
VENGEANCE IS HERE IS COMING NEXT!

Sincerely, thank you for your purchase and for reading! Authors and their books live and die by their readers and reviews. Please leave a review if you can.

To keep up to date on new releases, deals, and news, sign up for Robert's newsletter at <u>AllThatChazz.com</u> .

For daily posts, join Robert's inner circle on Facebook: Fans of Robert Chazz Chute.

EXPLORATION

Find links to all books by Robert Chazz Chute at
AllThatChazz.com

~ DYSTOPIAN AND APOCALYPTIC FICTION ~

This Plague of Days, Season 1
This Plague of Days, Season 2
This Plague of Days, Season 3
This Plague of Days, Omnibus Edition

THE AFTER Life TRILOGY
Inferno
Purgatory
Paradise
AFTER Life (E-Box Set)
AFTER Life Omnibus

Endemic
Citizen Second Class

Amid Mortal Words
Robot Planet, The Complete Series

THE DIMENSION WAR SERIES (with Holly Papandreas)
Haunting Lessons, Book 1
Death Lessons, Book 2
Fierce Lessons, Book 3
Dream's Dark Flight, Book 4 (solely by the author)

~ Time Travel ~

Wallflower

~ CRIME THRILLERS ~

Vengeance Is Hers
The Night Man
Brooklyn in the Mean Time

THE HIT MAN SERIES

Bigger Than Jesus
Higher Than Jesus
Hollywood Jesus
Resurrection

~ COLLECTIONS ~

Murders Among Dead Trees
Sometime Soon, Somewhere Close
Self-help for Stoners
All Empires Fall
Our Zombie Hours
Our Alien Hours

~ NONFICTION ~

Do the Thing: The Last Stress-busting Book You'll Ever Need

FIND ALL BOOKS BY ROBERT CHAZZ CHUTE AT ALLTHATCHAZZ.COM

http://allthatchazz.com

RECOGNITION

Great appreciative nods go to my wonderful editor Gari Strawn, beta readers extraordinaire Russ Sawatsky and Ciara Chute, and my lovely and loyal Facebook fan group.

Also, thanks to The Daily Zeitgeist for the spark of the bouncy castle scenario, Jason Pargin for sharing his understandable fear of whales, and to @whattheish on TikTok for the vengeance scenario using misted milk.

Finally, as always, thanks and love go to SWMBO for her constant love and support.

CONFESSION

Winner of fifteen writing awards, Robert Chazz Chute is a former crime and science journalist. A graduate of the University of King's College and the Banff Publishing Workshop, he has worked in both traditional and independent publishing. He writes suspenseful crime fiction and apocalyptic tales from his blanket fort in Other London.